THE HOPE JAR

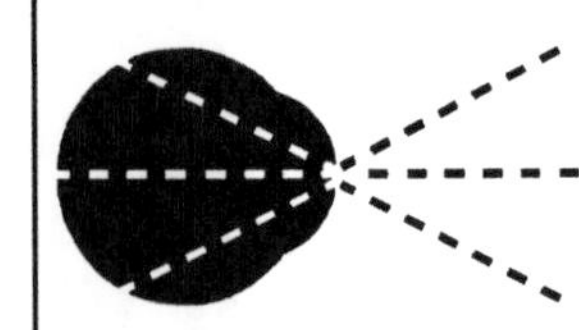

The Hope Jar

Wanda E. Brunstetter

LARGE PRINT PRESS
A part of Gale, a Cengage Company

Farmington Hills, Mich • San Francisco • New York • Waterville, Maine
Meriden, Conn • Mason, Ohio • Chicago

Scripture quotations are taken from the King James Version of the Bible.
All German-Dutch words are taken from the Revised Pennsylvania German Dictionary found in Lancaster County, Pennsylvania.
Large Print Press, a part of Gale, a Cengage Company.

The text of this Large Print edition is unabridged.
Other aspects of the book may vary from the original edition.
Set in 16 pt. Plantin.

LIBRARY OF CONGRESS CIP DATA ON FILE.
CATALOGUING IN PUBLICATION FOR THIS BOOK
IS AVAILABLE FROM THE LIBRARY OF CONGRESS

ISBN-13: 978-1-4328-5300-6 (hardcover)

ISBN 13: 978-1-4328-5301-3 (pbk.)

Published in 2018 by arrangement with Barbour Publishing, Inc.

Printed in Mexico
1 2 3 4 5 6 7 22 21 20 19 18

To Dr. Wilkinson and Dr. Spates, who, through their wisdom and caring attitudes, offer their patients hope.

Behold, the eye of the LORD is upon them that fear him, upon them that hope in his mercy.

PSALM 33:18

Prologue

Newark, New Jersey

Tears streamed down Sara Murray's face as she sat on the living-room floor, going through another box of her mother's things. Mama had passed away two weeks ago after a short three-month battle with colon cancer. By the time she'd been diagnosed and treatment had begun, things were more advanced than anyone had suspected. It shook Sara to the core how quickly it all happened. Her mother never complained of any pain she might have had. When she started feeling under the weather, she made an appointment with the doctor, figuring it was only a virus.

The agony of losing her mother was raw, and the hurt so deep Sara felt as if she were drowning in a sea of tears. She couldn't help feeling bitter. At forty-three, Mama was too young to die. And Sara, who had just turned twenty-four, was too young to lose her mother.

The task of sorting through everything in the boxes was difficult to endure, but many of the items brought back happy memories. Sara felt grateful her stepfather had let her go through Mama's personal things, saying she could take whatever she wanted.

Among the items Sara found first was a pretty scarf she had given Mama on her birthday last year. Sara had no idea then that it would be her mother's final birthday celebration.

She lifted the silky blue scarf, with little designs of black scattered throughout, and stretched the material out, remembering how pretty her mother looked wearing it around her neck. Even though Mama had several other scarves, for some reason she loved this one the most and seldom wore the other ones. She found so many different ways to wear the scarf and matched it with many of the outfits she wore, sometimes adding a pretty pin to hold the lovely item in place.

Inhaling deeply and pressing the silkiness against her face, Sara breathed in the fragrance of her mother's lily-scented perfume. If she closed her eyes, it almost seemed as if Mama was sitting right there beside her. Did her mother suspect when Sara gave her the scarf that it would be her last birthday? There were so many unanswered questions. *Was Mama partial to the blue-and-black scarf because I gave it to her?*

Gulping in air and swallowing past the lump in her throat, Sara couldn't hold back her tears any more than she could all the others she had shed since her mother's death. Watching Mama slip away so fast had been hard, but the absence of her presence was like nothing she'd ever dealt with before.

"Oh Mama," Sara whispered, feeling more alone than ever. "I miss you so much. Why did you have to die?" She looked upward. "If there is a God, why did You take my mother?"

Making it through the viewing and funeral service had seemed almost surreal — she felt nothing. Going through her mother's things, however, brought back the agony of her loss tenfold.

After several minutes, Sara's sobbing lessened, and she pulled herself together, hiccupping a few times. Then she tied the scarf loosely around her neck.

"Score one for Dean Murray," Sara muttered, blowing her nose into a tissue she pulled from her shirt pocket. At least Dean realized Sara could never part with some of her mother's belongings, like this simple but lovely scarf.

For the first six years of Sara's life, it had been just her and Mama. Then Dean entered the picture, and everything changed. He and Mama got married, and two years later Sara ended up with a little brother. She'd never felt close to Dean, and when a baby came along, things got worse. Kenny was the apple of his daddy's eye and could do no wrong. Even now, Dean gave in to his son's every whim.

Sara bit her lip, drawing blood, as she reflected on the many times she'd questioned Mama about her biological father. *Who was he, where did he live, and how come Mama refused to talk about him?* Instead of providing answers to Sara's questions, her mother would be evasive and change the subject. Now that Mama was dead, it was doubtful that Sara would ever know the truth of her heritage or find out who her real father was.

Sara pulled another box across the room and took a seat on the couch. She still hadn't found the Bible Mama told her about before she died and didn't know if it was in any of the boxes Dean had filled with his wife's personal items. For all Sara knew, the Bible Mama spoke of had been thrown out. If Sara understood her mother's dying words right, there was a letter inside the Bible that she'd written to Sara.

But it doesn't make sense. If Mama wanted me to know something, why didn't she tell me in person, instead of writing a letter?

Sara reached into the box and pulled out two photo albums, filled with pictures of her when she was a baby. Some of the photos had Mama in them too. She looked so pretty with her long auburn hair.

Not like mine. Sara touched her long wavy hair. *I wonder if my father's hair was also blond.*

After flipping through the albums, she noticed an envelope with more photos inside. These were several recent pictures, some from last year. Shuffling through a few of them, Sara stopped at one in particular that had been taken on her mother's birthday. It was funny how a single photo could take you back to the exact moment it had been snapped.

Sara smiled, looking at her mother, posing like a model with the new blue-and-black scarf around her neck. She remembered her own words exactly, asking Mama to *"pose pretty for the camera,"* right after she opened the gift bag with the scarf tucked neatly inside.

Sara wiped her nose as she continued to look at other photos. Most of the pictures had the date they were taken, embedded right into the photo. On some of the others, her mother had written the dates on the back. "I'll have to buy more albums, so I can arrange these other pictures in order." Sara swiped at a few more tears trickling down her cheeks. Then she returned to the box and took out a small, velvet-lined container. Nothing but costume jewelry in there, so she set it aside. Underneath that were the scarves Mama used to wear regularly before receiving the one from Sara.

Sara had hoped Dean would have given her Mama's wedding ring. What was he planning to do with it anyway? Perhaps he was saving it to give to his son's future wife someday.

She swallowed against the thickening in her throat. If she weren't in the middle of taking business classes at her local community college, she'd consider leaving town. With Mama gone, why should she stay?

Sara thought about her part-time job at a local dentist's office. She enjoyed working there when she wasn't in school, but being a receptionist wasn't something she wanted to do for the rest of her life.

Sara pulled the other miscellaneous scarves out of the box and gasped. Hiding underneath was a Bible. With trembling fingers, she lifted it out and held it against her chest. Why had she never seen this before?

Sara began thumbing through the pages, until she spotted an envelope tucked between the books of Matthew and Mark. She tore it open and read her mother's letter out loud.

"Dear Sara,

If you are reading this letter, it's because I am gone. There aren't enough words to say how much you mean to me. And with what you are about to read, please know I was never ashamed of you. The actions I chose to take when I was old enough to know better are where my guilt lies. You, my sweet daughter, are special. Don't ever forget that.

After all the years you have asked about your heritage and I've refused to reveal anything, I now want you to know the truth. My maiden name was Lapp. I changed it after I left home when I was eighteen.

My parents, Willis and Mary Ruth, live

in Strasburg, Pennsylvania, and here is their address. Hopefully, someday you'll get the chance to meet them. If you do, please tell my mom and dad that I love them and always have. Tell them I'm sorry for all the things I said and did to hurt my family before I ran away from home all those years ago.

Please let your grandparents know I was too ashamed to tell them about you. I didn't know what they would think of me, being unmarried and pregnant.

I am telling you this now because you have the right to get to know them, and they you. I hope and pray someday you will make peace with Dean and your brother. While my husband may not have been the perfect father figure for you, he has been a good provider, and did the best he could.

All my love,
Mama"

Sara nearly choked on the sob rising in her throat. *Oh Mama, why couldn't you have told me all this sooner? If you really wanted me to know my grandparents, then why'd you wait till now? We could have visited them together.*

She read her mother's letter several more

times before setting it aside. While Mama had written her parents' address on the back of the letter, there was no phone number included. Surely they must have a phone.

As Sara held the letter close to her heart, she made a decision. She would write to Willis and Mary Ruth Lapp, saying she'd like to come in June, but it might not be until July 5th or after because she had summer classes to finish. If they wanted to see her, she would pay them a visit, and maybe make the trip by bus as far as Philadelphia. Perhaps then she would learn the identity of her real father.

Chapter 1

One week later
Philadelphia, Pennsylvania

Michelle Taylor stared at the contents of her wallet and groaned. She barely had enough money to buy groceries this week, much less pay the rent that was due five days ago. She'd lost her job at a local coffee shop a month ago and hadn't been able to find another position. What little money she had saved went to pay last month's rent. Soon Mr. Henson would be hounding her for June's rent, and if she didn't come through, he'd probably throw her out in the street, like he had the last tenant.

Michelle looked around her shabby studio apartment. It came fully furnished but didn't include more than the basics — a few dishes and cooking utensils, a small kitchen table with two chairs, a well-used sofa, and a bed that pulled down from the wall. In the cramped kitchen area, peeling linoleum held little appeal, nor did the water-stained ceiling. The vinyl on the wall near the kitchen table had been ripped, and the chipped cabinet doors where she kept her canned goods hung askew. The rust-stained sink and crooked blinds on the window completed the gloomy picture in this room, not to mention the hum of the old refrigerator that just about drove her batty.

Then there was the pathetic bathroom. The toilet ran unless she shook the handle a couple of times. Chipped grout, blackened in places with sickening mold, made the faded tile behind the tub/shower combination anything but pleasing. Hard water stains covered the shower door, and some of the tiles on the floor had begun to buckle. The sink faucet dripped constantly, even though Michelle had tried several times to fix it — a job her landlord should have taken care of. There was nothing high class about this dwelling, but at least it gave Michelle a roof over her head — same as it did for the rest of the building's occupants. No one in this building was high class, most certainly not Michelle.

Emotionally and physically exhausted, she moved from the kitchen area and sank to the outdated, black, imitation-leather sofa.

Leaning her head back, and using her fingertips, she massaged her throbbing forehead. *What I should do is get out of Philly and make a new start somewhere else. Guess I could go back to Ohio and see if Al and Sandy will take me in again. Course, it's been so long they might have moved, or at the very least, taken in more foster kids, so they wouldn't have room for an unwanted guest.*

Michelle hadn't seen her foster parents since she graduated from high school and went out on her own six years ago. She hadn't called or even sent a postcard to let them know where she was or how she was doing. "They probably wouldn't care anyhow," she muttered. "Truth be told, Sandy and Al were probably glad to get rid of me."

Michelle squeezed her eyes shut, wincing as her headache worsened. *Shoulda kept my grades up in school. I may have had a chance at a college scholarship and might be workin' at a decent job by now. Guess this is what I get for being a know-it-all and running off the minute I got out of high school.*

When Michelle left Columbus, she'd gone from town to town, taking whatever menial jobs she could find. When things went bad, or she ran low on money, she moved on, always searching — always hoping — wishing she could put down permanent roots.

All Michelle had ever wanted was to feel loved and accepted — to feel like she truly belonged. Of course, it was only wishful thinking. At the rate things were going, she'd never have a place she could call "home" and mean it. It was doubtful Michelle would ever know what the love of a caring family was all about.

Her head jerked when someone pounded on the door. *Oh great. I bet that's Mr. Henson, coming for the rent I don't have. If I don't answer, he'll think I'm not here and go away.* She sat perfectly still and didn't make a sound.

The pounding continued. "Michelle! Come on, sweetie, I know you're in there, so open this door."

Relieved that it wasn't Mr. Henson after all, she called, "Coming, Jerry."

Michelle jumped up and hurried across the room. Jerry had been kind of edgy when he came to see her last night, and she didn't want him to make a scene outside her door. A few times before when she'd refused to let him in because he'd been drinking too much, he'd become loud and boisterous. After some of the other tenants complained about the noise, the grumpy landlord warned her that she would have to leave if it happened again.

Another loud knock on the door, and Michelle jerked it open. "Said I was coming. Didn't you hear me through the paper-thin door?"

Jerry's eyelids lowered as he stepped inside and slammed the door shut. "Yeah, I heard ya." He reached out and pulled her close.

Michelle smelled the rotten-egg scent of beer on his breath as soon as he kissed her, and she nearly gagged. Michelle had never acquired a taste for alcohol or appreciated the smell of it. The same thing held true for cigarette smoke. It wasn't that she thought she was too good for those things. They just made her feel sick.

"How'd your day go?" Jerry held Michelle so close she could barely breathe. "Did ya find another job yet?"

"No, I did not. Nobody seems to be hiring right now." Michelle pulled on her shirt collar. "And if I don't find something soon, I'll be kicked out of this apartment building for not paying the rent." She didn't let on that Jerry's yelling outside her door could also get her kicked out. He wouldn't think twice about threatening the landlord.

Jerry released his hold on her and sauntered across the room to the nearly empty refrigerator. "Ya got any beer?"

"No, and I hardly have any food either. If my luck doesn't change soon, I could end up living on the streets with all the other homeless people in this town."

Jerry raked his fingers through the ends of his curly brown hair. It looked like he hadn't washed it in several days. "You ain't gonna end up on the streets, sweetie, 'cause I want ya to move in with me. I told you that last night, remember?"

Michelle did remember. How could she forget? After she'd declined his offer, they'd had a big argument that ended with Jerry grabbing her so tight, she'd been left with bruises on both of her wrists.

"Michelle, did ya hear what I said?" Eyes narrowing, he got right in her face.

She nodded. "I'm just thinking, is all."

"Well, don't think too long. Just pack up your things and let's go. You'll be glad to say goodbye to this place."

"I told you last night that I'm thinking about leaving town — at least for a while. I may go back to Columbus to see my foster parents."

Jerry's brown eyes darkened as his nostrils flared. "And I said I don't want you to go anywhere but with me." His features softened a bit. "I'd miss you, baby. And you'd miss me too. Ya know you would."

Michelle twisted a strand of her long auburn hair around one finger. If she stayed in Philly and moved in with Jerry, he'd want more than she was ready to give him. They'd known each other less than a month, and even though Michelle was attracted to Jerry's good looks, his possessive nature worried her. Almost from the first night they'd met in a pool hall across town, he'd acted as if he owned Michelle. What worried her the most about Jerry, however, was his temper. In her early childhood years, she been the brunt of her parents' anger, until child services intervened and put Michelle and her brothers, Ernie and Jack, in foster care. Unfortunately, they had not all gone to the same home.

If a person could choose their parents, Michelle would certainly not have picked Herb and Ginny Taylor. Dad abused Mom physically and emotionally, and they both abused their kids. Michelle could still see her father standing over her with his belt raised, an angry scowl on his face over something he'd accused her of doing. He hadn't aimed for any particular spot. The belt connected wherever it landed, on her legs, arms, and back. He'd treated the boys just as harshly, often smacking them around until bruises or angry welts appeared.

Their mother was no better. She often pulled Michelle's hair and lashed out in anger. It was usually not because of anything Michelle had done wrong, but rather because Mom was mad at her husband.

One time, when Michelle had defended Ernie for something he'd been unjustly accused of, Mom screamed at Michelle, "Shut your big mouth!" Then she'd grabbed Michelle around the neck and tried to choke her. Fortunately, little Jack started bawling really loud, and Mom came to her senses. She'd never apologized though — just made a few threats and sent Michelle to her room.

Michelle blinked when Jerry waved his hand in front of her face. "Hey, snap out of it. You're spacing out on me, babe. Now go pack up your things and let's get outa here before that money-hungry landlord of yours comes to pay you a visit."

Looking him steadily in the eyes, Michelle thrust out her chin, then vigorously shook her head. "I am not moving in with you, Jerry. So please stop asking."

He drew closer so that they were nose to nose. "You're my girl, and you'd better do as I say."

Michelle couldn't mistake his tone of agitation, and a familiar fear bubbled in her soul. She took a step back, biting the inside of her cheek. "I — I appreciate the offer, Jerry, but as I said before, I'm not ready to move in with you." She spoke slowly and kept her voice low, hoping it would calm him.

"Well, ya wanna know what I think, sugar? I think you don't know what ya want."

"Yes I do, Jerry, and it . . . it's not you." Michelle didn't know where her courage came from, but she felt a little braver.

"What do you mean, it's not me? We've been together almost every night since we first met." His words slurred as he grabbed Michelle's shoulders and gave her a cruel shake.

"Stop it! You're hurting me." She pushed him back.

He sneered at her. "Ya think this hurts? If you leave me, Michelle, you'll hurt even more. You know you love me, babe."

Michelle swallowed against the bile rising in her throat. She wanted Jerry to leave but feared his reaction if she ordered him to go.

"Come here and give me some love." Jerry grabbed her again, and before she could react, he kissed her neck roughly, while holding her arms tightly behind her back. His lips moved from Michelle's neck to her mouth, and then he pushed her down on the couch. "You're mine. And don't you ever forget it."

Michelle fought against Jerry's brute strength, and when he wouldn't let her up, she bit his arm.

"Why, you little —" He cursed and slapped Michelle's face so hard her head jerked back.

She cried out and somehow managed to wiggle out from under him and off the couch. "If you don't leave right now, I'll scream at the top of my lungs for someone to call the cops. And they will too. You can count on it."

Jerry leapt off the couch and, panting heavily, gave her another hard slap, right where he'd hit her before. Whirling around, he stomped across the room and out the door, slamming it behind him.

Gasping for breath, Michelle ran to the door and bolted it shut. She had to get out of here — not just because she had no money to pay the rent, but to escape the man she'd foolishly gotten involved with.

She dashed to the bathroom and looked in the mirror. Her hand immediately went to the red mark quite visible on her face. "Ouch. I do not deserve this kind of treatment — not from Jerry or anyone."

Wincing, Michelle ran some cool water on a washcloth and dabbed it on the red, stinging skin.

Today was not the first time Jerry had physically abused her, and if she stayed in Philadelphia and kept seeing him, Michelle knew it wouldn't be the last.

Michelle awoke with a pounding headache. After Jerry left last night she'd had a hard time getting to sleep. Was he right? Should she stay and move in with him? Would that be the sensible thing to do? It would certainly take care of her financial problems.

Michelle shook her head. *What am I thinking? He's a jerk. I need to get away from him now. If I don't, I could end up in an abusive relationship for the rest of my life.*

She pulled herself out of bed and plodded across the room. Staring out the window at the depressing scene, Michelle weighed her options. She was tired of the unexciting view that greeted her every day. Seeing all the buildings surrounding her apartment made her feel closed in. And what little bit of sky she could actually see was dismal, just like her mood. She could either stay here in Philly and keep searching for another job, or get out of town and start over someplace else. One thing was sure: she had to break things off with Jerry. He was a loser and, short of a miracle, he would never treat her with love and respect.

While brushing her teeth, Michelle glanced in the cracked mirror. At least there weren't any marks left where she'd been slapped, and Jerry hadn't loosened any of her teeth. Dad had done that once to Mom, and they'd been too poor to go to the dentist.

Shaking her negative thoughts aside, Michelle got dressed and went to the kitchen to fix breakfast. She'd no more than taken out a bowl for cold cereal when a knock sounded on the door.

"Hey babe, let me in. I have somethin' for you."

Michelle groaned inwardly. Jerry was back. She figured if she didn't open the door, he'd keep knocking and wake the whole apartment complex, including her landlord.

She opened the door a crack, but kept the chain bolted. "What do you want, Jerry?"

"Came to say I'm sorry for last night." He held a pink carnation in his hand. "I wanna start over, darlin'. I promise never to hit you again."

Yeah, right. Michelle did not have to think about his offer very long. She didn't trust him not to hit her again. She'd had enough abuse when she was growing up. After hearing the same old assurances from her parents that they were sorry and it wouldn't happen again, Michelle knew good and well that Jerry would never keep the promise he'd just made.

"Sorry, Jerry, I'm not interested in starting over." Michelle shut the door in his face.

"You'll change your mind when you've had a chance to think things over," he called through the door. "I'll be back tomorrow, and we can talk about this again."

"You can come back if you want, but I won't be here," Michelle mumbled under her breath, as she heard his footsteps fading away. She lifted a hand to her still-tender cheek. "You'll never do this to me again. Don't know where I'm headed, but I'm gettin' out of here tomorrow, one way or the other."

CHAPTER 2

Strasburg, Pennsylvania

Mary Ruth Lapp ambled down the driveway to get the mail. She'd meant to go to the mailbox earlier, but it had rained hard most of the day, and she hadn't felt like going outside. As some of the clouds parted, a glorious sunset appeared with pink, gold, and orange hues. Mary Ruth took in its beauty, while breathing in the fresh after-rain scent.

Some days it was hard to feel positive, with all the terrible things going on in the world, but today wasn't one of them. Mary Ruth's spirits soared as she looked toward the trees and listened to the birds singing overhead as they found places to roost for the night. Of course she had always liked the month of June with the fragrance of flowers bursting open all around and mild temperatures that went well with tilling the garden.

Sighing contentedly, Mary Ruth reached the end of the driveway and pulled the mail out of their mailbox. She sorted through several advertising flyers, along with a few bills. There was also a letter addressed to Mr. and Mrs. Willis Lapp, but the return address was missing. In the place where it should have been was a sticky, rough spot, as though the address label had been pulled off.

She bit her lower lip. "Now I wonder who this came from." Not only was the postmark smudged, so she couldn't tell where the letter had originated, but parts of their address were unreadable. She was impressed that the post office had managed to deliver it.

Mary Ruth decided to open it right there on the spot, but as she struggled to open the envelope flap, it slipped from her hands, landing on the soggy, wet ground.

"*Ach!* Now look what I've done." She bent down and scooped up the letter. Unfortunately, the envelope acted like a sponge, turning it somewhat soggy. Wiping it quickly on her dress, Mary Ruth fussed, "Hopefully I saved the inside, and nothing got smudged."

Despite her curiosity, she decided to wait until she got back to the house to open the envelope. Besides, she was losing daylight, and it would soon be too dark to read.

Back at the house, Mary Ruth placed the bills and junk mail on the kitchen table. Then she sat in a chair and tore the envelope open. Squinting as she read the somewhat blurred words on the page, her heart began to pound. *Oh my! This cannot be. After all these years of hoping we would see or hear from our daughter, and now we find out she has died?*

Unable to read further, Mary Ruth covered her mouth with the palm of her hand, in an attempt to stifle the sobs. But her shoulders shook, and tears rose to the surface anyway.

Once she'd gained some semblance of composure, Mary Ruth rushed into the living room, where she found her husband asleep in his recliner. "Wake up, Willis! We've received some unsettling news."

He sputtered and snorted with eyes half-closed and reading glasses perched on the end of his nose. "Please don't bother me right now, *fraa;* I'm restin' my eyes."

She shook his arm, and when he became fully awake, Mary Ruth waved the letter in his face. "Rhoda's daughter wrote this letter. She wanted us to know that her *mudder* — our *dochder* — passed away two weeks ago from colon cancer."

Willis snapped to attention, his bushy gray brows lifting high as his eyes opened wide. "What are you talking about?"

"It's right here in this letter from Sara Murray. If I'm reading it right, she found a letter from Rhoda in an old Bible. The note said Rhoda left home when she was eighteen, and she told Sara about us. Rhoda asked her daughter to tell us how sorry she was for the things she said and did before she ran away from home. She'd been too ashamed to tell us she was expecting a baby." Mary Ruth paused and dabbed her eyes with a tissue, before taking a seat on the couch. "Oh Willis, how could we not know or even suspect that Rhoda was expecting a *boppli*? I wonder who the baby's father was. Do you have any idea, Willis?"

He shook his head. "You know how Rhoda could be. She was very private and kept things to herself. Most young women her age would have brought their boyfriends home to meet her parents. But there was no hint of our daughter being courted by anyone. I'm guessing it may not have been any of the young fellows from our church district. Could have been an English man for all I know. They could have run off together and got married."

Willis rose from his chair and sat beside Mary Ruth. "It's hard to accept the fact that we will never see our daughter again in this world, but maybe there's a chance we can meet our granddaughter." He reached over and clasped her hand. "Did she include an address or phone number so we can make contact with her?"

Mary Ruth shook her head, then pointed to the soiled letter. "Not that I could see, but she did say she's coming to meet us and should arrive in the afternoon at the bus station in Philadelphia on the fifth of June. At least, I think that's the date it says. With all the smudges, plus the missing address label, I have no idea how we can contact Sara." She leaned closer to Willis, clutching his arm. "Despite the sadness of learning Rhoda has passed away, the letter from Sara does give my spirits a tiny lift. Doesn't it do that for you, Willis?"

He nodded. "It pains me to realize that our dochder will never walk through our front door again, but it's good to know the granddaughter we never knew existed wants to meet us. Maybe she can shed some light on who her father is. If Rhoda did marry her baby's father and he's still living, then Sara will be able to tell us what we want to know. We might even get the opportunity to meet him sometime."

Mary Ruth dabbed at some fresh-fallen tears. "I can barely take it all in." Her chin trembled as she squinted at the blurry words toward the bottom of the damp paper. The ink had run in several places, making the rest of the letter difficult to read. "Do you think Sara is aware that we are Amish?"

"I don't know, though I would think Rhoda would have told her. May I see the letter?" Willis held out his hand.

She handed it to him. "Some of the words are blurred because I dropped the letter on the wet grass, but June 5th is tomorrow. We need to be at the bus station in Philadelphia to pick Sara up when she arrives." Tears stung Mary Ruth's eyes as she squeezed the folds in her dress. "Oh Willis, how could Rhoda have stayed away all those years without telling us she had a child?"

Before he could respond, she hurried on. "My heart aches to realize we will never see our daughter again, but at least we're being given the chance to meet our granddaughter. It's like a miracle, don't you agree?"

"Jah." Willis's eyes also glistened with tears. "I'll need to call one of our drivers right away and see if he can take us to Philadelphia tomorrow." He looked at the

envelope he still held in his hand. "Sure wish she had included a picture so we'll know who to look for."

Mary Ruth shook her head. "I don't need a picture. If she is our Rhoda's daughter, I'm sure I will know it the minute I see her."

Philadelphia

As the Lapps' driver, Stan Eaton, parked his van in the bus station parking lot, Mary Ruth's stomach tightened. She turned to Willis and gripped his arm. "What if Sara doesn't know we are Amish? She made no reference to it in her letter — at least the part I was able read clearly. It may come as a shock to her."

"Now, Mary Ruth, we spoke of this yesterday, and you're fretting too much. If Sara doesn't know about her mother's heritage, she will soon enough." Willis reached into his pants' pocket and pulled out the pocket watch he'd had since they got married forty-eight years ago. "According to the afternoon schedule Stan pulled up on his computer for us, the bus should be here soon, if it hasn't already arrived."

"That's right," Stan called over his shoulder. "But schedules are always subject to change. Your granddaughter's bus could get here early or it might pull in late."

Mary Ruth smoothed some imaginary wrinkles from her plain blue dress and made sure there were no stray hairs sneaking out from under her head covering. "Do you think Sara will like us, Willis? Will she be comfortable staying in our plain, simple home? Oh, I hope she can be with us for several weeks. It will take at least that long for us to get acquainted, and we'll want to find out more about Rhoda."

He patted her hand gently. "Try not to worry, Mary Ruth. I'm sure everything will work out. She probably has as many questions to ask us as we do her." Willis pushed the button to open the van door. "Now let's get out and go wait for the bus. I don't see any sign of one at the moment, so I'm sure it hasn't gotten here yet. Either that, or it came in early and has already headed out on its next route."

Mary Ruth opened her door and stepped down. She paused long enough to say a quick prayer, then followed her husband toward the station. When they entered the building, where several people with suitcases milled around, Mary Ruth saw a young woman with long auburn hair standing near the ticket booth.

With excitement coursing through her veins, she caught hold of her husband's arm. "Oh look! That's Sara over there." She pointed. "See, that pretty young woman? Why, she has the same color hair as our Rhoda." She reached up and patted the sides of her head. "And before gray hairs started creeping in, my hair was a golden red too."

Willis squinted as he stared at the young woman. "You're right, Mary Ruth. It's almost like we're seeing our dochder back before she ran away from our home."

Mary Ruth could hardly contain herself. Tears of joy filled her eyes as she and Willis headed in their granddaughter's direction.

As Michelle approached the booth to purchase her bus ticket to anywhere but Philly, she noticed an Amish couple staring at her. They seemed to be sizing her up.

Michelle's scalp prickled, and she rolled her eyes. *What's wrong with those two? Surely this isn't the first time they've seen an English woman. Maybe it is the first time they'd been in a bus station though. Could be they aren't sure what to do.*

While she didn't know a whole lot about the Amish, Michelle had seen a few episodes of a reality show on TV. It was about six young Amish people who hadn't yet joined the Amish church and had been touring the country on motorcycles. Of course, she wasn't sure how accurate the show had been, but it gave her an inkling of what Amish life was all about when the people were interviewed and they offered an account of what it was like growing up in homes with lots of rules and no electricity.

When the elderly couple began walking toward her, Michelle stiffened. *I hope they're not going to talk to me. I wouldn't have any idea what to say to people like them. They look so prim and proper. I probably seem like a hick to them.*

She took a few steps to the right and turned her back on the couple. *They could be here just to purchase a bus ticket, same as me. That show on TV did mention that some Amish people like to travel. Although, at their age, these two would not likely go anywhere on the back of a motorcycle.* It did seem odd, though, that neither the man nor the woman had a suitcase. If they planned to make a trip, surely there would be at least one piece of luggage between them.

"Excuse me, miss, but is your name Sara Murray?"

Michelle winced when the Amish man tapped her on the shoulder. *Oh great, I shoulda figured by the way they were looking at me that one of 'em would end up saying something.*

She turned back around and opened her mouth, but before she could respond to the man's question, the woman spoke. "I'm Mary Ruth Lapp, and this is my husband, Willis. We're your grandparents, Sara, and we're so happy you wrote and asked if you could meet us."

When the lady paused to swallow, Michelle was going to say that they had mistaken her for someone else. But she never got the chance, because the Amish woman quickly continued.

"Since we knew nothing about you until your letter arrived, you can imagine how surprised we were when you stated that you would be coming in on the bus here today." Mary Ruth gave an embarrassed laugh. She was clearly as nervous as Michelle felt. "Of course, when I dropped your letter in the wet grass, it made it difficult to be sure if this was the actual day you said you needed us to pick you up."

Willis nodded. "We were hoping it was, and since you're here, it can only mean that we read the letter right."

Dumbfounded, Michelle wasn't sure what to say. She looked all around and didn't see any other young women in the bus station, so she could understand why the Amish couple may have mistaken her for their granddaughter. *Would it be wrong if I played along with it?* Michelle asked herself. *If I go with them to wherever they live, I'll have a safe place to stay for a while, and I won't have to worry about finding a job or looking for another town to start over in. This could be the answer to the predicament I'm in financially too — not to mention getting far from Jerry.*

Michelle hardly knew what to think about this turn of events, except that a stroke of luck must have finally come her way. Her conscience pricked her just a bit though. *What's going to happen when the real Sara Murray shows up at the bus station and no one is here to pick her up? Does she know where her grandparents live? What if she visits and finds me impersonating her?* Michelle's fingers clenched around her suitcase handle so tightly she feared it would break. Then, throwing caution and all sensible reason aside, she let go of the handle and gave Mary Ruth a hug. "It's good to meet you, Grandma." She smiled at Willis. "You too, Grandpa Lapp."

Willis nodded, and Mary Ruth flashed Michelle a wide smile. "We hired a driver to bring us here to pick you up, and it'll take an hour or so to get to our home in Strasburg. But that's fine with me, because as we travel, it'll give us a chance to get to know a bit about each other."

Oh boy, Michelle thought, as the three of them began walking toward a silver-gray van. *I'll need to remember to respond to the name Sara and try not to say or do anything that would give away my true identity. This is my chance to get out of Philly and away from my abusive so-called boyfriend, so I can't do anything to mess it up.*

Chapter 3

Strasburg

As the Lapps' driver pulled onto a graveled driveway, a tall, white farmhouse with a wide front porch stood before them. Several feet to the left was an enormous red barn. No horses or buggies were in sight, but several chickens ran around the front yard, pecking at the neatly trimmed grass. *Probably looking for worms.* Michelle pressed a fist to her lips to cover her smile. *I can do this. After all, how hard can it be to live on a farm for a few days or a week? I'll just have to make sure I answer when they call me Sara.*

"You two ladies can go on inside while I pay Stan and get Sara's luggage from the back." Willis opened the van door and stepped down.

Michelle got out on her side, and Mary Ruth followed. As they began walking toward the house, Mary Ruth slipped her arm around Michelle's waist. "I'm so happy you contacted us, Sara. You have no idea how much having you here means to me and your grandfather."

Michelle made sure to put on her best smile. "I'm glad for the opportunity to get to know you both." Her statement wasn't really a lie. She was glad to be with the Amish couple right now. It was far better than dealing with Jerry and his outbursts of anger and abuse. Depending on how things worked out, she would have free room and board for a few days, or maybe longer. Michelle actually believed, for the first time in a long time, that she had found a safe, comfortable place to stay.

They were almost to the house when a beautiful brown-and-white collie with a big belly waddled up to greet them.

Michelle jumped back. She wasn't used to being around dogs — especially one this large. Ever since she'd been bitten by a snarling dog on the way home from grade school, she'd shied away from them — big or small. Those little ones might look cute and innocent enough, but they had sharp teeth too.

"It's okay," Mary Ruth assured her. "Sadie won't bite. She's just eager to meet you." She reached down and patted the dog's head. "She'll soon have puppies, so I bet she was taking a nap when the van pulled in."

Michelle wasn't convinced that the collie wouldn't bite, but she hesitantly reached out her hand so Sadie could sniff it.

Sadie did more than sniff Michelle's hand however. She licked it with her slurpy wet tongue.

"Eww . . ."

Mary Ruth snickered. "She likes you, Sara. Sadie saves her kisses for those she accepts."

Feeling a little less intimidated, Michelle bent down and rubbed the dog's ears. They were soft as silk. "Guess I should feel honored then."

"Yes, indeed." Mary Ruth motioned to the house. "Shall we go inside now?"

Michelle nodded, eager to get away from the dog. While Sadie might appear friendly right now, she wasn't sure she could trust the animal. For that matter, Michelle wasn't sure she could trust herself either. Thanks to her impetuous decision, she was now in a precarious position, pretending to be someone else.

Stepping onto the porch, she noticed a few wicker chairs, as well as a finely crafted wooden bench near the front door. Hanging from the porch eaves were two hummingbird feeders, as well as three pots of pink-and-white petunias. The picturesque setting was so appealing, Michelle wanted to take a seat on the porch and forget about going inside for the moment. But she followed Mary Ruth's lead and entered the house.

When they got inside, Michele felt as if she'd taken a step back in time. The first thing she noticed was a refreshing lemon scent. It reminded her of the furniture polish her foster mother had used whenever she cleaned house. The living room, where Mary Ruth had taken her first, had a comfy-looking upholstered couch with two end tables on either side, as well as a coffee table in front of the sofa. The wooden pieces appeared to be as expertly made as the bench on the front porch.

Matching recliners were positioned on the left side of the room, and on the right side sat a wooden rocking chair with quilted padding on the seat and backrest. With the exception of a braided throw rug placed near the fireplace, there were no carpets on the hardwood floors, yet the room seemed cozy and rather quaint.

An antique-looking clock sat on the fireplace mantel with two large candles on either side. Two gas lamps positioned at opposite ends of the room were the only apparent source of light, other than the windows facing the front yard.

Several balls of yarn peeked out of a wicker basket on the floor next to the rocker. There were no pictures on the walls, but the grandfather clock standing majestically against one wall made up for the lack of photos or paintings. Despite the quaintness of this room, it had a comfortable feel — like wearing a pair of old bedroom slippers.

As if on cue, the stately grandfather clock bonged, its huge pendulum swinging back and forth in perfect motion. Michelle would have to get used to the loud *tick-tock*s and *bong*s, but it was better than the city noises she'd heard out her apartment window in Philadelphia every night when she tried to fall asleep.

"How do you like our grandfather clock?" Mary Ruth questioned. Without waiting for Michelle to answer, she rushed on. "It's been in our family a long time. As a matter of fact, it used to belong to Willis's grandparents."

"It's beautiful, but big, and kinda loud," Michelle answered, hoping she didn't sound rude.

"You'll get used to it." Mary Ruth giggled.

"When we first got the clock, it kept me awake at night. But now we hardly notice when it chimes every half hour."

Every half hour? Oh boy. It will take some getting used to. Michelle plastered on a fake smile, while nodding her head. *During the day shouldn't be too bad, and hopefully my room will be at the far end of the house, so maybe I won't hear the clock at night.*

One thing she noticed was clearly missing in this Amish room was a TV. But then she remembered from the reality show she'd watched that the Amish did not allow televisions, computers, or other modern equipment in their homes. She thought the narrator said the Amish were taught to be separated from the desires and goals of the modern world. They also believed the use of modern things in their home would tear their family unit apart and take their focus away from God. *Well, maybe they are better off without all the things we, who live in the modern world, have in our homes.* Of course, Michelle didn't have a lot of fancy gadgets. How could she when she kept moving from place to place with only her clothes and a few personal things? If she had a TV available to watch, it was fine, but Michelle felt sure she could get by without it. Actually she didn't care that much about a lot of modern things.

"Here's your suitcase, Sara," Willis announced when he entered the room. He looked over at Mary Ruth. "Would you want to show our granddaughter her room?"

Mary Ruth nodded. "Jah, but if you don't mind carrying her suitcase up the stairs, I would appreciate it. With all the cleaning I did yesterday after we got Sara's letter, my back's hurting a bit."

"That's okay. I can carry my own suitcase," Michelle was quick to say. These people were too old to be lugging heavy things up the stairs. And her oversized suitcase was weighty, because everything she owned was in it. Not that Michelle had an abundance of things, but clothes, makeup, and personal items did take up a lot of space when crammed into one piece of luggage.

"Well then, if you don't mind, I'll head back outside and get a few chores done before it's time for supper."

Michelle took the suitcase from Willis. "It's not a problem. I've been lugging this old thing around for the last six . . ." She clamped her mouth closed so hard her teeth clicked. *Watch what you say, Michelle, or you're gonna blow it.*

"What were you going to say, Sara?" Mary Ruth put her hand on Michelle's arm.

"Oh, nothing. I just meant that I've had the suitcase a long time, and it's seen better days."

"Maybe it's time to buy a new one," Willis suggested.

"I'm short on money right now, so new luggage is not a priority."

"If you'd like a new one, we'd be happy to help."

Michelle looked at Mary Ruth and shook her head. "That's okay. I'm fine with this one. Sometimes it's hard to part with old stuff." It was bad enough she was posing to be the Lapps' granddaughter; she didn't want to take their money or any gifts. Just a comfortable place to stay for a while, and then she'd be on her way. Hopefully, by the time the real Sara showed up, Michelle would be long gone and wouldn't have to offer any explanations.

While Michelle sat with Mary Ruth and Willis at the kitchen table that evening, preparing to eat supper, she studied her surroundings. The kitchen was cozy, but no less plain than the living room or the bedroom Michelle had been assigned. Several pots and pans dangled from a rack above the stove. A set of metal canisters graced one counter, next to a ceramic cookie jar. On another counter sat a large bowl filled with bananas and oranges. There was no toaster, blender, microwave, or electric coffee pot, nor an electric dishwasher. Michelle knew what that meant — washing dishes by hand. She didn't see it as a problem, because none of the apartments she'd rented over the years had been equipped with a dishwasher. So washing dishes had become a part of her daily routine.

The stove and refrigerator were both run off propane gas, which Mary Ruth had earlier explained. Michelle couldn't imagine how these people got by without the benefit of electrical appliances in their home, but they appeared to be content. It would take some getting used to on her part, though, for however long she ended up staying with the Lapps.

Michelle noticed a few herb pots soaking up natural light on the windowsill by the kitchen sink. But the brightest spot in the room was the glass vase in the center of the table, filled with pretty red-and-yellow tulips. Their aroma was overshadowed, however, by the tantalizing smell of freshly baked ham.

Michelle's stomach growled. She could hardly wait to dig in.

Willis cleared his throat, directing her attention to his place at the head of the table. "We always pray silently before our meals."

Michelle gave a nod and bowed her head. Praying was something else she was not used to doing. They'd sure never prayed before meals — or any other time — when she lived with her parents. Her foster parents weren't religious either. Even so, they'd sent Michelle and the other foster kids off to Bible school at a church close by for a few weeks every summer.

Michelle hated it. Most of the kids who attended looked down on her, like she was poor white trash. And when one snooty girl found out Michelle and the others lived with a couple who weren't their real parents, she made an issue of it — asking if they were orphans, or had they run away from home and been placed in foster care as punishment? If there was one thing Michelle couldn't stand it was someone who thought they were better than her.

Then there was the teacher, telling goody-goody stories from the Bible, and making it sound like God loved everyone. Well, He didn't love Michelle, or she wouldn't have had so many troubles since she was born.

Michelle's eyes snapped open when Willis rattled his silverware and spoke. "I hope you have a hearty appetite this evening, Sara, because it looks like my wife outdid herself with this meal." Grinning, he picked up the plate of ham and handed it to Michelle.

"No, that's okay. You go first."

He hesitated a moment, then forked a juicy-looking piece of meat onto his plate. "Here you go, Sara." Willis handed the platter to her, then dished up a few spoonfuls of mashed potatoes, which he then gave to Michelle.

She quickly took a piece of ham and added a blob of potatoes to her plate. Next came a small bowl of cut-up veggies, followed by a larger bowl filled with steaming hot peas. Michelle's mouth watered as she took her first bite of meat. "Yum. This is delicious. You're a great cook, Mary Ruth."

The woman made a clicking sound with her tongue. "Now, remember, I want you to call me Grandma. Referring to me as Mary Ruth makes it seem like we're not related."

That's because we're not. Michelle managed a brief nod and mumbled, "I'll try to remember."

"Same goes for me," Willis spoke up. "I'd be real pleased if you call me Grandpa."

"Okay." Michelle picked up her glass of water and took a drink. It didn't seem right to call these people Grandma and Grandpa when they weren't related to her. But if she was going to keep up the charade, she'd have to remember so they wouldn't be offended or catch on to the fact that she wasn't Sara Murray.

As soon as all the food had been passed around, Michelle's hosts began plying her with questions, which was the last thing she needed.

"How old are you, and when is your birthday?" Willis asked.

Michelle rolled the peas around on her plate a few seconds, then decided to tell them the truth. "My birthday is June 15th, and I'll be twenty-four years old." At least that much hadn't been a lie. She hadn't even thought about her upcoming birthday until now.

Mary Ruth smiled and clapped her hands. "Why, that's just ten days away. We'll plan something special to celebrate."

Michelle shook her head. "Oh no, please don't go to any trouble on my account. I'm not used to anyone making a big deal about my birthday."

The tiny wrinkles running across Mary Ruth's forehead deepened. "Not even your mother when she was alive?"

Michelle was on the verge of saying no, but caught herself in time. "I meant to say, since Mom died."

Willis ran a finger down the side of his nose. "But according to your letter, our daughter's only been gone a few weeks."

Michelle's cheeks warmed and she nearly choked on the piece of ham she'd put in her mouth a second ago. "You're right of course. I'm just feeling a little rattled right now. It all happened so quickly, and I'm still trying to deal with her death." Michelle couldn't help thinking: *This is only the beginning of many more lies. How am I going to know what to say or not to say without messing up? It might be best if I don't stick around here too long.*

"It's perfectly understandable that you're a bit muddled, given the fact that you're still mourning your loss." Mary Ruth reached over and gently patted Michelle's arm. "And now here you are sitting with grandparents you didn't even know you had."

Michelle blotted her lips with a napkin. "Yeah, I am pretty overwhelmed right now."

Willis handed her the bowl of mashed potatoes again. "Bet you'll feel better after you've eaten a bit more and have had a good night's sleep."

All Michelle could manage was a slow nod. She only hoped that would be the case, because at the moment, she felt like she might cave in.

When Mary Ruth and Willis retired to their room on the main floor that night, she began to fret. "I hope we didn't bombard Sara with too many questions. She seemed so edgy during supper — especially when we brought up her birthday." She turned to face Willis, who was already situated under the bedcovers. "Do you think Rhoda wasn't a good mudder to Sara? Is that why she said no one made a fuss over her birthday?"

"If you'll remember, she corrected herself." Willis yawned and fluffed up his pillow. "I can't imagine our dochder treating her own flesh-and-blood child poorly." He removed his glasses and placed them on the nightstand. "No reading for me tonight. I'm bushed."

"It's been a long, busy day."

"I hate to bring this up, but I'm sure you must realize that, according to Sara's age, our daughter was definitely with child when she ran away from home."

"Jah, I know. It was mentioned in Sara's letter to us, remember?"

"I do remember, but since some of the words in the letter were unreadable, I thought — even hoped — we may have read that part wrong."

Mary Ruth drew in a breath, but couldn't seem to fill her lungs completely. It was difficult reliving this past event — especially when she'd always felt as if they might be responsible for Rhoda leaving. Perhaps she and Willis had been too hard on her — trying to enforce rules that their daughter was good at breaking. There may have been a better way of dealing with Rhoda than chastising her all the time. Maybe she thought her parents didn't love her and wouldn't have understood if she'd told them the predicament she was in.

Would we have been understanding or driven her further away by our disapproval? Tears sprang to Mary Ruth's eyes, and she whisked them away with the back of her hand. "You're right, Willis, and I wish she had told us so we could have helped her deal with the situation."

"According to what our granddaughter wrote in the letter, Rhoda was too ashamed to tell us." Willis's eyebrows gathered in. "Maybe she felt with me being one of the church ministers, it would have been an embarrassment to us. She might have believed that if word got out that a preacher's unmarried daughter was expecting a boppli, it could have affected our standing in this community."

Mary Ruth sank to the edge of the bed and undid her hair from its bun. "I wanted to ask Sara this evening about her father but thought it could wait. She seemed overwhelmed enough with all our other questions."

"True, and that was good thinking on your part. We can talk to Sara about her father some other time." He scrubbed a hand over his face. "We need to be careful what we say about Rhoda to her daughter. Wouldn't want Sara to think her mom was a bad person." Willis heaved a sigh. "That girl was a handful. There's no doubt about it. Always close-lipped about what she was doing with her friends and staying out later than she should have, which caused us both to worry. But we still loved her, although I could always tell she was dissatisfied with the Amish ways. If we could go back and do it over, I'd try to approach the situation with our daughter differently."

"Jah." Mary Ruth sighed as she started brushing out her long hair. "Sara made no mention of her father during our supper conversation either. Is it possible that Rhoda raised her alone?"

Willis shrugged. "I don't know, but I think it's a question that does need to be asked. Maybe after breakfast tomorrow morning, when we're showing her around the farm, I'll bring up the subject."

Mary Ruth moved her head slowly up and down. "Just be careful how you approach it, Husband. Sara just got here, and we don't want to say or do anything that might scare her off. We've lived with the pain of losing our dochder all these years, and I certainly don't want to take the chance of losing our *grossdochder* too."

Alone in her room, a strange feeling came over Michelle. Mary Ruth had said when she'd first brought Michelle upstairs that this used to be her daughter's bedroom before she left home. She felt weird knowing this was where her pretend mother used to sleep. *The real Sara should be sleeping here, not me.* It was too late to back away from this. She was here, and the Lapps seemed pretty pleased. If Michelle could fake it for a while longer, until she figured out what she needed to do, everyone would be happy. At least until the real granddaughter showed up. Then a bomb would drop right over Michelle's head.

Turning her thoughts in another direction, Michelle gazed with anticipation at the four-poster double bed. Instead of using shabby covers over a skinny single bed coming down from the wall, she would sleep under the beautiful quilt that covered this bed. The two windows in the room both faced the backyard. Only a dark green shade covered them, but Michelle didn't mind the lack of a curtain. At least there would be no noisy vehicles outside, with blaring horns and screeching brakes moving down the street throughout the night. Except for the clock downstairs, she probably wouldn't hear much noise at all.

Studying the rest of the room, she noticed a wooden nightstand positioned on the right side of the bed and a tall dresser against the opposite wall. At the foot of the bed sat an old cedar chest. Michelle had placed her suitcase on top of the chest, but had only opened it to take out her cotton pajamas and personal items. She was too tired to hang up her clothes tonight. It could wait till morning.

Even though scantily furnished, the bedroom was as spotless as the rest of the house she'd seen so far. The only source of light, other than the windows, was a battery-operated lamp on the nightstand, which Michelle had turned on as soon as she came into the room.

I shouldn't be here, she thought. *This room did not belong to my mother, although I wish it had. And I would give almost anything to have caring grandparents like Willis and Mary Ruth.*

Michelle had never known her mother's parents, or her dad's either. The only thing she'd been told about them was that they lived somewhere in Idaho. She had never even seen any pictures of them. Michelle often wondered if her grandparents were bad parents, and that's why her mom and dad had turned out the way they had. Maybe both sets of grandparents were abusers or heavy drinkers. She and her brothers were probably better off not knowing them. There had been enough anxiety in their young lives just dealing with explosive parents.

Sure wish I knew where Ernie and Jack are right now. She had tried several times to locate them but always came up empty-handed. Hopefully they'd gone to good homes and had made something of themselves. "Not like me," Michelle muttered. "I'm going down a one-way street that leads to nowhere."

Michelle reflected on all the questions that had been thrown at her since arriving at the Lapps — especially during the evening meal. She'd been so nervous about saying the wrong thing, it had diminished her appetite for what should have been a delicious supper. Maybe it was a good thing she hadn't eaten too much. If Michelle ate like that on a regular basis, all those carbs could pack on the weight.

Thinking back on the conversation they'd had about her birthday and Sara's mother, Rhoda, Michelle hoped she'd been able to cover her tracks well enough by saying she felt a bit rattled. It was certainly no lie, for by the time she helped Mary Ruth do the dishes, she was exhausted from the stress of trying not to say the wrong thing. She suspected there would probably be more questions tomorrow, and she'd be riding an emotional rollercoaster again.

Guess I'll wait and deal with all that in the morning. Right now I need to go down the hall to take a shower and brush my teeth. After a good night's sleep, maybe I'll wake up with a clearer head and a better idea how to proceed.

How thankful she was that the Lapps had indoor plumbing and not an outhouse, like that reality TV show had mentioned. Michelle didn't think she could last a day without indoor bathroom conveniences.

When she pulled back the covers a short time later and climbed into the comfortable bed, Michelle's breathing became consistent and the need to sleep took over. Even the grandfather clock down in the living room, bonging out the hour, didn't disturb her rest.

Chapter 4

Michelle sat up in her bed with a start. What was that irritating sound? She climbed out and padded over to the window.

Lifting the shade, she grimaced. An enormous rooster stood on top of the woodshed, crowing for all he was worth.

She looked at the clock on her nightstand and groaned. It was five thirty in the morning, and dawn had slowly cast a glow on the yard. She sniffed the air. Was that the hearty aroma of coffee she smelled? It wasn't a mocha latte, like they'd served at the coffee shop in Philly, but it smelled almost as good. Someone was obviously up and in the kitchen downstairs.

Michelle glanced around her room again. It still looked the same, only this morning, with the bedcovers in disarray, it appeared lived-in at least.

I can't believe I'm actually here. What a stark difference, waking up this morning on a farm, when less than twenty-four hours ago she was still in her stale, dinky apartment in Philly.

Gazing out the window again, she became aware that the loudmouthed rooster had suddenly gone quiet. *Thank goodness. Why couldn't you have done that sooner so I could've slept in?*

Michelle observed how the clouds took on amazing hues of pinks and purple, then faded into orange as the sun made its full appearance. How long had it been since she noticed the sky's beauty and how pretty a sunrise could be?

Watching the clouds change to a puffy white as the sun rose higher, Michelle relived yesterday, meeting the Lapps at the bus station, and then the trip here to Strasburg. It was so different driving out of the city, once they got past King of Prussia, and observing how the landscape changed. No more skyscrapers and huge business offices blocking the view as they drove farther from the Philadelphia region. Instead, she'd seen several small businesses along the road they traveled. But even they became sparser as farms, silos, and fields dotted more of the landscape. Once in the country, she could see into the distance for many miles. A day later, here she was, the guest of an Amish couple who owned a farm. Michelle never would have believed this situation possible when she closed the door in Jerry's face.

I wonder what he had to say if he went back to my apartment last night and found me gone. Sure am glad he has no idea where I went, so there's no way he can track me down. Her fingers clenched. *I hope I never meet up with another guy like Jerry. He was a loser.*

Eager for a cup of coffee, Michelle got dressed, went to the bathroom to freshen up, and hurried downstairs. She found Mary Ruth and Willis at the kitchen table with mugs of coffee in their hands.

"Well, good morning, Sara." Mary Ruth was all smiles. "Did we wake you with our chatter down here? We thought you might sleep in this morning."

"No, you didn't wake me. The crowing rooster did."

"That's Hector." Willis chuckled and shook his head. "No need to set an alarm clock, thanks to our predictable and feisty old bird. He's been with us longer than any of our chickens."

Michelle wondered if Willis's reference to the rooster being feisty meant the chicken was mean. If so, she'd have to remember to give him a wide berth.

"Would you care for a cup of coffee,

dear?" Mary Ruth rose from her chair.

Michelle held out her hand. "No, that's okay. I'll get it myself." After helping Mary Ruth do the dishes last night, she remembered where the mugs were kept, and the coffee pot was clearly visible on the stove. So she helped herself and joined them at the table.

"What would you like for breakfast, Sara?" Mary Ruth gestured to the refrigerator. "Thanks to our hens, who are laying well right now, we have plenty of eggs There's also a slab of bacon. Did we tell you that Willis raises hogs?"

"No, I don't believe you mentioned it." *Most likely because you were too busy asking me questions.*

The thought of eating bacon and eggs this early in the morning made Michelle's stomach feel queasy. She usually didn't eat much for breakfast anyway. "No thanks. I'll just have a bowl of cold cereal. If you have any, that is," she amended.

"Why, yes we do. In fact, Willis eats a bowl of bran flakes almost every morning, in addition to eggs, pancakes, or whatever else I serve for breakfast. He and I both had bran cereal for our breakfast this morning. We wanted to eat before Willis did his chores."

Willis bobbed his head before adding a

spoonful of sugar to his cup.

Bran flakes? Michelle took a sip of the darkly brewed coffee and tried to keep her composure. The last thing she wanted was a bowl of bran flakes. "Think maybe I'll stick with coffee."

"Oh my . . . That's not enough for breakfast." Mary Ruth shook her head. "If you don't want bacon and eggs, or cereal, then how about a banana muffin? Ezekiel King brought some fresh honey over the other day. You might enjoy having some of that on your muffin."

"Okay." Michelle mustered up a smile. "A muffin sounds good."

While Mary Ruth went to get the muffin and honey for Michelle, Willis finished his coffee, then set the mug in the sink. "As soon as you're done eating, Sara, why don't you come outside and I'll show you around the place? I'd like to introduce you to our buggy horses and some of the other animals we have — including the hogs."

Pigs? I bet they smell bad. Oh goody. I can't wait for that. Michelle offered Willis a phony smile. Maybe life here on the farm wasn't better than living in the city after all. "That'd be nice," she said to Willis. "I'd love to see your animals." If she was going to keep up this masquerade, she'd have to at least act interested in her pretend grandparents, as well as in their critters and anything else that pertained to them.

When Michelle walked with Willis and Mary Ruth through the double doors and entered the well-built, oversized barn, the odor of straw mixed with horse flesh and manure caused her to sneeze. She reached into her shirt pocket for a tissue and blew her nose as a fluffy gray cat darted between her legs. "Yikes!"

"Do you have allergies?" Mary Ruth's brows wrinkled a bit.

"Maybe. I don't know. I've never been around animals that much — especially horses."

"Your mother was allergic to cats. The minute she got around them her nose would start running and then came a sneeze." Mary Ruth patted Michelle's back. "I bet you take after her."

Michelle noticed the sadness in the woman's brown eyes. No doubt she missed her daughter and wished she could have her back.

"Speaking of Rhoda . . ." Willis leaned against one of the horse's stalls. "When we were talking yesterday, you never made mention of your father." He reached under his straw hat and scratched his head. "Did your mother raise you alone?"

Michelle's gaze dropped to the ground. She felt her body heat rising. *What am I supposed to say? I can't very well tell them about my own lousy father. Or my horrible mother, for that matter.*

Michelle blew her nose again, stalling for time. She'd need to think fast on her feet and come up with some decent answers if she was going to make the Lapps keep believing she was their granddaughter.

"Um . . . Actually, my dad and mom are divorced." *Wrong answer, Michelle.* She knew right away from Mary Ruth and Willis's slumped posture and stony expression that this was something they did not want to hear. As Michelle recalled the reality TV show, she remembered someone saying that the Amish didn't believe in divorce. She hadn't thought much about it at the time, but apparently it was true.

"I am deeply sorry to hear that," Mary Ruth said. "Does your father live near you, and do you see him often?"

Oh boy. Michelle rubbed her forehead. "No, after the divorce, my dad split. I haven't seen or heard from him since."

"That's a shame." Mary Ruth's tone was soothing. "Do you know if your father used to be Amish?"

Yikes! Now how am I supposed to know that? Michelle squirmed, feeling like she was on the hot seat. She moistened her lips with the tip of her tongue. "I'm not sure. My folks never talked much about their past to me." *At least that was the truth.* Michelle's hole of deception seemed to grow deeper with most everything that came out of her mouth.

To avoid telling more lies, Michelle changed the subject. "So whose horse is that, and what's its name?" She pointed to the horse in the stall closest to them.

"That's my mare, Bashful." Willis reached over the gate and stroked the horse's brown ears, which were tipped with white.

The horse nickered in response, then lifted her head over the wooden slat and nudged Willis's chest. "Bashful does well with me but tends to be kinda shy around people she doesn't know." After rubbing her soft muzzle a few seconds, Willis opened his hand to reveal a sugar cube. "You didn't think I'd forget your treat, now did ya?" He spoke tenderly to the horse.

It was cute to see how gently Bashful scooped up the cube. *Maybe someday, if I'm here long enough, she'll eat out of my hand too.*

Michelle looked at Mary Ruth. "Does the horse across from Bashful belong to you, Mary Ruth?"

"Yes. Her name is Peanuts, but once again, I really wish you would call me Grandma."

"Sorry. I keep forgetting." While Michelle was far from perfect, she didn't make a habit of telling lies. But her decision at the bus station in Philly had entrapped her in this huge web of lies.

"Yes, and I do want you to call me Grandpa," Willis echoed.

"Okay," she murmured, barely able to look at either of them. Why did these two have to be so nice and easy to like? It made it that much harder for Michelle to pretend she was Sara.

Michelle went over to Peanuts's stall with Mary Ruth. She had to get her mind on something else.

"We do tend to spoil our animals." Mary Ruth cradled her horse's head and greeted her with affectionate words. Then she handed Michelle a sugar cube. "Would you like to feed her?"

"I guess."

"Just hold your hand out flat," Willis instructed. "That way she won't pinch your skin."

Michelle giggled when Peanuts used her soft upper and lower lips to gently take the sweet she offered. “I think she likes me.”

“Well, sure she does.” Willis took a piece of straw out of Peanuts’s long mane, and the mare nuzzled his hands as if to say *thanks.*

“Do you have any brothers or sisters?” Mary Ruth asked, leaning against the horse’s stall.

Without giving it much thought, Michelle shook her head. “I’m pretty much alone now that my mom is gone.”

Willis gave her a soft pat on the shoulder, and Mary Ruth slipped an arm around Michelle’s waist. “You’re not alone anymore. We’re here for you, Sara, and you’re welcome to stay with us for as long as you like.”

She swallowed hard, her throat swelling from holding back tears. *If you knew who I really am, you wouldn’t be so gracious.*

After they left the barn, and Michelle had met the hogs, Willis went to town to run some errands, using his horse and open buggy.

As Michelle started walking toward the house, Mary Ruth paused near her vegetable garden. “Would you be willing to help me in the garden for a few hours?” she asked.

"The weeds will take over if I don't keep at it."

Michelle moistened her lips. "Well, I . . ."

"If you'd rather not help, perhaps you can pull up a lawn chair and keep me company. It will give us more time to get better acquainted."

"The things is, I haven't had much experience pulling weeds 'cause my mom never had a garden. But sure, I'll do what I can to help."

"No garden?" Mary Ruth's lips compressed. "I'm surprised to hear this. Why, when Rhoda was a girl, and even into her teen years, she spent a lot of time working in our garden." Mary Ruth's face relaxed and she snickered. "It seemed like that girl always had dirt under her fingernails, and I was often reminding her to clean her hands thoroughly."

Michelle rubbed her sweaty palms down the sides of her jeans. Was she ever going to say the right things? "You see, the truth is, my mom kept so busy with her job, she didn't have time for gardening."

"Oh? What kind of work did she do?"

Michelle pinched the bridge of her nose. *Now what do I say? What kind of job should I give this pretend mother?* "Mom was a hair stylist," she blurted. "She had her own shop and was so busy she hardly had any time for herself." *There we go — another untruth on top of all the others.* Michelle wondered how many more lies she'd have to tell before she gave up the Lapps' hospitality.

As Mary Ruth knelt on the ground next to her garden, she glanced at Sara. She'd pulled her beautiful auburn hair into a ponytail, and every once in a while, between pulling a few weeds, she would swat at the annoying gnats swarming around their heads.

"What's with all these bugs?" Sara scrunched up her face. "I'm afraid if I open my mouth too wide, I might swallow one of 'em."

"They're gnats, and they always seem to be worse when it's warm and humid — especially after it rains." Mary Ruth flapped her hand at a few of the bugs near her nose. "But don't worry; if you stay here long enough, you'll get used to them. It's a small price to pay for living in the country."

"Yeah, I suppose."

"Your mom didn't care much for the pesky bugs either. She loved nature but couldn't understand why God created gnats and wondered what possible purpose they could have here on this beautiful earth."

Sara frowned as she stuck her shovel into the ground next to a weed. "I think the earth would be a lot more beautiful if there were no irritating bugs."

Mary Ruth rubbed a hand against her heart. She could almost hear Rhoda saying those exact same words one muggy day when they were working in the garden. *Like mother, like daughter,* she thought. *If only Rhoda could be here now, working alongside me and Sara.*

Tears welled in Mary Ruth's eyes, and she blinked them away. So many times she had looked down the driveway and prayed their daughter would return. Rhoda was the second child she and Willis had lost, only at least they'd had her for the first eighteen years. After she'd left home, it felt as if she were dead — oh, the emptiness in Mary Ruth's heart was awful. So many wasted years when they could have been with their daughter, and now, with Rhoda's passing, there was no chance for that.

Before their other son, Ivan, came along, they'd had a baby boy named Jake, who had died two weeks after he was born. Their sweet little boy had a heart condition that ended his life all too soon. Ivan was born two years later, and he grew up to be a fine young man. He was married now, and living in Paradise, not far away. He and his wife, Yvonne, had a daughter, Lenore, as well as two sons, Peter and Benjamin.

Ivan and Rhoda had been close during their childhood and enjoyed swimming, fishing, and doing many other fun things together. He too was devastated when she left with only a note to say goodbye. When Mary Ruth had called to tell him about receiving Sara's letter and shared the sad news of Rhoda's death, Ivan had cried. Mary Ruth sobbed along with him, as the truth set in that the hope of seeing her daughter come home would never be fulfilled.

"You okay?"

Sara's question pulled Mary Ruth out of her musings. "I'm fine. Just thinking about the past, is all."

Sara gave a nod. "Yeah, I do that myself sometimes."

"Well, as our church bishop said in a sermon a few weeks ago, we shouldn't dwell so much on the past. What we are doing today and hope to do in the future are what count in the long run."

Sara kept swatting at the bugs and pulling weeds. Mary Ruth wished she knew what her granddaughter was thinking. Then, thinking of church meetings, she wondered if, were she to sew a few plain-style dresses, Sara would be willing to wear them. She studied the young woman, releasing a sigh. *If Sara remains with us, could she adjust to the Amish way of life? Maybe she would even decide to join our church, get married, and settle down here in our community. That would make me so happy.*

Mary Ruth reminded herself not to expect too much from their granddaughter, but she couldn't help being a wee bit hopeful.

CHAPTER 5

When Michelle woke up Sunday morning, every bone in her body ached. Yesterday, she'd helped Mary Ruth clean the house and bake two shoofly pies. When that was done, she'd stupidly let Willis talk her into helping him clean the barn. Big mistake. It was a smelly, dirty job. At least he hadn't asked her to do anything with those horrible hogs she'd seen in the pen outside. But the whole time they'd worked, Willis kept asking her questions about Rhoda. That part was more painful than all the cleaning they'd done.

Mary Ruth had done the same thing while she and Michelle cleaned house and baked. Some of the questions the Lapps asked were the same. Michelle hoped she had given good answers to both of them.

More difficult than helping with chores was being asked so many questions about someone she knew nothing about. Maybe after she'd been here a few more days Willis and Mary Ruth would let up on the questions and talk about other things. It was understandable though, the Lapps wanting to know about their daughter, whose presence they'd been deprived of all these years. Truth was, Michelle had some questions of her own. She was eager to find out how much of what she'd seen and heard on TV about the Amish was true.

Michelle pulled herself out of bed and lifted the shade at the window to look out. No clouds in the sky at the moment — just a bright, sunny day. *I hope the Lapps don't expect me to go to church with them today.* Since the Amish were a religious sort of people, she figured they probably were faithful about attending church on Sunday mornings. Michelle had no desire to sit in church and listen to some preacher talk about how God answers prayer. She'd heard that before when she'd been forced to attend Bible school.

Michelle had actually tried praying a few times when she was a girl but never felt like her prayers reached heaven. If there even was a God. Because if God was real, why did He allow people to treat each other so cruelly? Of course, the Lapps did not seem harsh, but then, Michelle didn't know them that well either.

Michelle's gaze went to the wooden chest at the foot of her bed. Curious to know what was inside, she lifted the lid, revealing a dark blue, Amish-style dress. She took it out, and saw a few more dresses under it, as well as some black shoes and a white, heart-shaped covering like the one Mary Ruth wore on her head.

I bet these belonged to their daughter. She was tempted to try on one of the dresses, but thought better of it, thinking Mary Ruth might not approve. *But then, how would she know, if I don't mention what I did? After I see how I look in the bathroom mirror, I'll take the dress off and put it back in the chest.*

Michelle took off her pajamas and slipped the dress on over her head. She didn't wear a dress very often, and the ones she had worn never looked so plain. *I wonder why Amish women wear dresses like this. Another question I should ask Mary Ruth.*

She reached in, picked up the *kapp,* and placed it on her head. *Oh boy. I can only imagine what I must look like.*

Michelle left the room and trekked down the hall to the bathroom. While the mirror over the sink wasn't full-length, at least she could see her upper body.

She giggled at her reflection. If her long

hair had been pulled back in a bun, she would almost look Amish.

Michelle took off the head covering, and opened one of the cabinet drawers, where she found several hair pins. After securing her hair in a bun, she put the covering back in place. Silently staring at herself, Michelle wondered what it would be like if she were Amish. Could she handle dressing plain all the time, not to mention all the daily chores and doing without modern conveniences? It would be quite a change from the things she'd become accustomed to.

Michelle shook her head. *Probably couldn't do it, although, except for the bugs, I would enjoy feeling one with nature, like I did when Mary Ruth and I were pulling weeds in her garden.*

Michelle left the bathroom and walked back toward her bedroom. She'd only gone a short ways when she heard footsteps on the stairs. A few seconds later, Mary Ruth appeared in the hallway.

Michelle jumped, and Mary Ruth gasped. "Oh, my word, Sara, you look so much like your mother in that dress."

Embarrassed, Michelle dropped her gaze. "Sorry, Mary Ruth — I mean, Grandma. I should have asked first before trying on the dress."

"No, it's okay. It was your mother's, and you have every right to wear it." Mary Ruth stepped up to Michelle. "In fact, I'd like you to have all her clothes that I've put away. You can take them whenever you decide to return to your home." She placed her hand on Michelle's arm. "Of course you're welcome to stay here indefinitely if you like. We don't expect you to join the Amish church, unless you should choose to do so. But maybe in time you could find a job locally and live here with us. And if you don't want to get a job, that's okay too. Would you at least give it some thought?"

Michelle nodded. She felt like a mouse caught in a trap. When the time came for her to leave, she would go, but not without telling them first who she was.

She glanced down at Rhoda's dress, touching the bodice. "Is there a specific reason Amish women wear dresses like this?"

"We choose to wear plain clothes and do not care to be changing styles designed to achieve glamour and not modesty."

Michelle pointed to the covering on Mary Ruth's head. "And the kapp? Why do you wear that?"

"We wear our coverings in obedience to the Bible. It says in 1 Corinthians 11:5, 'Every woman that prayeth or prophesieth with her head uncovered dishonoureth her head.' "

Michelle gave another nod, although she didn't really understand it all. The Amish way of life seemed quaint to her, but it held a certain appeal.

"I came up to tell you that breakfast is ready," Mary Ruth said. "Oh, and I also wanted you to know that we'll be having company later on."

"Really? I figured you and Grandpa might be going to church today."

"It's our off-Sunday."

Michelle tipped her head. "What's an off-Sunday?"

"We Amish gather for worship every other Sunday. On the off weeks we will sometimes visit another church district, or we may go visiting. Today, our son, Ivan, and his family will be coming over. They are anxious to meet you."

"I see." Michelle leaned against the wall for support. *I suppose my so-called uncle will also have questions to ask. I just hope I'm able to give him all the right answers.*

"Sara, this is your uncle Ivan. He owns a general store in the area." Willis grinned as he motioned to the two women standing beside Ivan. "And this is his wife, Yvonne, and daughter, Lenore, who is a teacher at one of our one-room schoolhouses in the area. His sons, Benjamin and Peter, couldn't be here today, because they are visiting some friends in Kentucky."

Michelle forced a smile and shook their hands. She felt like a bug under a microscope when tall, blond-haired Ivan studied her face. Did he think she looked anything like his sister, Rhoda, or had Ivan figured out that Michelle was a fraud?

Michelle turned her attention to Ivan's wife and daughter. Yvonne, a tall, slender woman, had brown hair and matching eyes. Lenore looked similar, only her eyes were hazel-colored. She was a few inches shorter than her mother, and was also quite slender. Lenore appeared to be in her early or mid-twenties — it was hard to tell. It wouldn't be right to just ask. Besides, what did it matter? It wasn't as if they were really cousins.

"Welcome, Cousin Sara." Lenore stepped forward and gave Michelle a warm hug.

Lenore's mother hugged Michelle too, but Uncle Ivan remained where he was.

Michelle shifted uneasily. *I don't think he likes me. Can Ivan see into the depths of my soul and know that I'm a phony?*

Ivan cleared his throat a couple of times. "Sorry for staring, Sara. It's just hard to believe my sister's daughter is here in this house."

No, she isn't. Michelle bit the inside of her cheek. It was wrong to lie to these nice people, but she couldn't bring herself to own up to the truth.

"Does Sara remind you of your sister, *Daadi*?" Lenore looked at her father.

Michelle didn't know any Pennsylvania Dutch, but she assumed *Daadi* meant Daddy.

Ivan nodded. "In some ways she does. I suppose it's the color of Sara's hair that reminds me of Rhoda. Her facial features are different though, but then I guess she probably looks like both of her parents."

You got that right, only they're not the parents you're thinking of. When Michelle was a girl, she'd often been told that she had her father's red hair and blue-green eyes, but her mother's facial features. Truthfully, she didn't care if she resembled either of them. Her biological parents meant nothing to her. The day that social worker came and took Michelle and her brothers away was the day she'd emotionally divorced her parents.

"Why don't we all go outside and sit at the picnic table?" Mary Ruth suggested. "While Willis fires up the grill, we can visit."

Michelle fought the urge to roll her eyes. *Oh great. I bet this will be a time for more questions fired at me.*

As they sat at the picnic table, eating hamburgers and hot dogs, Michelle felt as if all eyes were upon her. At least the smoke from the grill kept the gnats at bay. That was one positive.

She'd already answered dozens of questions — about her mother, where she'd grown up, siblings. Michelle hoped she'd remembered to give the same answers to their guests as she had when Mary Ruth and Willis asked these questions this past week. Michelle concentrated so hard on trying to give right answers, she could barely eat. Despite the gnawing in her stomach, she was glad when the meal was over.

While Michelle, Yvonne, and Lenore helped Mary Ruth clear the table and carry things inside, Willis and Ivan went out to barn to check on Sadie, who was supposed to have her pups any time.

The women had started washing the dishes when Ivan burst into the kitchen. "Hey Mom, Dad wanted me to tell you that Sadie's about to deliver. He thought maybe everyone would like to come out and watch as her babies come into the world."

Mary Ruth looked at Michelle. "How about it, Sara? Have you ever witnessed puppies being born?"

Michelle shook her head. *And I don't think I want to either.*

"Well good, let's go." Mary Ruth gestured to Lenore and Yvonne. "You two are welcome to come with us."

Yvonne shook her head. "I've seen plenty of pups born in my day. I'll remain here and finish washing the dishes."

"Same here. Mom can wash, and I'll dry." Lenore picked up a dish towel and moved toward the sink.

"Danki." Mary Ruth opened the back door and stepped outside.

Michelle reluctantly followed. "Does *danki* mean thanks?" she asked as they headed for the barn.

Grinning, Mary Ruth bobbed her head. "If you stay here long enough, I'll bet you'll be speaking Pennsylvania Dutch in no time. Jah, I do."

Jah meant "yes," and *danki* was the word for "thanks." Michelle didn't know how many other Amish words she could learn while she was here, but she was off to a good start. Well, maybe not a good start, but a few words learned anyway.

■ ■ ■ ■

Michelle wasn't certain she cared to watch the birth of Sadie's puppies, but at least it would take the attention off her. And she sure wasn't going to stay in the house with her pretend aunt and cousin, who would no doubt ply her with more questions.

Michelle must have missed seeing it when she was in the barn the other day, but Sadie had a large wooden box to stretch out in, with plenty of room for the pups to move around in once they became active. The bottom of the box had been lined with newspapers, making for easy disposal. Mary Ruth called it "Sadie's whelping bed."

Michelle stood between Ivan and Willis, watching as Sadie panted, stood up, and then lay down again.

"It won't be long now." Willis's eyes sparkled. He was no doubt excited, even though this was probably old hat for him.

Wish I could be that enthused. Michelle watched curiously as the first puppy arrived. Once Sadie removed the pup's sac, she began pushing again.

Mary Ruth took over and cleaned the first puppy's nostrils, then gently blew on its tiny face to stimulate breathing.

Michelle's throat constricted when the newborn pup gave a little yelp. No wonder they wanted her to witness this. A mere description would not have been good enough.

"Have you ever seen anything like this before?" Ivan asked.

Michelle shook her head. "I've seen a cat give birth, but never a dog."

"Your mom and I used to play a lot in this barn when we were kids." Ivan made a sweeping gesture of the area around them with his hand. "Being here with you now takes me back to those days." His eyes darkened a bit. "We didn't know how fortunate we were back then, to have loving parents and a wonderful place to grow up."

Michelle almost said she wished she could have known Ivan's sister, but caught herself in time. "Growing up in those days sounds nice. Wish I could have known you and Mom back then." *And I wish I'd had your parents,* she secretly added.

Chapter 6

When Willis entered the kitchen Friday morning, he found Mary Ruth stirring batter in a large mixing bowl. "Whatcha up to? Are you making *pannekuche*?"

"Sorry, no pancakes this morning. I'm mixing batter for a birthday cake. But I suppose I could whip a batch of pannekuche just for you." She turned and gave his belly a little poke.

He quirked an eyebrow.

"Today is our granddaughter's birthday." Mary Ruth paused to switch hands stirring. "Remember when she told us soon after she arrived that she was born on June 15th? She will be twenty-four years old."

"Oh yes, that's right." Willis put his hand lovingly under Mary Ruth's chin. "Look here a minute. Whatcha got on your *kinn*?"

After being married all these years, her husband's gentle touch still made her heart do a flip-flop, even when he was teasing her.

"I must look a mess." Mary Ruth giggled as he wiped some flour off her cheek and it landed on the front of her apron.

"Not to me. You've never looked more beautiful." Willis's gaze remained on her for several seconds. "All that flour on your face and apron shows how hard you've been working." He kissed her cheek on the spot where the flour had been. "So besides the cake, what else are we gonna do to help Sara celebrate her special day?"

"I invited Ivan and his family over again, but he and Yvonne had already made plans to get together with her folks this evening, so they won't be coming. Lenore said she's free though, so I guess it'll be just the four of us."

"That should work out okay then. It'll give Sara a chance to get better acquainted with her cousin."

Mary Ruth nodded. "I was thinking that too. Since the girls are about the same age and both single, they have that much in common. If Sara and Lenore become friends, it'll give Sara another reason to come here often. And who knows, if our granddaughter likes it here, she may even decide to stay in the area or live at our house permanently. We certainly have the room, and it would be nice to see Sara using our daughter's bedroom, instead of it looking so empty." Mary Ruth swallowed. "Maybe sleeping in the same room and in the same bed will give Sara a sense of being closer to her mudder."

"Jah, it might, at that." Willis's eyes twinkled as he tipped his head and grinned at Mary Ruth. "After all this time, it's nice to see such a look of pure joy on your face. It's been a good many years since you've been so enthused about something."

"A long time, I agree." She sighed deeply. "When Rhoda ran away, it wounded my soul. And every year that went by without us hearing from her hurt all the more. I thought we had done something that drove her away, and she wanted to forget us. Now that I know our dochder left a note for Sara, telling her about us, it's given me a sense of peace." Mary Ruth touched her chest. "The realization that Rhoda cared about us enough to want Sara to get to know us is like a healing balm to my hurting soul."

He kissed her cheek. "I understand. Having Sara here has been good for both of us."

"Are you two talking about me?" Sara asked, stepping into the kitchen.

Mary Ruth's face warmed. "Jah, but in a good way. We were just saying how nice it is to have you here. And I'm also happy we can be with you to help celebrate your special day." Mary Ruth moved away from the counter and gave Sara a hug. "Happy birthday, Granddaughter."

"Yes, happy birthday, Sara," Willis put in.

Sara's cheeks turned a light shade of pink. "Danki."

"You're welcome." It tickled Mary Ruth to no end, hearing her granddaughter use a Pennsylvania Dutch word.

"Have you been out to check on the puppies yet this morning?" Sara asked, looking at Willis.

"Not yet, but I will right after breakfast."

"You can go now if you want to." Mary Ruth gestured to the cake batter. "I want to put this cake in the oven before I start breakfast, so there's still a little time if you want to go to the barn."

"All right then. I'll head out there now." Willis looked at Sara. "Would you like to come along?"

"Sure, unless Mary Ruth . . . I mean, Grandma, needs my help with breakfast."

Mary Ruth shook her head. "You go along with your grandpa to the barn. When you get back, I'll have the cake in the oven and a skillet of scrambled eggs with ham ready to eat."

"Okay, thanks." As Sara followed Willis

out of the room, Mary Ruth heard her say, "If you don't mind, from now on, I'd like to help by taking care of Sadie and the pups' bedding. That's one less thing you would have to do."

"Danki, Granddaughter. That'd be just fine." Willis quickly came back to grab his hat off the hook. "I forgot this." His face fairly beamed as he glanced at Mary Ruth and winked.

When Mary Ruth heard the sound of the back door open and then close, she went to the window and watched her husband and granddaughter walk to the barn together. With gratitude, she closed her eyes and said a quick prayer. *Thank You, Lord. There is so much happiness in our house again.*

After taking two round cake pans out of the cupboard, she began humming a song they frequently sang at their ice-cream socials. Mary Ruth's motherly instincts seemed to be kicking in. Having her granddaughter here to fuss over was like having Rhoda home again. Willis was right — she truly was happier and felt ten years younger too.

Those puppies are sure adorable. Michelle took time to cuddle each one after changing the bedding, freshening up the water, and making sure Sadie's bowl was filled with food. Taking care of Sadie and her babies didn't feel like a chore at all. It was something she could look forward to every day. Even if they were only animals, it made Michelle feel like she was needed.

When she left the barn, Michelle walked down to the mailbox, at Willis's request. It was another simple chore, and she didn't mind doing it. In fact, after being in the smelly, stuffy barn for a while, it felt good to breathe in some fresh air. Even the bugs weren't bad yet, since it was still early in the day.

Michelle's stomach growled as the aroma of pancakes wafted from the house. She'd almost forgotten how much she loved homemade pancakes. Sometimes, her foster mother would make them on Saturday mornings, but she hadn't had any, other than the frozen kind you put in a toaster, since she'd left their home and struck out on her own.

As Michelle approached the mailbox, she wondered if she would find anything inside. It was still early, and she couldn't believe the Lapps' mail would be delivered this soon in the day. But since Willis had asked her to go get it, he must know what he was talking about. It could be that a rural mail carrier had to start early, and Willis and Mary Ruth's house might be on the first part of the route.

Michelle opened the box and was not disappointed. A handful of mail had been left inside. Curious, she thumbed through the stack — lots of advertising catalogs and flyers, a few bills, and one letter. She squinted at the name on the return address. It said: *"Sara Murray."*

Her heart pounded. *Oh no . . . It's the real granddaughter, and she lives in Newark, New Jersey. I wonder what she has to say. Maybe she wrote to tell her grandparents that they missed her at the bus station. Or she could be letting them know that she plans to come here soon — maybe even today.*

Gulping in several deep breaths, Michelle leaned against the mailbox as she deliberated what to do. If she took this letter inside and gave it to Mary Ruth or Willis, her cover would definitely be blown.

With her free hand, Michelle reached up to rub her forehead. She needed to find out what the letter said. Only then would she know what to do.

Michelle slipped the rest of the mail back inside the box. Clasping Sara's letter, she walked down the road a ways, until she came to a clump of trees. Stepping behind them with fingers shaking, she awkwardly tore open the letter to silently read.

Dear Grandpa and Grandma Lapp,

I wrote to you a few weeks ago, but since you didn't respond, I am wondering if you even got the letter. I wanted to let you know that it could be toward the end of summer, or even early fall before I'm able to come there to meet you. I had thought maybe July 5th, but it doesn't look like that's going to happen. This business class I'm taking requires a lot of homework, so it'll be difficult for me to get away anytime soon. Not only that, but my car is giving me problems, so when I do come, I still may have to take the bus. If I'm not able to drive, I'll let you know so you can decide if you're able to pick me up at the bus station in Philadelphia.

I hope you will write back soon so I know that you received this letter. I am looking forward to meeting you both.

All the best,

Sara

What a stroke of luck. Michelle drew a breath and blew it out slowly. It was a relief to know the Lapps' granddaughter wouldn't be coming until at least the end of summer. That meant Michelle could continue posing as Sara and reaping the benefits of staying with Willis and Mary Ruth. All she had to do was dispose of this letter. And from now on, she would volunteer to walk out every day to get the mail. It was the only guarantee that the Lapps would never find a letter from their rightful granddaughter.

Michelle sat at the breakfast table, barely listening to Willis and Mary Ruth's conversation. All she could think about was the letter she'd thrown in the burn barrel before bringing the rest of the mail to the house. She'd gone back to the barn, found a box of matches and lit a fire, destroying all evidence of Sara Murray's letter. Fortunately, Willis had already returned to the house by then and hadn't seen what she'd done.

How much longer can I keep up this charade? Michelle clenched her napkin into a tight ball. *What if Mary Ruth or Willis should decide to go out and get the mail before I have a chance to get there each morning? And what if another letter shows up from Sara? Boy, have I gotten myself into a mess.*

Mary Ruth tapped Michelle's arm. "Did you hear what I said, Sara?"

Michelle jerked her head. "Uh, no. Sorry, I didn't."

"I asked if there's anything special you'd like me to fix for your birthday supper tonight."

Unable to look at Mary Ruth's face, Michelle kept her gaze fixed on her plate. Her appetite for pancakes had diminished. Although they looked and smelled delicious, she could barely get the first one down. "Don't go to any trouble on my account," she mumbled.

"It's no trouble. There's nothing more I'd rather be doing." Mary Ruth nudged Michelle's arm, and when she looked up, she was rewarded with a pleasant smile. "So, what's your favorite supper meal?"

Michelle's guilt nearly made her confess her deception, seeing how genuine Mary Ruth was toward her. But she felt like a little girl — giddy that someone actually cared. "You might think this is strange, but I really like spaghetti and meatballs."

"That's not strange at all," Willis spoke up. "I like spaghetti and meatballs too."

Michelle looked at Willis, where he sat at the head of the table. "You do?" *I bet he only said that for my benefit.*

Grinning, he bobbed his head.

Mary Ruth clapped her hands. "All right

then, it's settled. Tonight, in honor of Sara's twenty-fourth birthday, I will fix her favorite supper."

Michelle finished her glass of milk and dipped the last bite of pancake in the leftover syrup on her plate. She wished the Lapps weren't being so nice to her. It made it all the more difficult to lie to them. But if she told the truth, she'd have to leave. Besides, to coin a phrase, what they didn't know wouldn't hurt them. The truth would hurt them — and her too. So for now at least, she'd keep silent.

As Ezekiel King approached his horse and buggy, his mother called out to him. "Don't forget the jar of *hunnich.*" She stood on the back porch, holding a tall jar of honey.

Ezekiel walked across the yard, meeting her halfway. *"Ich bin allfatt am eppes vergesse."*

"You're not always forgetting something; only when your mind is somewhere else." Lifting her chin to look up at him, Mom handed him the jar. "So what were you thinking about this time, Son?"

He smacked his forehead. "Beats me. Guess I had my head in the clouds." Ezekiel wasn't about to tell his mother he'd been thinking about buying a car or a truck. Unlike some Amish parents in their area, his folks did not look the other way or knowingly allow their children to take part in questionable things, like some English young people did. Ezekiel thought his mom and dad were too strict. He was twenty-three years old and ought to have the right to do as he pleased. Dad was always on him about joining the church, but Ezekiel hadn't made up his mind about that yet. If he did buy a car, he'd have to keep it hidden, somewhere other than here on his folk's property. Dad would never stand for any son of his owning a motorized vehicle, much less parking it here, where others could see.

Mom poked Ezekiel's arm. "Are you spacing off again?"

He blinked a couple of times. "Sorry. I was thinkin', is all."

Mom's brown eyes darkened. "You can do your thinking while you're heading over to the Lapps'to deliver the honey they ordered."

"Don't see why they want more honey. It wasn't long ago that I delivered a jar to their place."

"Maybe they used it up already. Anyway, it shouldn't matter the reason. They asked, and you have plenty of honey, so you'd best be on your way."

"Jah, okay, but I'm gonna run a short errand when I leave there, so I'll probably be gone a few hours."

She gave a nod. "That's fine. Things are kind of slow at the greenhouse today, so I'm sure your *daed* and I can manage without you for a while this afternoon."

"Good to know." Ezekiel glanced toward the back of their property, where the greenhouse was built. That was another thing frustrating him. He didn't enjoy working there so much. However, Dad insisted that Ezekiel, being the oldest son, should take over the business someday, whether he wanted it or not.

Ezekiel was glad he'd become a part-time beekeeper, because it gave him something else to do besides fool with plants and flowers all day. Not that he had anything against the greenhouse business — it just wasn't what he wanted to do for the rest of his life. Truthfully, Ezekiel wasn't sure what he wanted, but right now it didn't include joining the Amish church. What he wanted more than anything was to know more about the English world and enjoy some of the things his parents had forbidden him to do.

He said goodbye to Mom and put the jar of honey in a cardboard box inside his buggy. Then he released his horse, Big Red, from the hitching rail, hopped into the buggy, and headed down the driveway. There was no doubt in his mind. As soon as he left Willis and Mary Ruth's place, he was going to look at a used truck one of his friends had for sale. And if Ezekiel thought it was the right one for him, he might end up buying it either today or sometime soon.

CHAPTER 7

"Would ya mind helping me feed the hogs this morning?" Willis asked Michelle when they finished breakfast.

Mary Ruth squinted at him. "For goodness' sakes, Husband, today is Sara's birthday. You should not have asked her to do a *garschdich* chore like that."

"Feeding the hogs isn't a nasty chore," he responded. "It's a *eefach* task. You just take the food out and dump it over the fence."

"If it's so simple, then why don't you do it yourself?"

"Because I have some other chores to do, and —"

"It's okay," Michelle interjected. "My birthday's no big deal, and as long as I don't have to get in the pen with the hogs, I don't mind feeding 'em."

Willis grinned. "See, I figured as much. This little gal is a chip off the ole block."

Mary Ruth rolled her eyes, and Michelle

merely nodded. She'd done plenty of unpleasant chores over the years — at her birth parents' request and again for her foster parents. Then when she'd struck out on her own, more chores waited at the various jobs she'd done, not to mention trying to keep on top of things at the apartments she'd lived in.

Michelle felt safe here at the Lapps' and didn't mind whatever chores they asked her to do. It was kind of like payment for her room and board.

While Michelle took the dishes over to the sink, she listened to Mary Ruth and Willis talk, but she couldn't understand what they were saying because they spoke in their native Pennsylvania Dutch. "I'll take the food out to the hogs now," she said, turning to Willis. "When I come back inside, I'll help Mary Ruth get the dishes done."

Mary Ruth flapped her hand. "Don't bother about that. I'll take care of those this morning. After you feed the hogs, feel free to do something you'd enjoy for the rest of the day. Your cousin Lenore will be here around six o'clock, and we'll eat shortly after, so that gives you plenty of time to do whatever you want today."

Michelle shrugged and headed out the back door with a large bowl of table scraps that had been sitting on the end of the counter. *What is it I'm supposed to do today? I'm not used to having time on my hands. I've kept busy doing something ever since I got here.*

Michelle had been staying with Mary Ruth and Willis for ten days, but already she was in somewhat of a routine. She liked keeping busy and helping the Lapps. And every night when she retired to bed, sleep came easy after a day of activities from living and working on a farm.

Outside, Michelle paused to look up at the clear blue sky. Today had started out to be a beautiful morning. Yesterday's rain had taken away the humidity.

Michelle drew a deep breath, enjoying the fresh air that reached her nostrils. How nice to no longer deal with smog or the smell of vehicle fumes, like she'd been accustomed to in Philadelphia.

She glanced toward the country road. *Maybe after I feed the hogs, I'll take a walk to see the nearby area. Or I could spread a blanket on the grass and lay out in the sun and relax with a book. I haven't done that in a long while.*

Still undecided, Michelle moved across the yard. She'd only made it halfway to the hog pen when the whinny of a horse startled her. At that moment, she felt something brush against her leg. Taking another step forward, Michelle stumbled over a rock and fell facedown in a mud puddle.

Ezekiel arrived at the Lapps' in time to see a young woman with long auburn hair fall flat on her face in the mud. The bowl she'd been holding, along with all its contents, went flying. He pulled his horse up to the hitching rail and hopped out of the buggy. "Are you okay, miss?" he hollered. Running over to the young lady, he held his hand out to help her up, but she refused to take it.

"Yeah, I'm fine. Never better." Groaning, she clambered to her feet, wiping off the mud that stuck to her clothes. "Bet it was a stupid cat that brushed my leg."

Ezekiel looked around. He didn't see any sign of a cat. "Are ya hurt?"

"No, I'm not hurt." She swiped a hand across her dirty face. "Who are you?"

"My name's Ezekiel King. What's your name? Don't believe I've met you before." He suppressed a chuckle when she squinted at him and a hunk of mud fell off her eyelid. Looking beyond the smudges of dirt, Ezekiel couldn't help noticing her beautiful blue-green eyes, which seemed to grow deeper in color as her fair skin turned a blushing red.

"My name is Mich— I mean, I'm Sara Murray, Willis and Mary Ruth's granddaughter."

He narrowed his eyes. "Lenore's the only granddaughter I've ever known about."

"Well, it just goes to show you don't know everything." She bent down, grabbed the empty bowl, and dashed toward the house.

Ezekiel started after her, but then remembered he needed to secure his horse and get the honey he'd brought along. He hurried back to his buggy, eager to get to know about this English woman who claimed to be the Lapps' granddaughter. Despite her obvious irritation with him, Ezekiel thought she was kind of cute.

Michelle raced into the house, hurried up the stairs, and made a beeline for the bathroom to get cleaned up. It was bad enough she'd fallen on her face in the mud, but to have done it in front of someone she didn't even know was humiliating. The long-legged Amish man with thick brown hair probably thought she was a klutz. He seemed to want to carry on a conversation with her. But Michelle had no intention of remaining in the yard, looking like such a mess. She glanced down at herself and grimaced. *What a way to meet a friend of the*

Lapps, especially a guy who wanted to help me up. And to make matters worse, she'd almost given him her real name.

"I'll end up getting myself thrown out of the Lapps' home if I'm not careful," Michelle mumbled as she turned on the shower and threw her dirty clothes in a heap. At least she had a robe in the bathroom to put on till she went to her bedroom for clean clothes. Right now she just wanted to get cleaned up. Hopefully, by the time she went downstairs, the nice-looking Amish fellow would be gone.

Ezekiel stood on the Lapps' back porch, wondering why no one had answered his knock. Could the granddaughter be the only one here today? If so, maybe she was too embarrassed to let him in. He lifted his hand to knock again when Mary Ruth came up from the outside cellar entrance.

"Wie geht's?" she said, smiling at him. "Did you bring the hunnich I ordered?"

He nodded and gestured to the small box he held in one hand. "How are you today, Mary Ruth?"

"I couldn't be better. Danki for asking." Her smile widened. "The weather's beautiful today, jah?"

He nodded again.

"Don't you just love how clean everything looks and smells, after a soaking rain like we had yesterday?"

Mary Ruth was right. Ezekiel thought everything looked refreshed — except for the young woman who'd run into the house, all embarrassed a few minutes ago. "I agree. Tonight when it's dark, I may get my flashlight and catch some night crawlers out in the yard. The rain and now this warmth we're having should make it easy to search for worms for fishing."

When Mary Ruth gave no response, Ezekiel cleared his throat. "By the way, I met a red-haired woman when I pulled my rig in a few minutes ago. Said she was your grossdochder, Sara."

"That's right. She was taking some scraps to the hogs." Mary Ruth set the basket of laundry on the ground underneath the clothesline and joined him on the porch.

He bit back a chuckle, still remembering how the poor girl had looked when she fell in the mud. "Umm . . . Your granddaughter never made it to the pigpen."

Mary Ruth tipped her head. "Oh? Did something happen?"

"Sure did." Ezekiel explained about Sara falling in the mud, and the table scraps flying every which way on the grass. "I introduced myself, and after Sara said she was your granddaughter, she took off for the house like a bee was in hot pursuit."

Mary Ruth put both hands on her cheeks. "Oh dear. Not a good thing to happen on her birthday."

Ezekiel's forehead wrinkled. "I'm *verhuddelt* though. I didn't even know you had another granddaughter, much less anything about her being here on her birthday."

"No need to be confused." Mary Ruth grasped the door handle. "Come inside with the honey and I'll explain."

As Ezekiel sat at the kitchen table, listening to Mary Ruth tell him about how they'd received a letter from Rhoda's daughter saying her mother had died, his interest was piqued. "I'm sorry for your loss, Mary Ruth. Please tell Willis I extend my condolences to him too."

"Danki, I will."

"How long will your granddaughter be staying with you?"

"We don't know for sure. Sara said she's currently out of a job, so we told her she can remain here for as long as she wants." Mary Ruth's tone sounded hopeful. "Willis and I would be happy if she stayed indefinitely. She's such a nice young woman, and having her around makes it feel almost like we have our daughter back."

Ezekiel didn't know a lot about the Lapps' daughter, Rhoda, but he had heard his folks talk about her a couple of times over the years. Mom mentioned once how bad she felt for Mary Ruth and Willis, having their only daughter run off and never hearing from her again. To find out Rhoda had recently died and that the Lapps had a granddaughter they'd known nothing about was quite a shock. "So today's her birthday?"

"Jah. She's twenty-four years old." Mary Ruth's eyes brightened. "We're having a little birthday supper for Sara this evening, and her cousin Lenore will be joining us. I think it's good for Sara to spend some time with other people her age and not just us old folks."

Ezekiel shook his head. "You're not old. Leastways, neither you nor Willis seems old to me."

She chuckled, fanning her face with her hand. "It's very kind of you to say that."

"I meant it. You and Willis are young at heart, and it shows by the things you say and do."

"Well, we both try to keep a positive attitude and enjoy doing things outdoors and keeping active. Maybe that's why we seem young at heart." She picked up the jar of honey and tapped the lid. "Look at this beautiful golden color. I bet this'll be as good as all the other honey you've brought us."

"Did you finish the last jar already? It wasn't long ago that I brought one by."

"No, we still have some, but now, with Sara here, I thought she might enjoy the honey as much as we do, and I didn't want to run out." Mary Ruth went to the cupboard and took out an old coffee can. "How much do I owe you?"

"Same as usual." Ezekiel heard footsteps, and he glanced toward the door leading to the living room, expecting the red-haired woman to join them in the kitchen. But she never did. It could have been Willis he'd heard, or if it was Sara, she'd gone into a different room.

"I suppose I'd better go." After Mary Ruth paid him, Ezekiel rose from his chair. "I have an errand to run before I head for home." He started for the door, but stopped and turned around when she called out to him.

"Say, I have an idea. If you're not busy tonight, why don't you join us for supper? I'd like you to get to know Sara, and it'll give you a chance to visit with Lenore."

I wonder if Mary Ruth and my mamm *are in cahoots.* He held his hands behind his back, rubbing a tight spot on the left side. Ezekiel's mother had been trying for a couple of years to get him and Lenore together. She kept saying Lenore and Ezekiel had a lot in common, but he didn't think so.

If Mary Ruth was trying to play matchmaker, it wouldn't work. Ezekiel and Lenore had little or nothing in common. Besides, she'd joined the Amish church soon after turning eighteen. Ezekiel, on the other hand, had no idea if he'd ever join. As far as Ezekiel was concerned, he and Lenore would not make a good match. Despite all that, it might be nice to come for supper this evening. Not only could he get to know Sara, but it would give him an opportunity to ask her some questions about the English world.

Smiling at Mary Ruth, Ezekiel said, "I'd be happy to join you for supper. What time would ya like me to come?"

"Six o'clock is when I told Lenore to be here."

"Sounds good. I'll see you then." Ezekiel turned and went out the door. *Wonder if I should bring Sara a gift for her birthday. If I can find something she likes, it might make her more willing to answer my questions and forget what happened outside when she fell.*

Chapter 8

Newark

Sara walked into her living room and kicked off her shoes. Today's class at the local college had been mind-boggling. Business Law was not going to be one of her easier courses. That fact had been obvious on the first day of class, and today had been another confirmation. But it was required for getting her degree in business. Sara had finished another semester in May, but she signed up for Business Law over the summer months. It was a six-week course. Fortunately, the class was small, and it would be easier to concentrate on this one course.

Sara had to wonder if it would have been better to take an online course so she could work at her own speed instead of the allotted time in the classroom. It was too late to change her mind though, so she would have to buckle down and do her best to get a good grade and complete all her assignments on time.

There was also the issue of finances. Sara had refused any help from her stepfather when he'd offered to pay the tuition. Her situation would have to be much worse before she'd accept financial aid from him. It was a matter of pride that came from the need to prove she could succeed on her own.

Sara looked around the cozy room. The beige couch was strewn with colorful throw pillows, and on either side of it sat two wooden end tables. A recliner was positioned at one end of the living room, and the wooden rocker her mother had picked up in an antique store was situated close by. The hardwood floor was covered by a large area rug. A flat-screen TV had been mounted to the wall directly across from the couch, but Sara didn't spend much time watching television. Between her part-time job and studies, she had little free time and preferred to read a book or make some beaded jewelry.

When Sara turned eighteen, it was decided that she could move into the other half of the duplex her mother and Dean had bought shortly after they were married. The rent was reasonable, since they only charged her half of what any other tenant would normally pay. Even though her mom was right next door, Sara liked having a sense of independence. This was the first time she'd lived alone, not to mention it got her away from having to watch Mama and Dean spoil her brother, Kenny. Now that her mother was gone, it was hard for Sara to admit, but she appreciated the cheap rent Dean still let her pay. Otherwise, she wouldn't be able to take this college course.

A picture of Mama on the end table to the right of the couch caught Sara's attention. It had been taken at Christmas two years ago. Mama wore a Santa hat on her head and a silly grin to match. Sara couldn't remember her mother ever being anything but pleasant. She was a kindhearted person with a positive attitude. Sara enjoyed the humorous side of her too. She remembered how one day when Mama had done her pretty auburn hair in a new style, she'd gone to bed that night with a silk nightcap over her curls. Kenny made fun of the way she looked, but Mama just laughed and said, *"I'm sure this must be how all the glamorous movie stars keep their hair looking so perfect all the time. And if it's good enough for them, it's just what I need."*

Chuckling at the memory, Sara flopped

onto the couch and jammed the blue-and-white, quilted throw pillow her mother had given her several years ago between her knees. *"It's for your hope chest,"* Mama had said. *"Someday after you're married or living on your own, you can put it on your own bed or couch."*

"Seeing as I've never had a serious boyfriend, I doubt I'll be getting married anytime soon," Sara muttered. "But at least I'm living on my own and have a nice couch to curl up on."

Sara hadn't been the social type during high school or even after starting college. She was a nose-to-the-grindstone kind of person, always making her schoolwork and part-time jobs her priority.

The pillow slipped, and she grabbed it, holding the soft cushion against her chest as more memories of her mother flooded her mind. Sara wondered if she would ever adjust to not having Mama around. Tears sprang to her eyes as she untied the scarf she wore and pulled it from around her neck. It was the same one she'd given to her mother, and she wore it often, just to feel closer to Mama. Sometimes Sara tied it through the side loop of her jeans, and occasionally she carried it in her purse. Having the scarf close made it seem as if a part of her mom was always with her.

At this stage of her grief, Sara needed all the reinforcement she could get, even if only from a blue-and-black scarf. Oh, how she missed the times she and Mama would sit and enjoy a cup of coffee or tea together while they engaged in conversation. It had become a fun routine for Sara to walk next door and catch up with Mama for a while each day. But now, all she had left were the memories.

Years ago when Mama married Dean, Sara had resented him — especially when he began telling her what to do. He wasn't her father, after all, and clear into her teen years, Sara's bitterness toward him grew.

But who is my father? she asked herself for the umpteenth time. *Why did Mama refuse to tell me his name or say anything about him?* Not knowing was a hard pill to swallow.

Closing her eyes, Sara squeezed the pillow tighter. A bigger grudge seemed to be seeping around every corner of her heart. *My mother is dead, and I'll probably never get to meet my real dad unless my grandparents can provide me with that information.*

She opened her eyes. *I don't understand why they haven't responded to either of my letters. Maybe they don't live at that address anymore. For all I know, they could have moved or even died.* Sara wished she was free to go to Strasburg immediately and find out for herself. But in addition to needing to be here for class, her car had started sputtering on the way home, insurance was due, and she also needed new tires. So even a short trip out of town was out of the question at the moment. Hopefully by the time she was able to make the trip, things would improve.

Strasburg

"Where are you going?" Ezekiel's twenty-year-old sister, Amy, asked when he shoved on his straw hat and headed for the back door. "Don't you know supper's almost ready?"

He turned to look at her. "I realize that, but I'm going to the Lapps' house for supper tonight."

She squinted her blue eyes at him. "Willis and Mary Ruth Lapp?"

He nodded. "I took them a big jar of hunnich earlier today, and Mary Ruth invited me to come back for the evening meal." Ezekiel made no mention of meeting their granddaughter or the fact that it was Sara's birthday. Amy, curious as she was, might try to make something of it.

His sister's petite hands went straight to

her hips. "As I'm sure you must know, Mom and Dad went away for supper this evening, leaving me to cook for you, Abe, and Henry." She gestured to the stove. "And in case your sniffer isn't working well right now, I'm making your favorite fried chicken. In fact, it'll be done shortly."

Ezekiel felt bad, running out on his sister's good meal, but he was curious about the Lapps' newly found granddaughter and looked forward to getting to know her better, so he wasn't about to stay home.

"Sorry, Sis, but I told Mary Ruth I'd be there. I had no idea you were making fried chicken." He moved back across the room and gave her shoulder a light tap. "I'm sure our brothers will enjoy the tasty meat, and whatever else you're making to go with it. I'll have to settle for leftovers tomorrow — if there are any, that is. You know I like fried chicken cold, just as well as when it's hot."

Nodding, Amy lifted her shoulders. "Okay, but don't blame me if Abe eats all the *hinkel.* Fried chicken's his favorite meal too."

Ezekiel snickered. "That eight-year-old brother of ours is a growing boy, and he likes a good many foods. Bet he could eat a whole cow in one sitting."

Amy lifted her gaze to the ceiling, then waved her hand at him. "Go on with you now, and tell Mary Ruth and Willis I said hello."

"Will do." Ezekiel went out the door, calling, "See you later, Sister." First, he needed to stop at the greenhouse to pick out a plant for Sara, and then he'd hitch up Big Red and be on his way.

"Happy birthday, Sara." Lenore smiled when she entered the house and handed Michelle a small box wrapped in pink tissue paper.

Embarrassed, Michelle felt warmth flood her face. She hardly knew what to say. It had been a long time since anyone cared enough to give her a birthday present. But of course, the gift Lenore brought really wasn't meant for her. This pretend cousin thought she was giving Sara Murray a birthday present.

Michelle took the gift and managed to murmur her thanks. "You didn't need to bring me anything though."

"I wanted to. Besides, it's a privilege for me to help celebrate my new cousin's birthday." Lenore's sincerity showed in her pretty hazel eyes.

Michelle gazed at the package. "Should I open it now or wait till after we've eaten supper?"

"Why don't you wait?" Mary Ruth suggested, joining the girls in the living room. "Supper's almost ready, and we'll eat as soon as Ezekiel gets here."

"Ezekiel?" Michelle tipped her head.

"Yes, dear one." Mary Ruth looked at Michelle affectionately. "He's the young man who brought the honey today." She glanced at Lenore. "Since you and Ezekiel are friends, I thought it would be nice if he joined us. Oh, and I wanted him to get to know Sara too," she quickly added.

Michelle didn't know who was more surprised at this — she or Lenore, whose forehead had wrinkled. *I wonder if my pretend cousin doesn't care much for Ezekiel.* Truthfully, Michelle's brief encounter with him today hadn't impressed her. Of course with him seeing her face-down in the mud, he probably didn't think much of her either.

Mary Ruth gestured to the sofa. "While we're waiting for Willis to get out of the shower and Ezekiel to arrive, why don't you two take a seat so you can visit?" She turned toward the kitchen door.

"Aren't you going to join us?" Michelle asked. She didn't feel comfortable being left alone with someone she barely knew. What was there for them to talk about?

"I still have a few things left to do in the

kitchen," Mary Ruth replied.

"Is there anything I can do to help?" Lenore was quick to offer.

Mary Ruth shook her head. "Just relax and enjoy yourselves. I'll let you know if I need help with anything." Smiling cheerfully, she ambled out of the room.

Michelle took a seat on the couch, and Lenore did the same. "Aren't you afraid to drive a horse and buggy all by yourself?" Michelle asked, for lack of anything better to say.

"No, I'm used to it and have driven one for a good many years now. When I'm not teaching, I like to help out by running errands for my mother and sometimes my dad. It's a help, especially to Mom if she's busy with something at home," Lenore added.

"So how far is it from your home in Paradise to here? That's where Mary Ruth — I mean Grandma — said you live, right?" Michelle's fingers, toes, and every part of her body tingled. She'd been so afraid she would trip up and say something wrong, and sure enough, she'd done it. *I have got to remember to call the Lapps Grandma and Grandpa. If I'm not careful, sooner or later, someone will catch on that I'm an imposter.* She twirled the ends of her hair around her fingers and tried to relax. *Of course, my calling Mary Ruth by her first name might not seem so strange to Lenore. After all, she thinks I've just recently learned that the Lapps are my grandparents. So it's only natural that I wouldn't think of them as my relatives yet.*

Lenore nodded. "Our home is only about nine miles from here."

"Oh, I see." Michelle wasn't sure what else to talk about, but Lenore had some questions of her own. "How do you like it here in Lancaster County? Are you getting used to life on the farm?"

"Well, I haven't been here long enough to decide. But so far it seems to be going well." Michelle gave her tingling earlobe a tug. "I am curious about one thing though."

"What's that?"

"My only encounter with any Amish has been the few I have met since coming here. I was wondering if other Amish communities in different parts of the country were the same as in Lancaster County."

Lenore shook her head. "Various areas are definitely different, although many of the differences are subtle."

"Such as?" Michelle kept her focus on Lenore, eager to hear her response.

"There are different styles for the men's hats and prayer coverings for the women.

Also, the length and color choices of Amish women's dresses can vary. Even the types of suspenders the men wear can be different."

"Interesting." Michelle shifted her position on the couch. "Is that all?"

"No. In Lancaster County we ride scooters, but in other places — like certain Amish communities in Indiana, Illinois, and Ohio — they are allowed to ride bicycles."

"Why is that?"

Lenore shrugged. "It's whatever the church leaders decide. You see, some groups of Amish are allowed to use cell phones, especially if they are business owners, but others can't have a phone at all. Or if they do, it must be kept in a phone shed or inside the barn, but it must be outside the home."

"Lots of rules then, huh?"

"Yes, but they all serve a purpose. In some areas the farmers are allowed to have a tractor, but some cannot. Oh, and some Amish can have rubber tires, while others can only have iron wheels."

"What about indoor plumbing? Do most Amish homes have hot and cold running water in the house like my grandparents do here?" The more Michelle learned, the more interested she became. The Amish were truly a fascinating group of people.

"Most Amish do have indoor plumbing

these days," Lenore replied, "but there are still some in the plainer, more conservative districts that use outhouses."

Michelle wrinkled her nose. "Eww . . . Don't think I could ever get used to that."

As quickly as the subject of church rules and differences in communities had been brought up, Lenore changed the subject. "I never got to meet your mother, but my dad talked about her all the time. He really misses his sister and has talked about their childhood a lot."

All Michelle could do was smile. She was at a loss for words.

Lenore giggled. "I have two brothers, and I'm close to both of them, so I can only imagine how hard it would be if one of them ran off and we never saw him again."

Michelle frowned. This conversation had turned too negative. But before she could think of anything else to say, Lenore spoke again.

"From the things Dad has said, it seems as though he and Aunt Rhoda had a fun childhood."

Michelle held her breath. She thought sure Lenore would say more about the Lapps' daughter, and how she left home without a trace, but fortunately, the conversation changed again.

"How long do you plan on staying here with our grandparents?"

Michelle released her breath and answered carefully. "I'm not sure. I'd like to stay through the summer, but it all depends."

"Grandpa and Grandma would like that." Lenore smiled. "They'd probably be happy if you stayed with them indefinitely."

Michelle squirmed, feeling more uncomfortable by the minute. *If they knew who I was they'd be glad to see me go.* She cleared her throat and asked a question, hoping to calm herself. "What's it like teaching Amish children?" she asked, changing the subject. "Did you have to go to college and get a degree in order to teach?"

"Oh no." Lenore shook her head. "I graduated eighth grade, like all other Amish scholars, but I didn't get any other schooling, except learning how to work at my dad's general store. You see, when an Amish child graduates eighth grade, they most always learn a trade. Or at the very least, they'll end up working in a relative's place of business."

"Really? How come?" Michelle didn't see how anyone could be a schoolteacher without getting a degree. And the thought of only going through the eighth grade instead of graduating from high school seemed strange to her.

"We Amish have always believed that too much education can make a person proud. To us, an eighth-grade education is sufficient." Lenore shifted her position. "However, once a student graduates, they further their education by training as apprentices for their future jobs. In my case, I had excelled when I was attending school, and it pleased me when the members of our Amish community approved me as a teacher." Lenore's upturned face radiated the joy she obviously felt because of being a schoolteacher.

"One thing you might find interesting about our Amish schools is that we have a special Christmas program every year, where the scholars get to share poems, recitations, and songs for their families. The children will often exchange gifts with others in their class." Lenore's face brightened even more. "It's a joyous occasion, and one that both teacher and students look forward to during the Christmas season."

Michelle picked at a hangnail that had made an appearance this morning shortly after she'd helped Mary Ruth do the dishes. "That's all very interesting, Lenore. Thanks for explaining."

Her pretend cousin gave a nod. "If you

have any other questions, let me know. I'd be happy to answer them for you."

"Okay, I will." In some ways, Michelle wished she'd been able to end her education after the eighth grade. But if she had, it would have been a lot harder to get a job — even one waiting tables or taking orders at a coffee shop. A lot of employers wanted their employees to have at least a high school degree. Of course with the Amish, it was different, since most places of business where Amish people worked hired them based on their ability to do the job well. This was something else Michelle had learned by watching the reality show. It was one of few things they'd mentioned that actually made sense. And since Lenore had just said Amish young people learned some kind of a trade after they finished their formal education, Michelle figured that part of the segment she'd seen on TV must be true.

At the sound of a horse and buggy, Michelle turned her head. *Oh great, that must be Ezekiel. I can't believe Mary Ruth invited him to join us for supper.*

When Ezekiel knocked on the door, he was greeted by Willis, whose damp hair gave evidence that he'd recently taken a shower.

"Evening, Son. Glad ya could join us tonight." Willis swiped at a drip of water rolling down his forehead.

Ezekiel grinned and sniffed the air. "Me too. Something smells mighty good in here."

"That would be my fraa's special pasta sauce. Spaghetti's one of Sara's favorite meals, so that's what Mary Ruth is fixin' tonight." Willis gestured to the first room off the hall. "Lenore's here. Let's join her and Sara in the living room while we wait for Mary Ruth to call us for supper."

When Ezekiel entered the living room, he found Sara and Lenore sitting on the sofa beside each other. Feeling a bit awkward, he stepped forward and handed Sara a purple African violet. "Happy birthday."

Her eyes widened a bit, and her fingers trembled slightly as she reached out to accept his gift. "It's beautiful, thank you. I certainly wasn't expecting a gift from you." Sara looked at Lenore. "Or you either."

Lenore smiled. "Everyone should get a present on their birthday."

Mary Ruth entered the room, and seeing Ezekiel, she said, "I'm glad you're here. We can eat our supper now."

"Look what Ezekiel brought for Sara." Willis pointed to the plant Sara held.

Mary Ruth leaned in closer and gave an

approving nod.

Ezekiel handed Sara something else. "Here is a small saucer you can put under the African violet. There are holes in the bottom of the pot it's planted in, and instead of waterin' it from the top, like you'd do for most other potted plants, you'll need to water this one from the bottom."

"Okay." Sara's uncertain tone let him know she was a bit confused. "How does that help the plant?"

"After you put the water in the saucer, it will get drawn up into the dirt through the holes at the bottom, and the roots will grow downward, toward the moisture."

She nodded. "Thanks, I didn't know that."

"Once your plant gets established and it grows a little bigger, you can even take one of the leaves and put it in water."

Her nose twitched as she stared at the plant. "How come?"

"After some time passes, you'll eventually see tiny little roots coming out of the bottom of the violet's leaf," Mary Ruth said before Ezekiel could respond. "Once the roots grow more, you can plant the leaf, and it will start a new African violet."

Ezekiel bobbed his head. "We do that in the greenhouse to get new plants started."

Sara smiled. "That's amazing."

"Years ago, when the African violet my mother gave me got too big, I used to take leaves from it to start new plants," Mary Ruth continued. "Once they began to grow, the smaller plants made for nice gifts."

"She still has her mother's African violet. It's in our room, sitting by the window," Willis added.

"Since Sara has already received one gift, would it be all right if she opened mine now? It shouldn't take long." Lenore gestured to the present sitting on the coffee table.

"Go right ahead, Sara. Supper can wait a few more minutes."

Sara set the African violet on the table and picked up Lenore's gift. Her fingers trembled once more as she tore the paper off and opened the lid on the box.

Ezekiel wondered why she seemed so nervous. Surely she was used to receiving gifts on her birthday. But maybe not from people she barely knew. He watched with interest as she removed three rubber stamps, two ink pads, and some cardstock. Sara stared at the items like she'd never seen anything like them before.

"Have you ever done any stamping and card making?" Lenore asked.

Sara shook her head.

"Well, that's okay. I'll teach you. It'll give us something fun to do as we get to know each other better."

"Thank you." Sara pressed her fingers against her smiling lips. "This has been the best birthday ever."

"Well, it's not over yet." Mary Ruth moved toward the dining room. "We have our meal to eat, and then Willis and I have a gift for you too."

Willis nodded. "After that, there will be *kuche* and *eis raaham.*"

"What is that?" Sara rose to her feet.

"It means, 'cake and ice cream,' " Ezekiel announced.

"Oh, okay." She looked up at him with a hopeful expression. "In addition to learning more things about the Amish way of life, I hope I can learn a few Pennsylvania Dutch words while I'm here visiting."

"Don't worry. We'll teach you whatever you want to know." Mary Ruth put one arm around Sara's waist and the other arm around Lenore's. It didn't take a genius to see how happy she was to have both of her granddaughters visiting.

Since he wasn't part of their family, Ezekiel almost felt like a fifth wheel on a buggy. But he'd always felt welcome in this home. Willis and Mary Ruth treated him kindly — almost like he was part of their family. Sometimes, he felt more comfortable here than he did at home, where his folks — especially Dad — were often critical of him.

Well tonight he wasn't going to think about that. He planned to enjoy a good meal, relax, and have a nice time. He was curious though about what gift the Lapps would give Sara after supper. From the gleam in Mary Ruth and Willis's eyes, he had a feeling it was something special.

Chapter 9

"This spaghetti is scrumptious, Mary — I mean Grandma." Michelle blotted her lips with a cloth napkin. Mary Ruth had set a lovely table tonight, using her best china dishes and fancy glassware. Apparently some things this Amish family owned weren't so plain. "My only complaint about the food is that I ate too much."

Mary Ruth smiled. "I'm glad you like it. While pasta dishes aren't traditional Pennsylvania Dutch meals, in this house we do enjoy spaghetti, pizza, and lasagna sometimes."

Willis bobbed his head. "Anything my fraa cooks is *appeditlich.*" He winked at Michelle. "That means 'delicious.' "

"Appeditlich," Michelle repeated. "Jah, the meal is appeditlich."

Everyone nodded, even Mary Ruth. Michelle was certain the woman wasn't bragging. She simply enjoyed eating the spaghetti.

Michelle patted her stomach. "If I keep eating all this good home-cooked food, I'll get fat."

Willis looked at her over the top of his glasses. "A slender girl like you could probably eat twice as much as you did this evening and never gain a pound. I doubt you'll ever be *fett.*" He winked. "That word means 'fat.' "

Michelle smiled. It had been a long time since she'd eaten food this good or with such nice people. Most of her meals since she'd been out on her own either came out of a can or a box that needed to be heated in the microwave.

Michelle glanced across the table, where Ezekiel sat next to Lenore. Had he been seated there because they were a couple? *Not that it's any of my business.* She looked away. *While I'm staying here, maybe I should ask Mary Ruth to teach me how to make some of her tasty recipes. I need to have something positive to take away with me when I leave — something besides the memories.*

"Would you like another piece of sourdough bread?" Mary Ruth asked, breaking into Michelle's thoughts.

"No thanks, I'd better not." She thumped

her stomach.

"Oh, that's right." Willis grinned mischievously. "You need to save room for dessert."

"Oh my." Lenore held her stomach. "I don't know if I'll be able to eat any dessert."

"Me neither." Michelle shook her head. "I ate way more than I should have."

Mary Ruth looked at Ezekiel. "How about you? Have you got room for cake and ice cream?"

He nodded. "But I might need to let my supper settle awhile first."

"Not a problem. We'll wait an hour or so to eat our dessert." Mary Ruth got up from the table. "I'll put the dirty dishes in the sink to soak, and we can all go out to the barn."

Michelle's forehead wrinkled as she glanced at Lenore, who'd gotten up and quickly begun clearing away the dishes. Michelle did the same. She couldn't figure out why Mary Ruth wanted them to go out to the barn. *Maybe she wants to show Ezekiel Sadie's puppies.* If so, it was fine with Michelle. She looked forward to seeing them again.

"The puppies have grown since I saw them last." Lenore knelt beside the box and reached inside to pet one of the pups. "I was helping my mamm do the dishes while they were being born, but I'm glad she and I took the time to go out to the barn once we were done in the kitchen."

"Does *mamm* mean 'mom'?" Michelle asked.

"Yes." Lenore grinned at Michelle. "See, that's one more Pennsylvania Dutch word you have learned this evening."

Willis chuckled. "Pretty soon you'll be speaking the Dutch like you've lived here in Amish country all your life."

I wish I could stay here for the rest of my life. Michelle's chest grew heavy, knowing a happy life here with Willis and Mary Ruth was out of her reach.

"It's amazing how quickly puppies grow." Ezekiel's comment redirected Michelle's thoughts.

Mary Ruth gave Michelle's arm a little tap. "Do you have a favorite pup?"

"Yes, I do." Michelle leaned over and picked up the runt. "This little one has to struggle to get what he wants, so he's the one I'm rooting for." *Kind of like me. I've been struggling all my life and still don't have what I really want.*

Willis put his hand on Michelle's shoulder. "Well, he's yours. Happy birthday."

Michelle shook her head. "Oh no, I can't take the puppy with me when I leave. I don't even know where I'll be going."

Mary Ruth's forehead creased. "What do you mean, Sara? Won't you return to your home?"

"Um . . . yeah . . . I just meant . . ." Michelle wiped the dampness from her forehead. "I may not stay there. I might move someplace else."

"Where would you move?" Lenore asked.

Michelle put the pup back in the box and stood, massaging her temples. Her head felt like it was going to explode. "I . . . I'm not sure. The lease on my apartment will run out soon, and then I'll have to decide whether to renew it or move. Besides, I don't think my landlord would allow me to have a pet." Michelle was getting in deeper with added lies, but what other choice did she have? She had to make the Lapps keep thinking she was their granddaughter — at least until she was ready to leave.

"If you stayed here with us, you wouldn't have to worry about paying rent for an apartment or whether you could have a dog." Mary Ruth looked directly at Michelle. "You will think about it, won't you?"

Michelle nodded slowly. The thought of staying here held appeal, but it wasn't possible. It was only a matter of time before she would have to leave. While she was here though, she planned to enjoy all of Mary Ruth's and Willis's attention, as well as the sense of responsibility she was learning from them.

Willis gave Michelle's arm a tender squeeze. "We want you to have the pick of the litter. And if you're not able to take it, should you decide to leave, we'll keep the pup here and you can see it whenever you come to visit."

Michelle clasped her hands loosely behind her back as she gazed down at Sadie and her brood. "Thank you. It was a thoughtful gift, and I'm definitely going to claim the littlest pup."

"What are you gonna call it?" Ezekiel questioned.

Michelle directed her gaze to him. "I don't know. Any suggestions?"

He shrugged. "Guess you could just call it Runt."

"Or how about Tiny?" Lenore interjected.

Michelle sucked in her lower lip. "I suppose either of those names could work, but I'd like it to be something unique."

"Well, I think I'll leave you three young people here to figure it out while I go inside and get things ready for dessert." Mary

Ruth tapped her husband's arm. "Are you coming, Willis?"

He hesitated a moment, then nodded. "I'll put a pot of coffee on, while you get out the plates and whatnot."

She smiled and gave his full beard a little tug. "I'll wait to cut the cake and take out the ice cream until our granddaughters and Ezekiel come in."

Michelle watched as Willis and Mary Ruth ambled out of the barn, holding hands. While she'd never asked how old they were, she figured they were both probably in their late sixties. They hadn't given into old age by any stretch of the imagination though. Despite their slower gaits, they kept moving and doing chores. Truth be told, some people their age would have a hard time keeping up with Mr. and Mrs. Lapp. Michelle hoped by the time she became as old as they were, she'd have even half their determination and energy. Was it wishful thinking that one day she too might have somebody special to grow old with?

Leaning his full weight against a wooden post, Ezekiel watched Sara sitting on a bale of straw, holding her puppy. The light from the battery-operated lantern overhead shone down on her head. He noticed that she wore very little makeup. She didn't need it. Sara was a natural beauty. Her creamy complexion, slender features, and pretty auburn hair were enough to turn any man's head. Ezekiel figured Sara probably had a boyfriend, or at least dated a lot of men. In fact, he was surprised she wasn't married by now. Of course, Ezekiel was close to her age, and he wasn't married. For that matter, Lenore was still single, and to his knowledge, she'd never had a serious boyfriend.

Lenore stood up. "Most of the puppies are either sleeping or eating now, so I think I'll head back to the house and see if Grandma needs help with anything." She turned toward Sara. "Feel free to stay out here for a while longer with your furry little birthday present. It'll probably be another fifteen minutes or so before our dessert is ready to eat. I'll ring the bell on the back porch to let you both know when it's time."

Ezekiel nodded, and Sara smiled. "Okay."

After Lenore left the barn, Sara stood up and put the puppy back in the box. "I don't want this little rascal to miss out on a meal, and I'm thinkin' maybe we should go back to the house. I wouldn't want to miss out on the cake and ice cream."

Ezekiel stepped up next to her. This was the first time he'd had the chance to speak to Sara alone, and he didn't want to miss it. "Lenore said she'd ring the bell when it's ready. Besides, the cake and ice cream are in honor of your birthday, so I'm sure they won't eat without you."

She dipped her head slightly and giggled. "I guess you're right." Sara kept her attention focused on the box. "Would it be dumb if I called the pup Rascal?"

He shook his head. "If ya ask me that sounds like a good dog's name."

"Glad you like it." Sara started moving toward the barn door.

"Before we go in, could I ask ya a question?"

She stopped walking and turned to face him. "What do you want to know?"

He came alongside her. "I was wonderin' if you like being English."

She tipped her head. "In what way?"

"In all ways. Do you enjoy everything the English life has to offer?"

Sara's long hair swished back and forth as she shook her head. "Not even."

"Not even what?"

"It's a figure of speech. I don't begin to like everything about the English way of life." She pursed her lips. "But I was born into it, so I really have no choice."

"Your mother was Amish, and she left her

family to become English, so she must have seen something good in it."

Sara crossed her arms, staring blankly across the room as though she could look into her past. "I can't say what it was. She never talked to me about her reason for leaving the Amish faith or what she thought was good about being English." She looked back at him. "Does that answer your question?"

"Sort of, but it doesn't tell me what it's like to live in the English world."

"Let's just say, it's not all it's cracked up to be." Sara turned and started walking toward the door again. "I'm going back to the house now. Are you coming?"

"Yeah." As Ezekiel shuffled his feet across the yard, while she practically ran toward the house, his thoughts turned inward. He was past the age most young people got baptized and joined the Amish church, and his parents had been hounding him to do it. But Ezekiel wasn't ready to commit, and he wished he knew what road he was meant to travel. Would he be happier if he were English, or would his life be more satisfying if he remained here and joined the Amish church?

CHAPTER 10

When Michelle came downstairs Sunday morning, a knot formed in her stomach. Mary Ruth and Willis would be leaving for church after breakfast, and they had invited her to go with them.

She'd never been to an Amish church service and didn't know what to expect. Mary Ruth had explained a few things, like the fact that the service would take around three hours and a light meal would follow. Willis mentioned the sermons and songs would all be in German. Michelle wondered how she would make it, sitting for so long while listening to a language she didn't understand. Short of pretending to be sick, she saw no way out of going.

"Shoulda taken German instead of Spanish in high school," Michelle mumbled before entering the kitchen.

Mary Ruth set a platter of sticky buns on the table and smiled at Michelle. "What was that, Sara?"

Michelle shook her head. "It was nothing. I was thinking out loud."

"I do that sometimes myself." Mary Ruth gestured to Michelle's dark green, ankle-length skirt. "Is the skirt I made last week comfortable enough for you?"

Michelle looked down at the plain material and nodded. While it was nowhere near her normal attire, the elastic waist and lightweight material felt comfortable. She'd chosen a simple white blouse to wear with it, along with a pair of black flats. At Mary Ruth's request, Michelle had worn no jewelry or makeup today. In fact, since coming to live here, she'd pretty much given up wearing makeup and jewelry. Comfortable or not, this was Michelle's new image, and these days, no one from her past would likely recognize her.

"Since we will be leaving soon, I'm keeping breakfast simple this morning." Mary Ruth pointed to the sticky buns on the table. "There are also some hard-boiled eggs in the refrigerator, if you would like one."

"Thanks." Michelle opened the refrigerator and removed a brown egg. After cracking and peeling it on a paper towel, she took a seat at the table.

A few seconds later, Willis entered the room. "The horse and buggy are ready to go, so as soon as we're finished eating, we can be on our way to the Kings' place."

"Why are we going there?" Michelle asked. "It was my understanding that we'd be heading to church after breakfast."

"We will. Our church service will be held in Vernon's barn today." Willis peered at Michelle over the top of his glasses. "I thought we explained that we Amish don't worship in a church building. We take turns holding our bi-weekly services in one another's homes."

"If you mentioned it, I must have forgot." She couldn't imagine what it would be like to have church in a barn.

"That's right," Mary Ruth agreed. "If the house isn't big enough, we meet in a barn or shop on that person's property. Any building that's big enough to hold all the families in our church district."

"Oh, I see." Michelle realized she had a lot more to learn about the Amish way of life. She had a hunch she'd only scratched the surface. But with each thing revealed to her, she found herself becoming more fascinated.

Michelle sat next to Lenore on one end of a

backless wooden bench, feeling out of place and hoping her presence didn't stick out like a sore thumb. She pursed her lips. *I wonder where that old saying came from. It doesn't make much sense, if you think about it.*

With her back hurting from sitting this way for the past hour and a half, it was difficult to stay awake. The slow monotonous hymns sung in a language she didn't understand seemed so repetitive. Although it was amazing to listen to this crowd of people singing in unison. As they sang one stanza after another, their a cappella music seemed to fill every corner of the barn, and drift to the rafters. Surely anyone within a five mile radius could hear the melancholy tones coming from the Kings' farm. And perhaps the music, sung with such sincerity, was heard all the way up to heaven.

Michelle shifted to the left a bit, trying to find a comfortable position and not bump into Lenore. *Wish Mary Ruth would have mentioned that we women would be facing the men during the church service.* She had noticed Ezekiel watching her a few times when he should have been looking at his songbook. *The* Ausbund. *I think that's what Lenore called it when the books were handed out.* To be polite, Michelle had taken one, but the only purpose it served was to have something in her hand to hold onto.

Some of the other young men in the service today had also glanced her way. No doubt they were curious about the young woman wearing her hair up in a bun, but with no covering. She wondered what everyone thought of her long skirt and blouse, instead of a plain colored dress with a white apron, like all the other women wore today. *They probably wonder who I am.*

Michelle clasped her fingers together and twiddled her thumbs, wishing the time would go faster. If she was going to stay with the Lapps through the summer months, they would expect her to accompany them to church. So she would have to get used to sitting here like this every other Sunday. It was either that or come up with some excuse to stay home.

The congregation stood, and Michelle resisted the temptation to sigh with relief as she joined them. A tall, bearded man began reading from the Bible. At least she thought it was a Bible. The book was black and looked like some of the Bibles she'd seen.

Michelle remembered Mary Ruth telling her that when a person needed to go out to stretch their legs or use the restroom, it was usually during the reading of the scriptures.

She glanced around and saw several young mothers with babies in their arms leave the barn. A few men left with young boys too, and some of the older women as well. Mary Ruth remained in place, however, and so did Lenore.

Michelle fidgeted. *Do I stay or go?* With a need to give her back a rest, she scurried out the barn door behind a young pregnant woman.

Once outside, Michelle drew in a few deep breaths, although the air wasn't as fresh as she'd hoped it would be. The sun was out in full force, and the air felt humid and sticky.

Michelle walked around for a bit, to stretch her legs, until a swarm of gnats congregated around her head. *Great. My back is sore, and now I have to deal with these irritating bugs.*

Given the opportunity, she followed a couple of women into the house. Michelle needed a drink of water and the chance to use the restroom. She paused in the living room to ask one of the women holding a baby where the bathroom was. After being told it was down the hall, Michelle headed in that direction. There was a line outside the door, so she leaned against the wall and waited, hoping she wouldn't have to make conversation with anyone.

No such luck. The elderly woman in front of Michelle turned and offered her a friendly smile. "My name is Esther Fisher, and you must be Mary Ruth's granddaughter Sara."

Michelle nodded. *I wonder how she knew that. Guess news travels fast around here.*

"Mary Ruth and I have been friends for a good many years, and after Rhoda left home, I was deeply concerned." Esther's expression sobered. "Mary Ruth and Willis have suffered a great deal over the years, but having you come into their lives has brought them both joy and peace." She clasped Michelle's hand. "We are all glad you're here."

"Thank you." Michelle could barely get the words out. Not only had she deceived the Lapps, but she was basically lying to every person she met in their Amish community. Michelle felt a twinge of guilt, but not enough to end her charade. She was in a safe place — far from Jerry — and didn't need to worry about looking for work or wondering where her next meal would come from. She couldn't give this up — not yet anyway.

Ezekiel had been watching Sara when he should have paid attention to the songs they were singing. There was something about the Lapps' granddaughter that made him want to know her better. And it wasn't simply the fact that she was English.

As he stood during the reading of scriptures, he grew antsy. He'd seen Sara go out and wished he could follow. He would like the chance to talk to her again. But that wouldn't be acceptable behavior here at church. The men stayed together, and the women did the same. They even ate at separate tables during the noon meal. Although the service was here at his folks' place, it would still look bad if he went out and was seen talking to her.

Ezekiel popped his knuckles as he thought about Sara's birthday supper. It brought a smile to his lips, remembering how peaceful she'd looked holding the pup she named Rascal. He'd have to make another trip to the Lapps' home soon and see how the puppies were doing. It would also give him a chance to visit more with Sara.

"This is not the time or place to be popping your knuckles," whispered Ezekiel's cousin, Raymond, as he bumped his arm.

Ezekiel let his hands fall to his sides and glanced toward the barn door. Still no sign of Sara, and she'd been gone quite a while. *I wonder if she got distracted talking to someone in the house. Or maybe she's not coming back at all. Sitting in the stuffy barn all that time may have been too much for her.*

Ezekiel had seen that happen with a few other people — especially visitors who weren't used to sitting for so long and with no air-conditioning. Some young fellows who hadn't joined the church yet would go out during scriptures and not come back in till church was almost over.

Once when Ezekiel was in his early teens, a friend of his brother Abe walked out during scriptures and didn't come back. Ezekiel's dad later said that if any of his boys ever pulled a shenanigan like that, they'd be doing extra chores for at least a month. More chores held no appeal for Ezekiel, so if he left the building for any reason, he'd always made sure to return in a timely manner. Ezekiel's father held a tight rein on his children, but he'd never been physically abusive. For that much, he was thankful.

Ezekiel snapped to attention when Raymond bumped his arm again and pointed to the wooden bench they'd been sitting on. Scripture reading was over now, and everyone had taken their seats, in readiness for the first sermon.

Ezekiel glanced at the women's section.

Lenore sat on the bench where she'd been before, but Sara's place was empty. He couldn't help but wonder what Mary Ruth and Willis thought about that. Surely they'd seen her go out, and they must realize she hadn't come in.

A few minutes later, with her head down and cheeks pink, Sara entered the barn and took her seat. Many heads turned in her direction, including Ezekiel's.

Sara clasped her hands and folded them in her lap. No doubt she was embarrassed, but at least she had come back.

Chapter 11

"Where do you think you're going, Son? I was talkin' to you."

Ezekiel's skin tingled as his face warmed. "I'm going out to check my bee boxes," he mumbled, turning to face his father.

"You can do that later — when you're done working in the greenhouse."

Ezekiel drew a quick breath and released it with a huff. "Why can't Henry help in the greenhouse today? He's out of school for the summer and doesn't have much else to do."

"Not true," Mom spoke up from the other side of the greenhouse. "I've been keeping your little *brieder* busy with lots of chores around the yard and even some inside the house."

Ezekiel grunted. "Okay, okay. What do you need me to do, Dad?"

"For starters, all the plants in here need watering. And then . . ."

Dad's words faded as Ezekiel pulled his thoughts inward. He would do whatever needed to be done here, but during his lunch break, he planned to check his bee boxes, because that was important, even if Dad didn't think so. Afterward, he'd head over to the Lapps' place. If he could talk to Sara awhile, it might put him in a better mood. Since she wasn't Amish, maybe she'd understand the way he felt about certain things. No one here did, that was for sure.

As Michelle headed for the barn to check on the pups, she kicked a small stone with the toe of her sneaker, sending it flying across the yard. Yesterday at church had been horrible. Well, maybe not horrible, but certainly not what she'd hoped it would be. "Boy, I'm still sore."

Michelle rubbed the small of her back. Sitting for three hours on hard, backless benches had been difficult enough, but seeing so many people staring at her when she returned to the barn was embarrassing. Michelle hadn't planned to be gone so long, but after she came out of the Kings' bathroom, a pretty young woman named Amy had introduced herself as Ezekiel's sister. They'd ended up talking for a while, which made them both late returning to the church service. No one seemed to notice Amy when she slipped into the barn and took her seat. *Probably because they were all looking at me — the newcomer who didn't fit in.*

When church was over and the noon meal had been served, the only young people who spoke to her were Amy and her pretend cousin Lenore. Michelle had definitely been an outsider, but at least Mary Ruth, as well as a few of the older women, had engaged her in conversation. With the exception of Mary Ruth though, they were probably all merely trying to be polite to the newcomer.

Ever since Michelle was a child, she'd never really felt like she fit in anywhere. Even though she'd made a few friends since being out on her own, they'd mostly been poor choices. When people like Jerry, who had abused her physically and mentally, came into her life, she was duped into thinking they cared about her. Michelle had never received much nurturing and craved even the smallest kindness anyone might have offered her. But then, whenever her so-called friends' true colors showed, reality set in, and Michelle realized they'd only been using her.

I've gotta quit thinking about this and focus on something positive, Michelle told herself as she entered the barn. And what could be more uplifting than holding little Rascal? The puppies were innocent little creatures. They knew nothing more than being fed, finding a comfortable place to sleep, and having a little love showered on them. *If only life could be that simple.*

Michelle made her way over to the box and stood staring down at the litter. The pups were all nursing, and she didn't want to disturb them or Sadie, who napped while her babies fed.

Maybe I'll sit over there awhile and wait till they finish eating. She took a seat on a bale of straw and took a piece of gum from her shirt pocket. Michelle was about to unwrap it when a movement out of the corner of her eye caught her attention. "Why, it's a mouse," she whispered, not wanting to scare the little thing. The rodent scampered across a shelf, then darted behind a couple of old jars. Michelle watched as it went into a hole and disappeared.

While some people might have run screaming out of the barn upon seeing a rodent, Michelle had never been afraid of mice. She'd seen plenty of them during the years she'd lived at home with her parents. Her mom didn't keep the place clean, and her dad never fixed much of anything. The place was always a mess, so it was no surprise to see a few mice scurrying through it. Even some of the apartments Michelle had rented were occupied with the plump, long-tailed creatures.

Since the mouse was gone, Michelle focused on the glass canning jars. They looked old. Curious, she decided to take a closer look.

Michelle put the gum back in her pocket and went to get the stepladder that had been leaning against the wall near the barn doors. After hauling it across the room, she positioned the ladder in front of the shelf. Once she'd climbed it and taken a closer look, she knew for sure they were antique jars.

Michelle picked the first one up to inspect the bubbles in the glass, and spotted another jar behind it, only this one was a pale blue. But the pretty color wasn't what interested Michelle the most.

"Looks like there's a bunch of folded papers inside." Michelle turned the jar every which way and shook it, before pulling the wire back and removing the glass lid.

Holding the jar with both hands, Michelle returned to her seat on the bale of straw. She reached inside, retrieved a piece of paper, and silently read the message written there. *"Dear Lord, I know I'm not worthy, but please answer my prayers."*

Michelle pursed her lips. *I wonder who wrote this, and why did they put their prayer in this jar?* Eager to know what some of the other papers said, she pulled out another one.

"Lord, I need Your direction. Show me the right path."

Michelle's brows furrowed. *Whoever wrote these must be a religious person. Was it Mary Ruth? But why would she put her prayer requests in an old jar and leave it here in the barn, hidden behind other jars? Could it have been Mary Ruth's way of journaling her thoughts? Should I ask her about it?*

Michelle rolled the question around in her head, studying the other pieces of paper still inside the jar. *I better not. If she did write those prayers, they were personal. She might not want anyone to know about it. For some folks, some things aren't meant to talk about.*

Michelle heard whimpering coming from Sadie's box, so she put the two papers back in the jar, secured the lid, and returned it to the shelf. Some other time when she came out to the barn to look at the pups or do a chore for Willis, she would take the jar down again and read more.

Returning to Sadie's brood, Michelle reached into the box and picked up Rascal, careful not to disturb the other pups who lay close to their sleeping mother. The pup cried in protest as a little milk dribbled down his chin. According to Willis, the puppies' eyes should be opening soon — usually around two weeks after they were born. Michelle looked forward to watching the pups grow — especially Rascal. She hoped he would catch up to his brothers and sisters, but even if he remained the smallest, he'd always be her favorite.

"You're okay. I've got ya, boy." Michelle spoke soothingly as she carried Rascal to the bale of straw she'd been sitting on previously. She held the pup up to her face and giggled when the little fellow licked the end of her nose. Michelle inhaled the aroma of Rascal's sweet puppy breath. It felt comforting to sit here holding the pup and stroking its soft head. "Wish I could take you with me," she murmured, while Rascal curled up in her arms.

"Are you goin' somewhere?"

Michelle jumped at the sound of a booming male voice. A few seconds later, Ezekiel made his way deeper into the barn and came to a halt next to her.

"You startled me." She shifted on the bale

of straw. "I didn't hear a horse and buggy come into the yard."

"That's 'cause I came on foot." Ezekiel took a seat beside her, gently bumping her shoulder as he did so.

"You live quite a distance away. How come you walked over?"

"My horse threw a shoe this morning and the farrier can't come out till tomorrow morning. So it was either walk or ride my scooter." He gave a forced laugh. "It's kinda hard to ride one of those on a gravel road like what's out in front of the Lapps' place."

"I guess it would be." Michelle scooted over a bit. "Would you like to hold my pup?"

"Sure." Ezekiel held out his hands, and when she handed him Rascal, he nuzzled the puppy with his nose. "The little guy sure is cute."

"I'm one hundred percent in agreement." Michelle's posture relaxed. She felt contentment sitting here beside Ezekiel. He was easy to talk to, and he liked her dog. "So what brings you by today? Did you come to see Willis?"

"Nope. Came to see you."

"Oh?" Michelle couldn't imagine why he would want to see her.

"I wanted to talk to someone who doesn't complain about everything I do."

"Who's complaining about what you do?"

"My dad. I can never do anything right it seems. And to top it off, he wants me to take over the greenhouse someday." Ezekiel placed the sleeping pup in his lap. "But I have other plans."

Michelle wasn't sure if he wanted her to ask what his plans were or just listen. She would listen, but she wasn't concerned with his problem, because she had enough of her own to worry about.

"Want a piece of gum?" Michelle asked.

"Sure, why not."

Michelle took out the piece she'd previously put in her pocket and tore it in half. "I only have this one, but I'm willing to share it."

"Thanks." Ezekiel sat silently a few moments, chewing the gum, then lightly bumped her arm. "You never did answer my question."

"What question was that?"

"When I first came in I heard you say something about wishing you could take — I'm guessing, Rascal with you. Then I asked if you were going somewhere, but you didn't respond."

"Oh, I . . . uh . . . was just talking to the pup — saying I wish I could take him with . . ." Michelle stopped talking and cracked her gum.

Tipping his head, Ezekiel pursued his questioning. "You mean, take him when you leave your grandparents' house and go back to your own place?"

"Yeah, only I don't really have a place." Michelle bounced a curled knuckle against her mouth. "I mean I do have a place, but I may not stay there."

"How come?"

"Well, I might want to move. Besides, my landlord doesn't allow pets, so I wouldn't be able to take Rascal."

"Yeah, I remember you mentioning that on Friday. But you'll be comin' back here for visits, right?"

No. When I go, I can't come back. Michelle wished she could be honest with Ezekiel but instead added more to her lies. "Yeah, I hope to, anyhow."

"Willis and Mary Ruth would sure be disappointed if you didn't come back to see them."

All Michelle could manage was a brief nod as she heard a van pull into the yard. "I bet that's Grandpa and Grandma returning from their shopping trip. They hired one of their drivers to take 'em to some stores in Lancaster today."

"Makes sense. Especially if they had a lot

of things to get. There isn't much room in the back of our carriages — even the market buggies." Ezekiel massaged his forehead. "That's why I want a car or truck of my own."

Michelle studied the curves of his face and along his jawline. "Are you serious?"

"Yep. I've wanted one for a long time, but my dad would pitch a fit if I bought one, much less drove it home."

"Guess that makes sense, since you're Amish and aren't supposed to drive cars. Right?"

"It would be true if I'd joined the church already, but I haven't, so . . ."

"You mean you're allowed to own a car?"

"Well, I would be if my dad was okay with it." Ezekiel grunted. "Some of my friends have a car. But Dad's made it clear he doesn't want me to buy one. Even said if I did, he'd never let me have it anywhere on his property."

It didn't take a genius to see how frustrated Ezekiel was over his dad's refusal to let him buy a car. *But there are worse parents out there, that's for sure. Just ask me. If only I could tell you, Ezekiel . . . I have the world's worst parents.*

"Mind if I ask you another question about the Amish way of life?" Michelle asked after a lengthy pause.

"Sure. Ask away."

"Can anyone join the Amish church?"

His eyebrows shot up. "Why are you askin' me that question? Do you think you might want to join?"

Michelle leaned against the post behind her back. "No, of course not. I was only curious, that's all."

"Well, I guess anyone could join if they were willing to give up their modern way of life and abide by all the rules of the Amish church." He reached up and scratched a spot behind his left ear. "I think it'd be a difficult transition, though, 'cause there'd be many changes that would have to be made."

"Like what?"

"For one thing, they'd have to learn our Pennsylvania Dutch language. And of course change to the simple way of dressing." He pointed to Michelle's denim jeans. "An Amish woman would never be allow to run around in those."

She snickered. "No, I suppose not."

"Yep, in order to become Amish, an English person would need to give up most of the modern conveniences they'd become used to having." Ezekiel shook his head. "I suppose it could be done, but I doubt many could do it."

"You're probably right." Michelle stood. "Guess I should put Rascal back with his mother and go outside to see if Grandma and Grandpa need my help carrying in groceries."

"Yeah, sure. I'll help with that too." Ezekiel followed Michelle across the room and stood watching as she placed the puppy in the box.

"I hope things work out for you with your dad," Michelle said as they walked out of the barn.

"Me too, but it's kinda doubtful." Ezekiel's shoulders slumped. "But I'm gonna get what I want someday, regardless of how my dad thinks I should live my life."

Michelle wasn't sure how to respond, so she hurried her steps. Apparently, she wasn't the only person here with problems. Well at least Ezekiel wasn't lying to his dad. For Michelle, however, every day she was here brought more dishonesty. If she wasn't careful, pretty soon she might actually believe the lie she'd been telling Willis and Mary Ruth. Truthfully, she wished it wasn't a lie, for she'd begun to wish she were the real Sara.

CHAPTER 12

"Oh, there you are, Sara. And it's nice to see you too, Ezekiel." Mary Ruth smiled when Michelle and Ezekiel joined her and Willis at the back of their driver's beige van. It was different than the one that had picked them up at the bus station in Philadelphia earlier that month.

"We were in the barn, looking at the puppies." Michelle reached in and picked up a paper bag. "I'll help you carry the groceries inside."

"I can help with that too." Ezekiel grabbed two grocery sacks. "It'll give me something constructive to do before I head back home."

"All right, but first I'd like you both to meet Brad Fuller. Our other driver, Stan, introduced Brad to us, and he will be driving part-time this summer whenever Stan's not available." Mary Ruth motioned for them to follow her to the front of the van, where a young man with medium brown hair stood talking to Willis.

Mary Ruth stepped up to him. "Sara, this is Brad Fuller. He's attending college in Lancaster and is planning to become a minister someday." She motioned to Sara. "This is our granddaughter Sara Murray. She's here visiting us for the first time, and since she doesn't have a car, she may call on you for a ride sometime."

Brad held out his hand. "It's great to meet you, Sara."

"Nice to meet you too." Michelle struggled not to stare at his eyes. They were the most vivid blue — almost mesmerizing. He gave a brief smile, while Michelle pulled her gaze aside.

Mary Ruth introduced Ezekiel, and the men shook hands.

"In addition to driving for some of the Amish in the area, I'm also available to do odd jobs," Brad explained. "I'm open to do just about anything during the summer months, but in the fall I will go to a university in Clarks Summit, Pennsylvania, to earn my master of divinity degree. It's just north of Scranton — about 146 miles from here." He pointed upward. "I'm following a call God placed on my life when I was a teenager."

Michelle couldn't imagine anyone being so devoted to God that they'd want to become a minister, much less spend all that money on college. But then Willis was a minister in his Amish church, and he seemed like a pretty normal man. And from what Mary Ruth had told her, Willis didn't attend college or even take a home-study course to achieve that position. He'd acquired the unpaid job during the drawing of lots. She'd explained that only married men who were members of the local Amish church were eligible for a ministerial position.

The ordination was usually held at the end of a communion service. Men and women who were church members would go to a designated room in the house and whisper the name of a candidate to a deacon, who would then pass the name on to the church bishop. The names of those men who'd received three or more votes were placed in the lot. Those in the lot were asked if they were in harmony with the ordinances of the church and articles of faith. If they answered affirmatively, they were to kneel in prayer, asking God to show which man He had chosen.

Next, a slip of paper with a Bible verse on it would be placed in a songbook, randomly arranged with other songbooks, the same number as equal to the candidates considered. Seated around the table, the men who were candidates were supposed to select a songbook. When they opened the books, the lot fell on the man who had the slip of paper with the Bible verse inside.

Mary Ruth also mentioned that the term of office for a minister was usually for life. She had told Michelle that each Amish church district had a bishop, two ministers, and one deacon, who were called from within the congregation via the drawing of lots.

"Well, I need to get going. There's someone else I need to pick up." Brad broke into Michelle's thoughts when he spoke and handed her a card. "Here's my number. Feel free to give me a call whenever you need a ride."

"Thanks, I will." She grabbed another grocery bag from the back of the van and followed Mary Ruth, Willis, and Ezekiel to the house. Maybe when it was time to leave the Lapps' house for good, she would call on Brad for a ride to the bus station.

As Brad pulled his van out of the Lapps' driveway, he thought about his meeting with their granddaughter. He was surprised Sara wasn't wearing Amish clothes. Could she or her parents have been Amish at one time and left the faith? Brad wasn't an expert on the Amish way of life, but he'd heard from Stan that some Amish young people chose the English way of life rather than joining the Amish church. Maybe that was the case with Sara.

When a groundhog ran across the road in front of him, Brad slammed on the brakes. Some people might not have cared that it was only a groundhog, but Brad wasn't one of them, even if he didn't have a fondness for this type of animal. No matter what, they were all God's creatures, and he wasn't about to hit one on purpose.

"I need to keep my attention on my driving," Brad scolded himself as he sat back, letting the car idle. He removed a small notepad from his shirt pocket to look at the address again where he needed to pick up a young Amish mother who was taking her baby to a doctor's appointment. "There should be crossroads right up ahead, and then I need to turn left."

Looking into the rearview mirror, he saw a vehicle slowly coming up behind him. "Guess I better get moving." Putting pressure on the gas pedal, Brad glanced over into the field and saw the groundhog, standing on its hind legs. Shaking his finger in the critter's direction, he rolled down the window and hollered, "Good thing I saw you." Grinning at his reflection in the side mirror, Brad mumbled, "at least my eyesight didn't let me down."

Farther up the road, he saw the crossroad where he needed to turn. Approaching it, Brad put his signal on and turned left. The farm was only a few miles down the road.

Once more, the Lapps' granddaughter came to mind. *I wonder how long she'll be staying with the Lapps.*

Brad hoped Sara would call on him for a ride sometime. It would give him a chance to get to know her and ask a few questions. Sara was a beautiful young woman, but during their brief meeting, he had sensed something might be troubling her.

Brad had the gift of discernment, and his intuitions about people were usually correct. His mother often said he would make a good minister because he understood people and could almost see into the windows of their souls. Brad saw his intuitions as a gift from God — one that would help him counsel and minister to people.

"Thank you for helping me put the groceries away." Mary Ruth smiled as she and

Sara put the canned goods on a shelf in the pantry.

Sara nodded. "No problem. I'm happy to do it."

"Brad seems like a nice young man, don't you think?"

"I guess so." Sara reached for a can of black olives and placed it on the shelf. "I didn't really talk to him long enough to form an opinion."

"Stan knows Brad's dad, and he gave him a good recommendation. He said Brad is dependable and a hard worker."

"I see."

"So we'll probably be calling on him for help with several things here at the farm this summer."

Sara grabbed a few more items and placed them on the shelf. "I hope he works out well for you."

It was probably wrong to be thinking such things, but Mary Ruth hoped if Sara and Brad got along well, it might give her a reason to stay. Not that spending time with her grandparents wasn't reason enough. But it would be good for Sara to spend time with a young person who had dedicated his life to serving God. While it was nice to see Sara and Ezekiel getting along well, Mary Ruth hoped he and her other granddaughter might get together. Of course, Lenore had become a church member and was settled into the Amish ways, but Ezekiel hadn't yet joined and seemed a bit unsettled. It was a concern to his parents and everyone else in their community.

Mary Ruth's brows furrowed. *I shouldn't even be thinking about any of this. It's none of my business who Sara, Lenore, or even Ezekiel ends up with. I just want the best for both of my granddaughters.*

"Did you and Grandpa stop by somewhere for lunch?" Sara's question pulled Mary Ruth out of her musings.

"Yes. We ate at the Bird-in-Hand Family Restaurant. How about you? Did you fix some lunch?"

"Not unless you count chewing a piece of gum."

Mary Ruth's brows furrowed. "How come you didn't eat the leftover chicken I told you was in the refrigerator?"

Sara shrugged. "I wasn't really hungry. It wasn't the first time I've gone without eating a meal."

Mary Ruth wondered what her granddaughter meant by that. Surely when she was a child Rhoda would have fed her regularly. She was about to ask when Willis sauntered into the kitchen.

"Looks like you two have all the groceries put away." He glanced at the fully stocked pantry. "I was plannin' to help with that, but after Ezekiel helped bring in the sacks, the two of us got to talkin' and time got away from me."

"It's not a problem. Our granddaughter was a big help." Mary Ruth gave Sara's shoulder a squeeze. "Makes me wonder how we got along without her."

"Thanks, I just like to help out." Sara dropped her gaze to the floor. "I appreciate being here, more than you know."

Mary Ruth looked over at Willis and noticed his wide grin. She felt sure he was equally happy to have Sara staying with them.

As Michelle lay in bed that night, she reflected on the jars she had found in the barn that afternoon. While she and Mary Ruth put the groceries away today, she'd been on the verge of asking her about those jars — especially the blue one full of folded papers. Michelle's curiosity had been piqued when she found the jar, and even more so after she'd read the two prayers. Would writing a prayer down on paper and then putting it in a jar, be better than saying a prayer out loud? Of course, from what she'd observed so far from living here, the Amish only prayed silently. But they might be inclined to write a prayer down if there was some special meaning behind it or they didn't want anyone else to know their thoughts.

Pushing her head deeper into the pillow, Michelle closed her eyes. The sound of crickets chirping through her open window each night was soothing. *Think I'll have another look at that blue jar the next time I'm alone in the barn. Maybe I'll find a clue as to who wrote those prayers.*

Chapter 13

When Michelle finished breakfast and looked at the simple calendar on the kitchen wall, she was reminded that it was the last Friday in June. It didn't seem possible she'd been with Mary Ruth and Willis close to a month already.

Since coming here, Michelle had established a normal routine, and one of the first things she did every day after breakfast was get the mail. Fortunately, her pretend grandparents were okay with it, and even said they appreciated her willingness to help with so many things.

If they only knew why I offered to get the mail, they might not be so appreciative, Michelle thought as she stepped out the back door.

It was another warm day, already high with humidity. Michelle could only imagine how oppressive it would be by the end of the day. She hoped to get all her chores done before it got too hot, and then maybe she could go for a walk over to the nearby pond. It would feel mighty good to take off her shoes and wade in the shallow part of the cool, inviting water.

Michelle approached the mailbox and pulled down on the handle to open the flap. There were only two envelopes inside. She reached in to retrieve them, but as she was shutting the metal flap, both letters slipped from her hand.

"Oh great." She picked up the first one, but as a gust of wind came along, it carried the second letter out of reach.

As Michelle ran to retrieve it, the wind had its way with her again. To make matters worse, Sadie, who had followed her down the driveway, dropped the stick in her mouth and ran after the envelope like it was a game. Before Michelle could reach the letter, the dog snatched it and ran around Michelle in circles.

Michelle groaned. "Come on now. This is ridiculous. Sit, Sadie! Sit!"

To her surprise, the collie stopped running and dropped the envelope at Michelle's feet. "Whew!" Michelle leaned down, and gasped when she picked it up. Even though the envelope was soiled, there was no mistaking the return address. The letter was from Sara Murray.

She jammed it in her jean's pocket, then hurried up to the house. First stop was the kitchen, which she was relieved to see was empty. Mary Ruth was probably in the basement doing laundry.

Michelle dropped the other letter on the kitchen table and ran up the stairs to her room. After rolling her shoulders to get the kinks out, she flopped on the bed and tore the letter open.

Dear Grandma and Grandpa,

I am concerned because I still haven't heard from you in response to my first two letters. I would still like to come see you when my business class is done. Since neither of my letters were returned to me, I have to assume you received them. Please write soon. I am eager to hear from you.

Your granddaughter,
Sara

Maybe I should write her a letter, pretending to be Mary Ruth. If I can get Sara to give up on the idea of coming here, or at least postpone it for as long as possible, I can relax and enjoy my time in Strasburg.

Michelle took some paper and a pen from

her nightstand and wrote Sara a letter, signing it, "Mary Ruth." The message stated that they had received her letters, but since summer was a busy time for them, they would prefer she wait until sometime in October to come for a visit.

It was devious, but Michelle had too much at stake to let Mary Ruth and Willis see Sara's letter, which of course would let them know Michelle was not who she'd been pretending to be. With barely a thought concerning her actions, she ripped up Sara's letter, and took the evidence outside to the burn barrel.

Once all traces of the evidence was gone, Michelle started back toward the house. Halfway there, she noticed Willis's horse and buggy at the hitching rail. She wasn't sure if he'd gotten back from someplace or was preparing to leave.

Michelle moved over to the rail and reached out to touch Bashful's long neck. The mare seemed gentle enough, nuzzling Michelle's hand, while slowly shaking her head.

"I wonder what it'd be like to drive a horse and buggy," she murmured, continuing to stroke the horse. "If Lenore can do it, why can't I?"

"Would ya like to find out?"

Michelle jumped at the sound of Willis's voice. She whirled around, surprised to see him standing a few feet away. "Oh, I didn't know you were there."

"That's 'cause I was in the barn." He grinned. "Just came out and saw you over here petting my horse."

"Are you going somewhere?"

"Nope. Just got back. Went over to talk with our bishop about a person in our community who told a lie that could hurt someone."

Michelle's heart pounded as her breathing accelerated. *Is it me? Have they figured out that I'm an imposter?*

His posture relaxed. "It's okay now though. The person in question admitted what they did was wrong and apologized to the one they had lied about."

Michelle sagged against the horse's flanks with relief. Quickly changing the subject, she gestured to Bashful. "She seems pretty gentle."

"Wanna try driving her?"

"You mean now?"

He bobbed his head. "Now's as good a time as any, don't ya think?"

"I guess so." Michelle's palms grew sweaty. She hadn't expected Willis to be so quick to jump on the idea. While Michelle did want to learn how to drive the horse and buggy, she wasn't sure she was ready.

"All right then, hop in the driver's side and take up the reins. I'll release the horse from the hitching post and get in the passenger's side." Apparently Willis thought she was ready.

Michelle's anxiety escalated, and she rubbed her damp palms along the sides of her jeans. "We're not going out on the road, are we?"

"Not yet. It's best if you work up to that. For today, we'll just drive around the place." Willis gestured to the open area on the other side of the barn. "It will help you get a feel for it. Sound good?"

Michelle hesitated a minute, before nodding. "Okay. Guess it shouldn't be too hard."

"Go ahead and get in." Willis opened the door on the right side of the buggy and instructed Michelle to take up the reins. Then he went around front to release Bashful from the rail.

It felt strange, sitting in what would be the passenger's side in a car, and even weirder not to have a steering wheel to control where the vehicle went.

Michelle's throat felt so dry she could barely swallow as she gripped the reins hard enough to turn her knuckles white.

Bashful's head bobbed up and down in a quick motion, and she snorted and pawed at the ground.

"Whoa girl, easy does it. I'm new at this, so give me a chance."

Michelle moistened her parched lips and cleared her throat, hoping to prepare herself for what was to come. *I can do this. Willis will explain everything, and it's gonna be fine.*

After Willis released the horse, he came over to the passenger's side and opened the door. He put one leg in the buggy, but before he could get all the way in, the horse backed up, and the buggy gave a lurch. The next thing Michelle knew, Willis was on the ground, and she was at Bashful's mercy.

CHAPTER 14

"Whoa! Whoa!" Michelle's hands shook so badly that she could hardly hold onto the reins. Poor Willis lay on the ground, while Bashful's hooves practically flew over the gravel as she jerked the carriage and headed in the direction of the driveway. No matter how many times she said, "Whoa!" or pulled back on the reins, Willis's stubborn horse ignored her commands.

A few seconds later, Michelle caught sight of Mary Ruth running out the back door. Waving her arms, she shouted, "Whoa, Bashful. Whoa now, girl."

To Michelle's amazement, the horse slowed to a stop. Mary Ruth caught hold of Bashful's bridle and led her back to the hitching rail.

As soon as the horse was secured, Michelle jumped down from the buggy and raced over to Willis, who'd managed to get to his feet. "Are you okay?" she panted, taking in several ragged breaths.

"Don't think anything's broken, but I fell on my arm, and it hurts like the dickens." Willis held it protectively against his chest.

Before Michelle could respond, Mary Ruth rushed over to them. "Ach, Willis, what happened?"

"I was gonna give Sara a driving lesson," Willis explained, "but before I could get in the buggy, Bashful backed up, and I fell."

Mary Ruth took a few deep breaths, as though trying to calm herself. "Better let me take a look at your *aarem.* It could very well be *verbroche.*"

"I'm sure my arm is fine." He shook his head forcefully. "I don't have time for a broken arm. I've gotta take care of the hogs, not to mention all the other chores around here that need doin'."

Mary Ruth's hands went straight to her hips. "I'm going to the phone shed and call one of our drivers. You need to be looked at, just in case."

Willis held out his arm, wincing when he moved it around. "Don't think I could do this if it was broken."

Her forehead wrinkled as she turned to face Michelle. "Would you help me talk some sense into this stubborn man?"

Michelle wasn't sure if anything she said

would make a difference, but at least she could try. "Grandpa, I think maybe Grandma is right. It would be a good idea to at least go to the clinic and have your arm checked out."

His face relaxed a bit as he slowly nodded. "I can see I'm outnumbered here, so okay, I'll go."

After Brad Fuller came to pick up Willis and Mary Ruth, Michelle headed for the barn. As she entered the building, she glanced at Bashful's stall, where Mary Ruth had put her before Brad arrived.

"Stupid horse," she mumbled. "You shouldn't have backed up unless I told you to. And you shoulda stopped when I said 'whoa.' "

Bashful whinnied, as though in response, and swished her long tail.

"Bad horse. Bad." Michelle shook her finger at the mare. "Shame on you for causing your owner to fall."

Bashful turned around and walked to the corner of her stall with her head hung low.

"Good, you need to stand in the corner and think about what you did." Michelle reprimanded the horse again, then paused and shook her head. "Look at me, talking to this horse as if she understands what I'm saying." As much as Michelle would like to learn how to drive a horse and buggy, it wouldn't be with this high-spirited horse.

Since the Lapps would be gone for a while, Michelle remembered the jars, but first she checked on the puppies and transferred them to the cardboard box, kept nearby. After she put fresh paper in the whelping bed, Sadie got in and looked up at Michelle as if waiting for her to bring the puppies.

Michelle snickered and, one by one, placed the pups inside the box with their mother. Sadie sniffed each one, and when they'd all been returned, the collie laid on her side, so the puppies could nurse.

Michelle watched them feed a few minutes, then glanced over at the shelves where the antique jars were kept. After hauling the stepladder over, she climbed up and took down the blue jar. With the Lapps gone, this was a good opportunity to read more of the papers inside.

She took a seat on the same bale of straw she'd sat on before, shook the jar to distribute the papers, and then removed the glass lid. After taking the paper nearest the top out, and unfolding it, she read out loud the words that had been written.

" 'Let us therefore come boldly unto the

throne of grace, that we may obtain mercy, and find grace to help in time of need' Hebrews 4:16."

She sat quietly, rereading the Bible verse. Underneath it, in smaller print, a prayer had been written. *"Lord, I am overwhelmed by my guilt. Please, have mercy on me."*

Michelle looked up, gazing at the rafters above her head as she attempted to gather her thoughts. *If Mary Ruth is the one who wrote these notes, then what did she have to feel guilty about? Could she have told a lie to someone? Broken some church rule? I wish I could come right out and ask her.*

Michelle lowered her head, focusing on the piece of paper again. *Why do I keep thinking Mary Ruth wrote the notes? It could have been Willis, or someone else. For all I know, these messages could have even been written by more than one person.* She wasn't sure why, but Michelle felt a compelling need to know.

She slipped the piece of paper back in the jar and took out another one. It read: *"Last Sunday during church, the bishop said we should ask God to reveal His will and show us what He wants us to do. That's what I'm asking now, Lord. Please show me what I should do."*

One thing for sure, Michelle was certain whoever had written the notes must be Amish. Why else would they have mentioned what the bishop said during church?

Michelle looked up again. *Does God really show people what they should do? Did He show the person who wrote this note what he or she was supposed to do?* She bit the inside of her cheek. *Would God give me direction if I asked?*

She shook her head. *I'm not a religious person, and I've never been good at praying. He probably wouldn't listen to me.*

Michelle put the piece of paper back in the jar and secured the lid. Then she climbed up the ladder and placed it back on the shelf, behind the others. She couldn't rely on prayers to get her through life. She'd made it this far on her own and would continue to do so. No jar full of prayers or wishful thinking could change the course of her life. Michelle was on her own, and always would be.

As Brad approached the Lapps' home, he glanced in his rearview mirror. He was glad to be available to help them out, and pleased that Willis hadn't been seriously hurt when he fell. A bad sprain would heal, but he'd still have a hard time doing his chores with one arm in a sling.

When Brad pulled into the Amish couple's yard, he turned in his seat to face them. "I'm free to stay and help with any chores you might need to have done today, Mr. Lapp. No charge," he quickly added.

Willis shook his head. "I appreciate the offer, but I'm sure I can manage."

Mary Ruth scowled at her husband. "There isn't much you can do with only one hand, Willis." Before he could respond, she looked at Brad and said, "We'd be happy to have your help, but I insist on paying you something for your trouble. You have to earn a living, and from what Stan told us about your schooling to become a minister, I'm guessing you can use some extra cash."

Brad couldn't argue with that. Between the loans he'd taken out, plus money he'd borrowed from family members, he had quite a debt to repay. In some ways, he envied Amish ministers because they weren't required to get any formal training in order to preach God's Word. Even so, it was worth the financial sacrifice to answer God's call on his life.

"How about this," Brad said. "I'll do whatever chores you need to have done today for free, and if you have more things for me to do in the future, you can pay me. How's that sound?"

"It's more than fair." Mary Ruth smiled and nudged her husband's good arm. "Don't you agree?"

Willis nodded. "My wife can at least pay you for the ride you gave us to the clinic, and then I'll show you what all needs to be done yet today."

When Michelle heard a vehicle outside, she looked out the kitchen window and saw Brad's van pull up near the house. She hurried out the back door, eager to find out how Willis was doing.

Michelle watched as Mary Ruth and Willis got out of the van, and she rushed forward when she saw that Willis had his arm in a sling. "Is it broken?"

"Just a bad sprain." He looked over at Brad, who'd also gotten out of the van. "This nice young man volunteered to do some of my chores today, no charge."

Michelle glanced at Brad, noticing his dimpled smile. He was not only good looking, but charming as well. The fact that he'd volunteered to help Willis without pay made him almost too good to be true. Nothing like Jerry, that was for sure. Of course Michelle didn't know Brad well enough to make that call, but he seemed respectful — a rare quality, compared to a creep like Jerry. Maybe while she was here, they could get better acquainted. Michelle would have to think about it, but after Brad was done working, she might ask for a ride to the post office so she could mail her letter to Sara Murray.

CHAPTER 15

It had been three days since Willis sprained his arm, and the doctor said it might take about three weeks to heal completely. He did a fair job doing a few of the simple chores with his good arm, but Mary Ruth, Michelle, and Brad did most of the heavier work.

The job of feeding the chickens, cleaning the coop, and gathering eggs had been assigned to Michelle. While they weren't her favorite things to do, her chores beat feeding the hogs. Brad took care of that chore whenever he had time to come over, and at other times, Willis and Mary Ruth managed the task together. This morning however, when Ezekiel stopped by, he'd volunteered for the job.

Michelle stood outside the chicken coop, watching as Ezekiel finished feeding the hogs and stepped away from their pen.

She moved across the yard to talk to him.

"I see you got roped into helping today."

He shook his head. "I didn't get roped into anything. Came over here because I wanted to see you. After I arrived and found out about Willis's arm, I figured the least I could do was offer to help out."

"I'm sure my grandpa appreciates it." The longer Michelle was here, the easier it became to refer to Willis as her grandfather. Truthfully, she wished he was. She'd give anything to have grandparents like Willis and Mary Ruth. They were kind, caring, gentle people, with hearts as big as the sky. It was wrong to lead them on, but Michelle couldn't help herself. The longer she stayed, the more she wanted to remain here and be their real granddaughter.

Ezekiel snapped his fingers in front of Michelle's face. "What are you thinking about, Sara? You looked like you're a thousand miles away."

She blinked. "Uh . . . just thinking about the chickens, is all. So why'd you come here to see me?"

"Wondered if you were planning to go to the Fourth of July festival that's comin' up in two days."

She shrugged. "I hadn't heard about it, but I suppose it might be fun. Guess it'll depend on what my grandparents have planned."

"Yeah, that makes sense."

Michelle gestured to the barn. "Want to come with me to see the puppies?"

"Sure. Bet they've grown quite a bit since I last saw them."

"Yes, they have."

When they entered the barn, Sadie got up, stretched lazily, and ambled toward the door. Michelle figured the dog might be glad they were here. The pups would be occupied, giving Sadie a chance to go outside and be by herself for a while.

Michelle and Ezekiel knelt outside the new enclosure Willis had built for the pups before his accident. The height was just enough to keep them in, but low enough for Sadie to jump out whenever she needed to.

"Boy, they really have grown." Ezekiel reached in and lifted the largest one out, while Michelle took Rascal in her arms.

"I know. It's hard to believe they are three weeks old already." Michelle rubbed her chin against Rascal's soft head. "They opened their eyes last week."

"They're sure cute. And look how active they are." Ezekiel chuckled when one of the pups nipped at another one's leg. That puppy, in turn, pounced on a different pup, and soon they were all running around, yipping and chasing each other.

"Let's take the puppies we're holding and go sit over there." Michelle pointed to a couple of folding chairs.

After they sat down, each with a pup in their lap, Michelle was at a loss for words. Meanwhile the other puppies carried on even more, no doubt wanting some attention too.

"Now that you've been here awhile, how do you like it?" Ezekiel asked.

"My grandparents are wonderful, and I'm slowly getting used to living on the farm." Michelle scrunched up her nose. "There's one thing I can do without though."

"What's that?"

"The bugs. Especially those tiny little gnats. I hate it when they get in my hair or try to fly into my eyes." The skin around her eyes tightened. "It seems the more I swat at them, the more they like aggravating me. Truth be told, feeding the pigs is better than puttin' up with those pesky bugs."

Ezekiel chuckled. "Don't think anyone likes 'em, but it's something we all have to deal with."

"The next time I help Grandma in the garden, maybe I'll spray some bug repellent all over my clothes."

His forehead wrinkled. "That might not be the healthiest thing to do, Sara. Some of that bug spray is pretty powerful. Maybe you could try wearing a hat so they don't get in your hair."

"Guess I could try your suggestion, but will a hat keep them out of my eyes?"

"I think so."

Michelle shrugged her shoulders. "Anyway, at the very least, a hat might keep 'em from driving me so buggy." She snickered. "No pun intended."

He gave a wide grin. "Speaking of buggies, I heard Willis sprained his arm while trying to teach you how to drive his horse and buggy."

Michelle shook her head. "It never got that far. The poor man was knocked to the ground when he was trying to get in the buggy and his horse decided to act up. I tried to get Bashful to stop, but she wouldn't listen or cooperate with me. It was only when Grandma came out and hollered at the horse that she finally settled down." She lifted her shoulders with a sigh. "So I'll probably never learn how to drive a horse and buggy, and I was looking forward to it."

Ezekiel rolled his eyes. "Believe me, it's not that exciting. But if you really want to learn, I'll be happy to teach you."

"Really?"

"Sure thing. It'll have to be on a day I'm not working at the greenhouse though. Or maybe we could try early some evening."

"How come you're not working at the greenhouse right now?"

"We were caught up on things, and Dad said I could take off the rest of the day." He touched the tip of the puppy's nose and smiled. "Of course, I didn't mention that I'd been planning to come over to see you."

"Would your folks object to you seeing me?"

"I don't know. Maybe. Mom and Dad are worried that I might decide not to join the Amish church and end up going English."

Michelle pushed a wayward strand of hair out of her face. "Oh, and you think they believe being around me might lure you in the wrong direction?"

"Yeah, something like that."

"Don't you have other English friends?"

"A few."

"Then I don't see why my being your friend would make any difference to your folks."

"Maybe it wouldn't, but they might worry that we could end up seeing each other as more than friends." He glanced at her, then averted his gaze to the sleeping pup on his lap.

"Well, we wouldn't want them to get the wrong idea, so maybe it would be best if you don't teach me how to drive the horse and buggy."

Ezekiel shook his head with a determined expression. "No, it's okay. I'm old enough to do what I want, and I'd really like to teach you. As a matter of fact, I taught my sister Amy how to drive our buggy when she was in her early teens."

"I met your sister at church, the first time I went there with my grandparents. She seemed nice and was easy to talk to."

"Yeah, she's a good *schweschder.*"

Michelle tipped her head to one side. "What's a schweschder?"

"The word means 'sister.' "

"Oh, I see. What other Pennsylvania Dutch words can you teach me?"

He rubbed his chin. "Well, let's see . . . Can you guess what *hundli* means?"

"I have no idea."

Ezekiel pointed to Rascal, sleeping contently in Michelle's arms.

"Does it mean 'puppy'?"

"Jah. And the word for dog is *hund.*"

"Okay, I think I can remember that. *Hund* means 'dog' and *hundli* means 'puppy.' "

Michelle smiled, feeling kind of proud of herself for learning a couple of new Amish words.

"Okay now, so what do you think about me teaching you how to drive a horse and buggy?"

"Sounds like a plan, only not with Bashful. After what she did to Willis, I don't trust her."

"We can use my horse then. Big Red's a large animal, but he's gentle as a kitten and listens well. I'll bet using him, I could teach you pretty fast."

"All right." Michelle bobbed her head. "Whenever you're free to begin, just let me know." She lifted Rascal into her arms and stood. "In the meantime though, I promised Grandma I'd help her pick peas." Michelle didn't mention it, but she had something else she needed to do first. Then she added, "Tomorrow, she's gonna teach me how to can them, which should be an adventure in itself, because I've never been all that handy in the kitchen." She wrinkled her nose. "My idea of cooking is sticking a frozen dinner in the microwave and turning on the power."

He laughed, and they made their way back to the puppies' enclosure, where the rest of Sadie's brood had all settled down and lay sleeping in various places — some practically on top of each other.

In all Michelle's twenty-four years, she'd never expected to become friends with some good-looking Amish guy in Lancaster County, Pennsylvania. But after meeting Ezekiel and Brad, she was coming to realize there were actually some nice guys in this world. Jerry could use a few lessons from both of them on how to treat a lady.

"All right, boy, let's go!" Ezekiel snapped the reins, and Big Red took off toward home. He'd enjoyed his time with Sara today and hoped he would see her at the Fourth of July festival. The more time he spent with Sara, the more he liked her. If she stuck around long enough, he might even ask if he could take her out on a date.

It's funny that Amy never said anything to me about talking with Sara. It was probably just girl-talk anyway. I wonder what my folks would say if they knew I wanted to court an English woman. He reached under his straw hat and rubbed the side of his head. *Is that what I want to do, or am I only interested in the Lapps' granddaughter because she's English?*

Ezekiel thought about the truck he'd gone to look at, wondering yet again, if he dared buy it. The older model truck had been fixed up and looked as good on the inside as it did outside, which made it even harder to turn down. It was in mint condition, and according to his friend, "ready for the open road."

Ezekiel probably wouldn't be taking the truck on any long trips, but it would be great to have it to run errands and whatever else he decided to do. *Sure would be better than a horse and buggy or my scooter — especially in bad weather. And it would be safer too.*

Ezekiel was old enough to make his own decisions, so there was nothing his dad could do if he did buy the vehicle. *But then what if he doesn't let me park on his property?* That would make it difficult whenever Ezekiel wanted to go anywhere with the vehicle. And if he parked it at one of his relative's place, Dad would probably find out and start lecturing him again. The negatives seemed to outweigh the positives. It was a no-win situation. Unless Ezekiel decided to leave home and step out on his own, he might never be able to do all the things he longed to try.

"Decisions, decisions," Ezekiel mumbled. "Sure wish I knew what to do about that truck."

■ ■ ■ ■

Remembering the letter she'd written and still hadn't mailed, Michelle stepped into the house. "Grandma," she called. "Are you in here?"

"Yes, Sara. I'm in the kitchen."

Michelle entered the room. "I know I promised to help you in the garden this afternoon, but would you mind if I went for a walk first?" She placed her hand protectively over her pocket, where the letter was safely hidden.

Mary Ruth looked at Michelle with a curious expression. "Is everything all right?

"Of course. Why wouldn't it be?" Michelle shifted uneasily. Did Mary Ruth find out she'd written a letter to the real Sara? Michelle had hidden the letter inside her suitcase, waiting for an opportunity to mail it. Unfortunately, she'd forgotten about it until now. It was important to get it in the mail today.

Mary Ruth put her hand on Michelle's shoulder. "You look a bit distressed. Did Ezekiel say something while he was here to upset you?"

"No, I just need some air and feel like going for a walk to clear my head. Do you mind? I won't be gone long, and when I get back I'll help you with whatever needs to be done."

"Of course you can go for a walk. I'll manage fine on my own till you get back." Mary Ruth smiled.

"Okay, thanks. See you in a bit."

As Michelle walked out of the house and headed toward the road, she felt like a traitor, leaving Mary Ruth alone to do the work by herself. But she needed to mail that letter. Once the deed was done, she could help with the peas and then enjoy the rest of her day.

Chapter 16

Perspiration beaded on Michelle's forehead as she made the trek from the post office back to the Lapps' place. She had known where it was, having seen it a week ago when she went shopping with Mary Ruth, but hadn't realized the two-mile walk would take its toll on her in this heat. The hot weather wouldn't have been so bad, but the humidity was stifling. Michelle's clothes stuck to her as she reached into her jean's pocket for a rubber band to tie her long hair up in a ponytail. The creek she'd recently walked by looked inviting, even just to soak her feet in the shallow end for a while. But there was no time to pause and cool off. Michelle wanted to get back so she could help Mary Ruth with the peas.

She could have called Brad or the Lapps' other driver, Stan, to take her to the post office but had decided she didn't want to part with what little money she had for such a short ride. And Michelle certainly couldn't expect Willis or Mary Ruth to pay for her ride to the post office, especially if they'd known her reason for going there.

Well, the deed was done, and with any luck, it would guarantee her a few more months of living with the Lapps.

Michelle wiped her sweaty forehead and kept walking determinedly, her ponytail swinging back and forth across her sweaty back. In one respect, she felt guilty for her deception, because Willis and Mary Ruth were nice people. On the other hand, what they didn't know wouldn't hurt them. Of course, they would find out sooner or later when the real Sara made an appearance. But Michelle wouldn't be around to see their displeasure with her act of deceit. Hopefully once she left, she would stop feeling so guilty.

Michelle was about halfway back to the Lapps' when a horn honked, and a convertible pulled up alongside of her. Three young fellows sat inside, in addition to the driver, who looked to be around eighteen or nineteen years old.

"Hey babe. Where ya headed?" The guy in the front passenger's seat leaned forward and gave a shrill whistle.

Michelle looked straight ahead and picked

up her pace.

The car cruised alongside of her, and a couple of the young men made some crude remarks.

Michelle wasn't sure whether she should run or keep walking at her current speed. Even if she ran, she couldn't get ahead of the convertible. She didn't want these guys to know it, but she was scared. The best thing to do was try to ignore them, in the hope that they would drive on.

The last time Michelle had felt this frightened was when Jerry smacked her face and then refused to leave her apartment. She was fortunate that he went without a fuss, because the situation could have gotten much worse.

When the driver pulled up ahead and onto the shoulder of the road, it blocked Michelle's path. The hair on the back of her neck and arms lifted as she froze in place. She wanted to flee or hide, but there was no place to go. *Please God. Send someone to help me.* It was the first prayer Michelle had said in a long time, but in her desperation she couldn't think of anything else to do. Who knew when another car would come by? Out here on these country roads, the traffic was often light, and sometimes hardly any vehicles at all sped by.

A redheaded guy with a face full of freckles got out of the backseat and moved toward Michelle. "Come on, babe. Hop on in, and we'll take ya for a ride. It's a mighty hot day, and cruisin' in a convertible's a good way to cool off."

When Michelle didn't answer, he added, "What's wrong, darlin'? Ain't we good enough for you?"

The other fellows laughed, which only encouraged the red-head. "Maybe you're just playin' hard to get."

Hoping he wouldn't know how truly frightened she was, Michelle forced herself to look at him. "I am not playing hard to get, and I don't need a ride. I'm almost home, but thank you just the same." Maybe showing some courage while also being polite would make them leave her alone. Unfortunately, this only seemed to aggravate the freckle-faced fellow.

"Oh really? And where's home?" He grabbed her arm roughly.

Michelle pressed both elbows against her sides, wishing she could make herself invisible. "It's up the road, and if you don't let go of me, I'll scream."

"Oh yeah? And who's gonna hear ya, except me and my buddies? I don't see nobody else around."

"You're wrong, Buddy." The driver of the car pointed to the farm across the road. "See those cows over there in the field? I'll bet they're gonna come over here and rescue the pretty gal."

The others in the car whooped and hollered, calling Michelle a few names she'd never repeat, while the one holding her arm, pulled her against his chest.

Michelle's legs felt weak, like she might fall at any moment, but the firm grip he had on her right now kept her upright. This guy was so forward, he even reached back and took the rubber band out of her hair. Running his fingers through her long tresses, his face was so close, she could smell his stale breath.

"Nice." He picked up a thick strand of her hair and brought it up to his nostrils, inhaling a long slow intake of air. "Real nice."

Michelle choked back a whimper as he continued teasing her. *Please God, help me.*

She opened her mouth and was about to scream when a van that seemed to come out of nowhere pulled up behind the convertible. It gave her the opportunity and extra time to stomp on the pushy guy's foot.

"Ouch! Why you little —" He swung back his hand as if to slap her but backed off when the van door opened.

Michelle almost fainted with relief when Brad got out. What were the odds that he would come along just when she needed him? *Could it have been my prayers for help?*

"What's going on here?" As soon as Brad stepped out of his vehicle, the freckle-faced guy limped closer to the convertible.

"Uh, nothin'. We were just seein' if she needed a ride."

"Well, she doesn't. So please get back in your car and move on down the road." Brad spoke calmly but with authority.

With a grunt and brief shrug, the red-haired fellow got back in the car, told the driver to go, and they headed on down the road.

As they sped off, Brad heard the driver shout at the guy who sat slumped in the backseat, "Way to go, stupid."

When Sara looked up at Brad, he couldn't help noticing her trembling lips, or the tears in her eyes. "Th–thank you so much. I can't believe you came along when you did."

"Did they hurt you?" His brows wrinkled as he studied her flushed face, feeling concern.

She shook her head. "I'm fine. Just a bit shaky inside."

"I'm glad you're okay." Brad gestured to his van. "Why don't you hop in? I'll give you a lift home. I assume that's where you were heading?"

"Yeah. I went out for a walk and had started back when those guys showed up." She opened the passenger's door and climbed in, while Brad went around to the other side. He shuddered to think of what might have happened if he hadn't come along when he did. *I need to get Sara's mind off what might have happened.*

"Can I ask you a question?" Brad asked, after he'd pulled onto the road and noticed out of the corner of his eye how Michelle twisted her pretty, long hair, holding it up off the back of her neck.

"Sure, go ahead."

"Stan mentioned that when you came to visit your grandparents, it was the first time you'd been there. I'm wondering why you'd never gone to see them before."

She stared down at her hands, clutched tightly in her lap, and drew a quivering breath. "Until a month ago, I didn't even know I had grandparents living in Strasburg."

"Didn't your parents tell you?"

"Umm . . . I didn't know till after my mom passed away."

"I see." Brad didn't push any further, since Sara was still clearly upset about her encounter with the guys in the convertible. But Brad had more questions he wanted to ask. And maybe he would, once they got better acquainted.

"So tell me more about you." Brushing his arm with her hand, Sara glanced over at him. "I know you're studying to become a minister, but that's about all."

"What else do you want to know?"

"Just wondered where you are from. Is your home here in Lancaster?"

"Nope. I was born and raised in Harrisburg. Moved down here and rented a small apartment near the college I've been attending in Lancaster. But that was after I'd worked for my dad a few years."

"I see. So what does your father do in the capital of Pennsylvania?"

"He's a chiropractor. He and my mom hoped I'd follow in his footsteps and someday take over the business." Brad shook his head. "But that's not God's call on my life." He glanced over at Sara to see her reaction, but she sat staring straight ahead.

"I've known for some time that God called me to be a preacher," he added.

"Are your folks okay with it?"

"They are now but they weren't at first."

Brad put on his blinker and turned into the Lapps' driveway.

When he pulled up near the house, Sara looked over at him and smiled. "Thanks for the ride and for coming to my rescue. You're my hero."

"No problem. I'm glad I came along when I did." Brad's ears tingled with the warmth spreading through them. He didn't want to be seen as a hero, but it was nice to be appreciated.

Sara opened the van door, but hesitated. Then she turned back to face him. "Do you have any plans for the Fourth of July?"

"Nothing special. I may drive over to the festival everyone's been talking about. How about you? Are you doing anything with your grandparents that evening?"

"I mentioned the festival to Mary Ruth — I mean Grandma. She said I should go if I want to, but I don't think either her or Grandpa plans to attend the festivities."

"I'd be happy to take you if you need a ride." Brad saw this as another chance to get to know Sara better.

"Actually, if I did decide to go, I'd planned on calling you to see if you'd mind driving me there. I would pay you of course."

He lifted a hand. "No payment is needed. Since I'd be going myself, I would be more than happy to give you a ride."

"Okay then, it's a date." Her cheeks colored. "I — I mean, I'll see you around seven o'clock on the Fourth."

He grinned. "I'm looking forward to it."

As Brad drove away, he smiled. He could usually figure people out after one or two meetings, but he had a feeling there was more to Sara than met the eye. The visible tension on her face and the way she kept looking away when they were talking told Brad there was a bit of uncertainty about her.

Maybe I can draw her out. He tapped the steering wheel with his knuckles. *With God's help, I might be able to help Sara deal with whatever is bothering her.*

After Michelle said goodbye to Brad, she found Mary Ruth in the garden, picking peas.

Mary Ruth looked up and smiled. "I'm almost done — just one more row to go."

"I'll help you with it." Michelle hurried to the potting shed and got a container, a pair of cotton gloves, and a canvas hat she'd found on the shelf in her closet that morning. She'd taken it out to the shed after breakfast and placed it beside the gardening gloves. When she'd secured the hat on her head, she joined Mary Ruth in the garden.

"Where'd you get that?" Mary Ruth pointed to the hat when Michelle knelt on the ground. "I don't believe you've worn it before. At least not since you came here anyway."

"Oh, I didn't bring it with me, Grandma. I found it on the closet shelf in the guest room this morning. Thought it might help keep the gnats out of my hair and eyes."

"Good idea. So how was your walk?" Mary Ruth asked as they picked the last of the peas.

"It was okay. Brad picked me up on the way home and gave me a ride back here." Michelle was not about to tell Mary Ruth about the encounter she'd had with the bullies in the convertible. She'd be upset and wouldn't want Michelle to go anywhere by herself. Besides, other than shaking her up a bit, no harm had actually been done — thanks to Brad coming to her rescue.

"That was certainly nice of him. He seems like such a caring young man."

Michelle gave a nod. *I know that more than anything now.*

"I'm surprised he's still single."

"Maybe he doesn't have time for dating, with his school schedule and summer jobs."

"That could be. Or maybe he hasn't found

the right woman." Mary Ruth gave Michelle a sidelong glance.

Michelle hoped Mary Ruth wasn't insinuating she might be that woman. After all, she hardly knew Brad. Although if she were being honest, she did find him attractive. But could Brad be interested in someone like her? She couldn't even imagine what it would be like to be married to a pastor. *Now where did that thought come from?*

Michelle pulled several more peapods from the vine and dropped them into her bucket. *I shouldn't even be thinking about this. Brad Fuller and I are worlds apart. When summer is over, he will resume his studies, and I'll go back to my old life — living from day to day, while trying to find something meaningful to do with the rest of my life.*

"I was wondering if you and Grandpa made a definite decision about attending the Fourth of July festival."

Mary Ruth shook her head. "I think not. But as I said before, you should go if you want to. We could call one of our drivers to take you there."

"Actually, I would like to go, and Brad offered to drive me."

"Oh? What did you tell him?"

"I said yes."

Mary Ruth gave Michelle's arm a light

tap. "I'm glad, and I am sure you will both have a good time."

"I hope so." Michelle paused to push the brim of her hat back a bit.

Chapter 17

"Didn't Sara look nice this evening when Brad picked her up?"

Mary Ruth glanced over at her husband, who sat on the couch beside her, reading the latest edition of *The Budget.*

"Huh? What was that?" He placed the newspaper on his lap and turned to face her.

Mary Ruth repeated her question about Sara.

He squinted over the top of his glasses. "To tell you the truth, I didn't really notice. What was she wearing?"

"She had on a pretty skirt and top, but it wasn't her clothes that made her look so nice. It was the cheerful smile she wore as she went out the door." Mary Ruth's brows wrinkled. "I think maybe we've been holding her back."

"What do you mean?"

"It seems like all Sara's done since she got

here is help us with chores. Especially after you sprained your arm."

"She hasn't complained."

"True, but a young woman her age needs to have some *schpass.*"

"Sara seemed to be having fun on her birthday."

"Jah, but she didn't have that bubbly expression, like she did tonight." Mary Ruth released a puff of air. "Our granddaughter is not Amish, Willis. She may not enjoy spending all her time with us Plain old folks. Brad is English, like Sara, and she might rather be with her own kind."

"Puh!" Willis picked up the newspaper and gave it a flap. "If Sara didn't enjoy our company, do you think she would still be staying here with us?"

"I don't know. She might not want to hurt our feelings." Mary Ruth nudged his arm with her elbow. "Did you ever think of that?"

Willis shrugged. "I suppose you could be right. Maybe our granddaughter wants to go home and is afraid to say anything because she doesn't want to hurt our feelings."

Tears welled in Mary Ruth's eyes as she clasped her hands together. "I hope that is not the case. I want Sara to stay with us for as long as possible. Her being here is almost like having Rhoda back. And since she has no job or family to go home to, I see no reason for her not to remain here permanently. Only if she wants to, that is."

He slowly nodded. "But if she wants to go, we can't force her to stay for our sakes. We need to give Sara the freedom to go whenever she wants."

"I'll talk to her about it soon. See if she's happy here or would rather leave." Mary Ruth stood. "I'm going to the kitchen for a glass of cold buttermilk. Would you like one too?"

"That'd be nice. And I wouldn't mind a bowl of popcorn to go with it."

She lifted a hand. "Sure, no problem."

When Mary Ruth entered the kitchen, she reflected once more on Sara's happy expression as she went out the door this evening. If there was even a chance that their granddaughter and Brad might become a couple, it could guarantee that she would stay awhile — maybe even permanently. Especially if Brad took a church in the area once he became a minister. Mary Ruth's lips formed a smile, and she began humming a tune from her youth. *Now wouldn't that be something?*

Lititz, Pennsylvania

"Here we are." Brad pulled his van into a nearly full parking lot and turned off the engine. "Wish we could have come earlier today, to take in the parade and some of the other afternoon festivities. But at least we'll be able to see the fireworks display and get involved in some of the other fun activities."

Michelle smiled, feeling a bit self-conscious all of a sudden. She and Brad weren't here as a couple, and she didn't expect him to hang around with her all evening, but how could she bring up the subject without embarrassing Brad or making him feel obligated to spend the evening with her?

"Looks like there's quite a few people here," Brad commented after they'd left the van and made their way toward the festivities.

"You're right. We'll probably get lost in the crowd."

"I hope not, but let's plan to meet back here at the van by ten o'clock in case we do."

"Okay." Michelle assumed from Brad's comment that he planned to go off on his own. That made it easy, because now she wouldn't have to bring up the subject.

They had no more than entered the park

when she caught sight of Ezekiel and Lenore walking side by side. They were some distance away and didn't appear to see them. Michelle wondered if they had come here together. Maybe the two of them had begun courting and were on a date.

As they walked farther away, the sound of familiar music caught Michelle's attention.

"Oh look, there's a carousel over there." She pointed in that direction.

Brad smiled. "Sure enough. It looks small compared to the ones I rode on as a child at the carnivals in Harrisburg every summer." He chuckled. "At least I thought they were big back then."

Michelle nodded as a memory from the past came to mind. On one of the rare occasions when her dad was sober and things were halfway normal at home, her folks had taken Michelle and her brothers to a state fair. Dad had bought tickets so she, Ernie, and Jack could ride the merry-go-round. Michelle chose a horse that had been painted all white, except for a black tail. She'd sat up there so happy, feeling like she was on top of the world. When they'd gone home later that day, Dad had started drinking. He and Mom ended up in a huge fight, and before long, the police showed up at their door.

Her throat constricted. *Why couldn't I have grown up in a normal household, with good parents who got along with each other and didn't abuse their kids?*

"Hey, are you okay?" Brad placed his hand on her shoulder. "You look upset."

The comforting act caused the dam to break, and despite her resolve, tears coursed down Michelle's cheeks.

"What's wrong?"

She sniffed deeply and reached into her skirt pocket for a tissue. "Seeing the carousel reminded me of something from my childhood. Guess I'm just too sentimental." Michelle wasn't about to tell Brad the whole story. If he should repeat it to Willis and Mary Ruth, they'd think their daughter, whom Michelle had never even met, was a terrible mother.

Brad put his hand on Michelle's back and gave her a gentle pat. "Nothing wrong with being sentimental. We all get nostalgic at times."

"Yeah, I guess."

"Would you like to get something to eat or drink before the fireworks start?" he asked.

"Well, umm . . . I didn't bring any money with me."

"No problem. It's my treat."

"Thanks. I am kinda hungry." Michelle felt herself relax.

He grinned. "All right then, let's see what we can find."

As they headed toward the food booths, Michelle noticed Ezekiel again. This time he was looking in her direction. She waved, and he nodded in response. Lenore had her back to Michelle and seemed to be looking at something in one of the booths. Maybe she would have the chance to say hello to both of them later.

Ezekiel stood in line at the cotton candy booth. After Lenore went off to join some of her friends, he'd decided to get something to eat. Not that cotton candy was the best choice, since it was full of sugar, but it reminded him of when he was boy. Back then Ezekiel's life had been carefree, and he hadn't thought much about whether he would join the Amish church someday or become part of the English world. Now the prospect of leaving his Amish heritage consumed his thoughts. He didn't want to disappoint his parents, but he ought to have the right to make his own decisions about the rest of his life.

Ezekiel paid for his treat and moved on toward the area where the fireworks would be displayed. He'd seen Sara walking in the same direction with that English fellow, Brad. Before that, he had also witnessed Brad with his hand against Sara's back.

I bet they came here together. He probably asked her on a date. Ezekiel licked some sticky cotton candy from his lips and kept walking. When he'd mentioned the festival to Sara she had said she wasn't sure if she'd be coming or not. He'd hoped she might come here with him. *Guess it's my fault. I should've followed up with her.*

Ezekiel didn't understand why he felt envious. He barely knew Sara and certainly had no claim on her. *Maybe I'll have the opportunity to get to know her better when I start teaching her how to drive a horse and buggy.* In addition to giving Sara her first lesson tomorrow, it would give him the chance to find out if something was going on with her and Brad.

CHAPTER 18

Newark

When Sara returned home from her class on Thursday, she was pleased to discover a letter in her mailbox postmarked, *"Strasburg, Pennsylvania."* It had to be from her grandparents. *I am so glad they finally responded.*

Almost breathless, she hurried into the house, tossed the rest of the mail on the kitchen table, and pulled out a chair. Her fingers trembled a bit as she tore open the letter:

Dear Sara,

We were pleased to receive your letters and look forward to meeting you. But since summer is a very busy time for us, we would prefer you wait until sometime in October to come here for a visit.

Most sincerely,

Willis and Mary Ruth Lapp

In one sense, Sara felt relieved that her grandparents wouldn't be available to visit with her until October. It would give her plenty of time to finish her summer class and prepare for meeting them. In another sense, she was disappointed that she couldn't meet them sooner. At least between now and then they could communicate via letters. The next time Sara wrote to her grandparents, she would ask for their phone number. If they had one, it was obviously unlisted since she'd had no luck finding it via the internet.

Sara's forehead wrinkled as she reread the letter. As the words sank in, she became somewhat baffled. *Was I wrong in hoping they'd be a little more excited about finding out they had a granddaughter?* She sighed, glancing at the return address on the envelope. *But again, what did I expect to happen?*

Her lips formed a grim line as she continued to discuss the issue with herself, only this time out loud. "It would have been nice to put me ahead of their busy summer. After all, they just learned their daughter died, and I'm their daughter's offspring."

The more Sara went over this, the more she became unsure about her grandparents. The fact was, they'd taken their time getting back to her. That spoke volumes.

Sara continued to study the letter. Her grandparents sounded polite enough, but the more she read over the letter and got to the part about their busy summer, the more disappointed she became. This wasn't anything like she'd expected. Sara had daydreamed about her new grandparents' response and expected they would show more emotion than this. She had conjured up a wonderful emotional reunion once they finally met. It would be the type of reunion she'd watched on certain TV shows that brought together people who had been separated for a long time. One show brought people who had been adopted together with their biological parents. Sara cried along with them as they met for the first time.

What kind of people are the Lapps anyway? she fumed. *Was this letter their way of saying I'm no big deal?*

Sara's stomach growled, so she set the letter aside and went to the refrigerator to see what she could grab to eat. An idea had just occurred to her, and she needed something to nibble on while she pursued her search. "I don't know why I didn't think to do this before."

Sara went to the living room and brought her laptop out to the kitchen table. After signing on, she dug out a box of crackers and a jar of peanut butter from the cupboard. That would be easy to eat while she googled some information.

After making a few cracker sandwiches and pouring herself a glass of iced tea, Sara returned to the kitchen table. Using Google Maps, she took the return envelope and typed in her grandparents' address. After hitting Enter, the site pinpointed exactly where Willis and Mary Ruth Lapp lived.

She changed the screen to the Satellite view and zoomed in. "Well here's something I didn't realize. They live on a farm." Sara studied the rooftop of the farmhouse and a barn. Surrounding the property were fields and a lot of open space. *Maybe this is what they meant by being busy this summer. Depending on what they grow, it could take up a lot of their time to farm the place. I wonder if anyone lives there with them, or if they have to hire help with the place.*

Sara continued to stare at the screen. *So this is where my mother grew up.* Seeing the map of her grandparents' place made Sara even more determined to go there and meet them. No matter how the Lapps felt about her, she needed to see for herself what they were like and give them a chance to get to know her. If anything good came of meeting them, maybe she would find out who her real father was.

When a knock sounded on the back door, Sara shut her laptop, put the letter back in the envelope, and tucked it inside her purse. No doubt it was Dean. The last thing she needed was for him to see the letter and ask a bunch of questions. *Learning about Mama's parents is none of his business. If Mom had wanted Dean to know, she would have told him.*

Strasburg

"Before we begin your first lesson, I have a question for you," Ezekiel said as he and Sara stood beside his horse and buggy.

"What's that?" With an anxious expression, she glanced at Big Red.

"Since you won't be staying here permanently and will be returning to your English world at some point, how come you want to learn to drive a horse and buggy?"

She turned her head to look at him. "I think it'll be fun, and it will give me a better understanding of my grandparents' way of life. Of course," she added, "after seeing my grandpa get hurt when he tried to teach me, I'll admit I am a bit nervous."

"The accident really wasn't your fault. You weren't used to Bashful, and she wasn't used to you." Ezekiel shrugged. "Besides, your grandpa wasn't seriously hurt, and he's doing better now."

"Yes but not well enough to do all the chores on his own." Sara pointed across the yard. "Which is why Brad will be coming over later today to mow the lawn."

"Speaking of Brad, I saw you with him last night at the festival in Lititz. Were you two on a date?"

Sara's ponytail swished as she shook her head. "He drove me there, and we walked around together for a bit, but it wasn't a date." She pointed at Ezekiel. "I saw you and Lenore there too. Were you on a date?"

He pulled his fingers along his cheek bone, realizing he'd neglected to shave this morning. "Course not. I've known Lenore since we were kids, and there are no romantic feelings between us. Least not on my part anyway."

"Then why were you with her last night?"

"We shared a ride in her driver's vehicle. We were together for a few minutes when we first got there, but then we went our separate ways." Ezekiel opened the door on the right side of the buggy. "I don't know why we're standin' here talking about this anyway. I've got a lesson to teach, and you have some learning to do about driving a horse." He paused, sliding his tongue over his lips. "Say, before we begin, I have a favor to ask."

"What's that?"

"If I teach you how to drive a horse and buggy, would you be willing to teach me to drive a car?"

Sara's auburn eyebrows lifted high on her forehead. "You said before that you don't own a car."

"Not yet, but I've been eyeballing a truck that's for sale in the area. I wasn't sure if I wanted it, but I'm actually thinkin' about buying the truck now."

"Are you allowed to do that? I thought Amish people didn't drive cars. Isn't that why you hire English drivers to take you some places?"

Ezekiel struggled not to roll his eyes. Wasn't Sara listening when they'd had this conversation before? Or maybe she'd just forgot. "You're right." He tried not to sound perturbed. "Once a person has joined the Amish church, they are not allowed to own or drive a car. My folks hire a driver if they need to go outside the area or if a trip takes more than ten or fifteen miles by horse and buggy."

"What do they have against cars?"

"It's not the vehicle itself. The Amish believe owning a car could lead to a tearing apart of family, church, and community. And people who have cars tend to be away from home more, which can make the community more scattered." He frowned. "My dad says owning a fancy car could easily become a symbol of pride." Ezekiel pushed his straw hat farther back on his head. "Since I haven't joined the church, I would be allowed to buy a car. Only thing is, my folks — especially Dad — are against it. So if I get the truck, I'll need to park it someplace else 'cause I'd never be allowed to keep it on my parents' property. That's something Dad's made very clear to all his children."

Sara shook her head. "I didn't realize Amish parents were so strict. I heard some of them looked the other way when their young adult children went through their running-around years. *Rumspringa.* Isn't that what it's called?"

"Yeah. The Pennsylvania Dutch word for it is *rumschpringe.* It's a time that allows Amish young people who have not joined the Amish church yet to experience the modern world. Of course, some get this privilege and some don't. It varies from church district to district."

"Do you get to wear English clothes during that time of running around?"

He nodded. "Course not all Amish teens and young people do. Some are content to wear Amish clothes, and they just enjoy the freedom of going to movies, dances, or taking long trips with their friends. A couple of my friends went to Disney World during their running-around time, and my cousin Raymond spent some time in Sarasota, Florida."

"I see." Sara shook her head several times. "Boy, there are so many things I still don't know about the Amish."

"Such as?"

"I'm curious to hear how the Amish religion began."

"Well, the Amish people are direct descendants of the Anabaptists of sixteenth-century Europe. The Anabaptist religion came about during the Reformation."

Sara tilted her head to one side. "*Anabaptist* is a word I've not heard before. What exactly does it mean?"

"The term first started out as a nickname that meant 'rebaptizer' because this group rejected the idea of infant baptism."

"How come?"

"An infant doesn't have a knowledge of good and bad."

She stood quietly, gazing at the ground. She slowly lifted her head. "Is that it? Or is there anything else about the Anabaptists you'd like to share?"

"I can tell you more if you like."

"Sure, go ahead."

Ezekiel wasn't sure why Sara would be so curious about the Amish, but he was willing to share what he knew. Maybe her curiosity had to do with the fact that her grandparents were Amish and she wanted to know and understand them better.

"Before they came here to America, the Anabaptists were seen as a threat to Europe's religious and social institutions, so they were often persecuted."

Her eyes widened. "Seriously?"

"It's true. And some of the things that were done to them were so horrible it's hard to talk about."

Her eyes darkened. "That is so sad."

"Yeah. No one should be persecuted for their religious beliefs." Ezekiel folded his arms while shifting his weight. "Another thing you might find interesting is that the Amish religion is a branch of the Swiss Mennonites. The group got its name from its founder, Jacob Amman. Another leader was named Menno Simons, and the people who followed him were called, 'Mennonites,' " he explained. "Eventually, those who followed Jacob Amman formed a new group known as the Amish."

Sara stared at Ezekiel with widened eyes. "Wow, you sure do know a lot about the Amish religion."

"Well I should, seeing as to how I was raised in an Amish home. And actually, most Amish don't like to think of it as their religion, since they confess to be Christians, just as several other denominations do. They prefer to say that being Amish is a way of life rather than a religion." He waved away a bee trying to land on Sara's arm. "I'd be the first to admit that I don't have all the answers concerning Amish life, but having attended church with my folks ever since I was a baby, I've learned a lot."

"Yet you still haven't made a commitment to join your family's church?"

"That's right." Ezekiel rubbed the back of his hot, sweaty neck. "So changing the subject, how about it, Sara? If I decide to buy that truck or some other vehicle, will you teach me how to drive? I'll get a learner's permit first of course."

Her forehead wrinkled slightly before giving a hesitant nod. "Sure, I guess so."

Grinning, he clapped his hands. "Great! So hop up in the buggy and let's be off."

As Michelle crawled into bed that night,

she inhaled deeply. The sheets smelled so good — like fresh air. It was one of the benefits of hanging laundry outside. While it might be more work than tossing clothes in a dryer, it hadn't taken her long to get used to pinning freshly washed laundry on the line in the Lapps' backyard. In fact, she rather enjoyed the task.

Michelle snuggled beneath the cool linens and closed her eyes. Today had been a good one, and she'd enjoyed Ezekiel's company as much as she had Brad's the night before. It made no sense that she could get along well with two men from opposite backgrounds, but she felt equally comfortable with both of them. Michelle had enjoyed the pleasant conversation she'd shared with Brad during the Fourth of July festival, but she'd also liked being with Ezekiel today. He'd been patient and kind as he taught her how to hitch and unhitch Big Red. And Ezekiel made it seem easy when he took Michelle through the steps of driving the horse and talked about safety measures.

She'd been nervous at first, but by the time they returned to the house, Michelle felt more confident. Of course, having Ezekiel by her side, ready to take charge if needed, had bolstered her confidence. Though she still couldn't believe that he wanted her to teach him how to drive a car. While Michelle didn't have her own vehicle, she'd gotten her driver's license when she was seventeen years old and had driven her foster parents' car a good many times — running errands and picking up the younger kids in their family from school activities. She had renewed her license and driven Jerry's car a few times when he was too drunk to drive himself home. She hoped if and when Ezekiel asked her to teach him that she'd feel up to the task.

She also appreciated Ezekiel taking the time to answer some of her questions about Amish life. She had lots more of course, but those could wait for another time.

It pleased Michelle that Brad and Ezekiel were polite and respectful toward her. Nothing like Jerry had been during the time they'd been a couple. Michelle couldn't believe she had put up with his verbal abuse. When it became physical abuse, she'd had the good sense to get away from him.

Her throat constricted, and she swallowed hard. *Guess maybe at first, I thought I deserved no better. I wonder what it would be like to have a boyfriend like Ezekiel or Brad, who I'm sure would treat me like I was special — not someone to control, push around, or yell at.*

Michelle rolled onto her side. There was no point thinking about this. She couldn't have a relationship with Brad or Ezekiel, even if she wanted one. They didn't know the real her, and if either man learned the truth about her false identity, she felt certain they would never speak to her again.

"I should leave now, before someone gets hurt," Michelle murmured into her pillow. "If I had a lick of sense, I'd pack my bags and head out of here early tomorrow morning, before Mary Ruth and Willis are out of bed."

CHAPTER 19

Michelle couldn't believe how quickly the time had gone since she'd first arrived at the Lapps'. But it was the middle of July, and she'd been here over a month already. She wished she could make time stand still so she would never have to leave this special place.

When Michelle entered the barn in search of her gardening gloves, she paused to look up at the antique jars on the shelf overhead. It would only take a few minutes to get the jar full of prayers down and read one or two. She'd been so busy helping Mary Ruth keep up with all the garden produce lately that she hadn't taken the time to get the jar down for several days.

Think I'll take a few minutes to do that now. Maybe something written on one of those pieces of paper will give me a clue as to who wrote the messages.

Michelle placed her garden gloves and

shovel on Willis's workbench and dragged the ladder over to the shelf where the jars sat. Since Willis was at a doctor's appointment and Mary Ruth had accompanied him, Michelle had plenty of time to look at the notes without interruption. The produce she planned to pick in the garden could wait for a while longer.

Once she had the prayer jar down, she took a seat on the now-familiar bale of straw and leaned against the wooden post behind it. Since Michelle had pushed the notes she'd previously read to the bottom of the jar, she pulled one out near the top and read it out loud.

" 'Watch and pray, that ye enter not into temptation: the spirit indeed is willing, but the flesh is weak' Matthew 26:41."

Michelle shifted on the straw poking into her backside. *The person who wrote this must have been faced with some kind of temptation. Did they give in to it or hold fast?*

Michelle couldn't count all the times she'd been tempted — to steal, to cheat, to get even, to lie. And at some point or another, she had succumbed to each one. There was no doubt about it — her flesh was weak.

She folded the paper in half and pushed it to the bottom of the jar. *One more. I'll just read one more note and then head out to the garden. It wouldn't be good if I didn't get something done while Willis and Mary Ruth are gone.*

On the next paper Michelle withdrew, a prayer had been written. *"Dear Lord, You forgive my sins and give me hope."*

She contemplated it a few minutes before putting the folded paper back in the jar. Holding the antique container between her knees, Michelle folded her hands beneath her chin in a prayer-like gesture and looked up. "God, if You're listening, is there any hope for me?"

Except for the soft nicker of Mary Ruth's buggy horse, the barn was silent.

Well, what did I expect? Did I really think God would open the windows of heaven and shout something down at me? I'm just a foolish young woman whose life isn't going anywhere. Why would He care about someone like me?

Michelle's cheeks burned hot, and it wasn't from the outside heat creeping in. *I should have followed through with my plan to leave this place soon after I got here. The longer I stay, the harder it gets to go.*

Michelle leaned her head against the wooden post and covered her mouth with her hand to stifle a sob. *If I tell Mary Ruth and Willis the truth, they'll be upset, and I'll have to go knowing how much I hurt them. But how can I tell the truth without wounding the ones I've come to care about?*

The rumble of a vehicle approaching drew Michelle's thoughts aside. She stood and took a peek out the barn door. The Lapps were back, and she needed to get a grip on herself and decide what to do. *Do I tell them the truth and pack my bag, or keep pretending for a while longer?*

After Mary Ruth climbed out of Brad's van, she turned to Willis and said, "If you'll take care of paying our driver, I'll go see how Sara is doing in the garden."

Willis gave a nod. "That's fine, but Brad plans to do some work for me today, so I probably won't pay him till he's done for the day."

"That's fine." Mary Ruth patted her husband's arm. It was good he no longer had to wear the sling, but it might be another week or so before he could proclaim that his arm was completely healed. Even though Willis was able to do several chores by himself now, he still needed help with some things on the farm. Since Sara kept busy helping Mary Ruth so much of the time, she appreciated having Brad available to help Willis like he had. Their son Ivan helped on occasions too, but between all the responsibilities he had at his general store and his chores at home, he didn't come by to help as often as Mary Ruth would like.

She stood silently a few seconds, watching as Willis spoke to Brad. Turning away, she headed across the yard.

As Mary Ruth approached the garden, she saw Sara down on her knees, pulling weeds. The young woman looked up and smiled. "How'd Grandpa's appointment go?"

"It went well. He doesn't have to wear the sling anymore, but Dr. Kent cautioned him not to overuse it." Mary Ruth glanced over her shoulder, looking toward the van parked in their driveway. "So Brad will be here a few hours this afternoon to help with some of the heavier chores."

"That's good, and I'm glad Grandpa's arm is better."

"We are too." Mary Ruth smiled. "I'm going in the house now to change into my work dress. I'll be back soon to help you finish the weeding."

"Okay. No hurry though."

Michelle swatted at several gnats buzzing her head. *Oh great. Not this again.* They'd had some rain early that morning, and it seemed the pesky bugs were bent on revenge. Mary Ruth had said this was typical after a rain. *Guess I shoulda worn that old canvas hat, but I stupidly misplaced it.* She sighed. *Oh well, this chore will be over soon enough, and then I'll be out of the bugs' path.*

"The gnats are nasty today aren't they, Sara?" Mary Ruth knelt beside Michelle.

"That's for sure. They've been buzzing my ears and trying to get in my eyes and up my nose." Michelle drew in a breath and sucked in a bug. "Eww . . ." She coughed and almost choked.

Mary Ruth wrinkled her nose. "I've had that happen to me before, and it's not fun to know you've swallowed a bug."

"I think one of 'em may have bit me." Michelle rubbed her forehead. "How come they don't seem to be bothering you?"

"Well, for one thing, I don't wear any hairspray or perfume. Some bugs are attracted to certain smells."

Michelle shifted her position. *So much for thoughts about telling Mary Ruth the truth. The minute I saw her get out of Brad's van my resolve went out the barn door.* Truth was, even though she'd been here less than two months, Michelle had begun to think of Mary Ruth and Willis as her adoptive grandparents. She wished she could stay with them permanently.

"Sara, did you hear what I said?"

Michelle jerked her head. "Uh, sorry, I was deep in thought. Was it something about hairspray?"

Mary Ruth bobbed her head. "Some bugs are attracted to certain smells."

"I'll try to remember that the next time I do any work in the yard."

"The other thing you might do is wear a scarf, or what about that old canvas hat you said you'd found in your mother's closet? You still have it, don't you?"

"No, I haven't seen it for a while. Would it be okay if I wear one of Grandpa's old straw hats? I think there's one hanging on a peg in the barn."

Mary Ruth's eyes widened a bit. "Well, I guess it would be all right, but wouldn't you rather wear one of my scarves?"

Michelle shook her head. "The straw hat might work better, and it will serve a dual purpose by helping to keep the sun out of my eyes."

"Very well. Feel free to help yourself."

"Danki, I will." Michelle tipped her head to one side. "Did I say that right?"

"Yes, you certainly did." Mary Ruth winked. "I bet if you stay here long enough, you'll pick up a lot more of our Pennsylvania Dutch words."

Michelle clambered to her feet and headed to the barn. The mere thought of leaving here put a lump in her throat.

"I forgot to check for eggs this morning," Mary Ruth said when they finished weeding. "Would you mind doing that, Sara, while I start supper?"

"Sure, I'd be happy to do it." Michelle rose and brushed a clump of dirt off her jeans.

"Oh, and if you see Brad, please tell him he's invited to stay and eat with us."

"All right, I will." Michelle returned Willis's old hat to the barn, then hurried off to the chicken coop. As she opened the door of the small wooden structure, the hinge on the door gave an irritating creak.

When Michelle stepped inside, her nose twitched from the smell of dusty feed, fragments of straw, and chicken feces. This was not a place she cared to linger in very long. She hoped she wouldn't end up with a sneezing fit.

Michelle located the egg-collecting basket on a wooden shelf inside the door. She also discovered the chickens in an uproar — squawking, kicking up pieces of straw that had been spread on the floor, and running about as though they'd been traumatized by something.

"Simmer down. I'm not here to hurt you." Michelle shooed two overzealous hens away. If she hadn't put Willis's straw hat back in the barn when she left the garden, she would have used it to flap at the chickens right now. "Come on, ladies. I just came out here to get a few eggs. And if you don't behave, you may end up going without supper this evening."

Feeding the chickens and gathering eggs was not one of Michelle's favorite things to do. But it was better than throwing food into the hog trough. Those fat pigs could make such a racket, snorting and trying to push each other away, like their last meal had been served and they might miss out. They were all greedy. How was it any wonder those hogs were so fat?

Michelle reached into the first nest she came to, and pulled out two nice-sized, perfectly shaped brown eggs. Placing them carefully into the basket, she moved on. Meanwhile, the hens kept making a racket, the pitch of their screeching rising higher and higher. It was unnerving. Michelle was tempted to set the basket down and cover both ears.

When Michelle approached the next nest, she froze. Not far from where she stood lay a huge black snake staring back at her, with its tongue darting in and out. The reptile looked strange with a big bulge in its body. It was also creepy.

With her breath caught in her throat, she felt paralyzed, unable to move. The chickens' continued ruckus only added to Michelle's crippling fear. She took short steps and slowly backed away, never taking her eyes off the shiny, scaled serpent, and hoping she wouldn't knock any of the water feeders over. Michelle wanted to be sure the snake stayed where it was, and that it wouldn't follow her. Even after a hasty exit out the squeaky door, once she was outside the coop, she kept looking back, hoping the snake would remain where it was until she got help.

Except for one time at the zoo, Michelle had never seen a snake up close. And the previous time, there had been a wall of glass between her and the reptile.

Beads of sweat erupted on her forehead as she continued her retreat, whimpering and needing to put a safe distance between herself and the coop where the snake had taken up residence.

Oomph! She backed into Brad.

He took hold of Michelle's shoulders and turned her around. "What's wrong, Sara? Your face is just as white as snow."

"There's a snake in there." She pointed toward the coop.

Brad gave her arm a light pat. "Don't worry; it's not unusual to find a snake in a chicken coop. It's probably just a common black rat snake. I'll take care of it for you."

By "take care of it," Michelle assumed Brad meant he would kill the snake. But since he had no weapon, she didn't see how he could manage it. Surely he wasn't foolish enough to try and kill the snake with his bare hands. Well, she wasn't going in with him to find out.

Michelle waited outside the coop door while Brad went inside. The thought of what he might encounter sent shivers up her spine.

She cringed when a short time later Brad came out with the ugly black snake wrapped around his arm.

"Look here." He pointed to the bulge inside the snake. "This reptile swallowed an egg. See how big it is right behind its head?"

"Eww . . ." Michelle could barely look at the snake.

Brad started walking toward the adjacent field.

"Wait! Aren't you gonna kill that horrible thing?"

He stopped walking and turned to look at her. "Nope. Snakes like this are good at keeping the mice population down around farms."

Michelle glanced at the now-quiet chicken coop, wondering if she could ever muster up the nerve to go in there again. As much as she enjoyed being with the Lapps, maybe she wasn't cut out for country life.

Chapter 20

"Do you think Sara's been acting strange lately?" Mary Ruth asked Willis as they got ready for bed one evening in late July.

He took his glasses off and rubbed the bridge of his nose. "In what way?"

"Well, some days she seems happy and content, and other days her mood is so sullen." Mary Ruth placed her head covering on the dresser and picked up her hairbrush. "There are times when we're talking and she doesn't seem to even hear what I'm saying. And when Sara does respond, she won't always make eye contact with me." She moved over to the bed and sat down. "I'm concerned about her, Willis. Yesterday I offered to give her all the clothes Rhoda left behind when she ran away from home, but Sara said she would prefer that I keep them. Don't you think that's strange?"

"Maybe she's had enough of us and wants to go back to her own life. We can't force our granddaughter to stay here, you know." Willis leaned over and fluffed up the pillows on their bed. "And as far as her not wanting Rhoda's clothes — what would she do with them, Mary Ruth? Sara's not Amish, so she wouldn't be likely to wear them."

"True. And I would never try to keep her from leaving when she decides to return to her home. As you know, we've both told her that while we would like her to stay with us permanently, she's free to go whenever she likes." Mary Ruth heaved a sigh. "I just want our precious Sara to be happy — even if it means not staying here with us."

Willis took a seat beside Mary Ruth, placing his hand gently against her back. "I heard her talking about us to Ezekiel the other day when he came by to see if we were running low on honey."

Mary Ruth's ears perked up. "What did she say?"

"Said she dreaded the day she'd have to leave, and that she enjoyed being here very much." He gave Mary Ruth's back a few comforting pats. "So you see, there's nothing to worry about. If Sara truly likes it here, maybe when she does return to her home, she'll pack up all her things and come back to stay. Would ya like that, Mary Ruth?"

"Of course I would. And I'm sure you

would too. Having Rhoda's daughter living here permanently would give me nothing but pleasure." She leaned her head on his shoulder. "Even though it's wrong to selfishly ask God for things, I'm praying that's exactly what will happen."

"I'm going out to get the mail now," Michelle announced after breakfast the following morning. She still couldn't believe how early the mail came on this rural road. Back in Philadelphia, she sometimes wouldn't get her mail until close to supper time. Of course, it was mostly junk mail, which was why she hadn't even bothered to put in a notice with the post office when she left Philadelphia in a hurry. By not forwarding her mail, there was no way Jerry could contact her either. For sure, he was the last person she wanted to see or hear from again.

"If you have something else to do, I can get the mail on the way to or from my reflexology appointment." Mary Ruth began clearing the table.

"No, that's okay. I'll get the mail now and bring it in before you go." Michelle sprang to her feet. It was important that she be the one to get the mail, in case another letter came from the Lapps' true granddaughter.

"All right then, I'll start the dishes while

you're doing that."

Willis looked up from the newspaper he had just unfolded to read. "Sara, would you like to say goodbye to the puppies who'll be going home with their new owners today?" he asked.

Michelle nodded. While she hated to see the pups leave, it was nice to know they'd be going to good homes. It was hard to believe the rambunctious little critters were over six weeks old already. Willis had asked around to see who might want one, and with the exception of Rascal, all the puppies had been spoken for.

Michelle thought about how Willis and Mary Ruth had given her the puppy as a birthday gift. She'd become attached to the little fellow and wished she could take him along when she left the Lapps' home for good. But it wasn't a wise idea, since Michelle had no idea where she was going for sure or what kind of a place she might end up renting.

"Your cousin Lenore should be here around ten o'clock, so you have plenty of time between now and then to spend with the pups," Willis commented.

"Okay. I'm going out to get the mail now, and then I'll head to the barn as soon as I've done the dishes for Grandma." She looked at Mary Ruth. "I don't want you to be late for your appointment. I've heard that reflexology can help with a good many things."

"Yes, and my friend, who treats people for a donation only, says massaging the feet and its pressure points can bring relief when my neck, back, or head starts to hurt." The older woman's face radiated with joy. "I thank you for your thoughtfulness, Sara. You're such a sweet granddaughter."

Michelle cringed inwardly. *If Mary Ruth knew the real me, she wouldn't think I was so sweet.*

As Michelle made her way out to the mailbox, her shoulders slumped. How much longer could she keep doing this? If Mary Ruth or Willis ever went out and got the mail before she did and found a letter from the real Sara, Michelle would be caught in her trap full of lies. She tried not to think about it and simply concentrate on enjoying being here for as long as she could, but it became harder every day.

When Michelle approached the mailbox, a car sped by, going much too fast, and leaving a trail of dust following it. She could still hear the gravel crunching under the tires as the vehicle raced farther up the road. Didn't people have better sense than to travel at a high rate of speed on these back country roads? Anyone who lived in the area had to know horse and buggies traveled up and down this road. Even the tourists, who came to observe the Amish people living in the area, should know better than to exceed the speed limit.

Michelle looked up and down the road. Fortunately, there were no children out with pony carts this morning. In fact, she didn't see any horses and buggies.

Michelle remembered Ezekiel saying during her driving lesson last week that buggy accidents could occur from many causes: human error, horse error, runaway horses, barking dogs, certain road conditions, loud noises from motorcycles or trucks, and of course speeding cars. In his opinion, most accidents happened because non-Amish drivers were either inconsiderate or in too big of a hurry.

Michelle had to agree. She'd witnessed some Amish buggies being cut off by vehicles trying to pass. As long as she was given an opportunity to drive an Amish buggy, she would use caution.

Directing her thoughts back to the mailbox, she pulled on the handle and reached inside for the stack of mail. Thumbing through the ads and bills, she discovered another letter from Sara Murray.

Oh no. Her fingers trembled as she stuck the letter in her pocket. *I wish she'd stop sending letters. It freaks me out every time another one comes.*

Michelle ran up the driveway and into the house, nearly colliding with Willis, who stood near the back door.

"Whoa! Where are ya going in such a hurry?" he asked, stepping aside.

"I just wanted to put the mail on the table so I could get started on the dishes."

"No hurry about the mail." Willis raised his thick brows. "The postman usually brings bills and advertising catalogs, and an occasional letter from someone we know. So I doubt we got anything that can't wait to be looked at till later." He gestured to the stack of mail as Michelle placed it on the table. "Right now, I have chores to do, so I'd better get outside before the day warms too much. Heard it's going to be another hot one." Willis made a hasty exit out the back door.

Michelle figured Mary Ruth was in her room getting ready for her appointment, so she would wait until after she left to open Sara's letter. In the meantime, there were dishes to do.

■ ■ ■ ■

As soon as the dishes were done, and Mary Ruth had left the house, Michelle raced upstairs to her room. She couldn't take the chance of Willis coming back inside and finding her reading Sara's letter. Since the dishes were done and no one had shown up yet to pick up their puppy, this was the perfect time to see what Sara had written.

Michelle took a seat on the bed and tore open the envelope. Reading it silently, she frowned.

Dear Grandpa and Grandma,

I received your letter and wanted to reassure you that I won't come to visit until sometime in October. I am wondering, however, if you have a telephone. If so, could you please write back and give me the number? That way I can keep in better contact and let you know exactly when I might be coming to Strasburg.

Your granddaughter,

Sara

Michelle placed the letter in her lap and groaned. *How am I going to answer that? Maybe I'll just ignore it. I do have to destroy this letter though, and I'd better do it now.*

Rising from the bed, she ripped the letter into small pieces, then hurried downstairs. She would throw the remnants in the burn barrel, like she'd done before. It was the only way to keep the Lapps from finding out that she wasn't Sara Murray.

Chapter 21

Michelle sat on the back porch, holding Rascal in her lap. The puppy's soft, fleecy fur was nothing like his mother's yet, and it would be awhile before he lost his sharp puppy teeth. Since he was the only pup left from the litter, Michelle hoped to pay more attention to Rascal and maybe teach him some tricks. Rascal needed to get more social too. In a way, Michelle wished he would stay in this smaller stage, so adorable and cute. Unfortunately, she wouldn't get the chance to see the dog when he was all grown up. The poor little guy seemed lonely without his brothers and sisters to play with. They'd all gone home with their happy new owners yesterday.

Michelle sighed. *I hope all the puppies adjust to their new surroundings.* She understood how the pups may have felt last night, without the comfort of their mother, brothers, and sisters. Even though Michelle had been taken from an abusive home and put in a better, more stable one, she had always felt out of place in the foster home and lonely for her younger brothers.

Even Sadie, lying listlessly on the porch beside Michelle, wasn't herself today. It almost appeared as if the dog's eyes were weeping. One would think after caring for a batch of pups all these weeks, the dog would be somewhat relieved to see them go. But apparently Sadie's maternal instinct was stronger than her need to have time to herself. Although Michelle wasn't a mother, she figured any good parent would feel the same way — putting the needs of their offspring ahead of their own. It hurt to think that her own flesh-and-blood parents had never cared much about nurturing their children or meeting their needs. Michelle's mom and dad had so many problems they could barely function at times, much less provide a stable environment for their family.

Lest she give in to self-pity, Michelle put her focus on Rascal again. "You're sure a cute little thing." The puppy's floppy ears perked up when she stroked his head. "Maybe what we all need is a little exercise. It might help us not feel so gloomy."

Michelle lifted the pup and set him on the

porch beside his mother. Then she hopped up, ran into the yard, and picked up a small stick. "Come on Sadie — fetch!" Michelle tossed the stick across the yard.

Perking right up, the collie lifted her head, leaped off the porch, and chased after the stick. Then she brought it back to Michelle and dropped it at her feet.

"Good girl, Sadie." Michelle picked it up and threw it again.

Woof! Woof! Sadie took off like a streak. Apparently this playtime was just what she needed.

As if not to be outdone, Rascal practically flew off the porch and chased after his mother, yipping all the way.

Michelle figured Sadie wouldn't give up her stick, so she found a smaller one and tossed it for Rascal. It didn't take the little fellow long to get the hang of playing fetch, for soon he was romping back and forth, grabbing the stick in his mouth. Of course, getting him to bring it to Michelle was another matter. Once he got hold of the stick and claimed it for his own, Rascal raced off to the other side of the yard. In order to regain the twig, Michelle had to chase after the pup. Sadie, however, kept bringing her stick back to Michelle, and the game continued.

Michelle worked with Rascal a bit more, now that Sadie laid down to watch. "I'm sure you are too young yet, but for fun, I'll give it a try."

She sat the pup down and put the stick in front of him. When Rascal picked it up, Michelle gave a command. "No Rascal." She took the stick from his mouth, and placed it back on the grass. Michelle did this a few times, until Rascal finally sat there staring at the stick when she said no.

Then Michelle commanded Rascal to bring the stick to her. "Come Rascal. Bring me the stick." Michelle giggled when Rascal stayed sitting and cocked his head to one side. In hopes that the pup would understand, she took the stick and put it in Rascal's mouth, telling him to "Stay." Then, patting the side of her leg, she gave the command again. "Come, Rascal."

Rascal took off with the stick in his mouth, but instead of bringing it to her, he headed in the opposite direction.

Michelle chased after him but was soon out of breath and laughing so hard her sides ached. "Whew! Your pup is wearing me out, Sadie. But Rascal did pretty well for his first time chasing a stick." She plopped down next to Sadie and rubbed a spot between the collie's ears. It felt good to be so carefree and able to find enjoyment in the simple things. If she truly was the Lapps' granddaughter, she would stay here permanently and perhaps, if she ever felt ready, even join the Amish church someday. Right now though, she didn't know enough about their way of life or religious beliefs to determine if she could become a church member. Of course, under the circumstances, becoming Amish was nothing but a foolish notion. Once her true identity had been revealed, no Amish member would want her to be a part of their church.

Sadie barked when a horse and buggy pulled into the yard, and Rascal dropped his stick and joined in, making smaller *Arf! Arf!* noises.

Michelle shielded her eyes against the glare of the sun, watching as Ezekiel pulled up to the hitching rail. She wondered if he'd come to give her another driving lesson.

Ezekiel hopped out of his buggy and quickly secured his horse. "Hey, how's it going?" He waved at Sara.

"It's going good." She motioned to the yapping dogs. "I was entertaining Sadie and Rascal. Thought I'd try to teach the little fellow how to fetch."

"How'd he do?"

"Not too bad for as young as he is." Michelle offered a thumbs-up and grinned. "I'm sure he'll get the hang of it in time."

Ezekiel squatted down and greeted the animals. "I take it Willis must have found homes for the rest of Sadie's pups?"

"Yes. Only my little Rascal is left to pester his mother."

Ezekiel wiped his chin when Sadie became a little too exuberant and gave him a few slurps with her tongue.

Meanwhile, Rascal kept busy tugging on Sara's shoelaces. Laughing, she bent down and picked the puppy up, rubbing her cheek against his soft fur.

"Where are Willis and Mary Ruth today?" Ezekiel asked. "Are they in the house?"

Sara shook her head. "Grandpa went to meet with the other ministers in their district about something pertaining to one of the church members who is having some physical problems. And Grandma is helping her Amish neighbor Caroline, who just got out of the hospital."

"Oh? What's wrong with Caroline?"

"She had her gall bladder removed."

"That's too bad. I hear gall bladder issues can be quite painful."

Sara nodded. "What brings you by today, Ezekiel? Did you come to give me another driving lesson?"

"Not exactly, but if you agree to come with me, you can drive on the way back, because I plan on going after my own vehicle."

Her eyes widened. "I'm not sure what vehicle you're talking about, but there is no way I'm driving a horse and buggy by myself." Sara shook her head vigorously. "I am nowhere near ready for that."

"I figured if I followed along slowly behind, you'd be okay." Ezekiel couldn't hide his excitement. "I bought that truck I told ya about, and I wanna park it on my cousin's property. From there, we'll head back here to your grandparents' place."

Sara's forehead creased. "Wait a minute now. Didn't you ask if I'd be willing to teach you how to drive a car?"

"Well, yes, but . . ."

"So if you don't know how to drive, how are you going to follow me anywhere?"

Ezekiel's ears burned like someone had set them on fire. "Sorry if I misled you. The fact is, I've been practicing some in my friend Abe's car. And even though I don't have my license yet, I'm able to drive fairly well. I just need a little more practice. And I did get my learner's permit the other day," he quickly added.

Sara glared at him. "But you shouldn't drive by yourself with only a learner's permit — not to mention still needing more practice. If you were to get stopped by a cop, it wouldn't be good. And your folks would probably find out about it too."

Ezekiel folded his arms. "I'm well aware of all that. But it's only a short distance from where I'll be picking up the truck to my cousin's house, and I'll be very careful."

"I have a better idea. Why don't you let me drive the truck to your cousin's and you can drive your horse and buggy? That would be much safer, don't you think?"

"How 'bout we discuss this on the way to get the truck?" He moved closer to Sara, giving fluttery hand movements as he talked. "Will you please go with me? I'll make it up to you somehow."

"You don't need to make anything up to me." Sara tugged her ponytail. "I'll go because you're my friend, but let me first put the puppy away. I also need to leave a note for my grandparents, so they won't worry if they get back while I'm gone."

He drew a deep breath through his nose. "Thanks, Sara. I really appreciate this."

Michelle's fingers gripped the reins so tightly her knuckles whitened. She had to be crazy to let Ezekiel talk her into driving his horse and buggy without him along to tell her what to do. "But how could I refuse him when he sounded so excited to drive the truck?" Michelle's breath came out in nervous spurts of air. "Steady, boy. Easy does it." Why hadn't Ezekiel asked his cousin or one of his friends to go along with him, instead of relying on her? They would have handled Big Red much better than she ever could. Every bump she encountered and every passing of a car put Michelle's nerves on edge. But so far the horse was behaving himself. He just plodded along at a steady pace.

Michelle glanced in the side mirror and saw Ezekiel's truck behind her. She wondered if he was worried about driving it by himself, with so little experience.

As a convertible passed on the opposite side of the road, Michelle's fear escalated. It was the same group of guys who had taunted her the day she'd walked back to the Lapps' from the post office. If Brad hadn't shown up when he did, Michelle didn't know what she would have done, or how far the young men might have gone in their quest to torment her.

I hope they didn't recognize me. Don't know what I would do if they turned around and came back to give me trouble.

She glanced in her mirror again and relaxed a bit when their vehicle kept going. If they had come alongside the buggy and given her any problems, Michelle hoped Ezekiel would have come to her rescue the way Brad had that day.

Michelle jumped when Ezekiel tooted his horn behind. Luckily, Big Red didn't seem to be affected by the noise.

She glanced in the mirror again, and seeing the truck's right blinker come on, she guided the horse up the next driveway. This must be where Ezekiel's cousin lived. What a relief to know she would soon be turning the horse and buggy over to Ezekiel.

His cousin's farm was neat as a pin, just like the Lapps' place. Instead of pigs in the barnyard, however, Michelle saw a small herd of floppy-eared goats. Some were white, and others were black. It was cute how they all came up to the fence and noisily bleated, curious to see who had arrived.

Michelle had just pulled Big Red up to the hitching rail near the barn when she heard the shrill sound of a siren. She stepped down from the buggy in time to see a police car pull in behind Ezekiel's truck. *Oh no. I wonder what he did wrong. Or could it have been me?*

Chapter 22

Ezekiel's mouth felt so dry he could barely swallow. He couldn't imagine what he'd done wrong, other than maybe following the buggy too close. He got out of his new truck and stood by the door, waiting for the officer to approach. He was glad when Sara joined him, because he needed the moral support.

"Did you know the right blinker on your buggy isn't working?" The deputy sheriff looked at Sara.

She shook her head slowly, then glanced at Ezekiel.

"Sorry, sir. We didn't know." Ezekiel exhaled through his nose. When he'd heard the siren and seen the patrol car pull onto the driveway, he was sure he would be in trouble for driving alone, with only a learner's permit. "I'll make sure to get the blinker working again. Thanks for letting us know."

"So whose buggy is it — yours or hers?"

The deputy motioned to Sara.

"It's mine."

"Oh. I assumed it was hers, since you were driving the truck."

Ezekiel explained that the truck and buggy were both his. Sweat beaded on his forehead, and he reached up to wiped it off. He sure hoped the officer wouldn't ask to see his license.

The deputy nodded his head. "Yeah, I get it. Some of you Amish young people like to have the best of both worlds. I guess you'll have to sell the truck when you join the church though, right?"

All Ezekiel did was offer a brief nod. He wasn't about to tell the officer that he probably wouldn't be joining the church.

"Okay then, I'll be on my way. Just don't forget to get that blinker fixed." The deputy gave a wave and got back in his car.

Ezekiel turned to Sara. "Guess we'd better go. I need to get back home, and you do as well. I'll park the truck around back of my cousin's house, and we can be on our way."

Michelle waited by the buggy until Ezekiel came back. She still couldn't believe he had bought a truck or that he'd lied to her about not knowing how to drive. Of course, who was she to talk? She'd been lying to Mary Ruth, Willis, and everyone else she had met since her arrival in Lancaster County.

She moved up to Big Red and patted his side. *I'm sure there are a lot of people in this world — and maybe even this community — who have lied about something or are keeping some deep dark secret to themselves.* Her gaze dropped to the ground. *So why do I feel guilty for letting the Lapps think I'm their granddaughter?*

Michelle lifted her head when she heard Ezekiel approach. "Are you ready to go? he asked.

She nodded. "What about the blinker? Do you think we'll get stopped again because it doesn't work?"

He bopped the side of his head. "Oh, yeah. I forgot about that. I'll go in my uncle's workshop and see if he has any spare batteries lying around."

"Is he in there working?"

"Nope. The whole family is gone right now. They're on a camping trip with some of their friends. They won't be back till sometime toward the end of next week."

Michelle's face tightened. "So you're just gonna walk into your uncle's shop and take something without asking?"

"Yep. I'm sure he wouldn't mind. Besides,

I'll replace it with a new one before they get home."

"What about your truck? Is that something they don't know about either? Did you park it here without asking, and because they're not home, you don't think they are any the wiser?"

A splotch of color erupted on Ezekiel's cheeks. "That's not how it is at all."

"How is it then?"

"I told you before that my cousin said I could park the truck here. His folks aren't as strict as mine."

"But aren't they likely to tell your parents?"

Ezekiel shook his head. "I don't think so. I'll come over to see them as soon as they get home and explain the situation."

Michelle fiddled with the top button on her blouse, to avoid eye contact with him. "Okay, suit yourself. I'll wait in the buggy until you get the blinker working."

Paradise, Pennsylvania

Brad had spent the entire morning taking an Amish family to and from the Walmart store in Lancaster. He'd just dropped them off at their home and decided he would head down to Strasburg and see if the Lapps needed any work done. It would give him a chance to say hi to Sara too. He'd enjoyed her company at the Fourth of July festival a few weeks ago and thought he might see if she would like to go out for supper with him tomorrow evening. Secretly, he hoped to get better acquainted in an environment where so many people weren't milling around.

Brad thought about the night he'd joined the Lapps for supper. It would have been an opportunity to get to know Sara better, but unfortunately, Willis monopolized most of his time. Throughout the meal he'd talked, almost nonstop, about everything from the weather to the benefits of raising hogs. Mary Ruth had managed to get in a few words, asking Brad more about the call on his life to be a minister. Sara, on the other hand, had been quiet during the meal, barely looking in Brad's direction. He wanted to ask if something was bothering her but didn't get the chance. After the meal was over, Willis invited Brad into the dining room and challenged him to some Amish card game he'd never played before. By the time they were done, Sara had gone to her room, saying she'd developed a headache.

"I wonder if she was trying to avoid me," Brad mumbled. "Though I can't see why she would. Don't think I've said or done anything to offend her." He shrugged. "But then, who knows? I could have said something she didn't like without even realizing it." Brad worried sometimes about his relationships with people.

As a minister, he couldn't be putting people off or making them uncomfortable. He would need to have a good rapport with the people in his church and be sensitive to their needs.

Strasburg

When Brad turned his van up the Lapps' driveway, he saw Sara getting out of a buggy. Then he caught sight of Ezekiel stepping out of the other side of the buggy and realized they must have been somewhere together. Brad wondered if Ezekiel was interested in the Lapps' granddaughter. If so, did Sara like him?

"Hi, Sara. Is Willis at home?" he asked, stepping up to her. "I came by to see if he has any chores for me to do today or even sometime in the near future."

"My grandpa's not here," she replied. "Or at least he wasn't when Ezekiel picked me up to . . ." She paused, glancing over at Ezekiel. "Uh . . . he took me out for a horse and buggy driving lesson."

"I see." Brad glanced at the tall Amish

man and smiled. "It's nice to see you again."

Ezekiel gave a nod. "Good to see you too."

"I'll, um, go check the buggy shed and see if either Grandma or Grandpa's carriages are there." Sara twisted a strand of long hair around her fingers.

"Okay, thanks." Brad thought she seemed a little nervous today. Did it bother Sara that he was here and had seen her and Ezekiel together?

As she headed toward the buggy shed, Brad decided to ask Ezekiel a question. "I'm curious as to the reason you're teaching Sara to drive a horse and buggy. She's not planning to become Amish, is she?"

Ezekiel rubbed a hand across his chin. "I don't think so. Sara just said she wanted to learn, and I volunteered to teach her. Guess she thought it would be fun and a way to get to know her grandparents' way of life a little better."

"I see. Well, before he sprained his arm, wasn't Willis going to teach her?"

"Yeah, but that didn't work out, so I was glad to pitch in and take over for her grandpa. We've been using my horse, which has worked out better too, since Big Red's easy to drive and doesn't spook easily."

"Guess that makes sense." Brad really wanted to ask Ezekiel what his intentions toward Sara were, but it would be too bold, and probably not appreciated. Besides, it was really none of his business.

Brad waited quietly, staring at Ezekiel's horse. The animal stood patiently at the hitching rail, flipping his tail against the flies invading his space. He did appear gentle enough, at least here, where he didn't have to pull a buggy.

A few minutes later, Sara returned, shaking her head. "There are no buggies in the shed, and I don't know when either of my grandparents will be home. You're welcome to wait for them if you like."

"Okay, thanks, I will." Brad glanced at Ezekiel again, wondering if he too planned to stick around. He was pleased when Ezekiel told Sara he needed to go and climbed into his buggy.

Sara went around front and released the horse from the rail. "See you soon, Ezekiel," she called as he backed up his horse.

"Sure thing." Ezekiel looked at Brad. "See you around."

Brad nodded and waved. Then he turned to Sara and smiled. *Guess I'll get right to the point.* "Say, if you're not doing anything tomorrow night, I was wondering if you'd like to go out for supper with me."

Sara pushed a wayward strand of hair

away from her face. “Sure, that sounds nice.”

He smiled. “Great. I’ll pick you up around six o’clock.”

CHAPTER 23

That evening it started to rain, and just as Michelle was getting ready for bed, Mary Ruth knocked on her door and asked if she'd like to come out to the barn. "One of the sows is about to give birth. Your grandpa and I thought you might enjoy seeing the process."

Michelle's eyebrows lowered and pinched together. For the first time since coming here, she wished she was someplace else. Watching pigs being born was not her idea of fun. Not to mention going outside in the drenching rain. But she didn't want to hurt Mary Ruth's feelings or act disinterested.

"Okay, sure," Michelle called through the closed door. "I'll be out there pretty quick."

"All right. I'm heading out to the barn now. We'll see you soon. Oh, and Sara, make sure you wear a jacket. It's pouring outside."

"Okay, Grandma." Michelle smiled, despite the interruption. It felt nice to have someone care for her the way Mary Ruth and Willis did. They were truly the grandparents she'd never had. How different her life would be if she had known these good people since she was a young girl.

Guess I should enjoy their company while I can, 'cause it won't last forever. Michelle slipped into her jean jacket and left the room. Downstairs, she grabbed an umbrella in the metal stand near the back door.

Outside, the rain came down in torrents, and thunder sounded in the distance. Michelle cringed when a flash of lightning lit up the yard. Looking to the west, she saw several bright, zig-zaggy streaks where the fury of the storm seemed to be much worse. She hated thunderstorms — she had ever since she was a child. The noise and bright flashes had scared her the most, especially when she had been all alone in the unfinished, upstairs bedroom. The rain sounded louder, pounding on the roof like a herd of elephants. The thunder and lightning seemed to be right outside her bedroom window, which had only added to Michelle's fear. When the wind howled, it made the windows sing eerily. And hiding under the covers, like she'd often done, didn't help. Giving in to her anxiety, Michelle would end up flying down the stairs with her blanket to sleep on the couch for the remainder of the night. Of course, Dad made fun of her the following morning, saying there was nothing to be afraid of and she ought to grow up and quit being such a baby. Michelle's fear of storms was being passed on to her brothers, who he'd found huddled together and asleep under their bed that morning.

Pushing her negative childhood memories to the back of her mind, Michelle dashed across the wet grass, flung open the barn doors, and stepped inside. Willis and Mary Ruth's voices could be heard coming from the back of the building. Michelle headed in that direction. She found them both sitting on folding chairs near the pregnant sow's pen.

Willis looked up at her and smiled. "Glad you could join us, Sara. Your grandma and I feel it's necessary to be on hand during the birth of Penny's piglets, and we figured you might like to witness it too.

Laughter bubbled in Michelle's throat, but she held it back. She couldn't believe Willis had actually named the mother pig.

"There's another folding chair if you'd like to sit on it." Mary Ruth gestured with her head.

"No, that's okay. I'll sit here." Michelle

took a seat on a bale of straw.

Outside, the storm grew closer. She heard the wind howling as pelting rain hit the metal barn roof, while booms of thunder continued to sound. The storm didn't frighten her so much now. In fact, it felt kind of cozy inside the barn with all the familiar sounds and smells.

I might feel differently if I was alone in my room right now. Would I end up sleeping on the Lapps' couch?

Michelle yawned, pulling her knees up and wrapping her arms around her legs. She figured it might be a long night, waiting to see the piglets being born, but she didn't mind. It was nice being with Willis and Mary Ruth and listening to them chat. Even when they spoke in their native language, it didn't bother her. And since this would be the first time she'd seen a sow give birth, she'd be learning something new about farm life.

"Well, would you look at that?" Mary Ruth gestured to Sara. But her granddaughter had drifted off to sleep with her head on her bent knees.

Willis snickered. "Guess the excitement of watching Penny give birth wasn't enough to keep her awake."

"It is almost midnight, and I'm about ready to fall asleep myself." Mary Ruth kept her voice down. "Hopefully the rest of the piglets will be born soon."

"Should be." Willis yawned and reached for the thermos of coffee Mary Ruth had brought out to the barn a short time ago. He opened the lid and poured himself a cup. "Want some?"

She shook her head. "If I drink anymore *kaffi,* I'll be wide awake by the time we go to bed."

"Not me. I've always been able to drink coffee right up till I hit the hay, and it never bothers me."

She poked his arm playfully. "Jah, well, you're an exception."

He grinned. "Guess so."

Mary Ruth sat quietly with Willis, watching as three more piglets came into the world. A short time later, the sow laid on her side so all fifteen of her babies could nurse. It was a precious sight, and Mary Ruth never got tired of seeing the miracle of birth.

She glanced at Sara, who was still asleep, and her thoughts went to Rhoda. Mary Ruth remembered well how their daughter used to react when any of the farm animals had babies. Rhoda would get all excited and sit there watching all day if she didn't have chores to do.

Mary Ruth hadn't expected their daughter to run off like she did — not in a million years. She had spent many years blaming herself for Rhoda's departure. Was there something she had said or done to cause their daughter to run off? Had they been too hard on her? Or not hard enough? But that was all behind her now. Blaming oneself did no good, and she had determined that she wasn't going to do it anymore. Thanks to Sara's letter, telling them who she was, Mary Ruth knew that Rhoda had left home by her own choice. She'd been embarrassed to tell them she was expecting a baby.

Mary Ruth's eyes watered, and she sniffed, hoping they wouldn't spill over. *How wonderful it would have been if we could have offered Rhoda support and been a part of the birth of our granddaughter. We would have done all we could to help our daughter during that difficult time. I wish she would have been brave enough to come to us with her problem.*

Despite her best effort, a few tears trickled down Mary Ruth's cheeks. *Oh Rhoda, how I wish we could have seen you one last time before you died. If only you had contacted us, we could have talked things through and assured you of our love and concern.*

Mary Ruth's only comfort was having Rhoda's daughter here with them. It was as though God had seen her and Willis's grief and brought Sara to them as a healing balm. And that's exactly what she was. The joy Sara brought to Mary Ruth and Willis was beyond words. She hoped they never lost touch with her and could see each other often, even if Sara chose to return to her home.

Michelle woke up feeling groggy and disoriented. It took her a few minutes to realize where she was. But after seeing Mary Ruth and Willis standing against the sow's stall, it didn't take her long to realize she was in the barn.

After sleeping on the bale of straw all that time, Michelle's body ached. She stood and stretched her sore muscles. Once she'd gotten some of the kinks out, she glanced toward the pen, blinking and rubbing her eyes. "Wow, look at all those piglets! I can't believe I slept through the whole thing. Why didn't you wake me?"

"Your grandpa wanted to, but I said no, you needed your rest more than seeing Penny give birth." Mary Ruth pointed to the baby pigs lying beside their mother.

"She had fifteen little ones. Isn't that something?"

"I'll say. Bet the poor sow's more tired than I am." Michelle moved in for a closer look. "That's a lot of babies, but they're cute little things."

"Yes, indeed." Willis gave a loud yawn as he stood. "Well, everything seems to be okay here, so we should go into the house and try to get a few hours' sleep before it's time to get up and do our chores."

Mary Ruth nodded. "Guess that would be good, but not for too long, because soon it'll be time to fix breakfast."

"Oh, don't worry about that," Michelle said. "I'll take care of fixing breakfast this morning."

"Why, thank you, Sara." Mary Ruth slipped her arm around Michelle's waist. "You're always willing to help out. I just don't know what we would do without you."

Michelle smiled, although her insides quivered. *What would they think if they knew the real me?*

After Mary Ruth and Willis headed to their room, Michelle went back out to the barn. She wasn't sleepy anymore and thought it was a good chance to read a few more notes in the prayer jar. Each time she held the glass container, like she was doing now, her curiosity was piqued. As she shined the flashlight she'd brought along onto the paper, Michelle wished once more that she knew who had written the notes and why they'd chosen certain Bible verses, like the one she'd just read.

"Wherefore come out from among them, and be ye separate, saith the Lord, and touch not the unclean thing; and I will receive you. And will be a Father unto you, and ye shall be my sons and daughters, saith the Lord Almighty" 2 Corinthians 6:17–18.

With hands clasped under her chin, Michelle pondered the words, hoping to figure out their meaning. *How does one come out and be separate? Is this what Amish people are trying to do — be separate from the rest of the world by their Plain lifestyle and strict religious views?*

Her forehead wrinkled. *And what about the part of the second verse that says the Lord will be our Father and we shall be His sons and daughters? Maybe I should ask Brad about this verse when I go out to dinner with him tomorrow night.*

Michelle glanced at her watch. *It will actually be tonight, since it's now two o'clock in the morning.* She yawned and put the folded paper back in the jar. *Guess I need to try and get a few hours of sleep before it's time to start breakfast.*

She put the old jar back on the shelf behind the others and picked up her flashlight, prepared to leave the barn. *Maybe before I go back in, I'll take a quick look at the piglets and see how they're doing.*

Michelle walked back to the sow's stall and, shining the light, she looked in. Penny was sleeping, and so were fourteen of her babies. One of the brood, a little smaller than the others, had wandered off by itself and couldn't seem to find the way back to its mama. Its high-pitched squealing didn't seem to bother Penny. *Poor mama. She must be exhausted.*

Michelle opened the stall door and slipped quietly in. When she bent down to pick up the wailing piglet, her throat clogged up, and tears sprang to her eyes. These pigs had a mother as well as brothers and sisters. Michelle had no one except a pretend grandma and grandpa. And all the crying she'd ever done over the years hadn't brought anyone to comfort her.

Her thoughts went to her brothers, Ernie and Jack. How old would they be this year? "Let's see." Michelle counted on her fingers. "I can't believe my baby brother, Jack, will be twenty, and Ernie, twenty-two years old."

Oh, how she wished she knew what had happened to them after they were taken from their parents. Had they gone to the same foster family, or had they been separated from each other, like she had been?

The last time Michelle saw them would be etched in her mind forever. She was only ten years old at the time, but it was like yesterday. As the car drove away, taking her brothers from her, a scream lodged in her throat. Their eyes locked with hers for the very last time, as they watched from the back window of the car. Michelle saw the desperation in Ernie's and Jack's faces but was helpless to do anything about it. Her heart felt like it had been broken into a million pieces. The vehicle got farther and farther away, and her brothers faded along with it — the last of her family being stripped away. Then it was Michelle's turn to be taken away, leaving her parents and getting into a car with strangers who would take her to a new place. Fourteen years ago, Michelle and her brothers had become wards of the state, and there was nothing she could do about it.

A sense of longing welled in her soul. Did Jack and Ernie ever think about her, or were the boys too young back then to even remember her now? Surely at six and eight years old, they would have recalled something about their sister. But maybe it was best if they didn't. Michelle had nothing to offer her brothers, and she hadn't done anything to make Ernie and Jack proud.

Blinking back tears as she refocused her thoughts, Michelle put the tiny pig next to its mother and left the stall. Turning back for one last look, she saw that all was quiet now, as the little runt squirmed in between the others.

Who knows, maybe someday our paths will cross. If I ever get my life stable, I hope the day will come when I can find my brothers, and we'll never be parted again.

Chapter 24

"Thank you for fixing our breakfast." Mary Ruth smiled at Michelle from across the kitchen table.

"No problem. It was the least I could do, considering all you've done for me." Michelle paused to drink some of her apple juice. "You two have become like the family I never had."

Willis's brows lifted. "But your mother and father were your family."

Michelle's face warmed. "Yes, of course. What I meant was, you're the grandparents I never knew."

"So you never met your father's parents?" Mary Ruth asked.

Michelle shook her head. "Guess they didn't want anything to do with my dad." She had spoken the truth in that regard. Of course, Michelle had no idea what the real Sara's situation might be. For all she knew, Sara Murray might have a great relationship with her other grandparents.

Relief spread through Michelle when the Lapps changed the subject. Anything she would say to them about the family they thought she had would be a lie anyway.

While Willis and Mary Ruth talked about the baby pigs, Michelle wondered about the real Sara Murray. Michelle wished in some ways that she could meet and get to know the Lapps' granddaughter. It would be interesting to get acquainted with the young woman they believed her to be. What did Sara look like? What kinds of things did she enjoy doing? Did she have a job or a boyfriend? Were Michelle and Sara anything alike? She doubted it.

Michelle didn't even know what the Lapps' daughter looked like, because they had no pictures of her. All she knew was that her own hair, ironically, was the same color as Rhoda's. That fact made it easier for Michelle to pass herself off as their granddaughter.

As Michelle stared at her plate of scrambled eggs and ham, her appetite diminished. *If Sara knew I was here, pretending to be her, I bet she'd hate me.*

Newark

Sara took a seat at the kitchen table and

opened her plastic box full of beads. Since today was Saturday and she had no college classes or work schedule, it was a good time to make a few pieces of jewelry. Sara enjoyed this hobby — something she'd begun doing when she was in high school. She planned to make something for herself today, and perhaps another time she would make something to take to Strasburg when she went to meet her grandparents in October.

Sara hummed as she picked out certain colors. "Think I'll make a scarf ring to wear with the blue scarf Mama loved so much." She continued to hum while separating out the various shades of blue beads. When Sara was a little girl, her mother used to hum to her when she was sick or had a hard time falling asleep. She recalled how the roles reversed when Mama became so ill. In fact, Sara had been humming to her mother when she passed away.

Pushing the painful memory aside, she picked up several more glass beads and turned her thoughts toward the Lapps. *Maybe when I do this again, I'll make Grandma a bracelet or necklace. And Grandpa might like a keychain.*

Sara could hardly wait to meet them and learn about her mother's childhood. She tried not to think of the short letter she'd received that seemed so impersonal. Sara wanted to believe she had misinterpreted her grandparents being too busy to meet her just yet. Even more so though, she had high hopes of finding out everything about her father. *I'm sure they must know who he is.*

Strasburg

When Brad arrived at the Lapps' place to pick up Sara, he found her kneeling outside the barn door, petting the Lapps' collie.

"Last night one of my grandpa's sows gave birth to fifteen piglets. Would you like to see them?" She stood up and motioned him over, while Sadie darted across the yard, chasing after a black-and-white cat.

"Sure." Brad joined Sara, and when they entered the barn, she led the way to the sow's stall.

"Just look at them. Aren't they cute?" Sara leaned over the gate, pointing to one of the smaller baby pigs. "That's the runt. Early this morning, I had to help the poor little thing find its way to the mama."

Brad smiled at the enthusiasm he saw on her face. "Pigs are sure cute when they're babies. But then I guess most animals are."

Nodding, Sara pulled back from the gate. "We can go now if you're ready. I just wanted you to see the piglets." A lock of her long auburn hair fell against her cheek as she stood up straight.

Instinctively, Brad reached out to brush it back in place. He was surprised when she flinched and drew her head back. "What's wrong? I only wanted to push that hair away from your eyes. Sorry if it seemed I was being too forward."

"Y–you startled me." Her chin trembled a bit.

Brad looked at her, feeling concern. "I'm sorry, Sara. I reacted on instinct."

A tiny crease formed just above her nose. "Do you always fix women's hair when it gets out of place?"

"No, no, that's not what I meant." Brad felt like a bumbling idiot all of a sudden. "Uh, I think maybe we should go before I say or do anything else stupid."

She gave a quick nod and practically ran out the barn door.

They hadn't gotten off to a good start this evening. Brad could only hope the rest of their time together would go smoothly.

East Earl, Pennsylvania

"Oh my word. I've never seen so much food in all my life." Michelle stared at all the stations loaded with a variety of food. There was something for everyone here at the Shady Maple Smorgasbord.

Brad chuckled. "I'm guessing it's the first time you've been here then."

She nodded. "If I tried a little of everything, you'd have to carry me out of here in a wheelbarrow."

His chuckle went deeper. "You're not only beautiful, but you have a sense of humor too."

A warm flush crept across Michelle's cheeks. Was Brad flirting with her? Had his touching her hair in the barn earlier meant something more than concern she might end up with it in her eyes? *Don't be ridiculous. You're reading more into it than there actually is. I'm sure Brad has no interest in me.*

"Well, let's dish up and get on back to our table." Brad gestured to the stack of plates on the end of one of the buffet stations. "You go first, Sara."

"Okay." Michelle chose all the things she liked best, and when she was satisfied with the amount on her plate, she filled her glass with iced tea and returned to their table. Brad wasn't far behind her.

When they sat down, he reached over and took her hand. "Do you mind if I pray before we eat?"

"No, that's fine." Thinking he would offer a silent prayer, the way Mary Ruth and Willis did, she bowed her head and closed her eyes. However, Michelle was surprised when Brad prayed out loud.

"Heavenly Father, we thank You for the food we're about to eat. Please bless it to the needs of our bodies, and thank You for the many hands who prepared it. And thanks for the opportunity to spend more time with Sara so we can get to know each other better. Amen."

Michelle opened her eyes and looked around. It made her uncomfortable when Brad began praying out loud, and she hoped no one else had heard him. She relaxed a bit when she saw that nobody seemed to be looking at them.

As they ate their meal, Michelle thought about her reaction when Brad pushed the hair out of her face in the barn. She had tried to act nonchalant, but inside she'd been shaking. She would never have admitted it to Brad, but his unexpected gesture brought back the memory of when Jerry slapped her face so hard that it left an imprint on her cheek.

Michelle set her fork down and drank some iced tea. *I should have known Brad would never do anything like that. He seems kind and gentle — an all-around nice guy. Maybe too nice for me.*

"I see your plate's almost empty." Brad broke into her thoughts. "Are you ready to check out all the pies, cakes, and other treats?"

Michelle held her stomach. "Oh boy. I'm not sure I have room for any dessert."

He flapped his hand. "Sure you do. No one leaves Shady Maple's without sampling at least one piece of pie or some cake and ice cream." He wiggled his eyebrows and stood. "You gonna join me?"

She groaned. "Okay. Why not?" Michelle followed Brad to the dessert stations. After perusing all the pies, she chose cherry.

"What? No shoofly pie?" Brad pointed to his plate. He'd taken a slice of shoofly, plus a couple of other kinds of pie.

"I don't know where you're going to put all that," she said when they returned to the table.

He patted his stomach. "I think there's still enough room in there."

Michelle shrugged. "Whatever you say. You must know your limits."

As they ate their pie, she decided to bring up the verse of scripture she'd found in the old jar that morning. "Since you're planning to become a preacher, I bet you know the Bible pretty well."

"Well, I'm certainly no expert, but I have studied the scriptures."

She folded her hands and placed them under her chin. "So could you tell me what a certain verse means?"

"I'll give it a shot. What verse is it?"

" 'Wherefore come out from among them, and be ye separate, saith the Lord, and touch not the unclean thing; and I will receive you. And will be a Father unto you, and ye shall be my sons and daughters, saith the Lord Almighty.' " Her forehead wrinkled. "I think I understand the first part, because that's what my Amish grandparents are doing. What I don't understand is how God can be anyone's father."

"God created everything and everyone," Brad explained. "So by creating us, He became our father. And when we accept Jesus Christ as God's Son, we also become God's son or daughter. Does that make sense?"

"I guess so." Michelle wasn't about to admit that not much about the Bible seemed logical to her. If not for the verses she'd found in the glass jar, she wouldn't even be acquainted with the scriptures. Although she'd been going to church with Willis and Mary Ruth every other Sunday, everything was spoken in a language she couldn't understand, so it all seemed quite confusing. And anything she'd learned when attending Bible school a few times as a girl had gone in one ear and out the other.

"Do you own a Bible, Sara?" Brad questioned.

She shook her head "I read the verse on a slip of paper I found at the Lapps' — I mean, my grandparents'."

"Maybe what you need is a study Bible. It would help explain many of the verses found in the Bible."

"Why would I need a special Bible to study? All I was asking about was just one verse."

He touched the back of his neck. "I figured if you had a question about one verse, there might be others."

"Maybe." Feeling the need for a change of subject, Michelle finished the rest of her pie and asked if he was ready to go.

Brad looked down at his empty plate and nodded. "I couldn't eat another bite."

"I can imagine."

He smiled and gave her a wink.

As they left the restaurant and began walking toward his van, Michelle struggled with her emotions. *As much as I enjoy Brad's company, I feel guilty when I'm in his presence. Does he know I am hiding a secret?*

Chapter 25

Strasburg

Monday morning while Mary Ruth gathered eggs, Michelle went down to the basement to get some empty jars to use for canning tomatoes. After the snake incident, she'd been relieved when Mary Ruth said she would resume her previous job of getting the eggs every day. Just the thought of seeing that ugly black snake in the nest sent shivers up Michelle's spine. She hoped she wouldn't find anything frightening in the unfinished basement.

The cement floor had numerous cracks zig-zagging across it, and the rusty drain near the antiquated wringer washing machine looked nasty. The air smelled of mildew mixed with the milder scent of laundry detergent drifting out of an open box on a shelf near the washer. The natural light coming from two small windows positioned high on the wall helped the basement seem not quite so dreary.

To provide more light in the room, Michelle had taken a battery-operated lantern. The gas lamps hanging throughout most of the Lapps' home were good sources of light, as well as heat, but Michelle always felt a bit nervous whenever she had to ignite one. The last thing she needed was to cause an explosion or set the room on fire, for lack of paying close enough attention.

A spray of dust sifted into Michelle's face when she pulled a cardboard box marked CANNING JARS off one of the shelves. She managed to place it on a metal table a few seconds before a sneeze overtook her. She needed a tissue, but there were none in her pocket. *Oh great. Just what I don't need right now.* Michelle didn't want to go clear back upstairs for something to blow her nose on, but she needed to take care of this matter now.

She looked around, hoping there might be something down here she could use. An old towel or even a clean rag would do. Michelle felt relief when she spotted a roll of paper towels standing beside the box of laundry detergent. Quickly tearing one off before another sneeze came, she blew her nose and threw the soiled paper towel in the garbage next to the washing machine. *Now back to business.*

Lifting the light so she had a better look at all the shelves lining the walls, Michelle spotted a box marked, Rhoda's Toys. Curious to see what was inside, she took the box down, set it on the floor, and opened the flaps. Inside, she found a cloth doll with no face, several children's books, a coloring book, two small boxes of crayons, and a variety of miniature kitchen utensils. Apparently Mary Ruth hadn't been able to part with these things her daughter used to play with.

Michelle's heart clenched, thinking how devastating it must have been for the Lapps when their only daughter ran off and never contacted them again. Although Michelle hadn't run off from her own parents, she often wondered if they ever thought about her or wished things had been different. Had Mom and Dad sought help for their problems — particularly Dad's drinking, which had been a major cause for most of his abuse?

As she stood to return the box to the shelf, Michelle noticed an old jar toward the back. Looking closer she saw it was full of folded papers. The glass container appeared to be similar to the one she'd found in the barn, only this one was light green instead of pale blue.

Michelle climbed up on a stepstool she'd discovered and took the jar down. Then she used the top step of the stool as a seat and sat down. Michelle wasn't about to go back to the kitchen until she'd seen what kind of messages this antique vessel contained.

With anticipation, she reached into the jar and removed the paper closest to the top. Unfolding it, she saw a Bible verse: *"When thou passest through the waters, I will be with thee; and through the rivers, they shall not overflow thee: when thou walketh through the fire, thou shall not be burned; neither shall the flame kindle upon thee." Isaiah 43:2.*

Following the verse, a prayer had been written: *"Dear Lord, please walk beside me during this distressing time in my life. Guide me, direct me, and lead the way."*

Michelle's pulse raced. *Whoever wrote that must have been dealing with a challenge or going through something awful. I wonder what the problem was and how it all turned out. If only these walls could talk.*

She glanced around the dingy basement, inspecting each of the metal and wooden shelves. *Could there be more jars full of messages hidden here or someplace else?* This whole jar thing seemed like an unsolved mystery — one Michelle might never know the answer to.

"Where have you been, Son?" Ezekiel's mother pressed her thin lips together. "Our supper guest is here, and it's time to eat." She gestured to Lenore, standing near the kitchen table.

"Hello, Ezekiel. It's nice to see you again." Lenore offered him a fleeting smile, then took out four plates and began setting the table.

"Nice to see you too." Until this moment, it had slipped Ezekiel's mind that Lenore would be coming over. He'd thought her visit was going to be earlier in the day and was surprised to find out she'd be staying for supper. If Mom had told him the specifics, he must have forgotten. As far as Ezekiel knew, Lenore's reason for coming by was to pick out a plant from the greenhouse for her mother's upcoming birthday.

He pulled his fingers through the back of his thick hair. *I wonder if Lenore came over while I was gone this afternoon, and then Mom decided to invite her to join us for supper. Or could my matchmaking mother have set the whole thing up earlier so I'd have no choice but to spend time with Ivan Lapp's daughter?*

Ezekiel's mother would never admit it — especially to him — but she had been trying to get them together as a couple for the last two years. Well, it wouldn't work. It wasn't that Ezekiel had anything against Lenore. She was kind of pretty, in a plain sort of way, and also quite intelligent. But they didn't have much in common. Besides, she had already joined the church and was committed to being Amish. Not a good fit for him, since he still had visions of being part of the English world once he figured out how to tell his mom and dad.

Ezekiel could only imagine the tongue lashing he'd receive if either of his folks knew he'd bought a truck and had parked it behind the home of Raymond's parents. Dad didn't like that his brother Arnold was more lenient with his children and looked the other way when they went through their running-around years. He thought Arnold should make his young people toe the line, the way he'd always tried to do.

"Well, don't just stand there, boy." Dad stepped up to Ezekiel and tapped his shoulder. "Let's get washed up so we can eat our meal."

"Jah." Ezekiel followed his dad down the hall to the bathroom. He groaned inwardly.

After working most of the day at the greenhouse and then taking care of his bees this afternoon, all he wanted to do was relax. Company for dinner was not what he'd planned on at all.

As Michelle sat with Willis and Mary Ruth, eating supper that evening, she thought about the jar she'd found in the basement. *I wonder how many more there might be hidden around the Lapps' farm.* Who had authored the notes she'd found was also a puzzle.

Michelle glanced over at Mary Ruth, who was sitting straight up in her chair while eating a spoonful of scalloped potatoes. *Was it her? Could she have placed those secret notes in the jars when she was going through some difficult times? Does Willis know anything about them?* To ask might open up old wounds for either one of them. No, it was better to say nothing. Michelle had already created a problem for the Lapps when she'd come here under false pretenses. Once she left Strasburg, she would leave the old prayer jars and the notes in them behind.

"Your scalloped potatoes and pork chops are appeditlich, and so is my favorite sauerkraut salad." Willis looked over at his wife with a tender expression. "You spoil me so good."

Mary Ruth chuckled. "You always say that, Husband."

"Course I do, 'cause it's the truth."

Michelle nodded in agreement. "Your food is real tasty, Grandma. I wouldn't be surprised if I haven't put on some weight since I've been here."

"I'm glad you two are enjoying the meal, but with all these nice things you've said, I'm having a hard time not letting it go to my head." Mary Ruth fanned her face with her paper napkin. "And you know what they say about *hocmut.*"

"What does that word mean?" Michelle asked.

"It means 'pride,' " Willis explained. "Although not in these exact words, the Bible says, *'Der hochmut kummt vor dem fall.'* " He looked at Michelle, while tapping his knuckles on the table. "The translation is: 'Pride comes before the fall.' "

"I see." From all that Michelle had observed about this couple, neither of them had a prideful bone in their body. In addition to their kindness, both were the most humble, genuine people she'd ever known.

Willis and Mary Ruth bantered back and forth about several topics for a bit, before

Mary Ruth turned to face Michelle, placing her hand gently on Michelle's arm. "You looked tired this evening. Did I work you too hard canning tomatoes?"

Michelle shook her head. "I am kinda tired though. I think the heat and humidity is getting to me."

"That makes sense, since you're probably used to having air-conditioning," Willis interjected. "Here, in order to cool off, we have to hope a cool breeze comes up when we have the windows open. Or if it gets too hot, we'll find shade underneath one of the tall, leafy trees in our yard and sit a spell with a glass of cold tea or lemonade."

"Actually, I've never lived in a place with air-conditioning."

Mary Ruth tipped her head. "Really? Not even when you were growing up?"

Michelle opened then closed her mouth, as she struggled to find the right words. "Um . . . no, not even when I was a young girl. My folks didn't spend their hard-earned money on things they didn't really need."

"Makes sense to me." Willis reached over and gave Mary Ruth's hand a few taps. "Guess we did something right when we raised our son and daughter. Ivan learned how to be frugal, and it's nice to know that

Rhoda did too."

Thinking it would be a good time to raise a question she'd been pondering, Michelle asked, "Were Ivan and Rhoda — I mean my mom — the only children you had?"

Mary Ruth dropped her gaze to the table. "We had a son, but he had a heart condition and died when he was two months old. We were thankful for the time we had with him though, as well as the chance to raise our other two children."

Tears came quickly to Mary Ruth's eyes, and she excused herself from the table. As soon as she left the room, Willis slowly shook his head, looking sadly at Michelle. "Your grandmother is pretty sensitive when it comes to the baby we lost. Even though it's been a good many years ago, I don't think she's ever completely gotten over it."

Michelle wasn't sure what to say in response. She was sorry she'd asked the question. This poor couple had been through a lot, and they deserved to be happy.

Lacking the right words, she reached over and patted Willis's arm. *I'll bet Mary Ruth wrote all those notes after Rhoda left home. That must be why many of the messages seem so sullen. She was grieving for the loss of not one, but two of her children.*

■ ■ ■ ■

Ezekiel could hardly get a bite of food in his mouth because Lenore kept asking him questions. When she wasn't talking, his little brother Henry babbled on about a bunch of unimportant things.

"What did you do today?" Lenore's focus remained on Ezekiel.

"Worked in the greenhouse for a while, then took some honey from my beehives." He picked up his fork, but before he could put a piece of roast beef in his mouth, another question came.

"Will you be attending the young people's singing this Sunday evening?"

Ezekiel shrugged his shoulders. "Probably, but I'm not sure."

She smiled. "I am planning to go. I always enjoy our time of singing and the games we play beforehand."

"The food that's served is always good too," Ezekiel's brother Abe interjected.

Amy snickered and nudged him with her elbow. "You would say something like that. You always have food on your mind."

"Not so." Abe shook his head. "I think about my job workin' for the buggy maker, and also playing volleyball with my friends, which I'll be doin' Sunday night at the singing."

"Sounds like all you young people are planning to go to Sunday's gathering, and that's a good thing." Dad passed the potatoes to Ezekiel for a second helping. "Your mamm and I used to look forward to the singings when we were courting." Wiggling his brows, he gave her a quick glance. "Gave us a chance to spend more time together — especially on the drive to and from the event."

Mom nodded with an enthusiastic grin. "I remember those days well." She cast a sidelong glance in Ezekiel's direction. "Half the fun of attending young people's gatherings is the chance to visit with your date as you travel to and from."

Ezekiel clenched his fork so hard he thought it might bend. He hoped Lenore wasn't expecting him to take her to the singing or offer a ride home from the event. He didn't really want to go, but his folks would be disappointed if he didn't. So since he'd most likely attend, he wanted to go with Sara. He planned to ask her when they got together for another driving lesson later this week. He hoped she would say yes.

"Say, Mom, what's for dessert?" Henry looked at their mother with an expectant expression.

"I made a lemon shoofly pie this morning." She looked at Dad and smiled. "Because it's your daed's favorite."

Tilting his chin, Henry frowned. "Is that all we're havin'? You know I don't like lemon so much."

Mom gestured to the refrigerator. "There's a chocolate-and-peanut-butter pie in there too. Think you might be able to eat a piece of that?"

Henry lifted his chin, and his blue eyes brightened. "Jah, sure. I could probably eat more'n one."

Mom chuckled, and Dad ruffled Henry's hair. "Bet you could eat the whole pie."

Ezekiel was glad someone else had been able to get in a few words, squelching Lenore's constant prattle. But just when he thought he was in the clear, she turned in his direction again. It appeared that Lenore was about to say something when Amy spoke up.

"What have you been doing this summer, Lenore, now that you're not teaching school?"

Lenore blotted her lips with a napkin and smiled. "I've been working part-time at my folk's general store. I've also done a lot of gardening, and even had some time to do a bit of bird watching. Why, the other day when I was outside pulling some weeds, I spotted a . . ."

Lenore's words were muted as Ezekiel's thoughts pulled inward again. He was pleased that someone else was conversing with the schoolteacher, and he would be even happier when this evening was over.

CHAPTER 26

During breakfast the following morning, Ezekiel's mother kept looking at him as though she wanted to say something. But every time she opened her mouth, Dad cut in. It almost seemed as if he was doing it on purpose. Normally, he wasn't this talkative. Especially if he was in a hurry to eat and get outside to prepare the greenhouse for the day's business.

When everyone finished breakfast, Dad grabbed his straw hat and started for the back door. "You coming, Ezekiel?"

"Jah, I'll be right behind you."

"You too, Henry." Dad looked over his shoulder at Ezekiel's younger brother. "Your help is also needed in the greenhouse today."

"Okay, Daadi." Henry practically jumped out of his seat and raced across the room. The boy always seemed eager to do whatever Dad said. No doubt there would be no question about whether Henry joined the church when he grew up. He'd apply for membership, if for no other reason than to please their parents. Ezekiel, on the other hand, wasn't that compliant. He just needed more courage to speak up and say what was on his mind.

Soon after Dad and Henry went out, Ezekiel picked up his straw hat and started across the room. He'd no more than put it on his head and grabbed hold of the doorknob when Mom hollered, "Wait a minute, Son. I want to ask you a question."

He let go of the knob and turned to face her, glancing briefly at his sister, who had begun to clear the dishes and put them in the sink. "What's up, Mom?"

She left her place at the table and stepped up to him. "I was wondering if you've decided yet whether you'll be going to the singing this Sunday."

Ezekiel's toes curled inside his boots. *I shoulda known this was coming.* "Jah, Mom, I'll most likely go."

"Good to hear." A slow smile spread across her face. "Have you considered inviting Lenore to go with you? She's not being courted by anyone, you know."

He cringed. *Should have expected that too.* "No, Mom, I won't be inviting Lenore.

Thought I'd see if Sara might like to go."

Her dark eyebrows lifted, and she swiped a finger down her suntanned face. "The Lapps' other granddaughter?"

He nodded.

Before Mom could respond, Amy turned from the sink and pointed at him. "I knew it, Brother. You're sweet on Sara, aren't you?" Her chin jutted out as she smirked at him.

Feeling the heat of embarrassment cover his face, Ezekiel tugged at his shirt collar. It felt like it was choking his neck. "I'm not sweet on anyone. Sara and I are just friends."

"I hope that's true, Son." Tapping one bare foot and then the other, Mom jumped back into the conversation. "Sara's not Amish, and she won't be staying with her grandparents forever. So don't get too attached to her. Lenore's a better choice for you, and she's already joined the church."

Ezekiel's jaw tensed. He was on the verge of telling his mother that he had no plans to court Lenore, much less join the Amish church, but something held him back. He would never admit it to anyone, but there were times when the thought of going English sent shivers of apprehension up his spine. Ezekiel had been blessed with the support of his family for so long, he wasn't sure he could make it in the English world without them. Even so, his curiosity with modern things and desire to try some of them out kept him unable to give up his dream. It was stupid to be on the fence about this. He wished someone he trusted would tell him which way to go. For now though, there was only one place for Ezekiel to go, and that was out to the greenhouse.

"I need to go help Dad." He glanced at his sister, then back at his mother. "I'll talk to you later, Mom."

"Okay. Tell your daed I'll join you all in the greenhouse once Amy and I get the dishes done."

"Sure, I'll tell him." Ezekiel went out the door. Even though it was obvious that Mom wasn't fond of the idea of him asking a young woman who wasn't Amish to the singing, he looked forward to seeing Sara this Friday afternoon. Not only did he enjoy her company, but being in her presence strengthened his desire to leave the Amish world behind.

The morning had started out humid, and as Michelle made her way to the barn, she paused to wipe her sweaty forehead. She'd seen Brad briefly when he came to pick up

Willis for a dental appointment. She wished she could have talked to him longer, but maybe there would be an opportunity when he and Willis returned. She hadn't seen Brad since they went to the Shady Maple, and she had a few more questions about the Bible she wanted to ask.

When Michelle entered the barn, she was greeted by her frisky pup and his mother, both wanting to play.

She bent to pet each of their heads, then shooed them away. "Not now, you two. I want to check on the piglets, and I volunteered to help Mary Ruth bake some bread this morning."

The dogs tipped their heads and looked up at her as if they understood every word she'd said. Then Sadie gave a deep bark, and Rascal followed with a weak imitation, before both dogs raced out of the barn.

Michelle snickered. In the beginning, she was unsure about living around so many animals, but she felt differently now and was thankful for the opportunity to spend time with most of the critters here on the Lapps' farm.

It seems I really could be a farm girl, Michelle mused. She smiled, remembering how when she'd first arrived at the Lapps' farm, she had to convince herself that she could do this. Everything seemed so foreign and quaint. Michelle wasn't sure back then that she could even last a day, much less all these weeks.

Hearing the distinctive squeal of pigs, Michelle made her way over to Penny's stall. She stood for a while, watching the piglets nurse, and a peaceful feeling encompassed her. It was fun to watch the little babies wiggling around and crawling over each other, as they competed to get to their mother's milk.

Michelle couldn't believe in the nearly two months she'd been here how much she had come to love this place. She'd learned to bake, cook, tend the animals, and even drive a horse and buggy. She felt comfortable wearing less makeup and plainer clothes too. Even the emotional pain she had endured in the past seemed to be slowly receding. She had begun to feel as if living here with the Lapps was where she belonged.

Wish there was something I could do to keep the real Sara from coming here to meet her grandparents — or at least prolong it further.

She tapped her chin. *Maybe there is. I can write her another letter, pretending to be Mary Ruth, and say October's not a good time either. Or I could even say they've changed their minds about meeting her at all.*

Michelle heaved a sigh. But that would be heaping one lie on top of another. Mary Ruth and Willis did want to get to know their granddaughter. Trouble was, they believed they already were. Well, she had all of August and September to decide what to do. Meanwhile, Michelle would enjoy every minute possible with Mary Ruth, Willis, Ezekiel, and Brad. They had all become like family to her.

Michelle sucked in her bottom lip. *If they knew what I did, they'd probably turn their backs on me, and any trust they once had would evaporate like ice on a hot summer day.*

Michelle took one last look at the baby pigs and went back across the barn. If she had time to look at some of the notes in the prayer jar again, it might help her decide what to do. But Mary Ruth was waiting for her, so it would be better to get the jar down some other day when no one else was around. Right now, Michelle had no choice but to keep up her charade.

Brad and Willis pulled into the drive at the same moment as Sara stepped out of the house to shake a tablecloth. Before Brad even got out of the truck, the wonderful aroma of fresh bread wafted from the home's open windows.

"Smells like the women have been doin' some baking in there." Willis grinned. "I know what I'll be having for lunch today."

Brad smiled. "I'm heading to the barn to start on the chores you asked me to do."

"I'll be out to help just as soon as I tell Mary Ruth I'm home and see if I can snitch a piece of bread. Ya want one too?"

"Sure, if she can spare it I'd enjoy a piece." Brad watched as Willis headed for the house just as Sara stepped back inside. Brad was disappointed that she hadn't waved, but apparently Sara hadn't seen him. Hopefully he could catch her sometime later.

When Willis and Mary Ruth went to the living room to chat, Michelle began washing up the utensils and bread pans. Earlier, she and Mary Ruth had put on a pot of chicken-corn soup that still simmered. They'd also made two pies, several batches of cookies, and four loaves of bread.

Michelle was tired and wondered where Mary Ruth got her stamina to do all this baking in one morning. The kitchen felt stifling, with no air coming through the windows on this muggy day.

She paused from her chores to wipe the

sweat on her brow as she looked out the window. The tree branches were still, suggesting there wasn't a hint of air moving out there. As Michelle washed the next bread pan, she spotted Brad working in the corral on a fence board that had come loose.

Her hands remained in the soapy water, but she couldn't take her eyes off him. He had removed his shirt as he worked out under the blazing sun. Even from here, Michelle could see the sweat gleaming on his back. *I'll bet he could use a break and something cold to drink.*

Michelle dried her hands and took a tall mug from the cupboard, then filled it with iced tea. When she walked by the table, she grabbed a few cookies and wrapped them in a napkin, which she put in her apron pocket. She also draped a hand towel over her arm, in case Brad wanted to wash up, and then headed out the door.

"Sorry to interrupt, but I brought you something," Michelle called as she approached the corral.

"No problem, I was done with this project anyway and am ready to move on to the next one Willis wants done." He stopped his work and leaned against the fence post. "Is it a piece of bread? Willis said he might bring me one."

She shook her head and held out the cookies and mug of cold tea. "Willis — I mean Grandpa — popped into the kitchen for a minute, but then he and Grandma went to the living room to talk. Guess he must have forgotten about the bread."

Brad gave her a dimpled grin. "Well, I'm grateful for the break and appreciate the cookies and cold drink. This tea sure looks inviting." Brad gulped down the icy cold drink.

Michelle watched his Adams apple move each time he took a swallow. When some of the tea dribbled down his chin and over his throat, she resisted the temptation to wipe it off for him.

Brad emptied the glass and used the back of his hand to wipe the moisture from his mouth. He drank the rest of the tea so quickly, Michelle wished she'd brought two mugs instead of one.

"I brought you a towel so you can clean up when you're finished with the fence."

"Thanks. That was thoughtful of you. I'll wash my face and hands before I eat the cookies." Brad took the towel, went over to the hose, and turned it on.

Michelle watched as he rinsed off. She couldn't help noticing the water trickle down his broad shoulders and corded stomach muscles just below his chest. For a fleeting moment, she wondered how it would feel to have his strong arms holding her close.

She looked away, the heat of embarrassment flooding her face. *I hope he didn't notice me staring at him.* The hard work Brad had been doing this summer had obviously given him this healthy physique.

"Would you like some more ice tea?" Michelle asked, hoping her voice didn't sound as shaky as she felt at the moment. "I can go in and bring out more."

"Maybe, before I start work on the next project, but let's sit and visit a few minutes first."

Michelle took a seat at the picnic table while Brad grabbed his T-shirt from the fence post where he'd hung it earlier and pulled it on down over his head.

"Okay." Michelle sat quietly as Brad seated himself across from her and then she handed him the napkin and cookies.

"Thanks."

"You're welcome."

Brad had the prettiest blue eyes, and today they looked even bluer because his face had a healthy tan. For the moment, Michelle was at a loss for words.

"What's wrong? Do I have cookie crumbs

on my face?"

"Uh, no. I just can't think of anything to say right now." All thoughts of asking Brad more about the Bible vanished, like a thief in the night. There was no question about it — Brad was different than any man she'd ever known. And it wasn't only his good looks.

Brad was surprised at how quiet Sara had become. All the times he'd been with her before, she'd been quite talkative. "Maybe I will have some more iced tea," he said to break the silence.

"Sure, no problem." Sara got up and made a dash for the house, leaving Brad's empty mug on the picnic table. He watched her ponytail bounce as she approached the back porch.

Brad had a hard time understanding Sara sometimes. One minute she seemed happy and chatty, and the next minute her mood turned sullen. He wondered if he'd said something to offend her; although he couldn't think of what it could be.

When she didn't return right away, Brad went to the toolshed to get out what he needed to repair the corral gate, which was close to falling off. Poor Willis couldn't keep up with all the work around this place. It was a shame some of his family didn't live here on the farm with him and Mary Ruth. An elderly couple shouldn't be by themselves with so many responsibilities. *But then, maybe they enjoy the challenge of taking care of their home and property,* he told himself. *That's what probably keeps them going.*

Brad's concern for others was almost his downfall. He often worked too hard and didn't spend enough time having fun, but he'd always been the compassionate sort — often putting other's needs ahead of his own.

He'd just gotten into position to begin working on the gate when Sara returned with another mug full of tea. "Sorry for taking so long." She pushed a wayward piece of hair back in place. "I was helping Mary Ruth get lunch on the table, and they wanted me to extend an invitation for you to join them."

"That sounds good. Guess Willis doesn't plan on helping me do any work till after he eats." Brad rubbed the back of his neck where a mosquito had bit. *Or is the elderly man getting forgetful?*

Sara flapped both hands in front of her face. "Whew! I believe the humidity has become even thicker. What I wouldn't give to be in an air-conditioned room right now."

"I know what you mean. Say, before we go inside to eat, I'd like to ask you something."

"What's that?"

"If you're not busy Friday night, would you like to go out with me for an ice-cream cone or some other sweet treat?"

"Sure, I'd love to." Michelle gathered up the empty mug and headed back toward the house. Halfway there, she turned and called, "Are you coming, Brad?"

"Yep. I'm right behind you." He might not get the chance to see Sara too many more times before he left for seminary in a few weeks, so he was glad she'd accepted his invitation to go out Friday night. He thumped his forehead. *What am I doing? I need to stop thinking about that young woman all the time. Even though I enjoy being with Sara, she may not be the right girl for me.*

Chapter 27

Friday afternoon, as Mary Ruth took clothes off the line, she reflected on the enjoyable time she and Willis had with Sara last evening. It had been another warm day, so they'd eaten supper outside on the picnic table. Willis cooked steaks on the barbecue grill, and Mary Ruth served potato salad, dilled green beans, coleslaw, and corn on the cob. For dessert, they'd enjoyed refreshing raspberry sherbet.

After the meal, the three of them had sat on the porch and visited as they waited for the fireflies to make an appearance. The only downside was that Sara seemed quieter than usual. They'd be talking about something, and then Sara would stare off into space, as though her thoughts were someplace else. Mary Ruth wondered if their granddaughter might have grown tired of them by now and felt ready to return to her home. She debated about bringing up the topic, but decided it might be best to wait and see if Sara brought it up herself.

Bringing her thoughts back in line, Mary Ruth looked to her right, watching as Sara stood on the porch, shaking the braided throw rugs that went inside the front and back doors. She was a hard worker and never complained when asked to do a task. With the exception of not wanting to gather eggs since she'd seen the snake, Sara seemed to have adapted well to farm life.

Mary Ruth removed a kitchen towel from the line and dropped it into the wicker basket. *Would Sara ever consider giving up her English life to become Amish? Is it too much to hope that she might want to stay here permanently?* This topic had crossed Mary Ruth's mind multiple times, and she'd also discussed it with Willis. Like her, Willis wanted their granddaughter to stay, but he'd reminded Mary Ruth often that it was Sara's choice.

If only Rhoda hadn't run off, we could have known our granddaughter since she was a boppli. Mary Ruth shook her head. But if she'd stayed here, would she have married an Amish man, and if so, who would she have chosen? The man she had married was obviously English, since she hadn't run off with any young Amish men in the area — at least no one they knew about. Who knew what secrets their daughter had kept from them during her time of running around?

Life is full of choices. Mary Ruth stared up at the billowy clouds overhead. *By choosing one direction, it takes us down a certain path, but a different direction would lead to another.* She supposed it did no good to ponder the outcome of either.

"Can I help you finish taking the laundry off the line?" Sara asked, stepping into the yard.

Mary Ruth smiled. "I appreciate the offer, but I'm almost done." She gestured to the few remaining clothes on the line.

"Is there something else you would like me to do before we start supper?"

"I can't think of anything at the moment." Mary Ruth turned at the sound of a horse and buggy approaching. She wasn't surprised to see Ezekiel's rig pulling in. He'd been coming around a lot lately. Mary Ruth was pleased that he'd been teaching Sara how to handle a horse and buggy. Although neither had admitted it — at least not to her — she had a feeling something more than friendship was developing between Ezekiel and Sara. This in itself might be enough to keep Sara in Lancaster County. Of course, Brad seemed to have taken an interest in her too, but he had no plans to stay in the area permanently. Once Brad got his minister's license, he could be called to preach at a church in a different state.

One more thing I shouldn't worry about, Mary Ruth reprimanded herself. *The man our granddaughter chooses will be up to her, and the same holds true about where she will live.*

Michelle went up to Ezekiel's buggy as soon as he stepped down. He grinned at her. "Hey, I haven't seen you for several days. How are you doing?"

"Okay. How about you?"

"I'm fine too. Came over to see if you have time to go for another buggy-driving lesson?"

"You mean today?"

He nodded. "Thought maybe we could take a ride in my truck too."

"I can't today because it'll be time to help my grandma with supper soon."

Ezekiel's shoulders slumped. "I didn't realize it was getting so late. Could we go after supper?"

"Sorry, but I have plans this evening."

"Oh, I see." Tilting his chin down, Ezekiel cleared his throat. "There's something else I wanted to ask."

"What's that?"

"This Sunday evening there's gonna be a young people's singing. I was wondering if you'd like to go with me."

Michelle smiled. "Sure. I haven't been to one before, and I think it would be fun."

He rubbed his hands together. "Sounds good. I don't always go to the singings, but since you'll be with me, I'll look forward to going to this one."

Lancaster

Friday night came, and the humidity had not lifted one bit. They drove with the windows down, and Brad couldn't help noticing Sara's auburn hair lifting off her shoulders as the breeze from the open windows cooled them. He could have turned on the air-conditioning, but sometimes, a breeze — even a warm one — felt nice when driving.

"At least we are getting some air." Sara pulled her hair back and wrapped a rubber band around it, making a long ponytail. Brad wished she had left it down.

They pulled into the ice-cream store's parking lot. "Well, here we are." He grinned at her. "Should we order at the window instead of going inside?"

"Sure, that's fine with me."

They got out of Brad's van, walked up to the window, and ordered two strawberry ice-cream cones. Then they sat at an outside table, away from the others, to enjoy the refreshing, cool treat.

If Brad didn't know any better, he'd swear this was couple's night as he glanced at the other patrons who'd also chosen to sit outside. For an ice-cream store, it was kind of odd not to see any children with their families milling around. But all the tables were occupied by couples. Most of them looked to be about the same age as he and Sara, but Brad also noticed another couple — an elderly man and woman, both with silver hair. While eating their dishes of ice cream, the older couple laughed and enjoyed a conversation together as if they were the only two people in the world. *I hope someday I'll find my soul mate — someone I'm madly in love with — and we can spend the rest of our lives growing old together.*

Brad took a long look at Sara. Could she be that person? He certainly enjoyed Sara's company, but he needed to know more about her.

"This is a nice way to spend the evening. I'm glad you invited me." Sara wiped a dribble of ice cream off her chin.

Brad nodded. "There's nothing like a

frozen treat to help cool down in this heat."

"True."

When Sara finished her cone, he asked if she would like another.

She shook her head. "That was good, but one's enough for me. You go ahead and get another cone if you want to though."

"No, I'm good too. If you're not in a hurry to go, let's stay here and talk for a while."

"Okay." Sara settled against her chair. "Tell me more about your schooling."

"What would you like to know?"

"How long will it be before you start preaching at a church?"

"It'll be a few years yet." Brad leaned his elbows on the table, looking at her intently. "I'll be leaving for seminary on September 2nd, and then it will be an intense couple of years as I train for the ministry."

"Won't you miss Lancaster County after you're gone?"

"I'll admit, I've enjoyed driving for some of the Amish in the area and working on the local farms during the summer, so yeah, I most likely will miss it. The jobs I've done gave me a chance to do something physical, not to mention clear my head after all my studies, which can be mentally exhausting." Brad smiled. "But my goal is to be a minister, and it's what I need to do." He pointed at Sara. "What about you? What goals have you set for yourself?"

Sara dropped her gaze. "I have no goals."

"Nothing at all?"

"Nope."

His brows furrowed. "What about your grandparents? Surely you have some goals that involve spending time with them in the future."

She pulled in her bottom lip. "Well, I don't know. You see, the truth is . . ." Sara's voice trailed off. "Oh, never mind. I just live from moment to moment, that's all."

Brad had the feeling there was something she wasn't telling him. Should he press to find out what is was, or let it drop? He didn't want Sara to think he was being pushy.

A knot formed in Michelle's stomach. She had been caught off guard when Brad asked about her future goals, and she'd almost blurted out the truth of her deception. Thankfully, she had caught herself in time. Brad was a good person — maybe even righteous. He would look down on her and probably insist she come clean with the Lapps. Any good feelings he may have had for Michelle, who he believed was Sara, would be tossed out like yesterday's garbage.

She wouldn't blame him either. These last few months, as much as Michelle had enjoyed having Mary Ruth and Willis as her pretend grandparents, she'd begun to loath herself for lying to them. It was wrong to take advantage of those good people, and the only way to resolve the situation was for her to go. *Maybe I could ask Brad to drop me off somewhere when it's time for him to leave for seminary.*

She shifted in her chair, wondering how she would explain her reason for going at that particular time. *It might be best if I don't involve Brad. My problem is not his, and when he goes off to finish his schooling, I'll never see him again.*

Brad reached across the small table and placed his hand on hers. "Is something bothering you, Sara? I'm a pretty good listener, so if you'd like to talk about it, I'm willing to listen."

She shook her head. "No, I'm fine. I was thinking about how after you leave for seminary, we'll probably never see each other again."

"Well, you never know. Our paths might cross again someday. Maybe some time when you're visiting your grandparents, I'll make a trip to Strasburg, and we'll reconnect."

Michelle's voice lowered to a near whisper. "That would be nice."

As Ezekiel approached the ice-cream store in Lancaster, he decided to stop for a treat. He'd had a busy week helping his parents in the greenhouse and delivering honey to his loyal customers. So this evening, he figured he deserved a break, and it was a good chance to take his truck out for a spin.

Ezekiel let go of the steering wheel with one hand and swiped his arm across his sweaty forehead. He couldn't wait for this humidity to break. While he had been talking to one of his customers today, they'd mentioned the news said the hot, sticky weather would finally end on Saturday when storms were expected to come through, leaving a swath of cool, comfortable temperatures for the next several days. Ezekiel sure hoped it was true. He looked forward to taking Sara to the singing Sunday evening and would appreciate good weather.

When Ezekiel pulled his vehicle into the parking lot, he was surprised to see Brad and Sara there, getting up from a table and heading to Brad's van. They hugged before stepping up and into the vehicle.

Ezekiel drew back, feeling like someone had punched him in the stomach. Was this a date they were on? Is this what Sara meant when she said she had plans for the evening?

He sat hunched over the steering wheel, watching as Brad's van pulled out of the parking lot. He'd suddenly lost his appetite for ice cream or anything else.

Ezekiel's scalp prickled. *Of course Sara would rather spend time with Brad. She's English and so is he. I'll bet she only accepted my invitation to go to Sunday's singing so she wouldn't hurt my feelings. If I were English or she was Amish, maybe something more could develop between Sara and me.*

Even though Ezekiel had often wondered about being English, his feelings weren't as complicated or as confusing before Sara came along. Spending time with her had caused him to think about being English even more.

Chapter 28

Strasburg

On the way home from church Sunday afternoon, Mary Ruth turned in her seat to look at Sara. "I know we ate after church was dismissed, but it wasn't a big meal. How would you like to go on a picnic with your grandpa and me?"

Sara's pretty blue-green eyes sparkled. "Sounds like fun. Would we have it in your backyard?"

"Nope," Willis spoke up. "We'll go to the pond out beyond our place. Unless you got adventuresome and ventured there on your own, I don't think you've seen it yet." He glanced back at her and grinned. "The ole' pond is one of my favorite fishing holes."

"I have seen a few ponds in the area, but I don't believe I've been to the one you're talking about. Are we gonna do some fishing today?" Sara asked.

He shook his head. "I never fish on Sundays. Besides, you'll be going to the singing with Ezekiel later today, and we wouldn't want to hold you up for that."

"Okay, but can we go fishing some other time?"

"Sure thing. We'll try to make time for that."

Mary Ruth smiled. "Your mother enjoyed fishing. But then I guess you knew that, right?"

Silence.

Mary Ruth turned to look at Sara again. "Did you hear what I asked?"

Sara blinked rapidly. "Umm . . . What was it?"

"I mentioned that your mother liked to fish and asked if you knew it."

Forehead wrinkling, Sara slowly nodded.

Sara seems kind of off today. I wonder if something's bothering her. Mary Ruth glanced at Willis to see if he'd also noticed, but his concentration appeared to be on the road.

"I miss your mother so much," Mary Ruth murmured, "but I'm thankful to God for bringing you here."

Once more, Sara was silent. Perhaps she was also missing her mother. It probably wasn't a good idea to talk about Rhoda so much, but Mary Ruth couldn't help it.

■ ■ ■ ■

As Michelle rode in Ezekiel's open buggy on the way to the singing that evening, all she could think about were Mary Ruth's questions this afternoon — first on the way home from church and again during their picnic lunch. Previously, Michelle had managed to make things up when either Mary Ruth or Willis asked about their daughter. At first she'd been quiet and unresponsive when Mary Ruth began questioning her today, but as time went on and more questions were asked, she'd given the best answers she could. Apparently, whatever she'd said must have been satisfactory, because Mary Ruth finally quit asking and talked about other things. In fact, by the time they'd arrived back at the Lapps', Michelle's pretend grandma wore a peaceful expression.

Too bad I didn't feel a sense of peace, Michelle thought with regret. *I don't know if I'll ever feel any tranquility or sense of harmony in my life.* She shifted on her seat. *Is it wrong to want happiness? The Lapps have said many times that having me here has brought them joy. So is my lie really such a horrible thing?*

Michelle knew the answer, but it was hard to acknowledge, even to herself. If she'd never come here in the first place — never pretended to be Sara Murray — she wouldn't be in this predicament. She would be living on her own, who knew where, and the Lapps would have been reunited with their rightful granddaughter.

When they finally do meet the real Sara, they'll probably like her better than me anyway. I bet she's a decent person who would never take advantage of two sweet old people the way I have.

"We're here." Ezekiel startled Michelle out of her gloomy introspections. "Welcome to Emmanuel Fisher's home."

Michelle rubbed her forehead, trying to collect her thoughts.

"You okay, Sara?" Ezekiel touched her arm. "You were quiet most of the way here."

"I'm fine. Just doing a lot of thinking, that's all."

When Michelle stepped down from Ezekiel's buggy, she was greeted by Lenore.

"Hello, Cousin." Lenore clasped Michelle's hand. "You just missed a rousing game of volleyball, but I'm glad you could join us for the meal and our time of singing."

Michelle smiled. "Thank you. I have never

attended a singing before, so I'm anxious to find out what it's like."

Lenore linked arms with Michelle. "Let's go inside. I'm sure they're getting the food set out by now."

Michelle looked back at Ezekiel. "Aren't you coming?"

"I'll be in as soon as I get my horse put away."

"Oh, yeah, of course." Michelle hesitated a moment, but at Lenore's prompting, she followed her into their host's enormous barn. One would never know any animals had ever been housed here. The entire building looked as clean as Mary Ruth's kitchen, and it smelled good too, with none of the usual barn odors. Someone had done a good job cleaning.

Inside, several long tables with backless wooden benches had been set up. Another table held platters with plenty of sandwiches, chips, and other snack foods. On one side of the room a group of young men had gathered, and the women seemed to be staying by themselves. Michelle assumed once the festivities got started, the men and women would integrate. She was disappointed, however, when Ezekiel entered the building and headed straight for the men. Since he had brought her to this function, she figured it was sort of a date and that he would spend the evening with her. Was it normal for the men and women to segregate at a singing, or only when they first got here?

Michelle didn't have to wait long for her answer. After everyone gathered for silent prayer, the men dished up their plates and took seats at one long table together. When it was time for the women to get their food, they sat at an opposite table.

Michelle looked at Ezekiel, but engrossed in eating, he seemed not to notice. She went through the line with the other young women, then took a seat at the table with them, making sure to sit next to Lenore. Most everyone made Michelle feel welcome, but a few kept their distance, eyeing her with questioning looks. Michelle couldn't blame them. She didn't feel like she belonged here either.

She looked down at the simple blue dress she wore. It was one Mary Ruth had made for her. Although not as plain as what the Amish women dressed in, it made her feel more a part of this community.

Michelle leaned closer to Lenore and whispered, "When will we start singing?

"As soon as we finish eating."

"I have one more question."

"What's that?"

"Will we sit with the guys during the singing?"

Lenore shook her head. "They sit on one side of the room, and we sit on the other. It's pretty similar to the way it is during our church services."

"You mean there'll be preaching and Bible reading?"

"No, just singing, but we sit separate from the men."

"I see." Michelle sipped some lemonade. *I wish Ezekiel had explained all this to me ahead of time. When he invited me to attend the singing, I might have said no.*

"How'd you like the singing? Did you enjoy yourself this evening?" Ezekiel asked as they headed for the Lapps'.

"It was okay, I guess, but I would have enjoyed it more if you hadn't been on the opposite side of the room." Sara gave an undignified huff. "What was the point in asking me to go with you if we weren't gonna be together?"

He swallowed hard. "I thought you knew how it would be."

"How could I? I've never been to a singing till this one."

"I'm sorry, Sara. You're right. I should have explained things before we got there."

She shrugged. "It's okay. Guess it's no big deal, since I won't be here much longer anyway."

Ezekiel jerked his head. "What do you mean?"

"Come on, Ezekiel. You must realize I can't stay here forever. I need to get back to my own life soon."

"But you'll come back for visits, right?"

"I don't know."

He glanced at her, then back at the road again. "Your grandparents would be awful disappointed if you didn't come back to see them." *And so would I.*

"Them and me both."

"Then what's the problem?"

Sara stared down at the small black purse she clutched in her lap. "I guess there is none. Can we please talk about something else?"

"Sure. Actually there is another thing I'd like to ask you."

"What is it?"

"It's about Brad." Ezekiel pulled back on the reins a bit, to slow Big Red. He didn't want to get to the Lapps' before he had a chance to find out what he wanted to know.

"What about Brad?" she asked.

"I saw the two of you together at the ice-cream store in Lancaster Friday evening."

Her eyes widened a bit. "You did?"

"Yeah. I went there in my truck to get some ice cream and saw you and Brad hug each other before you got in his van."

She nodded. "I was thanking him for the ice cream he treated me to."

"So you were on a date." Ezekiel phrased it as a statement, not a question. It was fairly obvious Brad had taken Sara there on a date.

"I wouldn't call it a date exactly."

"Then what would you call it?"

Sara reached into her purse and withdrew a pair of nail clippers. "Just two friends getting together for what could be the last time." She opened the clippers and snipped a jagged nail. "Brad will be leaving for seminary in a month, and if he keeps busy driving some of the Amish in the area, plus odd jobs, there might not be another opportunity for us to see each other again before he goes."

"I see." Ezekiel rolled his tongue around in his mouth. He wanted to say more on the subject, but didn't want Sara to think he was being pushy. And if he wasn't careful, he might say something stupid and blurt out that he'd come to care for her and wished she felt the same way.

■ ■ ■ ■

As Mary Ruth and Willis got ready for bed that night, she brought up the subject of Sara. "Do you think our granddaughter had a good time with us today?"

"Jah, I believe so." Willis rubbed the back of his neck. "Why do you ask?"

"Didn't you notice how quiet she was during the picnic, and also on the buggy ride there and back home?"

The wrinkles in his forehead deepened. "Now that you mentioned it, she was quieter than usual. But I don't think it's anything to worry about. Maybe she was tired."

"You're probably right. Sara seems kind of moody at times. It's hard not to be concerned." Mary Ruth took a seat on the end of bed and pulled the pins from her thinning hair. "Talking about Rhoda today made me miss her all the more."

"Maybe you shouldn't talk about her so much then."

She narrowed her eyes at him. "You're kidding, right? There's no way I could ever forget about Rhoda or our precious little Jake either."

Willis put both hands on his hips as he moved closer to the bed. "I am not suggesting we should forget about our deceased *kinner.* But talking about them all the time is a constant reminder of the pain we endured losing them." He sat beside Mary Ruth and took hold of her hand. "I say we focus on our son, Ivan, his family, and the newest member of our family — sweet Sara."

Mary Ruth sniffed, leaning her head on his shoulder. "You're right, Willis. I am grateful for your good advice. Just knowing we've been given the chance to meet and get to know Rhoda's daughter gives me a sense of joy and peace."

Willis puts his arm around Mary Ruth and gave her a tender squeeze. "My heart feels at peace too."

CHAPTER 29

Newark

Sara woke up with a headache, but she wouldn't skip work this morning or her afternoon class. Both were important to her future. She hurried to get dressed, then went to the kitchen to make herself a cup of coffee.

Sara picked up her planner and took it with her to the table. In two months she would be going to Strasburg to see her grandparents. Sara had hoped to receive another letter from them, but she'd heard nothing since the last one, asking her to wait until October.

"Maybe they don't want to meet me after all," she murmured. "I'll write them again in a few weeks to be sure. As much as it will hurt, I don't want to go barging in there if I'm not wanted."

Sara had already determined that if she wasn't welcome, she would accept their wishes and not go, but oh how she hoped the Lapps wouldn't say no. She so desperately wanted to meet them and learn about her mother's life before she'd left home. *A link to my mother's past will be a connection to my future.*

A knock sounded on the back door, interrupting Sara's musings. She rose from her seat to see who it was.

"I saw your car in the driveway and figured you hadn't left for work yet." Her stepfather's dark brows lifted. "Or are you having car problems again? Because if you are, and you need a lift . . ."

Sara shook her head. "For the moment, the little beast is running, but who knows for how long." She gestured for him to come inside. "I got paid last Friday for the few hours I worked at the dental clinic that week, and the week before, so I can pay this month's rent now."

"Are you sure? Don't want you to cut yourself short."

"No, it's okay." Sara couldn't help wondering why Dean was being so nice. Normally, he wanted the rent money on the first of every month, without question. Why the sudden change? He must have some sort of agenda.

She opened her purse and handed him

the cash. "Here you go. Don't spend it all in one place." Sara gave a small laugh, hoping to diffuse any tension she may have created by repeating a line he used to say when she was a girl. She'd never really known how to take anything Dean said back then. Sometimes when he said something and she thought he was kidding, she would say something back and then be accused of having a smart mouth. There were other times when Sara thought her mother's husband was being serious, and it turned out he was only teasing. Or at least, that's what he said. Dean was a hard person to figure out, and she'd given up trying.

Sara often wondered what it was about Dean Murray that had appealed to her mother. Did Mama think he was good looking, witty, smart, or would make a good provider? He'd done a fair job of providing for them over the years, but Sara didn't care much for the man. And the fact that Dean favored his biological son, Kenny, had done nothing to put him in Sara's good graces.

"Well, I need to get to work myself," Dean announced. "Is there anything you need before I go?"

She shook her head. "But thanks for asking."

"No problem." Dean stuck the rent money

in his shirt pocket and went out the door.

Inhaling a deep breath, Sara returned to her chair and the now-lukewarm coffee. *I wonder what my real father is like. Is he nice looking? Kind? Caring? Does he even know about me? If so, has he tried looking for me all these years? Hopefully, all my many other questions will be answered once I meet the Lapps.*

Strasburg

"What on earth happened in here?" Ezekiel frowned as he and his parents entered the greenhouse. Someone, or something, had knocked over several potted plants, spilling dirt and containers onto the floor.

Dad's forehead wrinkled as he surveyed the situation. "Maybe Henry left the door open when I asked him to close up Saturday evening. Shoulda followed behind him I guess."

"Well, nothing seems to be broken, at least," Mom said. "If Henry did leave the door open, I'm sure he didn't do it on purpose."

Ezekiel rolled his eyes. His twelve-year-old brother could do no wrong in their mother's eyes. *I never got away with something like that when I was Henry's age.*

"We'd better get busy cleaning up the

greenhouse and trying to repot the fallen plants before any customers show up." Dad went to get the broom.

"How'd things go at the singing last night, Ezekiel?" Mom asked as she knelt to pick up two potted plants. "We were already in bed when you got home, and I forgot to ask this morning during breakfast."

Ezekiel gave a forced laugh. "Let's just say, it didn't go as well as I'd hoped."

She tipped her head, looking up at him. "What do you mean?"

"Sara didn't have that good of a time."

"How come?"

"She expected we would sit with each other."

"Well, that's what you get for takin' an English girl to an Amish function." Dad entered the greenhouse and started sweeping up the dirt on the floor. "You should have invited Lenore or one of the other available Amish women."

Ezekiel knew if he responded he and Dad would end up arguing. So instead of offering a comeback, he went down on his knees to pick up a couple of clay pots. As soon as things slowed down in the greenhouse today, he planned to check on his bees.

Ezekiel headed out to the far edge of their

property to tend his bees. As he approached, he was surprised to see one of the boxes had been knocked over. Several bees hovered around the fallen hive, trying to get back inside.

Staring at the box on the ground, Ezekiel figured some animal must have knocked over the hive. He didn't think it was a bear, although it was not uncommon to have bear sightings around Lancaster County. A recent newspaper article stated that a captured bear had been released in the game lands north of Harrisburg, but he doubted one would travel this far.

Ezekiel tapped his foot. *Course, I guess it could have been a bear. They do love honey, as well as feasting on the bees. They like to eat the bee's larvae as well.*

But after looking at the damage a little more closely, Ezekiel figured maybe a raccoon or even a skunk got into the hive. Probably the same critter that had gotten into the greenhouse and made a mess.

In a hurry to get the hive set back up, Ezekiel didn't take the time to put on a head net. Big mistake! Buzzing bees swarmed all around his face. The next thing he knew, he'd been stung in several places. Already, he could feel his cheeks beginning to swell.

Ezekiel groaned. "That's just great. I was

going over to see Sara later today for another buggy-driving lesson. How can I go there looking like this? I'll be lucky if I can even see to drive the horse and buggy."

Michelle went into the barn to look at more of the notes she'd found in the prayer jar. Each time she did this, she came away with something new to ponder. One of the messages she'd found today was in the form of a prayer and dealt with bitterness.

"Dear Lord," Michelle read silently, *"I don't mean to feel bitter, but the hurt in my heart has festered like an embedded splinter. I heard it said once that hurt fertilizes bitterness, making it grow like a weed. That's exactly what has happened to me."*

"I can relate to that," Michelle mumbled. "I've lived through a series of hurts in my life. Mom and Dad hurt me. My foster parents hurt me, and so did Jerry."

She shifted on the bale of straw, wondering how to go about freeing herself from bitterness caused by deep-seated hurt. She couldn't simply wave a magic wand over her head and ask it to go away. If it were possible to dispel the hurts life brought, there had to be something more.

Hearing a horse and buggy pull into the yard, Michelle hurried to put the jar away.

The note, however, she slipped into her jean's pocket. If Willis and Mary Ruth had returned home, she didn't want them to see what she had discovered. The two prayer jars she'd found had become Michelle's little secret.

Outside in the yard, she discovered Ezekiel's buggy, not the Lapps'. Michelle smiled and waved, but when he stepped down and moved closer to her, she looked at him with concern. "What happened, Ezekiel? Your cheeks are red and swollen."

"I know. I stupidly didn't bother to put on my protection mask when I went to take care of the bees this morning, and believe me, I paid the price for it." He grunted. "Found one of the hives had been knocked over — probably by a raccoon or some other critter. And when I went to pick it up, the bees came after me."

"That's a shame. Are you okay?"

He nodded. "Mom had some stuff to put on the stings, and she gave me a homeopathic remedy called Apis mellifica. It helped quite a bit with the pain and kept the swelling from getting worse."

"That's good about the remedy, but I'm sorry about your beehive."

Ezekiel scrunched up his nose. "That's not all of the trouble we faced this morning. When we went into the greenhouse, we discovered that some animal had been in there and knocked over several plants, making a mess to clean up on the floor."

"Sounds like it wasn't a good start to your day."

"That's for sure."

"Well, I'm glad it wasn't any worse." Michelle reached out to rub Big Red's ears. "So what brings you by today, Ezekiel? Shouldn't you still be at the greenhouse working?"

"Nope. My dad said I could have the rest of the day off. Think he felt sorry for me when he saw what the bees did." He secured his horse to the hitching rail. "I came by for two reasons. First, to see if you'd like another buggy-driving lesson, and second, to invite you to my birthday supper tomorrow evening."

"That sounds nice, but are your parents okay with me being there? I'm not part of the family or anything."

Ezekiel waved his hand. "Don't worry about that. It's my birthday, and they said I could invite whoever I want. I'll come over and pick you up around five. Is that okay?"

Despite Michelle's apprehension over what his parents would think, the idea of helping Ezekiel celebrate his birthday gave her a sense of joy. "I look forward to it, and will be ready by five."

Chapter 30

"*Hallich gebottsdaag,* Son." Ezekiel's mother gave him a hug as soon as he entered the kitchen.

"Danki, Mom."

Ezekiel's father, sister, and two brothers echoed Mom's happy birthday greeting as they all took seats around the breakfast table.

He grinned. "Thanks, everyone."

"I made your favorite johnnycake to go with fried eggs and ham." Mom placed a platter on the table, along with a basket filled with the tasty cornmeal biscuits that had been baked in a square pan and cut into several thick pieces.

Ezekiel smacked his lips. "Yum. You're spoiling me today, Mom."

She smiled and gave his shoulder a pat before taking her seat at the table. Then all heads bowed for silent prayer. When the prayer was over, Mom passed the food around, starting with Ezekiel.

As he looked around at his family, Ezekiel felt a true sense of belonging. If he decided to go English and move away, he would miss the closeness they had. But a few others he knew who had jumped the fence kept in touch with their families, so maybe it wouldn't be so bad. Ezekiel certainly wouldn't want to be completely cut off from his folks or siblings. So if he decided to go English, he would make sure to visit as often as possible. Hopefully, they would visit him too.

"Are you looking forward to your birthday supper this evening?" Amy asked. "Our big sister and her husband are expected to be here, so the whole *familye* will be together."

Ezekiel nodded before biting into one of the johnnycakes. "I invited Sara to join us too."

Mom's brows furrowed, and Dad cleared his throat real loud. "We were planning to keep this more of a family get-together."

"I'm sorry about that, but I thought it'd be a good chance for you all to get to know Sara better." Ezekiel took a deep breath, trying to keep his composure. It didn't take a genius to see that his parents didn't approve of Sara. Which was why they needed to get to know her.

Mom wiped a speck of egg yolk from her chin before looking at him. "I suppose having Sara here will be all right, since I also invited Lenore and a couple of your other friends."

Dad cast her a sidelong glance, but said nothing.

"It's a good thing the swelling in your cheeks has gone down." Abe bumped Ezekiel's arm. "With all that company we'll be having this evening, you wouldn't want to show up looking like a squirrel with his cheeks full of nuts."

Ezekiel bumped his brother back. "Very funny."

"So what are ya hopin' to get for your birthday this year?" young Henry chimed in.

"Maybe some new bee supplies, or a cover for —" Ezekiel stopped short of finishing his sentence. He'd almost said he would like a cover for the seat of his truck. He'd done a good job so far hiding his purchase from Mom and Dad and didn't want to blow it. If they found out the truth, it would put an end to any kind of birthday celebration.

"A cover for what, Ezekiel?" Mom asked.

"Um . . . I was thinking a throw cover or blanket would be nice to have in my buggy for when the weather gets colder." Internally, Ezekiel justified what he'd said, because it wasn't really a lie. It would be nice to have a new blanket to drape over his or any passenger's legs when it felt chilly while riding in the buggy.

At five o'clock on the dot, Ezekiel showed up to take Michelle to his house for his birthday supper. Looking out the kitchen window, she watched him pull his horse and buggy up to the hitching rail. She was certain he wouldn't have picked her up in his truck. Especially since he'd be taking her to his parents' house to spend the evening. He no doubt had said nothing to them about his recent purchase.

"Ezekiel's here, Grandma. So I'm gonna head out now." It was strange, but Michelle had actually gotten used to calling the Lapps Grandma and Grandpa.

Mary Ruth turned from where she stood at the stove, preparing supper for her and Willis. "Have a good time, and please tell Ezekiel we said happy birthday."

"I sure will." Michelle grabbed the gift bag she had for Ezekiel, along with a sweater in case the air turned chilly, and went out the back door. She found him waiting near his buggy.

"You look really nice tonight, Sara." He

touched the sleeve of her dress — another simple one Mary Ruth had made, only this one was green. "I'm glad you were free to come to my house for supper."

"I wouldn't have missed it. Happy birthday, Ezekiel." She handed him the present. "I hope you like what I got."

He smiled down at her. "You didn't have to get me anything. Just spending the evening with you is gift enough for me."

Michelle felt an ache at the back of her throat. Ezekiel was so sweet and kind. She enjoyed being with him more than any man she'd ever met. *Even more than Brad,* she realized for the first time. "Would you like to open your gift now? Or would you rather wait till we get to your house?"

"Think I'll open it now." Ezekiel reached inside the gift bag and smiled when he withdrew a pair of binoculars. "Well, what do ya know? I lost my old pair about a year ago and haven't gotten around to replacing them." He leaned close to Michelle and gave her a kiss on the cheek. "Thank you very much."

Michelle's pulse quickened. While uncertain of Ezekiel's intentions, she'd never received such a gentle, heartfelt kiss before. It was nothing like Jerry's smothering, forceful kisses, showing no tenderness at all. Being with Ezekiel was like a breath of fresh air. If she could stay here in Lancaster County permanently, Michelle felt that she could most certainly fall in love with this man. But she couldn't allow herself to give in to those feelings — not with her leaving this place soon. It wouldn't be fair to Ezekiel — assuming he felt the same way about her, which she suspected he might.

"Well, shall we get going?" Ezekiel opened the passenger's door for Michelle. "Sure don't wanna hold up my birthday meal. Mom wouldn't like that at all."

"And I couldn't blame her." Still unsure and a bit nervous about how his family would react to her being there, Michelle hoped everything would turn out all right.

Ezekiel guided his horse and buggy into a long driveway, which had a sign at the entrance that read: KINGS' A-BLOOM GREENHOUSE. Several large, majestic oak trees lined the driveway heading to the house. It surprised Michelle to see the lovely home Ezekiel's parents had. It was a large farmhouse done in stunning limestone. The cooper roof appeared to have developed a beautiful patina, no doubt after years of exposure to the weather. Beautiful flowers adorned window boxes on the entire main level, and colorful flowerbeds throughout the property made the lush green yard even more attractive.

They passed the house and drove toward the back, where a huge barn sat. The lower half was done in limestone, to match the house, while the upper half was wood and had been painted white. The barn also had a metal roof, but it was hunter green. Beyond the barn stood a greenhouse that seemed to stretch for miles. Michelle looked forward to visiting it someday, as she felt certain there'd be an overwhelming amount of pretty flowers and plenty of shrubs to check out.

Ezekiel glanced at Sara from across the table. Mom had somehow made sure to seat her opposite of him and put Lenore in the seat to his left. She was up to her old tricks again, and it irked Ezekiel to no end. His siblings were all polite and friendly to Sara, but his parents were another matter. Mom and Dad were obviously uncomfortable with Ezekiel's English guest, although she kept trying to make conversation with them. Did she sense his parents' disapproval?

Ezekiel figured their main complaint was Sara being English. Did they think she would sway him to leave home and not join the Amish church? Were they worried she might try to turn him against his family? Ezekiel thought he knew Sara pretty well, and there was no way she would do any of those things.

Ezekiel's cousin Raymond, who sat on the other side of him, leaned closer and said quietly, "My daed wants you to move your truck. It's in the way, and he needs it to be gone by noon tomorrow."

The whole room got deathly quiet. Apparently they'd all heard every word Raymond had said. Ezekiel's face heated, and Raymond covered his mouth with the palm of his hand. "Oops! Sorry, Cousin. I didn't mean to spill the beans or for anyone to hear me."

Ezekiel's father's lips pressed into a white slash. "What's this about a truck?" He leveled an icy stare at Ezekiel.

Ezekiel felt like a bird that was about to be devoured by a hungry hawk. He was caught and had no choice but to fess up. "I bought a truck, Dad. And I parked it at Raymond's place because I knew you'd never allow me to have it here."

Dad's face reddened as he swatted at thin air. "Ya got that right!"

Mom sat beside Dad, tapping all five fingers of her right hand against the table-top, but she never said a word. She didn't have to. Her clenched jaw and deep frown said it all.

Ezekiel looked at his brothers and sisters, hoping one of them might take his side, but they all remained quiet with their eyes averted. Sara also sat quietly, looking down at her half-eaten plate of fried chicken, mashed potatoes, and pickled beets.

I shoulda told my folks the truth sooner, Ezekiel berated himself. *And I should have never trusted Raymond to keep quiet about the truck.*

Dad leaned forward, his elbows on the table. "You are either going to sell the truck or find another place to live. Is that clear?"

"But Dad, I just turned twenty-four and shouldn't be treated like a child."

His father glared at him. "Then you oughta stop acting like one. And need I remind you that you're way past the normal age of someone joining the church?" He shook his finger, the way he used to when Ezekiel was a young boy. "You'd better make up your mind soon, before it's too late."

Too late for what? Ezekiel felt tempted to pound his fists against the table, but he held himself in check. Gritting his teeth, he pushed back the chair he sat upon and stood. "You'd better get your purse and sweater, Sara. It's time for me to take you home."

Without a word, she rose to her feet and followed him out the door. So much for a happy birthday. Ezekiel had only two choices now — sell the truck or move out and find a place of his own. Neither seemed like a good choice, but he'd have to make a decision, and soon.

Chapter 31

Saturday morning, after looking at and pondering more of the writings inside the prayer jar she'd found in the basement, Michelle decided to take a walk down the road. For a day this late in the summer, it was beautiful — warm, but comfortable, with low humidity. The mugginess in the country was a bit easier to take than in the city. She remembered the nights in her apartment back in Philadelphia when it was almost too hard to breathe. At least here in the wide-open spaces, she didn't feel so constricted and closed in.

Poor pup. Michelle looked toward the barn when she heard Rascal whimpering. She felt kind of bad for leaving Rascal at home but didn't want the puppy to get used to walking along the road, where he could get hit by a car or even a horse and buggy. Besides, she was miffed at him this morning. She'd found the little dickens out behind the barn, chewing on the canvas hat that had gone missing. Apparently Rascal had found it, and now the hat was practically shredded. Definitely not good enough to wear any longer. So after scolding the puppy and taking what was left of the hat away, Michelle decided to work off her frustration by taking a walk. Some time alone would also be good for reflecting on how things had gone at Ezekiel's birthday supper.

Michelle had been getting to know the people in the community and felt close to the Lapps. But if Ezekiel's parents found out who she really was, they'd have a good cause to dislike her. While they hadn't actually said the words to her face, Michelle felt sure from their coolness toward her that Vernon and Belinda King didn't think she was the right girl for their son. No doubt they would prefer someone like Lenore for Ezekiel.

Ezekiel has a lot to deal with right now, Michelle thought as she made her way down the path along the side of the road. *Now that the truth is out, he's been forced to choose between his truck and living at home with his family. How could his parents make their son face such a thing?*

She kicked at a twig with the toe of her

sneaker. *Ezekiel and I are two of a kind. Life hasn't been fair to either of us, and we've both become liars. I wonder if he feels as guilty as I do for keeping a secret.* While it hadn't gone well for Ezekiel when the truth came out, Michelle could only imagine how bad it would be for her once the Lapps found out about her deceit.

Her thoughts went to Willis and Mary Ruth. *How can I keep deceiving those good people? They think I'm one person, when I'm really another.* Tears blurred her vision, and she blinked to clear it. *I don't deserve all the kindness they've shown me. If only there was some way I could make it up to them.*

Michelle had to be gone by October, but unless her deception was discovered before then, she planned to stay until a few days before the real Sara arrived. The mere thought of leaving this place and the special people she'd come to know and love caused her heart to feel as though it would break and send her world spinning into a sea of depression and gloom.

When a car pulled up alongside Michelle, she stopped in mid-stride. In the front seat sat a rugged-looking, dark-haired man. He reminded her of Jerry. Not necessarily his appearance, but the way he looked at her with such a smug expression.

Michelle's mouth went dry as she had a flashback, remembering how a few weeks ago she'd been stopped by those obnoxious young men on her way back to the Lapps' house from the post office. Fortunately, Brad had come along and offered her a ride home. She gulped. *But today I'm on my own.*

"You look lost. Do you need a ride somewhere?" The driver's voice was smooth, and his expression overly confident.

She shook her head.

He rode slowly beside her as she kept walking and looking straight ahead.

"You sure about that?"

She gave a quick nod and picked up her speed. Michelle's hands turned clammy, as her adrenaline spiked. *Here I am in the same predicament.* She bit her lip, hoping to see Brad pull up once again, or even Ezekiel, and come to her rescue. *What should I do? I can never outrun his vehicle, any more than those threatening teenagers' convertible.* She sent up a quick prayer. *Please help me, God. Make this guy move on and leave me alone.*

"Okay. Sorry I bothered you. You looked lonely, and I figured you might need some company."

"I don't."

He shrugged, then waved. "Okay, pretty lady. Have a nice walk."

When the car moved on, Michelle pressed a palm against her beating heart and blew out a breath of relief. Wiping the sweat from her brow, she kept her eyes focused up ahead. *I pray that guy doesn't turn around and come back.* This would be the last time she would take a walk out here by herself. In the big city, she realized she had to be careful and keep eyes in the back of her head, but Michelle didn't expect the threat to be here. Next time she wanted to go for a walk, she would bring Sadie or even Rascal along. Some people were intimidated by a dog. Plus, she was sure Sadie, at least, would try to protect her.

Michelle turned and headed back toward the Lapps'. She hadn't gone far when she spotted Ezekiel's truck coming in the opposite direction. *Where was he when I needed him?*

The truck slowed, then stopped. Ezekiel opened the passenger's door. "Hop in, Sara, I'll give you a ride home."

With no hesitation, Michelle climbed in and buckled her seatbelt. "Where are you headed? Did your dad kick you out? Are you leaving your family and striking out on your own?"

"Nope. Not yet anyway. Just picked up the truck from my cousin's house, and now

I'm takin' it to a friend's home in Smoketown."

Her brows lifted. "Smoketown? That's a ways from here, isn't it? How are you planning to get home from there?"

"Sam will give me a ride with his horse and buggy. I'll head there as soon as I've dropped you off home." Ezekiel pulled out onto the road.

Michelle drew in her lower lip. "The Lapps' house is not really my home."

He rubbed his chin. "Yeah, but it is while you're visiting them, right?"

Michelle's mind raced with the possibility of telling Ezekiel the truth. Would it ruin their friendship if he knew? Would he be as understanding about her situation as she was with his?

"I'm sorry about the other night." Ezekiel broke into her thoughts. "I wanted to talk to you about it when I took you home, but I was too upset to make any sense. Besides, I was embarrassed."

"You mean because your folks insisted you get rid of your truck?"

"Partly, but mostly because of the way they treated you during supper." He groaned. "They're afraid I'm getting serious about you. Mom came right out and accused me of that this morning. She thinks you're the reason I've decided not to join the church."

"Am I?" she dared to ask. "And have you decided for sure not to join?"

"You're not the reason I won't join, but I do have deep feelings for you."

Michelle sat beside Ezekiel, too stunned to speak. *So my suspicions are true.*

"You're awfully quiet. Are you upset because of what I said?"

"No, I'm just surprised, is all."

Ezekiel pulled his truck onto the Lapps' driveway, then stopped the vehicle and took hold of her hand. "You had to know."

"Well, I . . ." Michelle moistened her parched lips.

"I was hoping you might care about me too, Sara."

"I — I do, but . . ." She paused, searching for the right words. "I'm not the person you think I am. You deserve someone better than me."

Ezekiel slipped his arms around Michelle and pulled her close. "You're everything I need. As soon as I get a little more money saved up, I may decide to get a place of my own, and then . . ."

Michelle put her finger against his lips. "I can't talk about this right now. Go ahead and take the truck to your friend's place.

We can discuss this in a few days."

Ezekiel kissed her cheek. "Okay, sounds good."

Mary Ruth glanced at the grandfather clock on the far living-room wall. "I wonder what's taking Sara so long"

Willis set his newspaper aside and looked at Mary Ruth. "As usual, you worry too much. She said she was going for a *geloffe,* and some walks take longer than others."

She grunted. "I realize that, but Sara said she wouldn't be gone long."

"Well, maybe she's already back and just hasn't come inside yet. She could be out in the barn or doing something with one of the hund."

"I suppose, but still . . ." Her stomach quivered as she reflected on the day they realized Rhoda had left home. *Surely our granddaughter would not leave without saying goodbye. Oh, I hope that is not the case.*

Mary Ruth stood. "I'm going outside to look for her."

"Suit yourself, but I still think you're worried for nothing."

Ignoring her husband's comment, Mary Ruth went out the front door. She'd no more than stepped onto the porch when she spotted a truck sitting at the end of their driveway. *Now that's strange. I wonder who the vehicle belongs to.*

Mary Ruth remained on the porch, watching. She was surprised when a few minutes later, Sara stepped out of the truck. As she began walking toward the house, the truck backed out of the driveway and pulled onto the road.

"I'm glad you're back. I was concerned about you," Mary Ruth admitted when Sara joined her on the porch.

Sara tipped her head. "Really? Was I gone that long?"

Mary Ruth nodded. "Almost two hours."

"Well, I'm sorry for causing you to worry. Ezekiel picked me as I was walking back, and he gave me a ride the rest of the way."

Mary Ruth frowned. "Does he own that truck?"

"Yes, but . . ."

"Oh dear. I bet his parents are upset. They're quite strict, and I don't think either of them would approve of any of their children owning a motorized vehicle."

"But Grandma, Ezekiel is twenty-four years old, and he's not a member of the Amish church. Shouldn't he have the right to do whatever he pleases?"

"Not as long as he's still living under his parents' roof." Mary Ruth folded her arms.

"He needs to respect and abide by their rules. Our children were taught that as well. Although . . ." Her voice trailed off. "Never mind, Sara. Since you weren't brought up Amish, I can't expect you to understand our ways. Let's go inside. It's time to start lunch."

Sara went silently into the house. As Mary Ruth stepped in behind her, she was hit with the realization that no matter how much she may want it, Sara was not Amish and could never comprehend what an Amish parent went through when one of their children went astray. She could only hope, for Vernon and Belinda King's sake, that their son Ezekiel didn't make the same mistake Rhoda had made. She also hoped that the Kings didn't say or do anything to drive him away.

Chapter 32

Lancaster

Brad sat at the kitchen table in the small apartment he shared with his friend, Ned, contemplating whether he should go over to the Lapps to see Sara before he left town. She had seemed so troubled the last time they talked. Brad wanted to help her in some way. He'd dialed the Lapps' phone number so many times, but always hung up before leaving a message.

Once school started, Brad knew any free time he'd have would be minimal. His conscience told him to wait and not be pushy — let Sara get in touch with him if she wanted to connect before he left. Another part of him wanted to forge ahead and try to counsel her if needed. Brad didn't know why he'd been vacillating so much. He just needed clear direction.

He opened his Bible to James 1, verse 5, and read it aloud. " 'If any of you lack wisdom, let him ask of God, that giveth to all men liberally, and upbraideth not; and it shall be given him.' "

Brad bowed his head. *Why am I still struggling over this, Lord? I know You have placed a call on my life, and it does not include a relationship with a woman who is not a believer. Yet I can't get Sara out of my thoughts. Please give me wisdom and the strength to say no to my fleshly desires. Remind me daily to keep my eyes upon You. Amen.*

Brad wasn't sure if his attraction to Sara was purely physical or if it went deeper, but he could not allow himself to get caught up in a relationship with a woman who didn't share his devotion to God. Besides, he was almost certain Sara was hiding something — perhaps from her past — that could also stand in the way of a relationship with her.

Maybe this is why I'm attracted to Sara. Is my sense that she needs help in some way the reason I'm drawn to her? Brad ran his hand down the side of his face. Never had he felt so confused. For a fleeting moment, he wondered if he had what it took for the ministry. Shouldn't he be able to discern things better if he was a servant of the Lord?

Brad left the kitchen and looked around his apartment at all the things he still needed to pack. He was glad he'd be leaving for seminary in a week. Getting into his studies and putting his focus on the goal before him should take his mind off Sara, although he would remember to pray for her and hopefully keep in touch.

Strasburg

Michelle sat in the back of the Lapps' buggy, trying to relax while Willis drove the three of them to town for lunch. It was the last Friday of August, and things were happening too fast. Brad would be leaving for seminary next week, and she hadn't had a chance to say goodbye to him yet. Between all the garden produce Michelle had been helping Mary Ruth pick and process, plus housekeeping, laundry, and taking care of her dog, there was little time for socializing. She figured Brad must be busy too, since he hadn't come by the house for several weeks. Willis had called Brad for a ride one day last week, but Brad said he was busy packing and doing a few runs for other people, so he'd have to pass. Michelle wondered if he might be avoiding her. It was probably for the best that he'd be leaving soon. Brad deserved someone better than her — a woman who shared his faith and didn't tell lies to get what she wanted. Besides, she'd already decided that she and Ezekiel were better suited.

Not that I can be with either man. She leaned her head against the back of her seat and closed her eyes. Between the steady *clip-clop* of the horse's feet, and the gentle sway of the buggy, it was difficult to stay awake.

Yawning, Michelle thought about how upset Mary Ruth had seemed last week when she found out about Ezekiel's truck. Michelle couldn't blame her. The idea that Ezekiel might leave his Amish roots was probably a reminder to Mary Ruth of what her daughter had done when she left without a good explanation or telling them goodbye in person.

Michelle drew a breath, unable to fill her lungs completely. *Here I am, supposed to be the Lapps' granddaughter, and I'll be leaving soon. Just like Rhoda, I'll be yanking the rug out from under them. Of course,* she reminded herself, *soon after I'm gone, the real Sara will show up, and then things will be better — at least for Mary Ruth and Willis.*

She pressed a fist against her chest. Michelle could hardly stand to think about the day she would need to go and wondered how best to let her pretend grandparents know she was leaving. If it wasn't for their real granddaughter coming in October, Michelle could have stayed here forever.

She was living a dream right now, but it shattered every time she faced the truth: *This isn't real. It's only a sham— one I created myself the moment I left the bus station in Philly with two of the greatest people I've ever known.*

A desire to escape the sadness filling her being was so intense, Michelle almost asked Willis to stop the horse so she could get out of the buggy. But that was ridiculous. Where would she go with so little money and only the clothes on her back? And what reason would she offer for getting out of the buggy and running off down the street?

Michelle tugged her earlobe. *This is ridiculous. I need to get a hold of myself and quit thinking such dumb thoughts. Jumping out of a buggy in the middle of the road is no way to make a sensible exit.*

"We're almost at the Hershey Farm Restaurant," Willis announced, halting Michelle's contemplations. "Just a few more blocks to go."

Michelle sat up straight. She'd never eaten at this restaurant before and hoped the food was good. Her appetite had diminished since Ezekiel's birthday supper, and thinking about the mess she'd made of her life, it was hard to get in the mood for a noon meal.

Willis pulled Bashful to a stop at a red light. He'd taken his closed-in buggy today, since showers were predicted for this afternoon.

As they waited at the light, Michelle glanced at the car that had pulled up beside them in the left-turn lane. Her eyes widened, and she stifled a gasp when she realized it was none other than Jerry's car. She'd recognize it anywhere, with rust forming around the spot that had been damaged, and the big dent in the passenger rear door that never got fixed after Jerry had been involved in a fender-bender. He had used the insurance money he'd received for something else.

Michelle scooched as far back in her seat as possible, but leaned forward briefly to peek out the window, to be sure she hadn't imagined it was Jerry. No, it was him all right. She cringed and ducked her head when she saw him looking at their buggy with a smirk on his face.

Remembering a derogatory comment he'd made once about the Amish while they watched that reality show together, Michelle could almost guess what he must be thinking. Jerry thought the Amish were living in the dark ages and shouldn't be allowed to drive their horse and buggies on the roads.

He'd commented on the women's long dresses, saying they looked like pioneers.

Michelle's heartbeat picked up speed. *What is he doing here in this area? Oh, I hope he didn't see me here in the backseat. Wish I was dressed in Amish clothes right now. It would be a good disguise.*

The fear Jerry had instilled in her life came back to Michelle in a flash. Being with the Lapps all this time, she'd been able to put him and those feelings of fear behind her. But now, seeing Jerry again had dredged up the past — a past she'd rather forget. Sitting here at the red light, a few feet from Jerry's vehicle, caused Michelle to break out in a sweat. *Now I won't be able to go anywhere without looking in every direction and wondering if Jerry is close by.*

She drew a deep breath through her nose and gave a noisy exhale when the light changed and Jerry turned left. *Even if he did catch a glimpse of me, I'm sure he didn't realize who I was. I know Jerry well, and he would never expect me to be in an Amish buggy.*

"Is everything all right back there, Sara?" Mary Ruth turned in her seat to look at Michelle. "You've been awfully quiet since we left home, and then a few seconds ago, you made a strange sort of gasping noise."

"I'm fine," Michelle assured her. "I'm tired and sorta dozed off for a few minutes." Michelle wasn't about to mention seeing Jerry. She glanced out the window again. No sign of Jerry's car, so that was a relief. If he had recognized her, he would have turned around and come back to check things out. Michelle could only imagine how things would play out if Jerry met Willis and Mary Ruth and found out that Michelle had been posing as their granddaughter. Everything would blow up in her face.

I'll need to be more cautious from now on, she told herself. *I'll have to watch out everywhere I go and be on the lookout for Jerry. This is one more reason I can't go out walking alone anymore.*

Chapter 33

As Michelle sat on the unyielding wooden bench during church the first Sunday of September, her thoughts went to Brad. He would be leaving the area tomorrow, and she might never see him again. She should have tried to get in touch with him this past week. But she kept talking herself out of it. What would be the point? From what he had told her, his studies would keep him busy, and he'd have little time for much else. Besides, she'd also be leaving soon. So the friendship she had developed with Brad would be a thing of the past.

She glanced across the room and found Ezekiel staring in her direction. At least she thought he was looking at her. He could have been watching a fly on the wall opposite him, for all she knew. One thing was certain: Michelle was not the only person in the room ignoring the sermon being preached.

Of course, I have a good reason, she told herself. *I don't understand German.*

Michelle had made up her mind that when the time came for her to go, she wouldn't look back or focus on all she'd lost. But it would be a challenge. Living here all these months and getting to know the Lapps had made her feel as if she had a real family. For the first time in Michelle's life it seemed as if she could be truly happy.

She bit her lip to keep from crying. *But I guess happiness for me is not in the cards. I'll always be a loser, longing for something just out of my reach.*

Ezekiel glanced at Sara, who was fanning herself with the back of her hand. He couldn't blame her for that. The heat inside Roman Beiler's barn, where church was being held this morning, was stifling. Ezekiel would be glad when summer came to an end and the cooler temperatures of fall took over. Only three more weeks to go, and it would truly be autumn.

He swiped at the sweat running down the back of his neck and onto his shirt. *Sure hope the weather realizes it too and that autumn is not just a word on the calendar.*

Ezekiel had been so busy helping his parents in the greenhouse lately and delivering jars of honey to his customers, it was hard to believe summer was waning — especially in the face of this relentless heat. And after last night's downpour, the air was so muggy it was hard to breathe — particularly in close quarters such as this.

Ezekiel's attention was drawn to Sara again. He hadn't had the chance to see her since he dropped her off at the Lapps' in his truck before taking it to his friend's place.

Ezekiel felt guilty for keeping the vehicle when Dad thought he had sold it. But at the same time, he just couldn't let go of the truck, nor could he muster up the courage to move out of his parents' home. Ezekiel felt like a teenager — wanting a certain thing so badly on one day that he could taste it, and desiring something else just as much on the following day. He needed to grow up and stop changing his mind, because he couldn't have it both ways.

Maybe when Sara goes back to her hometown, I'll go with her. Ezekiel tugged on his shirtsleeve. *It would be a lot easier to strike out on my own if I settled in a town where I knew someone.*

Now that it was nearing the end of the season for harvesting honey, Ezekiel hoped to have a little free time so he could see Sara more often. He would like to talk about his plan and see if she'd be okay with him tagging along. *And when Sara leaves, she'll have transportation, because I'll have my driver's license by then and can give her a ride in my truck.*

Ezekiel swiped a hand across his forehead, where more sweat had collected. But the greenhouse work would be picking up, since they raised poinsettias for the Christmas season. That might make it difficult to leave if Sara decided to go before Christmas. Some major businesses in the Lancaster area had quantities of poinsettias preordered to give out to their employees for the holiday. Many of their regular customers bought plants for Christmas gifts too. So the months coming up would be a super busy time for the greenhouse, and Mom and Dad would need Ezekiel's help.

Ezekiel reached around and rubbed a spot on his back, where it had begun to kink. *Here I go again . . . Changing my mind about leaving. If I did venture out on my own soon, I'm sure Dad could hire someone to take my place in the greenhouse.*

He shifted on his bench, trying to find a comfortable position. *Not sure what I'd do with the bees though. Maybe I could talk Abe or even Henry into taking over my honey busi-*

ness. It wouldn't take much to train them. Think I'll talk to Abe about it in the morning.

The following morning, Mary Ruth and Michelle made a trip to the Kings' greenhouse. Mary Ruth said she wanted to buy some basil, mint, and parsley. She also mentioned purchasing tulip and crocus bulbs, which she would plant in the next few weeks.

When Michelle followed Mary Ruth into the greenhouse, she felt the increase in temperature. *Too warm to be working here all day,* she thought. *I'm surprised Ezekiel hasn't found another job where he can make enough money to support himself.*

She spotted Ezekiel's mother waiting on a customer. Ezekiel was nearby, watering some plants. Apparently he hadn't seen them yet, but when Belinda finished with her customer and welcomed Mary Ruth, Ezekiel set his work aside and hurried over to Michelle.

While Belinda helped Mary Ruth find what she was looking for, Ezekiel suggested he and Michelle step outside.

Michelle looked past Ezekiel and noticed the wrinkles in his mother's forehead as she glanced her way, but Mary Ruth seemed oblivious to all of it, as she perused the pots of herbs. *Does Belinda really think I'm a bad influence on her son? Doesn't she realize he's not happy being Amish, and it has nothing to do with me? He felt that way before I came into the picture. Ezekiel told me so.*

"There's something I want to ask you," Ezekiel said when they stepped outside and away from the greenhouse.

She tipped her head back to look up at him. "What is it?"

"Whenever you decide it's time for you to return to your hometown, I'd like to go along. In fact, I'll drive you there in my truck."

Her eyes widened. "You want to go to my house?"

"No, I'm not asking to move in with you, Sara. I just thought if I could start over someplace where I know someone, it would be easier. I'm planning to talk to my brother Abe about taking over my bee business, and Mom and Dad can hire someone to take my place here in the greenhouse." Ezekiel leaned against the retaining wall that had been built near the greenhouse. "I have some money saved up, and if I can't find a job right away, I'll sleep in my truck."

Michelle shook her head. "Not a good idea, Ezekiel. No one should ever have to live in their vehicle. It's not safe, and the conditions would be anything but ideal."

Her voice lowered. "Besides, I'm not sure yet when I'll be going back to my home, so I can't make any promises about you going with me." Truth was, Michelle didn't want Ezekiel to take her to wherever she was going. It would give his parents one more reason to dislike her. And of course, she'd be blamed for his leaving. Not that it would really matter once she was gone, but Michelle didn't want to live with any more blame. She'd already done enough to feel guilty for.

Seeing Ezekiel's desperate expression, she clasped his arm. "Let me think about it, okay?"

He nodded slowly. "I'll talk to you again soon."

Michelle fingered the neckline of her blouse, which was sticking to her like glue. She needed to make a decision soon as to what day she should leave and whether to include Ezekiel in her plans. *I wonder what he'd say if he knew I don't even have a home to return to. When I leave Strasburg, I'll have to decide which direction to go. One thing is certain: it'll be as far away from here as possible. I don't want to be reminded of all I've left behind.*

Chapter 34

On Monday morning, the last full week of September, it was all Michelle could do to roll out of bed. During the night, a terrible windstorm had struck with lots of heavy rain pelting the roof. All the noise kept her awake for several hours. At one point, she almost grabbed her blanket and went down to the living room to sleep on the couch. It was okay doing that when she was a little girl, but being a grown woman, she shouldn't be acting so childish. It didn't stop her though from pulling the covers up over her head, no matter how hard it was to breathe.

Groaning, she lifted the window shade and peeked out. The yard below was littered with leaves, branches, limbs, sticks. *Oh boy. That mess is gonna take awhile to pick up. Guess I'd better get dressed and head downstairs to breakfast. I'll need all the strength I can muster in order to get through this day.*

Downstairs in the kitchen, Michelle found Mary Ruth in front of the counter, stirring pancake batter. She looked at Michelle through squinted eyes. "You look tired. Did last night's storm keep you awake?"

"Yeah. Did you and Grandpa get any sleep?"

"A little." Mary Ruth pointed to the back door. "Your grandpa's already outside picking up some of the debris in the yard. He said I should call him when breakfast is ready."

"I'll help him as soon as I've had something to eat." Michelle patted her midsection. "I don't work well on an empty stomach."

Mary Ruth smiled. "I understand. I'm the same way." She gestured to the kitchen table. "Oh, there's a letter for you."

"Y–you went out and got the mail?" Michelle's heart pounded. What if another letter had come from the real Sara?

"No, dear. The letter is from Brad, and it didn't come in the mail. He dropped it by fifteen minutes ago and said it was for you."

Michelle's fingers trembled as she reached for the envelope. Although thankful Mary Ruth had not gotten the mail, Michelle's feelings about the letter from Brad were conflicted. Why hadn't he asked to speak to her in person? Did he think it was easier to say goodbye this way?

"If you'd like some privacy, you can read his letter in the living room." Mary Ruth pushed a wisp of hair back under her dark colored head scarf. "I'll let you know when it's time to eat."

"Okay, thanks." Clasping the letter to her chest, Michelle ducked out of the kitchen and went straight to the living room. Taking a seat on the couch, she read Brad's letter silently.

Dear Sara,

As I'm sure you know, I'm leaving town today — heading to the seminary up in Clarks Summit, where I'll be until I'm through with my ministerial studies. I thought about coming by to see you last week but decided it would be better to say goodbye this way. I can express myself easier with written words than if I spoke to you in person.

First, I want to say that I've enjoyed spending time with you these past few months. I wish, however, that we could have become better acquainted. In talking to you, I've always felt you were dealing with some sort of problem but might be afraid to talk about it. I feel I may have failed you, because as a future clergyman, it will be my job to help people deal with their problems. Perhaps I am lacking in that area, because in all the times we've talked, you have never truly opened up to me.

When we first met, I felt an immediate attraction, and I don't think it was just physical. We enjoyed each other's company, and I wanted to get to know you better. It didn't take long for me to realize though that you don't share my passion for Christ and the ministry to which I feel called.

You seem happy when you're with your grandparents, and it's obvious they are very fond of you. Have you thought of moving to Strasburg permanently? Who knows — you might even decide to join the Amish church someday.

Well, I've said more than I planned to in this letter, so I'll end it by saying, I'll be praying for you. And if you ever need to talk, I'm only a phone call away.

May God bless you in the days ahead, and draw you close to Him.

All the best,
Brad

Tears welled in Michelle's eyes and dribbled down her cheeks. *Brad knows there's something not right about me. Maybe I should have told him the truth. Being the decent man he is, Brad probably could have given me some good direction.*

She rocked back and forth, holding his letter against her chest. *But if I had told Brad who I really am, I'm sure he would have insisted that I admit it to Willis and Mary Ruth. I cannot tell those good people what I did to their face. I just can't.*

"Did ya ever see such a mess?" Willis called to Michelle as the two of them worked on cleaning up the yard.

She shook her head. "That was some storm we had last night."

"I'll say." He hoisted a few broken branches into the wheelbarrow. "And now, thanks to all that rain, we have more humid weather. I, for one, will be glad when the cooler temperatures get here."

Nodding, Michelle kept working on the pile she'd started. After Willis unloaded the wheelbarrow by the woodpile near the garden shed, she would haul her stack of wood out there.

While Michelle worked, she reflected once again on the letter she'd received from Brad this morning. It probably was for the best that they hadn't said their goodbyes face-to-face. It would have been difficult for her to look at him and not break down. It wasn't just knowing she'd never see him again, although that was certainly a portion of it. The hardest part for Michelle would have been to face Brad, knowing all this time she'd been living a lie. She longed to tell him the truth, but she feared his reaction. Now he was gone. She would never have to know what his response to her deception would have been had she told him.

Michelle was on the verge of bending down to pick up a strip of bark when she heard a snap. Before she had time to react, a limb that had broken off from the tree overhead clunked her on the head, bringing Michelle to her knees. "Yeow!"

Willis was immediately at her side, and Mary Ruth, who had stepped outside, joined him there. "Ach! Sara, are you all right?" Mary Ruth's fear was evident in her quavering voice.

Michelle tried to stand as she brought a shaky hand to the top of her head. "I–I've got a mighty big lump, and I feel kinda woozy." Her vision blurred as she weaved back and forth, and dropped back down to her knees.

Mary Ruth fingered the lump and gasped. "I don't see any blood but that lump is huge. Willis, you'd better call one of our drivers. I think we need to take Michelle to see a doctor — she could have a concussion."

Willis nodded. "I will help you get Sara on her feet and into the house. Then I'll run out to the phone shed and make the call."

As Mary Ruth sat beside Sara on the couch, her concern for the young woman escalated. Sara had begun saying some strange things — mentioning people's names Mary Ruth had never heard of and talking about events that made no sense at all. And she didn't recognize Mary Ruth at first. The poor girl was clearly disoriented.

"Why can't Al or Sandy take me to the doctor? They took me there once before."

Mary Ruth placed her hand gently on Sara's shoulder. "Who are Al and Sandy?"

No response. Sara closed her eyes.

"Don't go to sleep, dear. If you have a concussion, you need to stay awake."

"I'm tired. Think I might throw up."

Mary Ruth dashed into the utility room and grabbed a bucket. She returned to the living room barely in time for Sara to empty her stomach into the bucket. "Wh–where's Mom and Dad? Why aren't they here? Don't they care that I'm sick?"

Mary Ruth looked up at Willis when he entered the house. "She's not doing well. Did you get a driver to take us to the hospital emergency room?"

"Jah. Stan Eaton should be here soon."

Mary Ruth released her breath. "Thank the Lord."

Chapter 35

It had been seven days since Michelle got hit on the head, and she still didn't feel quite right. While the nausea and dizziness were gone, the bump continued to hurt, and it was hard to concentrate or think clearly. The doctor said she had a moderate concussion, and it could take a few weeks to heal. Michelle was kept at the hospital overnight for observation and sent home the following day with instructions to rest. The doctor also reminded her not to engage in any strenuous activity that might lead to another injury.

Mary Ruth had told Michelle that right after the accident she'd been disoriented and didn't seem to know where she was for a time. Michelle had also talked about some people Mary Ruth didn't know, whom Michelle had never mentioned before. Michelle hoped she hadn't said anything that revealed her true identity, but if she had, surely Mary

Ruth would have mentioned it by now.

It was hard to sit around and do nothing, but what other choice did she have? Mary Ruth hovered around, making sure Michelle followed the doctor's orders and didn't do anything she wasn't supposed to do. Willis took care of all the outside chores, including clearing away the rest of the mess that had been left from the storm. Some of his neighbors, as well as Ivan, offered to help out, but he insisted on doing it by himself. No wonder Mary Ruth sometimes called him stubborn.

Ezekiel had come by twice to see how Michelle was doing, and also to offer his help if needed. Lenore dropped by once, on her way home from teaching at the schoolhouse. It felt good to know people cared about her, even though they didn't realize she was someone else.

Michelle's biggest concern was not being allowed to walk out and get the mail the first few days after her injury. Fear that another letter from Sara Murray would come left her feeling anxious. But fortunately, no letters had been delivered, and now that Michelle was able to walk without feeling woozy, Mary Ruth had given in and let her resume getting the mail each morning. It was about the only thing she was allowed to do however. Mary Ruth made sure of that.

This afternoon, as Michelle sat in a wicker chair on the front porch with Rascal snuggled in her lap, she thought about the quote she'd read this morning: *"Every day is a second chance."* While Mary Ruth had been busy fixing breakfast and wasn't aware of what Michelle was doing, she had gone down to the basement to look around and read some of the notes in the prayer jar again.

On one of the slips of paper she'd also read Psalm 33:18: *"Behold, the eye of the LORD is upon them that fear him, upon them that hope in his mercy."*

Michelle wasn't sure what it meant, but she'd put both pieces of paper in her pocket, as she had done with a few others she'd found in the prayer jar inside the barn. She planned to take them with her when she left this place, as a reminder of her time in Strasburg.

"Mind if I join you?" Mary Ruth broke into Michelle's contemplations.

"Of course not. Please do." Michelle gestured to the chair beside her.

Mary Ruth took a seat and reached over to stroke Rascal's head. "This little guy sure seems to like you, Sara."

Michelle nodded. "I like Rascal too, and I'm gonna miss him when I go back home, which should be soon. I've been here several months and have probably worn out my welcome by now."

Mary Ruth pressed a hand to her abdomen. "No, you haven't, and I wish you would reconsider and stay for a while longer. Why, you're still recovering from a head injury. Besides, it would be so nice if you could be here for the holidays this year. Thanksgiving will be here before we know it, and then Christmas."

"I'm curious — how do the Amish celebrate the holidays?" Michelle asked.

"Well, Thanksgiving is celebrated in our district in much the same way as many English people celebrate it. In the morning we gather our family for devotions, and everyone often shares something they feel grateful for." Mary Ruth folded her arms and leaned her head against the back of her chair. "Then the adults and older children have a time of prayer and fasting during the morning hours. But around noon we gather with our family members for a delicious, traditional Thanksgiving dinner."

"So you have turkey, gravy, mashed potatoes, and all the trimmings."

"That's correct. We might also have a variety of vegetables and salads, as well as fresh bread or rolls." Mary Ruth licked her lips. "And of course after the meal, we eat dessert and spend the rest of the day visiting while the children play games."

"Sounds like a relaxing day and a lot of fun too." Just hearing about it caused Michelle to wish she could be here for Thanksgiving and take part in helping to cook, as well as eat, the meal. "What about Christmas? Do you celebrate the same we English people do?"

"To a certain extent we do, but there are no decorated trees or blinking lights inside our homes," Mary Ruth clarified.

Rascal woke up and began to squirm, so Michelle set him on the porch floor. A short time later, he ambled down the steps and into the yard. "So you don't do any Christmas decorating at all?"

"Some Amish string the Christmas cards they receive around a room in their home. And a few people might set out some candles or greenery, but nothing fancy."

"What about gifts? Do you give each other Christmas presents?" Michelle found all this information about Amish traditions to be so interesting.

"Yes. On Christmas morning after we've had devotions, the children will open their gifts." Mary Ruth's voice was light and bubbly. "In the afternoon, we share a big meal, and if Christmas Day falls near the end of the week, some church districts hold their service on Christmas morning instead of the usual Sunday service."

Michelle clasped her hands behind her neck. "It all sounds wonderful. I'm sure you must have a good time."

"Yes, we certainly do, and we'd really like you to stay through the holidays, Sara."

Seeing Mary Ruth's pleading expression, Michelle nodded. "Okay, I'll stay until after Christmas."

Mary Ruth placed her hand on Michelle's arm and gave it a tender squeeze. "That's *wunderbaar.* I know Willis will also be pleased."

Michelle swallowed around the lump in her throat. There was no way she could keep the promise she'd made. The real Sara would be arriving sometime this month, and she had to be gone by then. As soon as she felt strong enough, she would leave the Lapps a note explaining the truth and head out on her own.

"Thanksgiving will be a wonderful occasion." Mary Ruth's face radiated with pleasure. "We'll invite Ivan, along with his wife and children, and there will be so much good food we won't know what to do with it all."

When Mary Ruth began to reminisce about what the holidays were like when Rhoda was a girl, Michelle concentrated on Rascal and tuned her out. It was too painful to hear about this, knowing she would not have the opportunity to be a part of their holiday celebrations. No doubt, Michelle would probably be sitting in some dreary old apartment, feeling sorry for herself on Thanksgiving, as well as Christmas.

Michelle wished she had some good recollections of the holidays, but her upbringing hadn't left any pleasant memories. As a child, Thanksgiving always ended up with her parents fighting. On one Christmas, a neighbor called the cops, and Dad was hauled off to jail. Not much good about those holidays to remember.

The time Michelle had spent with her foster parents was a little better, but nothing like she'd hoped it would be. Al and Sandy Newman were nice enough, but they had three kids of their own, plus Michelle and two other foster children, so they couldn't afford to do much for the holidays.

When asked by her friends in school about what she got for Christmas, Michelle couldn't admit how things really were, so she would pretend everything was great and make things up about all the gifts she'd supposedly received. Maybe the reason pretending came so easy to her was because she'd had a lot of practice. But if it was the only way she had to get a sense of truly belonging, however temporary, Michelle would keep pretending for as long as she could.

Compared to living with her birth parents, being with the foster family hadn't been nearly so bad. But here, with Mary Ruth and Willis, it was like having a real family — grandparents who cared about her and took care of her needs. Too bad it couldn't last.

Ezekiel urged Big Red on. He was eager to see Sara and find out how she was doing today. A hit on the head could be serious, and if she didn't take it easy, there might be repercussions. The last time he'd gone to see Sara, she'd looked tired and appeared to be distracted. Hopefully after more than a week of recovery, she was doing better.

Approaching the Lapps' driveway, Ezekiel guided his horse and buggy off the road. When he pulled up to the hitching rail, he spotted Mary Ruth sitting on the porch, snapping green beans.

"I came by to see Sara," he said, stepping

onto the porch. "How's she doing today?"

Mary Ruth barely looked up from her task as she mumbled, "She's better but still needs to rest." Eyebrows squeezing together, she added, "I don't think it's a good idea for her to go anywhere with you today."

"I didn't come to ask her to go anyplace with me." Ezekiel tapped his heel against the wooden porch slats. "Just wanted to see how she's doing." He glanced at the back door. "Is she inside?"

Mary Ruth shook her head. "She took a walk out to the barn with Rascal a short time ago."

"Oh, okay. I'll head out there and say hello."

When Mary Ruth gave no response, Ezekiel turned, trotted down the steps, and ran to the barn. He found Sara inside, sitting in a pile of straw. Her puppy was curled up beside her with his head in Sara's lap.

"I talked to your grandma and she said you were in here. Didn't see any sign of your grandpa though."

"He went to the bank."

"Oh, I see. So how are you feeling today?" Ezekiel squatted down beside her. "Is that bump you got still pretty sore?"

She reached up and touched the top of her head. "A little. The swelling's gone down quite a bit though."

"Good to hear." He lowered himself to his knees and moved closer to her. "I think Mary Ruth is still *umgerennt* with me."

"Why would she be upset?"

His eyes widened. "Oh, you knew what that meant?"

Sara nodded. "Willis says it sometimes when he's upset with the hogs. When I questioned him about the word, he explained its Pennsylvania Dutch meaning." She touched Ezekiel's arm. "Why do you think Mary Ruth is upset with you?"

"She's been less than friendly ever since she found out I own a truck. I can't understand why it would bother her so much. I'm not their son or any other relation of theirs." He lowered his voice. "Don't think she's said anything to my folks about it though. If she had, Dad would be all over me for not selling the truck and parking it at my friend's place." Feeling a headache coming on, Ezekiel massaged his forehead. "My daed says if there's one thing he can't tolerate, it's a liar."

Sara sat quietly, staring straight ahead.

He snapped his fingers in front of her face. "Did ya hear what I said?"

"Yeah. I was just wondering how you feel about people who don't tell the truth."

He shrugged. “Well, it all depends on who’s lyin’ and what they’re lying about.”

“So do you believe it’s all right to lie to your folks?”

“I’m not really lying. I told Dad I would move the truck off my cousin’s property, and I did.” Ezekiel didn’t understand why Sara was questioning him like this. “Do you think I should sell my truck and join the Amish church? Is that what you’re getting at?”

“I don’t know what you should do, Ezekiel. It’s a decision you’ll need to make. Guess what I’m wondering is how you feel about not telling your parents the truth. Doesn’t it make you feel guilty?”

He nodded. “Yeah, it does. But if I tell ’em I still own the truck, Dad may kick me out of his house.”

“Guess there’s always a consequence for not telling the truth.” Sara glanced toward the barn door, then looked back at Ezekiel. “There’s something I need to talk to you about, but you have to promise not to tell anybody — just like I never told anyone about your truck. At least not till you drove me home in it that day.”

Nodding, he shooed a pesky fly away from his face. “I care about you, Sara, and you can tell me anything.”

She heaved a sigh. "I'm not the person you think I am."

He placed his hand on her shoulder and gave it a squeeze. "I think I have a pretty good idea what kind of person you are."

"No, you don't. In fact, you don't know me at all."

"Yes, I do. I know you're kind, sweet, and —"

She held up her hand. "I'm none of those things. I'm an imposter."

He tipped his head to one side. "What are you talking about?"

"My name is not Sara Murray. I'm Michelle Taylor, and the Lapps are not my grandparents."

Ezekiel's thoughts scrambled, as he tried to digest what she'd said. "Are you making all this up just to tease me, or has that whack you took on the head messed with your brain?"

Sara's lips trembled, and her eyes glistened with tears. "I am not making this up, and it has nothing to do with getting hit on the head. When Willis and Mary Ruth went to the Philadelphia bus station back in June to pick up their granddaughter Sara, they thought I was her." She paused and drew in a shaky breath. "I needed a place to go real bad, so I went along with it and let them believe I was Sara."

Ezekiel sat quietly with his hands folded in his lap, as Michelle went on to explain things. When she got to the part about intercepting the real Sara's letters, he'd heard enough. "I thought we were friends, Sara — I mean, Michelle. A true friend would never deceive someone like that, especially not to this extent." He glanced toward the door. "And what about Willis and Mary Ruth? How could you have lied to those good people?"

It was all Ezekiel could do to keep from shouting. All these months he thought he and this pretend Sara were drawing closer — that they might even have a future together some day, if he decided to go English. Now he realized she'd been playing him for a fool. Worse yet, she'd conned two of the nicest people in the world into believing she was their granddaughter. How despicable was that?

Ezekiel leaped to his feet. Feeling a tightness around his eyes, he said through clenched teeth: "I wish you'd never come to Lancaster County." With that, he whirled around, jerked open the double barn doors, and made a beeline for his horse and buggy. He'd never felt so betrayed in all his life.

Sara — Michelle — was not the woman for him.

Chapter 36

Newark

Sara's thoughts raced as she began packing her bags and getting ready for the trip to her grandparents' house this morning. It had been difficult to wait until October, but here it was October 3rd, and she would soon be greeting the Lapps for the first time. She was excited, yet nervous.

There was so much she wanted to share with them. Sara was eager to tell her grandparents about the business classes she'd taken at the local community college this summer, and how she'd been working part-time at a dental office. She also thought they might want to know what her childhood was like. And of course there were personal things about her mother to share with Willis and Mary Ruth.

She took a seat on her bed, holding the blue-and-black beaded bracelet and matching necklace she'd made for her grandmother, along with the keychain for her grandfather. In addition to the silver ring for his keys, there was a small leather patch connected to it that she had etched with the letter *L* for Lapp.

Sara planned to drive to their home in Strasburg, instead of taking the bus as she'd originally planned. Since some repairs had been done to her vehicle, it only made sense to go there by car. If Sara had figured it right, the trip would take a little over two hours. She could travel at her leisure and make stops along the way, as needed.

She hoped to stay several days, or even a few weeks with her grandparents, if Mary Ruth and Willis had a spare room and wanted her to stay that long. Since she hadn't heard from them since that last letter, she wasn't even sure if she'd be welcomed, much less invited to stay in their home. The Lapps might be satisfied with just a short visit.

Her lips pressed together. *Well, I won't know till I get there, so I may as well stop worrying about it.*

Sara was about to close the suitcase when she looked toward the nightstand and saw her mother's Bible. *Oops, I cannot forget that.*

Sara took the Bible and opened it, making sure her mother's note was tucked safely inside before she put it under her neatly packed clothes and zippered shut the suitcase. She felt it necessary to show her grandparents the letter their daughter had written.

Then Sara remembered her birth certificate that she wanted to take along. She had gone to the local office supply store and made a copy of it to give her grandparents. Although they hadn't asked in their letter to see a birth certificate as proof of who she was, Sara wanted to make sure she could prove she was Rhoda's daughter. The Bible, the note her mother wrote, and the certificate should be enough to verify who she was.

Sara rose from the bed and stood in front of the full-length mirror to check her appearance. She'd chosen a pair of crisp linen slacks in navy blue, and a white tank top with a short-sleeved navy blue jacket for her traveling attire. Around her neck she wore her mother's favorite scarf, and the scarf ring she had recently made held it in place.

Her long blond hair had been freshly washed, and as always, she'd let it air dry. One advantage of having naturally wavy hair was the ease of styling it.

Satisfied that she looked all right, Sara picked up her suitcase and handbag. Taking one last glance in the mirror, she left her room. *Well, Mama, here I go.* It was time for her adventure to begin.

Strasburg

Michelle felt grateful that Mary Ruth and Willis were out running errands and wouldn't be back until sometime this afternoon. It gave her the time she needed to get ready for her departure and be gone before they returned.

Knowing the real Sara could be here any day, Michelle couldn't wait any longer. Besides, she worried that Ezekiel might say something to the Lapps about what she'd confided in him before she had the chance to leave.

Michelle couldn't deal with her deceit anymore, but there was no way she could face Mary Ruth and Willis with the truth. She'd taken the coward's way out and left them a note on the kitchen table. As soon as the Lapps had left this morning, Michelle called their driver, Stan, to pick her up. Then she'd packed her bags and now sat on the front porch, waiting for his arrival.

She wished she could see Ezekiel before she left and apologize to him for ruining their relationship, but he'd left in such a huff yesterday, she felt sure he wouldn't want to talk to her. Anything that may have been between them had been destroyed once Ezekiel learned the truth about her deceit. *If I were Amish and joined the church, I'd most likely be shunned for the lie I've told.*

Michelle shifted on the bench she sat upon. *Who is he to cast judgment on me, anyhow? Ezekiel's been lying to his parents all these months about his truck, and he won't make a commitment to join the Amish church or decide to officially become a part of the English world. He's just stringing his family along, all because he's too afraid to make a decision he might later regret.*

Under the circumstances, Michelle believed a clean break was for the best. Once the Lapps found her note, they would tell Ezekiel and others in their church district why she had left. Then undoubtedly Ezekiel would tell them he already knew. Michelle would never have to see any of them again, so hopefully, she could move past all of this and find her way through life on her own. Although she couldn't imagine that she would ever amount to anything.

As Michelle continued to wait for Stan, Rascal and Sadie plodded onto the porch with wagging tails. A sense of sadness washed over her, as she leaned down and let the dogs take turns licking her hands.

She was not only saying goodbye to the people she'd come to think of as her family, but also to the loving animals she'd grown so fond of here on this farm. She would miss taking care of them, especially Rascal, who had come to depend on her.

"Sure wish I could take you with me," Michelle murmured, stroking Rascal's silky soft head. "But it's just not possible, since I'm not sure where I'll end up or if and when I'll find a job."

Michelle had no money of her own. What little she'd had when she first came here, she'd spent on necessities, not to mention Ezekiel's birthday gift. Since she knew where the Lapps kept some extra cash, she'd opened the cupboard this morning and taken down the old coffee can. She'd removed all the money she thought she'd need to get by on until she found a job. Not only was she a liar, but she was a thief as well.

But I'm gonna pay it back as soon as I can, she told herself, hoping to justify why she'd taken it. *I'll get a money order and mail it to them, as I promised I would do in the note I wrote.*

Tears pooled in Michelle's eyes when Stan pulled his van into the yard. It was time to go. Time to leave this place that had been her home for the nearly four months she had lived here. "Goodbye, Rascal. Bye, Sadie. Take care of each other, okay?" She gave both dogs one last pat.

Bird-in-Hand, Pennsylvania

"I'm glad we decided to stop for lunch before doing the rest of our errands." Mary Ruth smiled at Willis from across the table at the Bird-in-Hand Family Restaurant. "The salad bar is so good here, and it's just the pick-me-up I needed right now."

He nodded in agreement.

"Too bad Sara didn't want to come along. It would have been nice to have her with us today."

"Jah, but Sara still needs to take it easy, so maybe it's best that she stayed home where she can rest."

"You're right, as usual." Mary Ruth smiled before taking a drink of iced tea. "I'm so glad she decided to stay through the holidays. Having her here to help us celebrate Thanksgiving and Christmas will be wunderbaar. We'll have to come up with something special to give her."

"Well, one thing's for sure. She doesn't need another hund. Maybe I should make Sara a cedar chest to put her cherished items in or use as a hope chest. I'll have to work on it in the early mornings, or maybe after she's gone to bed. Wouldn't want the surprise ruined ahead of time." Willis winked at Mary Ruth. "The way she and Ezekiel have been hanging around together so often, I wouldn't be one bit surprised if they didn't end up getting married someday."

"Since Sara wasn't raised in the simple life, it's doubtful she'd want to become Amish." Mary Ruth pursed her lips, as they finished their lunch. "If she and Ezekiel should develop deep feelings for each other, he'd likely go English. Which is what I suspect he wants anyway." She lowered her gaze to the table for a few seconds, then lifted her head. "Just like our Rhoda, he's not satisfied with the Plain way of living. Otherwise, he wouldn't have bought a motorized vehicle."

"Some young people can't see what's right before them." Willis motioned for the waitress to bring their receipt. "Guess they don't realize how much it hurts their family when they run off and do their own thing."

As they went up to the front desk to pay for their lunch, a young, blond-haired woman stood by the register, asking the cashier for directions.

"How far is it from here to Strasburg?"

Mary Ruth heard her inquire.

"You're only about fifteen minutes from there," the cashier explained. "There's a road right here past the restaurant — North Ronks Road. Stay on that until you hit Route 741, which will take you right into Strasburg."

"Thanks. That sounds easy enough." The blond-haired woman smiled politely, then went into the restroom.

"How was your meal?" the cashier asked when Willis stepped up to pay.

"It was very good, thank you." He handed her cash and waited for the change.

After the young man counted back his change, Willis turned to Mary Ruth. "I'll be right back. I need to put a tip on our table for the waitress."

"Okay." Mary Ruth looked toward the restroom and saw the blond woman come out. She stopped to look at a rack of books for sale by the entrance door.

Willis returned a few seconds later. "Have a nice day," he told the cashier as he and Mary Ruth headed for the door. At the same time, the woman asking for directions went for the door handle too.

"Here, I'll get it for you." She held the door open until Mary Ruth and Willis went out.

"Why, thank you." Mary Ruth smiled.

"You're welcome." The blond walked swiftly through the parking lot.

As Mary Ruth and Willis headed to the area where they'd secured their horse and buggy, Mary Ruth paused and glanced over her shoulder in time to see the young woman get into a small blue car.

"Did you hear that young lady ask for directions to Strasburg?" she asked Willis.

"Jah. It's too bad we couldn't ask her to follow us. But then if we had, she'd have to drive pretty slow." Willis took Mary Ruth's arm and helped her into the buggy before untying the reins. "The cashier gave good directions, so I'm sure she'll find her way."

"Jah." As Mary Ruth settled herself on the seat, she thought about the conversation she and Willis had during lunch. How would Ezekiel's parents feel if he and Sara did end up getting married? Would they accept her into the family, despite her not being Amish? If Ezekiel did end up going English, would Belinda and Vernon blame Sara for it?

Remembering once again the sinking feeling she'd had when their daughter left them a note, saying she was leaving home, caused Mary Ruth to tear up. *Oh, I wish I could quit thinking about this.* She wondered sometimes if the pain of it would ever completely go away. Well, at least their life was filled with happiness now that they'd met Rhoda's daughter. This was where Mary Ruth needed to keep her focus.

Strasburg

Michelle was about to step off the porch when a light blue compact car pulled into the yard. Going past the van, the vehicle pulled up close to the house. An attractive young woman with long blond hair got out and stepped onto the porch. "Excuse me, but is this where Willis and Mary Ruth Lapp live?"

All Michelle could do was nod her head. Her intuition told her this young lady was here for a purpose.

The woman smiled. "I'm their granddaughter, Sara Murray. I've written them several letters, and their response was that I should come here to meet them in October. So, here I am. Are they home?"

Heart pounding and barely able to speak, Michelle squeaked, "They're out running errands, but the front door is open, so feel free to go inside and wait for them." Without explaining who she was or where she was going, Michelle grabbed her things and headed for Stan's rig.

Yip! Yip! Rascal followed.

Tears clouding her vision, Michelle shook her head and signaled for the pup to go back. "Sorry, buddy, but you can't come with me. Go back on the porch with your mama."

The dog whimpered, and with his tail between his legs, he ambled slowly toward the house. Rascal stopped once and turned toward Michelle, but when she clapped her hands and shouted, "Go back!" he made a hasty retreat.

Michelle opened the back door of the van, tossed her things inside, and took a seat. "Let's go, Stan. There's no time to waste." She quickly buckled her seatbelt.

Stan's eyes narrowed slightly, as though confused, but then he backed the van out of the driveway. Just before he pulled onto the road, Michelle looked back toward the house and saw Sara crouched on the porch, petting Rascal. *I hope she's good to my puppy.*

Michelle gripped the end of her seatbelt, pulling it so tight she could barely breathe. *She's the one my pup belongs with, not me. She's Mary Ruth and Willis's rightful granddaughter.*

"So where are you headed?" Stan asked, glancing over his shoulder.

"I don't know. How far will a hundred dollars take me?"

Chapter 37

Harrisburg, Pennsylvania

Michelle could barely see through the film of tears in her eyes. Leaving Willis and Mary Ruth's home had been harder than she imagined. It was the only place she had ever felt secure and as if she truly belonged. Most importantly, while living with the Lapps, Michelle had felt, for the first time in her twenty-four years, what it was like to be loved unconditionally.

Thinking about her deceitfulness to the grandparents Michelle wished she had made her almost nauseated. How could she have treated those good people that way? But what would Mary Ruth and Willis have done had she told them who she was? Would they have accepted her or asked her to leave? Would they have understood Michelle's situation and forgiven her once they knew the truth?

She squeezed her eyes shut, hoping the

tears wouldn't flow. *And what do they think of me now that they've no doubt read my note? I bet they couldn't wait to tell Ivan and his family. Lenore, who I'd begun to think of as a good friend, will probably think I'm a terrible person.*

With her eyes remaining closed, Michelle thought about how one evening, a few months ago, she and Lenore had gotten together to do some stamping and card making with the birthday gift Lenore had given her. Lenore had been so patient, teaching her how to emboss the cards she'd stamped by holding them carefully and not too close over one of the gas burners on Mary Ruth's cooking stove. There would be no more fun times like that for Michelle — relaxing, while talking and learning something new with a special Amish friend. *Only, Lenore believed I was Sara. My pretend cousin had no idea she was teaching a fraud how to make such lovely homemade cards.*

Michelle nearly choked on the sob rising in her throat. The thought of never seeing any of the things or people she'd left behind in Strasburg was almost too much to bear.

"Are you sure this is where you want to be dropped off?" Stan asked when he pulled up to a rundown hotel.

Her eyes snapped open, and she blotted

the few escaping tears. "Yeah. The hotel sign says they rent rooms by the day, week, or month. So until I get a job, it's probably about all I can afford right now. If this place doesn't work out, I'll have to look for something else." Michelle leaned over the seat and handed him two fifty-dollar bills. "Thanks for the ride. I appreciate it."

He gave her back one of the bills. "I appreciate your generosity, but fifty dollars more than covers my gas to and from Harrisburg."

Michelle felt grateful for Stan's kindness. Right now, she could use the extra money — even if it wasn't rightfully hers.

"You sure you're feeling okay? It hasn't been very long ago that you suffered a concussion."

"I'm fine now." She opened the back door, grabbed her things, and hopped down. "Thanks again, Stan. Have a safe trip back."

He opened his mouth like he might say more, but merely nodded instead. "Take care, Sara. I hope to see you again sometime."

She didn't bother to correct him or say that seeing him again was doubtful. He'd find out soon enough from the Lapps that she wasn't their granddaughter. For that matter, most of the Amish community in

Strasburg would likely know the truth before the week was out. It was one more reason she could never show her face there again.

Michelle wasn't sure why she'd chosen Harrisburg to start over. Maybe it was because the city was fairly large, so she shouldn't have too much trouble finding a job. She would stay here for a while, at least — until she decided it was time to move on.

Michelle felt thankful Stan hadn't asked her a bunch of questions on the ride up here from Strasburg. The only thing she'd told him was that she'd overstayed her welcome at the Lapps' and needed a fresh start in another location.

Fingers gripping her suitcase handle while she fought back tears, Michelle entered the dreary-looking hotel.

Strasburg

Sara opened the door hesitantly and stepped inside. It didn't feel right to enter a house uninvited when no one was at home. She wished she could have asked a few more questions of the young woman who left here in such a hurry. For the first hour after arriving, Sara had remained on the porch with the whining dogs. When she couldn't stand the noise any longer, she decided to go inside, as the auburn-haired woman had suggested.

Standing in the living room, looking around, she had second thoughts about being here. It felt as if she were invading someone's space. A very simple, plain space at that.

Her grandparent's house was neat as a pin, but there were no frilly curtains on the windows, just dark green window shades. A braided throw-rug lay on the nicely polished hardwood floor in front of the stone fireplace. She also noticed a Bible on the coffee table, and next to it was a stack of magazines.

The room was devoid of knickknacks except for the small clock on the mantel with two candles on either side. Across the room stood a large grandfather clock, which had begun bonging when Sara came into the room.

She looked for a switch to turn on the light, but found none on any of the walls. Then Sara spotted two lamps setting next to a couple of recliners. She was looking for a knob to turn one on when she heard gravel crunching outside. Someone must have pulled into the driveway.

Sara hurried to open the door and was

surprised to see an elderly couple dressed in plain clothes, getting out of a horse-drawn carriage. They were Amish.

Well no wonder the house looks so plain, and there are no light switches on the walls. Sara's stomach tightened as her body heat rose. *Why didn't Mama mention this in the letter she'd written and tucked in her Bible?* Throughout her childhood, Sara had never heard anything about her mother being born into an Amish family. Whenever Sara asked about her heritage, Mama was always vague and changed the subject.

Now Sara realized the jewelry she had made her grandma would not be appropriate to give. But the key ring for Grandpa could be used for house keys at least, since they didn't have a vehicle to drive.

Sara's palms grew sweaty as she stood on the porch and waited for them to join her. The couple looked kind of familiar to Sara. Had she met them somewhere before?

Sara smiled, even though her nerves were on edge. If the last letter she'd sent to the Lapps had gotten here, they should have known she was coming today. But if that was the case, why hadn't they been at home waiting for her?

"I wonder who the blond-haired woman is

on our porch." Mary Ruth stood beside Willis as he unhitched his horse. "Wait. Isn't that the young woman we saw at the restaurant, asking for directions, and then she was kind enough to hold the door open for us?"

He shrugged. "Kinda looks like her, doesn't it? Maybe she's a friend of Sara's, or she could have come to the Strasburg area trying to sell something."

"True. Should I go talk to her or wait till you've put the horse and buggy away and we can go up to the house together?"

"It's up to you. I may be awhile when I take Bashful to the barn. She's worked up a pretty good sweat, so I'll need to rub her down."

"I'll go then. If she is selling something, I'll just politely tell her we're not interested."

Willis nodded and led his horse away.

As soon as Mary Ruth stepped onto the porch, the young woman stretched out her hand. "Didn't I see you a short time ago, back at the Bird-in-Hand restaurant?"

"Yes, we just had lunch there." Mary Ruth smiled and shook her hand. "I overheard you asking the cashier for directions to Strasburg."

"Yes. Yes, that was me." The woman looked at Mary Ruth with the oddest expression. "This might seem hard to believe, but I'm Sara Murray, and you must be my grandmother, Mary Ruth Lapp."

Blinking rapidly, Mary Ruth took a step back. "I don't know what kind of game you're playing, but our granddaughter is here at our home . . ." She pointed. "She's inside our house."

The young woman tipped her head. "Are you talking about the woman with long auburn hair?"

"Yes. Her name is Sara Murray, and —"

"No, it's not — unless there are two Sara Murrays. I've written to you several times about coming to visit, and you responded, saying I should wait until October. In fact I sent a letter a few days ago, letting you know I would be here today." Her forehead wrinkled a bit. "But I'm guessing the letter hasn't gotten to you yet."

"I don't know. Our granddaughter usually goes out to get the mail." More confused than ever, Mary Ruth leaned against the porch railing for support. Her mind raced, trying to process all this and frantically searching for answers that made sense. Surely there had been some mistake. This young woman on her porch could only be an imposter. "Where is Sara — the auburn-haired woman now? I need to ask her a few questions so we can get this all straightened out." Mary Ruth couldn't imagine why this person had showed up claiming to be Sara when their real granddaughter was inside, no doubt resting as she should be.

"She's gone. When I arrived here a few hours ago, she was sitting on the porch with her suitcase, and there was a van parked in the driveway." The woman paused and drew a quick breath. "As soon as I introduced myself, she said you were out running errands and that the front door was open, and I should go in." She gestured toward the partially open door.

"I set my luggage and purse in the living room, but I did not go in any other rooms because it didn't feel right to be in your house when you weren't home. I felt relieved when you got here and hoped you might be as eager to meet me as I was to meet you and my grandpa."

Unable to think or speak clearly after all that had just been explained, Mary Ruth stood staring at the woman in utter disbelief.

"Was your daughter's name Rhoda?"

"Yes."

"My mother's name was Rhoda, and I wrote a letter to let you know she had died." She folded her arms. "I have no reason to lie about this. I'm telling the truth. That other woman, whoever she is, got in the van with her suitcase and left."

"What you've said makes no sense." Mary Ruth shook her head. "My husband and I picked our granddaughter up at the bus station in Philadelphia four months ago, and she's been living here with us ever since."

"Well, she's not here now, and I'm sorry, but she's not your granddaughter. Trust me, I am Rhoda's daughter."

Gathering her wits, the best she could, Mary Ruth turned in the direction of the barn. Cupping her hands around her mouth, she hollered, "Willis! You'd better come to the house right away!"

Moments later, Willis, holding his straw hat in one hand, showed up. "What's all the shouting about? Didn't I tell you I was gonna rub the horse down?" He glanced briefly at the young woman, then back at Mary Ruth. "Is there a problem?"

She gave a decisive nod. "Jah, I believe there is, and I think we should all go inside and get to the bottom of this."

Willis faced the young woman. "If you're selling something, sorry, but we're not interested."

"No, I'm not a salesperson. I'm your granddaughter, Sara Murray."

The wrinkles across Willis's forehead

deepened as he looked at Mary Ruth through squinted eyes. "Didn't you tell her that our grossdochder is in the house?"

"I did, but she insists that she's Sara and said the auburn-haired woman told her to wait for us in the house, and that she" — Mary Ruth paused to wipe a tear from her eye, barely able to swallow — "She said Sara — or whoever she is — got in a van and left."

"Whoever she is?" Head flinching back slightly, Willis tugged his beard. "Let's all go in the house and talk about this. There has to be some explanation."

Back inside the living room, Sara took a seat on the couch, while the Lapps sat in the matching pair of recliners. Feeling a desperate need to prove to them who she was, she went to her suitcase and took out her mother's Bible. Then she reached inside her purse and pulled out a manila envelope. "Inside this envelope is my birth certificate, and here is my mother's Bible. If you open the Bible, you'll find the note my mother left, telling me about you. I brought both along in case you had any questions or doubts about my mother being your daughter." She got up and handed the envelope and Bible to the woman whom she felt sure was her grandmother.

Mary Ruth stared at the Bible, running her hands over the worn cover. Slowly and tenderly, she opened it as if afraid to see what was inside. "Why, this was my own mother's Bible. She gave it to me a few months before she died, and then in turn, I gave the Bible to Rhoda, thinking it might help her decide to settle down and join the Amish church." She looked up at Sara with the raw sentiment she must be feeling and gingerly took out the note.

Sara watched with pity when her grandmother's hand went to her mouth. "It's Rhoda's handwriting all right." Her voice shook with emotion as she handed the note to her husband. Clutching the Bible close to her chest, Mary Ruth's chin trembled. "And this is indeed the Bible we gave her shortly before she turned eighteen."

Next Mary Ruth pulled out the piece of paper from the manila envelope. After reading it over, she got up and showed it to her husband. "What do you make of this, Willis?"

"I don't know." Rubbing his forehead as though in extreme pain, he left his chair, ambled into the hallway, and disappeared into another room.

Sara returned to the couch and waited

nervously for him to come back.

A few minutes later, Willis shuffled into the living room, holding a piece of paper and slowly shaking his head. "She's gone, Mary Ruth, and her name is not Sara."

Mary Ruth looked up at him with furrowed brows. "Who is she then?"

"I found this note from her on the kitchen table. Her name is Michelle Taylor." Willis pressed one hand to his temple. "And if that's not bad enough, her message said she'd taken money from the coffee can in our cupboard."

Mary Ruth's mouth hung slightly open. "Oh my! I never in a million years expected she would do something like that."

"Yeah, well supposedly she plans to pay us back when she finds a job." Willis waved the piece of paper he held and grunted. "I doubt we'll ever see Michelle again, much less any of the money she took."

Sara shifted uneasily in her seat. It was difficult seeing her grandparents having to deal with all this. She wished there was a way to make them feel better, but she couldn't think of anything beneficial to say.

"But — but why would she deceive us like this all these months?" With slumped shoulders, Mary Ruth dropped her gaze to the floor. "I thought she cared about us."

"In the letter, she apologized for lying and said she'd wanted to confess but couldn't find the nerve to do it. She felt leaving this way was better." Willis's face contorted. "Maybe it was best for her, but certainly not us."

Mary Ruth's cheeks appeared hollow as she stared vacantly across the room. "If only she had come to us sooner and told the truth."

Willis moved closer to Mary Ruth and handed her the note. "Here. You can read it. There's more."

Her eyebrows lifted. "Seriously?"

"Jah. While Michelle was here, she intercepted the real Sara's letters and kept them from us. Oh, and she also wrote Sara back, pretending to be you."

Mary Ruth held the piece of paper her husband had found, and as she read it, tears coursed down her wrinkled cheeks. "Oh dear. Oh dear . . . I thought she cared about us as much as we did her."

Sara inhaled sharply as she sagged against the couch. *I know they are both suffering, but I'm their real granddaughter. Don't they even care about me?*

CHAPTER 38

"We weren't very cordial earlier to our rightful granddaughter," Mary Ruth said as she helped Willis rub down his horse. "The poor girl looked so verhuddelt when we showed her to the other guest room upstairs and said we were going out to the barn to take care of a chore."

"She did look confused, and we sure couldn't give her the room Sara — I mean Michelle — stayed in. Under the circumstances, it wouldn't seem right."

"That's true, especially when the bed would need clean sheets and everything." Mary Ruth sighed. "This is all such a shock, Willis. I can't get over the fact that we were lied to all these months and had no idea Michelle wasn't our granddaughter. It certainly seemed as if she was."

"It is hard to comprehend," he agreed, "but some things are beginning to make sense to me now."

"Like what?"

Willis set the curry comb aside and moved closer to Mary Ruth. "There were times when she acted sort of *naerfich* and like she might be hiding something."

"Jah, and after she got hit on the head, she was mentioning people's names that we'd never heard before. At first she didn't seem to know who I was." Grimacing, Mary Ruth shook her head. "But I assumed all that was because she was disoriented due to her concussion."

"Look how hard it was for her to call us Grandpa and Grandma at first and how vague she was when we asked certain questions." Willis massaged the bridge of his nose.

"I still can't believe that young lady helped herself to the money we had in the cupboard." Mary Ruth's face tightened as she slowly shook her head. "I wonder if we'll ever hear from her again, or if she will pay us back."

Willis shook his head. "No. As I said earlier, I doubt we'll ever see the money or Michelle, for that matter." Bashful nickered, and he reached out to pet the horse's flank. "We have to accept the fact that we may never hear from her again. Although, from what I read in her note, it did seem that she was genuinely sorry for pretending to be our granddaughter, as well as for taking the money."

"Since she had no cash of her own, she was most likely desperate. Without funds, how would she be able to start over?"

Willis bobbed his head. "The part that really got to me in Michelle's note is where she told about the letters our real granddaughter had written and she'd intercepted. What kind of a person could do something like that, Mary Ruth?"

"I don't know. And to think that she went so far as to write Sara back and pretend it was me who'd sent the letter." Mary Ruth's hands dropped to her sides. "I haven't felt this deflated since Rhoda ran away from home."

Willis slipped his arm around Mary Ruth's waist and pulled her gently to his side. "There is really nothing we can do for Michelle except pray for her. What we need to do now is focus on our true granddaughter, who is waiting for us in the house, and make sure she feels welcomed."

Sara stood at the foot of the bed in the guest room she was taken to before her grandparents went outside. This was not the kind of greeting she'd hoped for, and the disappointment she felt caused her to wonder if she should spend just one night and return to her duplex in the morning. What this Michelle person had done was deplorable, yet Willis and Mary Ruth seemed more focused on the imposter than they were on Sara.

As much as she hated to admit it, Sara felt envious of her impersonator. All those months Michelle had been here, pretending to be her and taking advantage of two elderly people who apparently wanted to meet their granddaughter so badly that they'd fallen right into the play-actor's trap.

Sara's jaw clenched. *It should have been me getting to know my grandparents, not the redhead. And now I have to wonder if I'll ever get a chance to bond with them.*

Sara turned away from the bed and stared out the window, watching as her grandparents crossed the yard and headed for the house. *I wish there was something I could say or do to worm my way into their hearts.*

She thought about the blue dress and black apron her grandmother wore. It reminded her of the special scarf she'd given to her mother. *Is that why Mama liked the scarf so much? Did it make her think of her mother's blue dress and black apron?*

Sara jumped when a knock sounded on the bedroom door. "Come in," she called.

The door opened, and her grandmother stepped inside. "I'll be starting supper in a few hours. Is there anything special you would like, or would you care for a little snack to tide you over?"

Sara shook her head. "I'm not a fussy eater, so don't go to any bother on my account. I made a sandwich this morning to eat during my trip, and I ate that when I got outside of Newark. But I am a little hungry, now that you mention it." She moved toward the door. "If you'll show me what you'd prefer that I eat, I'd be happy to fix my own snack. And later, I'll be more than willing to help you with the evening meal."

At first Mary Ruth shook her head, but then she nodded. "All right. Working in the kitchen together will give us a chance to get acquainted. I have many questions I would like to ask, and I'm sure you do too. So how about if I peel an apple, and you can cut some cheese to go with it?"

"That sounds perfect."

They left the room together and descended the stairs. As they started down the hall toward the kitchen, Mary Ruth stopped walking and slipped her arm around Sara's waist. "I hope you will be patient with me and your grandfather. Learning that the young woman we thought was Rhoda's daughter was only pretending to be her has been quite a shock to us both. We grew to love the young woman very much. It's going to take a bit of time for Willis and me to adjust to this, but we are pleased to finally meet our real granddaughter."

Sara's throat constricted, and she could barely swallow. "Thank you, Grandmother. I have so been looking forward to meeting you both, but if my presence here is too painful, I don't have to stay. I can return to my home in Newark in the morning."

The older woman shook her head so hard the ties on her kapp swished across her face. "No, we want you to stay with us for as long as you can."

In a voice choked with tears, Sara said, "I can stay a couple of weeks, but then I'll have to get back to my part-time job."

Her grandma's face fairly beamed as she nodded her head. "I understand, and we'd be pleased to have you here for two weeks. It will give us all a chance to get to know each other."

Ezekiel had calmed down some since Michelle's confession yesterday, but he still didn't understand why she had done it. After supper, he'd decided to make a trip over to the Lapps to see if she had told Willis and Mary Ruth the truth yet. He hoped she had, and if so, he was eager to hear what their response had been. All of this had gotten him to thinking about his own dishonesty with his parents. He had to reach from within and admit to Dad that he hadn't sold the truck but had moved it to his friend's place in Smoketown. Even if telling the truth meant having to move out of his parents' house, it was the right thing to do.

When Ezekiel pulled his horse into the Lapps' yard, he saw a blond-haired woman sitting on the porch next to Mary Ruth. He'd never seen this person before and wondered if she might be new to Strasburg, or maybe a friend of the Lapps from out of the area.

After securing Big Red to the hitching post, Ezekiel hurried across the yard. "Where's Sara, and how is she doing this evening?" he asked, looking at Mary Ruth.

Before Mary Ruth could respond, the young woman spoke. "My name is Sara Murray, and if you're referring to the auburn-haired woman whose real name is Michelle, she's gone."

Ezekiel reached under his straw hat and scratched the side of his head. "Huh?" He looked back at Mary Ruth. "Where did she go?"

Mary Ruth gestured to the empty chair beside her. "Have a seat and I'll explain everything."

Ezekiel sat and listened as she told about Michelle's letter, and how when the real Sara showed up, Michelle had gotten in a driver's van and driven off. She touched the young woman's arm. "This is our real granddaughter. Michelle was only pretending, and as you can imagine, Willis and I are deeply hurt by her deception."

He nodded. "I understand. I was too."

Mary Ruth's brows drew inward. "What are you saying, Ezekiel? Did you know Michelle was an imposter?"

"Not until yesterday when I came to see how she was doing. That's when I found out the truth." He looked at Mary Ruth. "Remember, you told me she was in the barn?"

Mary Ruth slowly nodded.

"Well, when I went out there to talk to her, she confessed the whole thing to me." He shifted his weight on the chair. "I was so upset that I rushed out of there and went straight home to think things through." Ezekiel sighed. "I never expected she would just up and leave without saying anything to you. Especially since she was still recovering from her head injury."

Mary Ruth leaned her head back and groaned. "Oh that's right. She's not out of the woods yet. I really wish she would have told us the truth. I realize now that basically none of the things Michelle said to us were true."

"Would you have understood if she had told you to your face that she'd been deceiving you and Willis all along?"

"Jah, I believe so. Well, maybe not at first."

"It's hard to forgive when someone you've come to care about hurts you," Willis said joining them on the porch.

Ezekiel jumped up. "Here, Willis, you can have my seat."

Willis held up one hand. "Stay seated, young man. I'll get one of the folding chairs inside the house." He stepped inside and returned a few minutes later with a metal chair. "Now where were we?" he asked, sitting down.

"You were saying it's hard to forgive someone who has hurt you," the real Sara spoke up.

Willis nodded. "Ah yes. Even though it is difficult, the Bible tells us in the book of Matthew, chapter 6, verse 14: 'For if ye forgive men their trespasses, your heavenly

Father will also forgive you.' "

Mary Ruth pinched the skin at her throat. "I only wish we knew where Sara — I mean, Michelle — went when she left here. Someone needs to be in contact with her to make sure she's all right."

"Who was her driver?" Ezekiel asked.

Mary Ruth shrugged, then looked over at Sara. "Do you remember what color the vehicle was that she got into?"

"It was a gray minivan. I didn't see the license plate though."

Willis snapped his fingers. "Our only driver with a gray van is Stan. Jah, I'll bet he picked Michelle up. So if it was Stan, then he'd know where she is."

Ezekiel stood. "Should I go call him now and see what I can find out?"

Mary Ruth shook her head. "Stan usually goes to bed early. It's best that we wait till morning to make the call." She looked at Ezekiel. "We'll let you know what we find out."

Harrisburg

Michelle lay on the lumpy mattress in her stuffy motel room, staring at the ceiling. She had originally thought she might ask the Lapps' driver to take her to the train station, and then she would head for Columbus, Ohio, where her foster parents lived. But she'd decided not to go there after all. She had been gone six years with no contact whatsoever and might not be welcome. Now she was in Harrisburg, a city she'd never visited before and where she knew no one. Such a lonely existence. She missed Mary Ruth, Willis, Ezekiel, and even little Rascal. *Too bad I couldn't have brought him along to keep me company.* It might seem weird to someone else, but Michelle even missed the bonging of the Lapps' grandfather clock. She pretty much missed everything about being on Willis and Mary Ruth's farm.

Michelle had to figure out what to do next. It hurt too much to think about what she'd left behind in Strasburg. It was best to concentrate on the future. Could she find a job and a decent place to live? She sure didn't want to stay here any longer than necessary. The price of the room might be cheap, but the place was a dump. Not nearly as comfortable as her cozy room at the Lapps' with clean sheets and a colorful quilt on the bed. As soon as she found a job, she would look for an apartment she could afford.

Maybe it was best she didn't know any people in Harrisburg. She was so ashamed of what she'd done to Willis and Mary Ruth she couldn't face anyone right now — not even strangers.

She sat up, reached into her purse, and pulled out a slip of paper she'd found in one of the prayer jars. Her chin trembled as she whispered the words, "Dear God, help me to trust You with the present, as well as the future."

The question was: Could she do it? Did she even have a future?

CHAPTER 39

It had been nearly two weeks since Michelle arrived in Harrisburg, and here she was, still living at the bug-ridden hotel. The place was crawling with ants, and she'd seen a roach in the bathroom. She'd been able to find a job waiting tables at a local diner, but it would take time before she had enough money saved up to look for a decent place to live — not to mention the need to return what she took from the Lapps.

Michelle felt closed in. She opened the window to let in some air. Even though it was early October, the weather remained warm and humid. The air-conditioning unit inside her hotel room was old and didn't work well enough to keep the room cooled. It was so rickety and noisy there was no point in turning it on. To make things worse, the room smelled like stale cigarette smoke — no doubt from whomever had stayed here before. The walls were paper thin, and she could hear the TV and conversations going on in the rooms on either side of her.

At least she had a microwave, so she could heat up any leftovers she brought home from her break at work. But oh how Michelle missed the delicious home-cooked meals Mary Ruth made.

She'd gotten off work a short time ago, and her hair reeked of grease from working in the restaurant all day. The schedule Michelle had been given was crazy. Sometimes she worked the day shift and other times the evening hours. Her boss was a big burly guy. Not real friendly, but okay. She was just glad to have found a job. Michelle also felt relieved that the lump on her head had receded and she no longer suffered from headaches. It would have been difficult to work anywhere if she was still in pain.

Susan, one of the single waitresses who was close to Michelle's age, was friendly and easy to work with, and they usually had the same shift. Right now, it seemed Susan was her only friend. The desk clerk at the hotel where she was staying seemed pretty nice too.

The restaurant was small, and the tables and chairs were set too close together, making it difficult to get around. Despite the fact that it sat on the corner of a secondary street and farther up from the office district in Harrisburg, a nice flow of customers came in. From what Michelle could tell, they were mostly regulars who either lived or worked in the city. A few of them, she'd learned, worked at the state capitol, some at the courthouse, and others in offices around the Capitol District. They were decent people, for the most part, and tipped well, but some who stopped in for a bite to eat were questionable.

Unfortunately, later in the evening people disappeared off the sidewalks, except at the corner where she worked. It became a hangout, drawing some of the local young men, who stood around smoking and looking for trouble. Quitting time was unnerving when Michelle left to walk back to her hotel after the evening shift. Cat whistles from the guys became a normal thing, and sometimes a not-so-nice comment reached her ears.

But for the most part, that was the extent of them bothering her. As long as they left Michelle alone, she could put up with their jeers. Of course, that was minimal compared to what she'd gone through when she lived with her parents or had dealt with Jerry.

Michelle got by on as little as possible and

felt grateful for the food she was offered as part of her compensation for working at the restaurant. Since she planned to put money in an envelope to pay back the Lapps, there wouldn't be much left for food and personal items.

Moving down the narrow hall and into the bathroom, Michelle gazed at her reflection in the bathroom mirror. Her throat tightened as tears sprang to her eyes. She'd been miserable ever since she left Willis and Mary Ruth's and hadn't really been able to relax. Ever since she'd arrived in Harrisburg, her nerves had been on edge. Michelle felt like she did when her brothers were taken away. She was downright depressed. *Wish I'd never pretended to be Sara Murray. I've really made a mess of my life.*

Michelle had gotten used to wearing little or no makeup while living with the Lapps, but since she was working again, she'd begun wearing makeup. But the makeup felt heavy on her face, and her eyes itched from the mascara and eye liner. She couldn't wait to get back to her room each night when her shift was over so she could wash the makeup off. Next came the shower with lukewarm water, and finally, she collapsed on the bed.

Each night before going to sleep, Michelle

would read the few prayer-jar notes she had brought with her. They gave her a sense of peace and, most importantly, hope. Tonight, the paper she took out was Isaiah 41:10: *"Fear thou not; for I am with thee: be not dismayed; for I am thy God: I will strengthen thee; yea, I will help thee; yea, I will uphold thee with the right hand of my righteousness."*

Oh Lord, I do need Your help. I'm just not deserving. Michelle sniffed and reached for a tissue. Her thoughts turned to Ezekiel and the special friendship that had developed between them. She had kept her growing feelings for him to herself, knowing she would someday leave, but now she could freely acknowledge that she had fallen in love with Ezekiel, not Brad.

But it was too late for any kind of relationship between them. She had ruined things with her lies. Ruined her chances with the Lapps, and with Ezekiel, and with Brad. Michelle was well aware of Ezekiel's interest in the English life, but deep down she didn't want to be the reason he might leave the Amish faith. His parents were already uncomfortable with her, and if he left, they'd probably blame her. Well, there was no cause for them to be concerned about that now.

Michelle rolled over and punched her pillow, trying to find a comfortable position. She still couldn't believe how upset Ezekiel had gotten with her when she'd admitted the truth. Didn't his conscience let him realize that he too was a liar?

If I were really Sara Murray and could have stayed in Strasburg permanently, I may have joined the Amish church and maybe Ezekiel would have too. After getting a taste of how the Amish lived, and the decency, kindness, and honesty she saw in the Lapps, how could she ever measure up or be good enough considering everything that had happened in her life?

A song popped into her head. She'd learned it in Bible school when she was living with her foster family. She began to sing the words, surprised that she remembered them at all. "Jesus loves me! This I know, for the Bible tells me so; Little ones to Him belong; They are weak, but He is strong. Yes, Jesus loves me! Yes, Jesus loves me! Yes, Jesus loves me! The Bible tells me so."

Feeling as though the song had been meant for her, Michelle closed her eyes. *If Jesus loves me, I hope He hears this.*

Michelle whispered a prayer asking God's forgiveness, before closing her eyes and drifting off to sleep.

■ ■ ■ ■

Strasburg

Sara was about to head upstairs to bed when Mary Ruth called out to her. "I almost forgot — when your grandpa went out to check for mail this evening after supper, there was a letter for you."

Sara paused. "Are you sure? No one knows I'm here except my stepfather, and I would think if he wanted to get a hold of me, he would have called my cell phone."

"It's addressed to you." Mary Ruth held out the letter.

"Okay, thanks. I'll take it up to my room and read it there." Sara took the letter. "Goodnight, Mary Ruth — I mean, Grandma."

Mary Ruth smiled. "I hope you sleep well, Sara."

"You too." Sara nodded and hurried from the room. She'd been here nearly two weeks now and still hadn't gotten used to the idea that this pleasant Amish couple were actually her grandparents. It seemed like she was living a dream. A very simple, plain one at that.

Michelle Taylor's name had only been brought up a couple of times since Sara's first day here, but Willis and Mary Ruth had asked her dozens of questions about their daughter, wanting to know anything she could tell them about her mother. What was Sara's life like growing up? Where did they live? Did she have any siblings? What did Rhoda do for a living? How did she die? So many of their questions had brought back a flood of memories for Sara — some happy, others sad.

Sara had asked them plenty of questions too — including if they knew who her biological father was. She was greatly disappointed when they said they had no idea. In fact, her grandparents said they'd been wondering about that too. With frowns, they did comment that Sara's mother had always kept pretty quiet about who she saw or what she did during her running-around days.

It was a surprise to learn that Willis and Mary Ruth had no idea their daughter was expecting a baby when she left home. That bit of information Sara had learned when she'd read the letter Mama left for her in the Bible. It had been a shock to her as well, although she'd suspected it because of growing up without a father until Mama had married Dean. The part Sara hadn't known until reading the letter was that her mother had run away from home. It was hard to understand how Mama could have left such loving parents.

Mama must have been a bit of rebel during her younger years, Sara thought as she climbed the creaking stairs. *I can only imagine the agony of what her parents went through when she ran away from home and never contacted them again.*

Her heart ached as she clutched the doorknob and stepped into the guest room. *And then they had to deal with that auburn-haired woman's deceit.* Sara wished there was something she could do to alleviate their pain. *Would it help if they knew who my father was, or is it only important to me?*

Sara had determined in her heart, even before she arrived here, that she would leave no stone unturned in trying to locate her father. Surely there had to be someone in this community who knew who he was. Unfortunately, on this visit she'd spent most of her time just getting to know her grandparents. The next time she came to Strasburg to visit her grandparents, she would do some asking around and see if anyone the Lapps knew might be able to shed some light on things.

Taking a seat at the small desk in the room, she turned on the battery-operated lamp and tore open the letter that had no return address. Silently, she read it:

Dear Sara,

I am settled in at the seminary and decided to take a few a minutes from my studies to write and see how you're doing.

I trust you got the note I dropped off the day I left Strasburg. Wish we could have said goodbye in person, but maybe it was better this way.

I've enclosed a card with a Bible verse on it, along with my mailing address here. I hope you will write when you have the time. As soon as I have a free weekend, I'd like to come there for a visit.

Give my love to Willis and Mary Ruth, and remember, Sara, I am praying for you.

All God's best,
Brad

Sara set the letter aside. It was obviously not meant for her. The man clearly knew Michelle, whom he believed to be Sara. He sounded like a nice guy and was apparently religious. But he had no idea Michelle had deceived him.

Her scalp prickled. *Oh boy. This poor man*

will be coming here to see the woman he knows as Sara, and my grandparents will be the ones to tell him the truth. Sure hope I'm not here when it happens.

CHAPTER 40

When Ezekiel woke up the last Saturday of October, he made a decision. He'd finally connected with Stan Eaton yesterday and found out where he'd taken Michelle. Stan had been gone for three-and-a-half weeks, visiting his sick mother who lived in Iowa. Now that he was back in the area, Ezekiel learned that Stan had driven Michelle to Harrisburg the day she'd left the Lapps'. Apparently she had asked him to drop her off at a hotel that was not in the best part of town.

Thinking more about it, Ezekiel shook his head. *I bet she's low on money by now. I'll take some extra cash with me, just in case.*

He had taken some time to process what he'd learned from Stan, and even though he was still upset with Michelle for the way she'd left, not to mention the reason for it, Ezekiel felt compelled to see her. Since he hadn't sold his truck, and now had his driver's license, he could get to Harrisburg without hiring a driver.

Two days ago, Ezekiel had told his parents the truth about not selling the truck, but so far Dad hadn't asked him to leave. It would probably come sooner or later. But it didn't matter, because Ezekiel had made up his mind about what he was going to do.

Harrisburg

Since Michelle didn't have to work until evening, it would be good to take some time for herself and get acquainted with more of her surroundings. It seemed that all she had done since arriving in Harrisburg was work and sit around feeling sorry for herself. So recently, she'd asked her coworker Susan if there was anything close by to see or do that wouldn't cost any money.

Susan had given Michelle a few suggestions, and she decided to walk up Front Street to see the view of the Susquehanna River. Michelle grabbed her keys and her jacket and left the hotel for her small venture.

After walking the few blocks and crossing the street, Michelle found herself in a grassy area. Beyond that, the flowing river came into view. Huge trees grew on this stretch of public land with massive branches donning leaves of autumn's brilliance. Today was Saturday, and traffic on Front Street was light, unlike Monday through Friday when people traveled to the city for their jobs.

That was one thing Michelle had noticed right away. Not only was the traffic heavy in Harrisburg during the work week, but the view out her hotel room window was boring — kind of like it had been in Philadelphia. Boy, how she missed looking out into the Lapps' backyard from her upstairs bedroom window in Strasburg, where she could look as far as her eyes would let her, and see the big open sky. From her hotel room and the restaurant, Michelle saw mostly brick and mortar, which she had hoped to never see again.

"Wow, this view is amazing," Michelle murmured as she took a seat on one of the park benches. Activity surrounded her everywhere. It seemed to be a popular place to come for those wanting to get away for a spell. Michelle watched people jogging, riding bicycles, and walking their dogs along the macadamized pathway. There were also some folks sitting on benches, reading a newspaper or book. But most, like herself, sat quietly staring out, no doubt, enjoying the spacious view.

Michelle took a deep breath and let it out

slowly. She hadn't felt this relaxed since leaving Strasburg. She would have to try and come to the riverfront more often, for it wasn't confining here, like in her room back at the hotel.

As Michelle looked across the river, she could see clear to the other side. *That must be what I hear people referring to as the West Shore.* She had heard that term used at the restaurant quite often too. This side of the river, she'd learned, was called the East Shore.

Michelle turned her head when she heard some honking, and watched a small flock of geese land in the grass a short distance away. An older man and woman, sitting closer to the birds, took out a bag of cracked corn and threw it toward the geese.

Michelle smiled when the geese hungrily snatched up the food then took off in flight toward the river. She watched them land on one of the islands, which jutted out toward the middle of the river. Other birds mingled along the island's shoreline. One bird stood out among the rest: pure white with extremely long legs. From where she sat, several bridges were in view, crossing over the water to the West Shore. When Michelle looked in the other direction, a mountain range could be seen. *I wonder how long it takes to get up there.*

Michelle thought it was truly a breath of fresh air, seeing the river and beyond, as far as the eyes could see. It was exactly the outlet she needed after being cooped up at work and inside her dinky hotel room, and it was a good way to get her mind off her troubles. She was thankful she had taken Susan's suggestion and come here today.

As Michelle looked up the river, something caught her attention, and as it got closer, she realized it was a tree branch. The limb moved slowly along with the water's flow, bobbing up and down in the ripples like a giant cork. *I wonder where that branch will end up. It's kind of like me, not knowing where I'll wind up.*

Just as she was about to get up, her friend Susan plopped down beside her. "Hey girl, I was hoping you would make it out to view the mighty Susquehanna River. What do you think of our beautiful waterway?"

"You were right. It's a nice place to come, and just across the street from all of that." Michelle pointed to the buildings behind her.

"That's one perk for working in Harrisburg. We have river frontage to escape to." Susan grinned. "Not all of Harrisburg looks old and rundown, like the neighborhood where Dan's restaurant is located. There are a lot of fun things to see and do in the city."

"Like what?"

"There's a state museum, and farther up the river is Fort Hunter, where they have several events throughout the year. There's also a sportsmen's show, the Pennsylvania auto show, and a big horse show."

"I would enjoy the horse show. When I lived in Strasburg, I was around horses a lot." Michelle's thoughts took her back to a day when she'd hosed off Mary Ruth's horse, Peanuts. As warm as it was that afternoon, it had felt good for both the mare and Michelle to have cool water spraying on their bodies. Michelle almost chuckled out loud, remembering how the leaky nozzle on the hose had caused a spray of water to be aimed in her direction.

Then Michelle reflected on another day when one of the Lapps' chickens had followed her around the yard, cackling and flapping her wings. The silly chicken didn't quit carrying on until Michelle stopped walking and bent down to stroke the hen's soft feathers. After that, Michelle was fairly sure she'd made a new barnyard friend. Then there was Willis's horse, Bashful. Michelle had been a bit leery of her at first, but after she was around the mare longer, they too became friends. In fact, it didn't take long before Michelle had Bashful eating out of her hand.

Susan tapped Michelle's arm. "Well, you need to go to the horse show then, and maybe I'll even go with you. And you know what else, Michelle?"

"What's that?"

"If you stick around Harrisburg, in January there's the annual farm show at the Farm Show complex. Think you might enjoy that too?"

"Yeah, I would. But I'm not sure how long I'll be living in Harrisburg."

"How come? Do you have someplace else to go?"

Michelle shook her head. "No, not really. It all depends on how well things go with my job, and whether I'm able to find an apartment I can afford." Michelle pushed a strand of unruly hair behind her ear that seemed determined to blow across her face. A nice breeze coming off the river rattled the leaves overhead. A variety of birds flew close to the water's surface.

Michelle felt a little better about her current situation, knowing she could at least attend some interesting events and also come to the riverfront to unwind a bit. She looked over at Susan. "I can't believe all the birds I've seen since I got here."

"Many of them are migrating south right now, and they stop over here at our river."

"We should come here on our lunch break some time. There is so much to observe by the river. And I didn't realize this was so close to where we work either. It really is a pretty place."

"Yes, Harrisburg has a lot to offer. I live not far out of the city, but I come here a lot when I have free time." Susan stared out at the river too. "I like your suggestion about coming here on our lunch break sometime."

Michelle smiled. She felt thankful she had made a new friend in Susan. She'd never realized how important friendships were until she lived in Strasburg and had become friends with Ezekiel, Brad, and even Lenore. Those days were gone though, and it was time to move on.

"You know, my grandma said that when my daddy was a little boy, he had a hard time pronouncing the word *Susquehanna.*" Susan's voice broke into Michelle's thoughts. "Guess he used to call this body of water, 'the second-handed river.' "

"That's really cute." Michelle chuckled, then she pointed. "What's that over there?"

"It's called City Island. They have baseball

games there, and a little park where kids can play. A lot of the people who work in Harrisburg park their cars on City Island too." Susan pointed in that direction. "They park their cars over there and just walk back across the bridge. By the way, that's the Market Street Bridge."

"That's interesting. I might wanna walk across that bridge sometime."

"Hey, do you want to take a walk now? It's Saturday, and we have most of the day to do something." Susan stood up. "This is a great place to get some exercise."

"Not only that, it looks like a wonderful area to come and clear your mind. Almost like the country, where I used to live," Michelle said. "Maybe we can get lunch somewhere after we walk awhile, since we still have a lot of time before we have to work the evening shift tonight."

"I know just the place. It's a nice little sub shop where we can have a leisurely lunch. Then you can tell me all about where you used to live."

"Okay, let's go, and we'll work up an appetite."

Strasburg

"I wish you didn't have to go so soon, Sara." Mary Ruth placed her arm across Sara's shoulders after they had finished eating an early lunch. "We've barely had a chance to get to know you."

"Your grandma's right," Willis put in. "Can't ya stay another week or so?"

"I would love to, but I can't afford to be gone from my part-time job any longer. I've already stayed longer than I planned. My boss is great, but if don't get back to work by Monday, he might decide to hire someone else permanently — maybe even the young woman who's been taking my place these past couple of weeks." Sara gave Mary Ruth a tender squeeze. "I promise to come back for Thanksgiving and again at Christmas. That is, if I'm still invited."

"Course you are." Mary Ruth nodded. "It will give you the opportunity to get to know your Uncle Ivan and his family better too. Even though you were able to meet them while you were here, you didn't get to spend much time together."

"I look forward to knowing them all better — especially my cousin Lenore." Sara smiled. "Never knew I had a cousin until I came here."

Mary Ruth thought about Lenore's reaction when she'd found out Michelle had been posing as Sara. She, as well as the rest of her family, had been quite upset about the situation. Mary Ruth didn't have the nerve to tell them Michelle had taken all the cash they'd been putting away inside their coffee can for incidentals and a small vacation fund. Truth be told, she and Willis would probably never see that money again.

But maybe Michelle needed it more than they did. And it wasn't as if she'd taken everything they owned, for they still had money in their bank account. They were getting along okay and didn't really miss the amount that had been stashed away in their cupboard. Despite all that, what Michelle had done was wrong, and some folks might not be so quick to forgive. Mary Ruth was sure, however, that Ivan and his family would eventually find it in their hearts to forgive Michelle's misdeed.

After all, there were plenty of verses in the Bible to remind people of the importance of forgiveness. Jesus was a prime example, for when He hung on the cross, close to death, Jesus asked God to forgive those who had crucified Him, for they knew not what they were doing. Of course Michelle did know what she was doing, but that didn't mean her deeds shouldn't be forgiven. *"Hate the sin, but not the sinner."* She'd heard Willis quote that phrase in several of the sermons he'd preached over the years.

Turning back to Sara, Mary Ruth smiled and said, "I believe you and Lenore can be good friends."

"I hope so." Sara reached for her suitcase. "And now, I'd best be on my way."

"Here, let me get that for you." Willis stepped forward.

"It's okay. I can manage, Grandpa."

He hesitated but finally nodded.

Mary Ruth held back a chuckle. Their granddaughter was independent, just like her mother had been, and dear Willis had a hard time not taking charge of things. Sooner or later, he would learn that some folks liked to be self-sufficient.

They followed Sara out the door and walked her to the car. Mary Ruth was pleased when Sara allowed Willis to put her suitcase in the trunk of the car. Hugs were given all the way around, and then Sara said a tearful goodbye and got in her car.

Mary Ruth, swallowing against the lump in her throat, stood beside Willis and watched as their granddaughter drove away. *I hope Sara keeps her promise and comes back for Thanksgiving.*

Harrisburg

Ezekiel arrived in Harrisburg shortly before supper. It didn't take him long to locate the hotel Stan had told him about. It wasn't in the best part of town, but he figured Michelle had chosen it for the cheaper rate advertised on the lighted reader board outside the building. Unable to find a spot to park his truck in the hotel lot, he realized he'd have to look for something on the street. He finally located an empty spot, put money in the parking meter, and went inside the rundown building.

After making some inquiries at the front desk, Ezekiel felt relief hearing that Michelle was still staying here. The female clerk said she wasn't supposed to give out room numbers to just anyone asking. But since Ezekiel looked like an honest sort and said he was Michelle's friend, she told him that his friend's room was on the fourth floor. The desk clerk also mentioned the room number.

Ezekiel thanked the young woman and headed for the elevator. Looking around after he got on, Ezekiel knew without a doubt that he was nowhere close to home. One of the first things he noticed were the smudges and fingerprints on the walls, not to mention crumpled gum wrappers, dirt, and even a few flattened plastic water bottles. Metal rubbed against metal, and there were squeals and squeaks as the doors shut. It was too late now, but Ezekiel wished he'd taken the stairs. As the elevator began its ascent, Ezekiel wondered what would happen if there was a power outage or even an elevator malfunction. Being trapped in a confined space like this would be frightening enough if there were other people inside with him. But the thought of being stuck here by himself sent shivers of apprehension up Ezekiel's spine.

Just breathe and try not to think about it, he told himself.

The elevator shuddered and made a sudden jerk, and then the door came open. *Fourth floor. What a relief.*

Ezekiel wasted no time stepping out. A few minutes later, he found the room Michelle had rented and knocked on her door. Unfortunately, she didn't answer, so he assumed she wasn't there.

Heading back to the lobby, he took the stairs. Then, checking with the desk clerk again, Ezekiel asked if she knew where Michelle might have gone.

"If she's not in her room, then she's probably at work," the tall, dark-haired woman said.

"Can you tell me where that is?"

She leaned over the counter, as if sizing Ezekiel up and down. "Yeah, I do know, but

I'm really not supposed to give out that information either."

His patience waning, Ezekiel tapped his foot, then leaned against the counter. "You told me her room number a few minutes ago, so what would it hurt to give me the name of the place my girlfriend works?"

The woman's scrunched up face relaxed slightly. "Well, why didn't you say she was your girlfriend in the first place? You just said she was a friend before. Course I'll tell ya where Michelle works."

On the one hand, Ezekiel was relieved that the desk clerk would give him the information he needed. But on the other hand, he couldn't believe he'd blurted out that Michelle was his girlfriend. At no point had he ever asked her, nor had she ever said she wanted him to court her. Even so, there had been a spark between them. Ezekiel had even admitted to Michelle, when he'd thought she was Sara, the feelings he had developed toward her. He felt sure she had developed the same feelings for him during her stay in Strasburg.

Of course, Michelle had lied about her name, so maybe she'd only pretended to be interested in me, Ezekiel thought.

He stood straight when the brunette woman handed him a slip of paper. "Here's the name and address of the restaurant where Michelle works. It's just about three blocks from here."

"Thanks." In his eagerness to leave the hotel, Ezekiel almost tripped over his own big feet. Righting himself before he toppled over, he stuck the paper in his pocket and made his way out the door. He figured since the place where Michelle worked wasn't far, he would go to the restaurant on foot. A walk in the evening air might be just what he needed to clear his head.

Walking down the street, Ezekiel couldn't get over all the big buildings he saw. Some looked like offices, and others were stores. He'd never seen so many places to eat either, tucked in and around everything else.

As he continued to walk, large homelike structures appeared, some three stories high with huge porches. The buildings looked old, and some were rundown, but most appeared to be well cared-for. Surprisingly, huge trees seemed to grow right out of the sidewalks.

Ezekiel glanced toward one of the porches where several people sat. They stared at him as if they'd never seen an Amish man before. *This is making me uncomfortable.*

Ezekiel picked up his pace and nearly fell on his face when he tripped over a section of concrete that a tree root had lifted up. As he moved on, he could still hear the porch-sitters talking and chortling. He hoped they weren't laughing at him.

When Ezekiel approached the eatery a short time later, he noticed a group of young men, hanging around outside, smoking and drinking. When he walked up to the front door, one of the men hollered, "Say, buddy, what's with the straw hat? You ain't one of them Amish guys, are ya?"

Ezekiel ignored the man's question and reached for the door handle. But before he could get it open, another fellow grabbed his arm and turned him around. With one quick swipe, he knocked Ezekiel's hat off his head.

Then, someone else gave Ezekiel's other arm a hefty punch and snorted. "I think he's a yellow chicken. That's what I think."

The rest of them joined in and kicked his hat around as if it were a ball. One guy remained close to Ezekiel, as if ready to pounce on him, in case Ezekiel tried to fight back.

As he looked from this guy, to the others who were playing with his hat, Ezekiel wasn't sure how to deal with the situation. One thing was sure. He didn't want any trouble. *Should I stand up for myself? Run? Or try to reason with them?*

CHAPTER 41

"Listen now, fellows, I don't want any trouble. I just want to go inside so I can see my girlfriend." Ezekiel held his ground, staying close to the restaurant's front door. He couldn't believe the predicament he was in. It had been hard enough waiting for Stan to return home so he could locate Michelle. Then Ezekiel had dealt with the flighty desk clerk. And now that he was in front of the place where Michelle worked, he faced an even bigger challenge.

The guy who'd begun the taunting, leaned so close to Ezekiel that he could smell his raunchy breath. "Oh yeah? Who'd go out with a big oaf like you?"

Before Ezekiel had the chance to respond, the second young man hauled off and hit him in the stomach.

Umpf. Ezekiel doubled over and dropped to his knees. He'd been taught from an early age not to fight. The Amish were pacifists and should not retaliate. The Bible said in Matthew 5:39: *"But whosoever shall smite thee on thy right cheek, turn to him the other also."* Ezekiel also remembered another verse in that chapter that said: *"Love your enemies, bless them that curse you, do good to them that hate you, and pray for them which despitefully use you, and persecute you."* This was a tall order, and Ezekiel wasn't sure he could abide by it right now. Every fiber of his being wanted to defend himself.

His muscles quivered as he struggled to get up, heat coursing through his body. He fought the urge to vomit. What he wanted more than anything was to punch the guy who'd hit him, but he was clearly outnumbered here. And if he did fight back, what kind of message would it send? Certainly not a good Christian witness. Besides, he'd likely end up in worse shape than he already was.

Glancing at her watch, Michelle realized she hadn't been at work an hour, and already her feet were killing her. *I can't even think about how many hours I still have to work.* She ground her teeth together so hard her jaw ached. Not only did her feet hurt from walking along the riverfront earlier today, but for the last ten minutes, one of the customers had been giving her a hard time. Frank was a guy who came in at least once a week and reminded her of Jerry.

She knew his type and tried to stay clear, but it was difficult in this small restaurant with its confined eating area. Frank constantly asked her out and showed no respect when she said no. This time, however, Frank had become more insistent. When Michelle walked by his table, he grabbed her arm. "I'm tired of you always saying no to me. What's the matter, babe? Ain't I good enough for you?"

Before Michelle could respond, someone in the restaurant hollered, "Hey, there's a fight goin' on outside!"

Frank let go of Michelle's arm, and she almost lost her balance. She recovered the plates on her tray in time to keep them from falling onto the floor. Fights outside weren't unusual, so she didn't follow Frank or any of the other patrons over to the window. But when she heard someone shout that there was an Amish guy outside getting roughed up, Michelle dashed across the room to see what was happening. As far as she knew, no Amish lived in Harrisburg. *Maybe it's an Amish man just passing through, and he stopped for a bite to eat. But why here, in this crummy part of town?*

Michelle slipped between two customers so she could peek out the window. She was stunned to discover Ezekiel lying on the ground. Two big guys with raised fists stood over him. With no thought at all for her safety, she jerked open the door and hollered at the guys to stop.

They sneered at her, and one of them let loose with a couple of cuss words. "Now don't tell me *she's* your girlfriend," the biggest guy taunted.

To her relief, Dan, the owner of the restaurant came out. "Okay you scumbags . . . Break it up, or I'll call the police."

Looking none too happy, one of the guys mumbled something to Ezekiel, and then he and his buddies all slunk away.

Michelle dropped to her knees beside Ezekiel, cradling his head in her hands. "Are you badly hurt? Do we need to call for help?"

"No, I'll be okay." He took her hand and clambered to his feet.

"What are you doing here anyway?" she asked, leading him inside and over to a seat.

"Came to see you."

Michelle's friend, Susan, came over and handed him a wet washcloth, which he held against a place on his face that appeared to be scraped.

"But how did you know where to find me?" Michelle took the chair beside him.

"I found out Stan drove you away from the Lapps'. Took me awhile to talk to him about it because he was out of town. But when I did make connections, he said he drove you to a hotel here in Harrisburg, and he gave me the name of it." Ezekiel paused and took a drink of water another waitress had brought him. "I went there, but you weren't in your room, so I talked the desk clerk into telling me where you worked. Then I came over here so I could talk to you. But thanks to those bullies I encountered, I never made it through the front door."

It was all Michelle could do to keep from hugging Ezekiel, but she didn't want to give those in the restaurant anything more to talk about. Besides, she wasn't sure how Ezekiel would respond. The last time they'd seen each other, he'd been pretty upset with her.

"How'd you get here?" she questioned. "Did Stan drive you up from Strasburg?"

Ezekiel shook his head. "Came in my truck."

"So you still haven't sold it, huh?"

"Nope, but I did come clean and tell my folks where I'd taken it." Ezekiel rubbed his stomach. "Boy, that guy could sure hit. Feels like I've been head-butted by one of my uncle's goats."

"I'm sorry you were subjected to that. Maybe you should have stayed home today."

"No way! I wanted to see you. We need to talk."

Michelle wasn't sure what they had to talk about, but she excused herself and went to speak with her boss. "Would you mind if I left a little early today? I know my shift started less than an hour ago, but this is kind of important, and I need to leave."

He nodded. "Sure, go ahead. I'm guessin' you want to spend some time with your friend."

"Yes, I do. I need to make sure he's really okay."

"Well, go on then." Dan flapped his hand. "Looks like it's gonna be a slow night anyway, so I'll see you tomorrow, late afternoon, for the evening shift."

"Okay, thanks."

As Michelle headed back to the table where Ezekiel waited, she caught sight of Frank stealing tip money off several of the tables. "Hey, what do you think you are doing?"

Quicker than she could blink, her boss ran past and wrestled the guy to the floor. "I can either call the police, or you can hand over the money you took — now!"

"I'll give up the money," Frank mumbled. He handed over all the bills, and when Dan let him go, Frank turned and glared at Michelle. "You think you're so smart, don't you?"

She shook her head. "No, I just know the price people must pay for their dishonesty."

With a loud snort, the troublemaker ambled out of the restaurant.

Michelle returned to the table where Ezekiel waited with a wide-eyed expression. "Unless you have somewhere else to go, let's head over to my hotel so we can talk and you can get cleaned up."

"I have no place else to go. I came here to see you, remember?" Ezekiel clasped Michelle's hand. "By the way, how are you doing? You look good, so I assume that bump you took on the head is much better."

She nodded. "I haven't had any problems since I came here. At least not with my head."

"I'm glad." He gave her fingers a tender squeeze.

Michelle felt a mixture of hopefulness and humiliation. If Ezekiel hadn't come here, he wouldn't have gotten beat up. But if he'd stayed down in Lancaster County today, she wouldn't have this opportunity to apologize to him or find out how Willis and Mary Ruth were doing.

Chapter 42

Strasburg

The rocking chair creaked beneath Mary Ruth's feet, as she sat rocking, staring at the note Michelle had left on their kitchen table. How many times had she read the young woman's message revealing her true identity? *Probably as many times as I've read Rhoda's note.* While parts of Rhoda's note gave Mary Ruth peace of mind, Michelle's note still confused her.

She couldn't help wondering where the young woman was and how she was doing. During the months Michelle had spent with Willis and Mary Ruth, a bond had been created between them. At least for Mary Ruth it had. She had no idea how Michelle truly felt about them. Since everything the young woman had told the Lapps had been a lie, Mary Ruth wondered what Michelle's life was really like. Who were her parents? Where did she come from? Why had she pretended to be Sara? Despite Michelle's deception, Mary Ruth couldn't help missing her.

Slowing the rocker, she released a heavy sigh. *I suppose we will never know anything about her past. But at least I can keep praying for her, asking God to keep Michelle safe and on the right path.*

"Whatcha doin' in here? I thought we were gonna have lunch."

Mary Ruth jumped at the sound of her husband's voice. "Ach, you scared me, Willis!"

"Sorry about that." He ambled across the room and stopped in front of her chair. "So how come you're here and not in the kitchen? It's past lunchtime already, and you said you would call me when the meal was ready."

"I apologize, Willis. I got busy doing some cleaning and lost track of time. Then, feeling kind of tired and depressed, I came in here to rock and think for a bit."

He placed his hands on her shoulders. "You're missing our grossdochder, right?"

"Jah. It is lonely without her."

"Don't forget. Sara will be back next month, for Thanksgiving."

Mary Ruth nodded. "I'm also missing the young woman who pretended to be Sara."

He cocked his head. "Figured as much. Those four months she was with us created a connection. It's just a shame she wasn't honest with us from the beginning."

"I'm partly to blame as well."

"How so?"

"I was so excited to meet our granddaughter at the bus station that day, I never even thought to question whether the young woman we thought was Sara truly was." Mary Ruth lifted her hands and let them fall back in her lap. "She went with us so willingly, I just assumed . . ." Her voice trailed off. "Oh well, what does it matter now anyway? We've finally met Rhoda's rightful daughter, and Michelle ran off, unable to face us. We'll probably never know where she is or how she's doing."

"Jah, and I have to say once again that I seriously doubt we'll ever see the money she took from us." Willis shuffled his feet. "So let's put it in the past and try not to think about it, okay?"

"It is in the past, but I can't guarantee I won't think about it." Mary Ruth stood. "Let's go to the kitchen, and I'll fix us something to eat."

Harrisburg

Michelle sat in a chair across from Ezekiel

inside her stuffy hotel room. Even with the window open, it seemed too warm. Of course, it didn't help that the hotel's furnace didn't work any better than the air-conditioning. Her room was always too warm or too cold.

Michelle was glad Ezekiel hadn't been seriously injured by those guys outside the restaurant, but the question he'd just posed had slammed into her like a horse running at full speed into the barn.

"I can't believe you want me to go back to Strasburg with you." Michelle stuck a fingernail between her teeth and bit off the jagged end. "I don't have all the money I took from the Lapps to return to them, and just thinking about facing Mary Ruth and Willis again makes my heart palpitate."

"It won't be as bad as you think, Michelle. The Lapps are good people. I'm sure they've already forgiven you by now."

She sniffed. "Don't see how they could. What I did was awful. I've asked God to forgive me, but I can't seem to forgive myself."

Ezekiel nodded. "Believe me, I understand. I've had trouble forgiving myself for lying to my folks all this time. It was a huge burden off my shoulders when I finally admitted to Dad that I still owned the truck."

"So what are you saying — that I should admit what I did to Mary Ruth and Willis face-to-face?" Michelle shifted on the hard-backed chair she sat upon. "I already told them I was sorry in the note I left on their kitchen table."

Ezekiel glanced around the room. "You don't belong here, Michelle. Your place is with the people you love in Strasburg, and who also love you."

She shook her head vigorously. "The Lapps would never invite me to stay at their house again. And even if they did, I wouldn't feel right about it. Besides, they have their rightful granddaughter now, so I doubt they're even thinking of me. I can't imagine how the real Sara feels about me either."

"Not true. I can't speak for Sara, but Willis and Mary Ruth have both mentioned you to me several times." Stretching his arms over his head, Ezekiel gave her a playful grin. "Rascal misses you too. I've seen the sadness in his puppy dog eyes."

Michelle pressed a palm against her chest. Merely thinking about the dog she'd left behind put an ache in her heart. "Do the Lapps know you're here?" She leaned slightly forward.

"No. I told no one I was coming to see you. Stan probably suspects, since I asked him to tell me where he'd brought you."

She drew in a deep breath and sighed. "Even if I did go back, it would only be to apologize again and give them back the money I took." Frowning, she rubbed the bridge of her nose. "Only problem is, I don't have all of it yet. The restaurant doesn't pay much, and most of what I earn I have to use for the weekly rate on this crummy room. It could take months till I have enough saved up to pay the Lapps back."

"I'll loan you the money, and you can pay me back when you're able." The sincerity she saw in Ezekiel's eyes was almost enough to make her agree to go back to Strasburg with him.

He got up from his chair and moved across the room. Clasping her hands, he pulled Michelle to her feet. "I care about you, and I'd like the chance to court you."

She tipped her head back and gazed into his brown eyes. "That's the sweetest thing anyone has ever said to me, Ezekiel."

"Does that mean you'd be willing?"

"Willing to let you court me, or willing to return to Strasburg and face Willis and Mary Ruth?"

"Both." He placed a gentle kiss on her

forehead.

Michelle's heart pounded. "Have you decided whether you want to remain Amish or go English?"

"I haven't made up my mind for sure yet, but after getting a little taste of the English world, I'm not sure I would fit in." He touched his stomach. "I am a bit baffled and dissatisfied with what I've seen so far. Truth is, I'm probably not cut out to be English."

"Ezekiel, what you experienced outside the restaurant doesn't paint a picture of the entire English world." Michelle lifted her hands and let them fall against her sides. "It's true, there are some bad ones, like I'm sure there are in the Amish world. But there are a lot of good English people too, same as the Amish."

"What you've said makes sense." He slipped his arms around her waist. "To tell you the truth, my decision about whether to go English or join the Amish church might depend on you."

"What does that mean?" She reached up and pushed a lock of hair out of his eyes.

"It means, if the only way I can be with you is to live in the English world, then I'll do it. But if you'd be willing to . . ."

"Willing to what? Join the Amish faith?"

"Yes."

Michelle gave Ezekiel a playful tap on the arm and snickered. "Yeah, right. Can't you just see the Amish church allowing someone like me into their flock? That's never gonna happen, Ezekiel, and you know it."

"I'm no better than you. But if I were to take the necessary classes and showed that I'm sincere in my desire to serve the Lord and follow the rules of the Amish church, I'd be allowed to join."

"But I'm an outsider," Michelle argued. "And even on the off-chance that they did allow me to join, it would be a difficult transition."

"Oh, I don't know about that. I saw what you did when you lived with Willis and Mary Ruth. You enjoyed the simple things and even wanted to learn how to drive a horse and buggy." He pointed to her. "That was the real you, not the pretend Sara."

Michelle couldn't deny it. She had enjoyed her time at the Lapps' and had even daydreamed on several occasions what it might be like if she were Amish. Even so, she felt sure it was just a foolish dream, so why get her hopes up?

"Do you care about me?" Ezekiel asked.

"Yes, I do." Her words came out in a whisper.

"Do you trust me?"

She slowly nodded.

"Then go back to Lancaster County with me, face the Lapps, and let's see where things go from there." He gestured to the line of ants crawling across the floor. "Anything you might face in Strasburg can't be as bad as the way you're being forced to live here."

"I'd have to go by the restaurant and tell my boss that I'm quitting."

"No problem. We can do that."

"And I'd also need to let the desk clerk here know I'm checking out for good."

"Yep." Ezekiel leaned a bit closer. "So how about it, Michelle? Are you willing to go back with me now?"

Michelle's thoughts raced as her heart beat a staccato. "I may be crazy, but jah, I'll go."

He grinned and gave her a kiss — this time full on the lips.

Michelle melted into his embrace. *How could I have ever thought I might be falling for Brad? Ezekiel is the man I love.* While Michelle felt apprehensive about going back to face Willis and Mary Ruth, she was ready to accept whatever they decided. She didn't know what the future held for her or Ezekiel, but having him by her side would make it easier. They would need to put their faith and trust in God, and with His help, Michelle and Ezekiel could face any obstacles that may lay ahead.

"I don't want you to worry about anything either," Ezekiel said as they pulled slowly apart. "I'll help you pack up your things, and soon we'll be heading for home."

Home. Michelle liked the sound of that. For the first time in many months, she felt a sense of hope and peace. She couldn't be sure yet, but perhaps returning to the Amish community in Strasburg was God's will for her life — and Ezekiel's. Maybe one of the prayers Michelle had found in the old blue jar inside the barn would become her prayer for life.

EZEKIEL'S FAVORITE JOHNNYCAKE

Ingredients:

1 cup cornmeal
1 cup flour
1/4 cup sugar
4 teaspoons baking powder
1/2 teaspoon salt
1 cup milk
1 egg, beaten
1/4 cup vegetable oil or melted shortening

Grease 8-inch square baking pan. In bowl, mix cornmeal, flour, sugar, baking powder, and salt. Add milk, egg, and oil to dry ingredients, stirring only enough to blend. Spread in baking pan and bake at 400 degrees for 20 to 25 minutes. Serve warm or cold with butter.

MARY RUTH'S TASTY SCALLOPED POTATOES AND PORK CHOPS

Ingredients:

5 cups peeled and thinly sliced raw potatoes
1 cup chopped onions
Salt and pepper to taste
1 (16 ounce) can cream of mushroom soup
1/2 cup sour cream
6 pork loin chops (1 inch thick)
Chopped fresh parsley

In greased 9×13-inch baking pan, layer half the potatoes and onion. Sprinkle with salt and pepper. Repeat layer. Combine soup and sour cream and pour over potato mixture. Cover and bake at 375 degrees for 30 minutes. Meanwhile in skillet, brown pork chops on both sides. Place pork chops on top of casserole. Cover and return to oven for 45 minutes or until pork chops are tender. Uncover during last 15 minutes of baking. Sprinkle with parsley and serve. Yields 6 servings.

DISCUSSION QUESTIONS

1. Have you ever wondered what it would be like to set your modern, worldly things aside and live on an Amish farm for several months with no electricity or modern conveniences? What would be the one thing you'd have the hardest time giving up?

2. If you had been Michelle, would you have been honest with the Lapps right from the start? If you had decided to pretend you were their granddaughter, would you have been able to deceive them for as long as Michelle did without breaking down?

3. Mary Ruth and Willis Lapp were deeply grieved when their only daughter, Rhoda, left home when she was eighteen and never made contact with them again. If you had an adult child old enough to make their own decisions, and he or she

left home without word of their whereabouts, how would you cope with the situation? Would you try your best to find them?

4. Have you ever lost a loved one quickly, as Sara did, and barely had time to deal with their illness before they were gone? How did you get through the ordeal? Were there any verses of scripture that helped you along the way?

5. Do you think Willis and Mary Ruth Lapp wanted so badly for their granddaughter to truly be coming home to them that they threw caution to the wind and approached the first person at the bus station who they thought was their granddaughter? Should they have asked more specific questions to make sure it really was Sara?

6. Michelle deceived everyone she met while living in Strasburg. If you had been any of them (the Lapps, Brad, Ezekiel, Ivan, Lenore) would you have been able to forgive her when you found out what she did?

7. Michelle's interest was piqued when she discovered some old jars that contained

prayers, sayings, and Bible quotes. It was because of these notes that she began thinking about someone other than herself. Have you ever found a note in an unusual place and didn't know who had written it or why? Did it make any kind of an impact on your life?

8. If you were the real Sara, how would you have felt after discovering that someone had been pretending to be you?

9. At one point Michelle convinced herself it was okay to deceive the Lapps because she had grown fond of them and didn't want to hurt them. Is there ever a time when it's all right to keep the truth from someone, for fear of them getting hurt?

10. Ezekiel had also been living a lie, keeping the truth from his parents about the truck he'd bought. Why do you think some Amish young people want to have modern things or take part in some activities that English young people might do?

11. How do you think Amish parents should deal with their young people who try out worldly things? Should they look the other way, hoping their children will become

dissatisfied with what the world has to offer? Or should Amish parents forbid their children to experience what English young people do?

12. When Ezekiel was attacked by a group of bullies outside a restaurant, he chose not to fight back. He had been taught from an early age that Matthew 5:39 says if someone hits us on the right cheek, we are supposed to turn our left cheek to him as well. How do you interpret this verse? How would most people react if they were picked on by bullies, the way Ezekiel was?

13. Would the unkind greeting Ezekiel got in Harrisburg outside the restaurant where Michelle worked give you the impression that's how the English world really is? Does it make sense that, following the incident, Ezekiel became a bit more hesitant in his decision to become English?

14. Did you learn anything new while reading this story in regards to the Lancaster County Amish? In what way is their life different from any other Amish community in America?

15. Were there any verses of scripture, prayers, or sayings that Michelle found on the slips of paper inside the old jars that spoke to you or touched your heart in some way? What was your favorite quote?

ABOUT THE AUTHOR

New York Times bestselling and award-winning author **Wanda E. Brunstetter** is one of the founders of the Amish fiction genre. She has written close to 90 books translated in four languages. With over 10 million copies sold, Wanda's stories consistently earn spots on the nation's most prestigious bestseller lists and have received numerous awards.

Wanda's ancestors were part of the Anabaptist faith, and her novels are based on personal research intended to accurately portray the Amish way of life. Her books are well read and trusted by many Amish, who credit her for giving readers a deeper understanding of the people and their customs.

When Wanda visits her Amish friends, she finds herself drawn to their peaceful lifestyle, sincerity, and close family ties. Wanda enjoys photography, ventriloquism, gardening, bird-watching, beachcombing, and spending time with her family. She and her husband, Richard, have been blessed with two grown children, six grandchildren, and two great-grandchildren.

To learn more about Wanda, visit her website at www.wandabrunstetter.com.